Inertial Anomalies

Archeons, book 6

by James L. Steele

Inertial Anomalies (Archeons, book 6)
Copyright © 2021 by James L. Steele

Cover art by **Lepricon**, furaffinity.net/user/lepricon/

Editing by **Alex Phengsavath**, polyglotprose.blogspot.com/

Special thanks to **W. R. Frixmargen** for science consultation, furaffinity.net/user/wrfrixmargen/

Published by KTM Publishing

Print edition set in Fanwood, Exo, and Playfair Display, all royalty-free typefaces

Print edition ISBN: 978-1-7322824-5-2

Russia

Rive opened his eyes and stretched. The summer air in the house told him Crystal was already awake and hard at work in the front room. He rolled to his stomach, the wooden floor creaking under his weight. The room was small, meant to conserve heat, and the bed was of a style not seen since Charles Dickens' time. Crystal was too old to sleep on hard wood, so she often slept up there. Rive was too heavy for it, so he was content with the floor.

He rose to his feet and walked to the bathroom. A tan body stared at him in the mirror, almost exactly how he appeared before the disaster tore him apart. His body hadn't aged a day since he met Crystal. In fact, it had become more efficient.

He'd had long talks with his metal over the years, sometimes lasting for days at a time. The first thing he had done was convince it that heat was good. He then showed the Multitude how to mimic the texture of his scales. Now instead of grey metal contrasting with his light brown scales, his body was a uniform color again. The metal imitated his scales so well he couldn't see where it ended and his skin began. It felt and looked more natural as well. It still smelled like metal, but appearance was all that mattered on this world. Years ago the Multitude had tuned his vocal cords closer to his original voice as well. It felt so nice to sound like himself again.

Rive straddled the toilet, maneuvering his slit over the bowl, and urinated. He preferred to do this outside, but sometimes indoor facilities were more convenient. Given how little blood he had to filter, he only needed to do this once every couple of days anyway. He flushed, deliberately leaving the seat up, then walked through the house.

It was ancient by human standards, as was this Siberian town, which was tolerable during the summer months. The people would not breathe a word to outsiders that an extraterrestrial still lived on Earth. He and Crystal were known enemies of the United States, so the people here figured they must have done something right. It was remote enough that the town would often go years without meeting another outsider but not so remote that it lacked electricity.

Crystal sat on the couch in the front room, typing on her laptop, papers and cassette tapes stacked around her. She recorded all of the interviews she did both digitally and on tape as a backup. Modern computers made it possible to have multiple recordings playing at the same time, which made cross-referencing much faster. Rive often listened to the interviews she conducted and made notes of who said what and where it was on the recording, which saved her hours of source-checking. If the interviewee did not speak English, Rive also translated, which by itself saved an enormous amount of time and money.

He climbed onto the couch. It groaned as he lay on the cushions, but it held him. He nuzzled her cheek. She reached up and draped an arm around his neck.

"Where are we going today?" he said.

She smiled, looked away from the screen and met his eyes. "We've been going where I want to go for weeks. Don't you want to go anywhere?"

Rive reached over with his hand and shared a smile with her. "Here is just fine."

"You want to watch me work all day?"

"Maybe a movie? In English this time."

Crystal shook her head as she turned back to the computer, rubbing his fingers. "That's all you ever want to do these days. How can you lay on your belly and watch screens when the world is falling apart?"

Rive laughed. "You haven't taken a break in months."

Crystal brought her hand back down to the keyboard. "I seem to remember you telling me raptors are instinctive homebodies. It was their foxes who pulled them away from their families and made them go on adventures."

Rive bumped noses with her. "In the absence of a fox, a human will do just fine."

She smiled. "You're getting too local. I kept my last husband from becoming a drunken couch potato and I'll be damned if I let you become one. We should go somewhere offworld."

Rive clicked his claws. "Good idea. I'll start working on a way. We'll leave tomorrow. Any requests?"

"Pick someplace warm and with a coastline. I'd like to walk on a beach again."

"So would I."

Rive stepped off the couch and walked to the other computer. He used a proxy server to log into a proxy server to hack into their bank. He initiated fund transfers from a few multinational corporations, added the data to the log files, created some false permission codes, then logged out. As long as he didn't do anything extreme, the bank would not scrutinize, and the company he stole from would not notice a tiny fraction of their profit had gone missing. As a rule, he never stole money from people. Only corporations.

Computers were simple to learn, and they made it easier than ever for money to appear and disappear, but it was often less suspicious to play Robin Hood. Rive spent months researching companies, figuring out where they held their money. He identified profitable companies that were automating, cutting staff, pushing more work onto fewer people, moving jobs overseas, and then using all of it as an excuse to squeeze local workers even more. He then calculated how much money those workers should be making and moved money from the offshore holdings into one of his many accounts.

He saved some for himself and Crystal and then random people working for that company would find their mortgage or car loan or student loans paid in full. It had yet to make the news anywhere in the world, and Rive hoped it never would. If people noticed, he would no longer be able to do this.

It did not fix the underlying problem, and he could do little to help the people in other nations who bore the brunt of the physical labor and pollution, but it helped thousands survive the aftermath of the economic crash a few years ago.

Rive spent a few hours extracting a few million from companies that were merely hoarding it, and then gave it to the people who worked to make it. The whole time Crystal typed away on her laptop. He always looked forward to reading over everything she wrote each day, committing it to memory in case something happened to the text, as he expected, given the direction technology was going.

Crystal released her own work under several different names. The internet made it so easy to publish, while at the same time even easier to drown in the ocean of information. She had more than a dozen books on the internet available for purchase on various outlets because that made them legitimate, but she herself released them onto piracy websites for anyone to download.

They had spent this past month traveling the world and interviewing various people willing to talk to them about the company once known as Crescendo. It had been bought out by another company, which had in turn been bought out by another and then another until now only three biotech companies remained, all of which cooperated but released nearly-identical products to give the illusion of competition. The stories those former employees told had been scary. It wasn't just C-Corn anymore. DNA from the alien plant had been incorporated into other industrial and consumer products, from dental fillings to plastics to engine oil, purely for the sake of owning a patent and controlling a market sector.

Studies had been done on some of these products, all of them discredited along with the scientists who performed them. Crystal had been interested in talking to the people involved, and Rive had made the portals that took her wherever they wanted to meet. Those studies showed how unstable the products were, how they were hurting people and animals and even the oceans, and yet they were taking over.

Some months Crystal researched biotech companies. Some months she investigated NATO activity. Once she investigated the Davos convention. WTO activities. Drone strikes. Political funding sources around the world. The impact of trade deals. Extraterrestrial Terror Day. No topic was off limits, and she had the time to research all of them. It amazed her what she was free to do now that money was not a concern.

Crystal pursued whatever interested her without having to worry about transportation, passports, or the United States catching up to her. The government knew she was out there and had quietly passed a law making it illegal for any US business to work with her. Recently, the United Nations had passed a resolution making it a "violation of human rights" to associate with persons guilty of treason in any nation. Crystal felt proud to have had international policy passed just for her.

In the sixteen years since the US government convicted her of treason for willfully handing US citizens over to extraterrestrials for the purposes of creating passive livestock for their own blood-lust, as the official verdict read, she had been digging through the dirt and getting to the roots of modern civilization. Rive helped her research all of those books, translated them into every known language on Earth, organized the interviews, and assisted in making sense of the sheer amount of information out there.

She had given interviews around the world about the topics she researched, which were never broadcast anywhere in the English-speaking nations. Only ever to countries who dared to say something critical about what the United States was doing to people all over the world—nations either ignored or demonized in the US media. The few times the news in the United States mentioned Crystal, it was always in the context of how far she had fallen. Once an upstanding senator, now a traitor whose only audience was tiny countries with biased, state-controlled media.

Rive never allowed himself to be seen with her. Only a handful of people knew Crystal was not alone. The CIA knew though. Rive had hacked a few classified databases and read through hundreds of screens of information while inside. The current strategy was to continually discredit her in the media, and it largely worked in nations friendly to US interests. For everyone outside of broadcast range, however, they heard her, they read her, and they knew what she said jibed with what they experienced every day. Rive had read the CIA was trying to persuade other nations to repeat the propaganda discrediting not just Crystal but everything she was saying in the hopes the people of other nations would hear the refutation several times before they heard her even once.

While he worked, Rive began a way to Kronia. He hadn't checked in with Sorven in years, so he wondered how his video wall was holding up, and if anyone had heard from Deka, Sonjaa, or Kylac. He was sure Crystal would like to meet Sorven again before going to the beach. The Krone had become a different person since Stephen and Norh had synchronized, and the change had been welcome —the best of both the human and the Krone.

Vacation, for them, meant leaving Earth to catch a glimpse of life on another planet. Crystal enjoyed meeting other Archeons and learning that not everyone was like Rive. People asked Crystal if she was Rive's fox or his mate. She sometimes called Rive her husband, but Rive never felt comfortable calling her his wife. Many human languages, including English, had a strong possessive case relative to Relian, so to imply he now possessed her ran contrary to how the relationship actually felt. Rive had never found a reason to clarify. He liked this relationship exactly as it was. To define it would ruin it. All he wanted was to be wherever she was.

Several years ago, he had taken Crystal on the path Stephen had taken with Deka, Kylac, and Norh through the contacted universe. She had met so many people in that month, and along the way they met quite a few of the humans who were part of the Relian group now. Most Relians had a human with them, and she saw what was happening.

Years back, Rive had taken her to something that hadn't happened since the disaster. The Relians had no homeworld anymore, so they gathered on Tavax, which had been the most comfortable for them since they lost their planet. There they had allowed the children to mingle and play, and Crystal watched young raptors and foxes pair off. He told her that the pairing would last for life, and the raptor would know how to tame a fox's animal nature.

Now humans were among them. Crystal watched over these few days as the young boys and girls became part of a

Relian group. They were confident the young raptors would do for the humans as they did for their foxes.

As they continued following in the steps Stephen had taken across the contacted universe, Crystal had asked what would happen now. Rive had told her that once a raptor and a fox had paired off, the parents would play a smaller role in raising them. The young Relians were old enough for the contacted universe to bring them up now, and they would be mostly free to explore it as they wished.

Crystal had wondered if a six-year-old alone with an immature raptor and fox would be a good thing. Rive had laughed and told her stories of what he and Friend did in those years, all the places they had been, all the people they had met, things they had learned, and the danger they had put themselves in. Others in the contacted universe would look out for the young ones.

Last year he had taken Crystal on the same path of planets Deka, Sonjaa, Kylac, and Sorven had taken through the contacted universe while chasing the antifox. Sorven had told them everything they had done. Rive took great pleasure in showing her these wonderful planets, how they had recovered from the events.

Neben had captivated her. The crystal life forms had learned how to tone down their voices so they could share weak brain signals with others, making direct communication possible now.

The people of Magor had determined the invasive trees were in fact a single organism which extended across the continent. It was unintelligent but nonetheless fascinating, and wherever the plantlike animal's body had been excavated from the soil it drew visitors from all over the contacted universe. There was much discussion as to how it evolved and how long it had been waiting to sprout.

On Fusina, Cilitrus had returned and told everyone about the new form of life that had made contact with her.

Compressional waves as living beings. They lived within a gas giant, not too far from the core, inside the superfluid. This kind of life was not uncommon deep inside gas giants, and it had only just now become aware of solid life forms thanks to portal physics. Venturing into the deep oceans for them was like the vacuum of space to a carbon-based creature, but they could survive for brief periods of time. Cilitrus could not stop talking about it, and neither could the other offworlders.

Rive had even taken her to Gaow and showed her the plant that had become an Earth company's intellectual property.

Sometimes he let her take him somewhere. The contacted universe had been open since Deka, Kylac, and Sonjaa disappeared on Labccr, so they walked from world to world easily. Each one had a story. Each story connected to hundreds of other planets.

Whenever they returned to Earth after one of these trips, Crystal was full of life and eager to dive into something she had not researched before. Crescendo was her default project, but often she would begin researching it and end up pursuing something else. This had yielded a dozen books on various topics, all of them interconnected. No matter where she went, she explored, she analyzed, she documented. Rive enjoyed taking her to places on Earth as much as he enjoyed taking her across the contacted universe.

The only thing Rive needed was time to sleep and communicate with his metal. The Multitude had learned a lot over the years and was confident in Rive's plan to save their mountain range. But a strange thing had been happening. The more they understood of reality, the more they wanted the rest of the mountain to become metal explorers with other biological life forms and experience the universe in this way as well. Rive discussed the possibility with them, but progress had been slow. They were still new to a reality outside of the one they created within the neural net of their mountain range. It had taken them years to understand the concept of heat and why creatures such as Rive needed it, so it would take even longer to help them understand other basic things.

Crystal had once laughed that here he was teaching an alien life form about the universe and had plenty of time to take her to Israel, or Somalia, or France, or somewhere else to interview someone about NATO, or political funding, or some other thing that was so trivial compared to the scope he worked with. Rive only had to reassure her once that everything she did affected billions of people, therefore it mattered.

As Rive moved modest sums of money around the world, he recalled the people he had talked to who had read her books. Many of them were conspiracy theory enthusiasts. Rive understood their affliction, trapped in an environment they didn't understand, desperate to break out of it, mind reaching for connections. Crystal's books gave order to the chaos, backing it up with facts instead of leaps of logic.

Among the other people who read her books and listened to her interviews were individuals who thought they had everything figured out, but the longer they lived, the more they wondered about what they had heard in the press since the year two thousand. They had seen the videos the news had broadcast purporting to show that Rive was still on Earth and very much working to bring the United States down, but now they wondered why the videos of Rive looked so grainy and unclear in a digital age. Why did videos of Rive keep surfacing that showed him speaking in Arabic? Why would Rive use aggressive portals to take down sixteen buildings all over the world in the first place. Why did this version of Rive just so happen to stage mini-invasions in the Middle East, and why were United States military forces the only army in the world capable of repelling extraterrestrial invaders?

In some ways, Rive felt as if he were helping. It was indeed a rare thing for someone to have the freedom to investigate the events that shaped history. People were increasingly caught up in a cycle of never-ending work and debt they had no time to pay attention to their environment, or to question why things worked this way. It wasn't just in the United States; this trend had been engulfing cultures all over the world.

Rive finished moving money. He had used imaginary money to pay off imaginary debt, thus freeing a few people from the pressure of keeping up. He wished he could help them all. He wished he could change things, but he knew even if he did change something, it would start all over again. The instinct to dominate slept inside every human being, and without a companion species the same system they fought to bring down would eventually rise back up.

Rive let go of the computer mouse and walked to the door. It was time to hunt. Reindeer, elk, rabbits, and other creatures adapted to cold weather lived here, but other than bears, the game did not interest him. He preferred large animals, either predator or prey, that challenged his strength. He wasn't used to having a preference, or hunting for himself. He was becoming a new person without a fox, and he liked this new raptor. Rive wrapped his fingers around the doorknob.

The door exploded in his face. The house became shrapnel and swirled around him. Roaring filled his ears. His vision blanked. Pain lit up every square centimeter of flesh and metal. Wood, ceramic, plastic—all of it pounded his scales. Fire. Heat. Tremendous, skin-melting heat.

Exactly seven seconds later, he lay under a pile of splintered, burning wood. The metal was in complete panic, sending him images of his body as they now saw it. Much of Rive's skin had been blasted off or burned to the bone. His arm was missing from the elbow down. His flesh-and-bone leg had been severed at the ankle.

Rive communed with his metal, telling it he had been attacked. Rive had always known they were not safe anywhere with drones flying in the skies, but he never imagined the Russian government would allow a strike over their soil. He wondered if it had.

He told the metal to shut his pain receptors off entirely and help him get out from under the rubble. Rive's metal parts were the only things on him that worked now, and he pushed the wood off of himself with one arm and pulled his shattered body out of the wreckage. He smelled burned human flesh and hair.

He climbed three paces through the burning wood and emerged into the air. His other leg was indeed half gone. It did not bleed anymore, the metal having spread to the wounded parts and plugged the blood vessels.

He stood on the smoldering rubble that was his house in the center of a ruined, smoking town. Bodies lay scattered everywhere, most of them on fire and in pieces. Houses were still falling over and spreading more flames.

Crystal's arm stuck out of the rubble. It had been severed at the shoulder, and part of the collar bone was still attached.

Rive screamed. He fanned his claws and scraped the burned flesh from his body. Bones became visible underneath the charred scales. He yanked blood vessels from the stump where his flesh arm had been. He pulled shattered pieces of bone from the wounds and dug pieces of wood and metal out. All around him the fires raged. He reached up and clawed his skull free of debris. He was aware he was touching bare bone, and his claws were very close to his real eye, but none of that mattered now.

When he had cleaned out as much as he could, he faced where he calculated the missile had come from and told the metal to spread out and remake the missing parts. The metal liquefied and flowed over and through him. Metal that had once been inside of him, part of his phantom circulatory system, now filled in the new gaps in his flesh and bone. Metal flowed through his arm and remade the hand, joining it to the small piece of skin that still existed. It flowed into his leg and remade the missing flesh. It then formed the foot again, complete with claws exactly as they had been. It moved up through his skull and covered the bone. It didn't have time to mimic the texture and color of scales, so he stood on the burning house, his skin reflecting the flames and destruction all around him.

Rive braced himself on two metal feet and screeched into the sky.

He saw another missile approaching. He screamed at it, hoping whoever was watching saw what happened next. The missile slammed into the ground three paces in front of him. The explosion threw Rive backwards thirty paces. He rolled into the dirt and held on with his hands, yanking himself to a stop. The missile had done little damage. Rive stood again and thumped his metallic chest as he screeched into the air.

Three more missiles hit, two on either side of him and one just a pace behind him. The explosions threw him in three directions at once, making him spin in the air and crash to the dirt. What remained of his skin was on fire.

The Multitude told him something was trying to invade the cells in his brain and spinal column. The structure reminded it of the concentrated C-Corn pollen that almost killed him back when the Relians were on Earth. It sent Rive chemical and genetic analyses. Rive snarled. This was a genetically modified virus, and he was the first test subject. He told the Multitude to kill it before it did any damage to his neurons.

Rive climbed to his feet, claws fanned and raised, mouth open and metal teeth on display. He faced where the missiles had come from and gave whoever piloted that drone the middle finger, then the two-fingered salute, then bit his thumb—every insulting gesture he knew in the human cultures, past and present. No more missiles came.

Rive looked around, dropping to his knees as he screeched for the people of this town. And Crystal. He knew this day would come, but he had hoped he could stay ahead of them forever.

He continued working on a way to Kronia. He wanted to be at a computer again so he could hack into a database and find the details of this strike.

First Landing

I

Intangible fluidic particles ceased as the four Relians tumbled through a barrier. They became aware of reality forming around them—enveloping and making room for them as they changed to accommodate it.

Kylac lay on his side, gasping. He had only just entered the Lake, and now gravity had pulled him to a solid surface again. He rolled to his back, looking up at a black sky. No visible stars. His Archeon mind was attempting to probe the universe as his senses took in all the variables around him. Temperature, atomic vibrations, wind speed, atmospheric composition—all of it hit him at once. Something was wrong. He couldn't open a portal. Neither could he open a sphere beyond the universe and into the Lake.

He was breathing methane.

Kylac raised an arm into his field of vision. It was not covered in fur, but his skin still had the same red and black pattern his canine body once had. He sat up, looked down at himself. He was not a fox, but some sort of creature he had never seen before. Bipedal, with limbs that started off small at the shoulders and thickened to double their circumference at the forearms and ankles.

Heat radiated from the ground itself. Volcanoes glowed in the distance, providing the primary source of light, large enough and bright enough to illuminate the land for thousands of paces as they spewed toxic gasses.

Kylac saw Deka, also sitting up and examining himself. His skin resembled the same dark blue of his former theropod body, including a red stripe beginning at the tip of his nose, moving over his head, down his back, and ending at the tailbone. He had the same type of body Kylac had. Neither reptilian nor mammalian, it resembled a mixture of crocodile and primate with thick, rigid skin. Kylac sensed this species shed its skin much like a reptile because it was too thick to grow gradually. It needed to be this way to survive in a volcanic, methane-rich environment. They also had sloth-like claws as long as their forearms. The fingers were articulate but permanently formed into a grasping position.

Deka met his former fox's eyes. "Kylac?"

"I'm here."

Deka looked to the side. A green body with light yellow stripes running up her fingers and neck lay still on the ground, curled up in a ball.

Friend lay next to her, rising to a sitting position and scanning the land. "This is another universe! It's just as I thought! There are thousands—perhaps billions of them moving through the Lake. I was not aware of the passage of time once we left our universe. Does anyone else feel no time at all has passed?"

Deka moved his legs and rose to his feet. He stood like an ape on Earth, with his knuckles acting as forefeet, claws folded under him, and yet his fleshy skin and crocodile snout could not have looked less apelike.

"Friend?" Deka said.

The formerly reverted fox took a breath. He rolled to his hands and knuckles.

"I'm... I'm fine. I don't feel any scent anxiety."

Kylac rose, standing naturally on his hind feet and knuckles. "I don't feel it either. The equations have stopped. The variables in this universe are different."

Friend turned in place, looking in all directions. "Yes, exactly! We are in a universe in which the laws of physics are different! We have yet to figure out how to open spheres here. I wonder if anyone has discovered portal physics. It's so wonderful not knowing."

Deka bounded on his feet and knuckles and slashed Friend across the snout. Friend recoiled and fell to the ground, muzzle smacking the dirt. Deka sensed that this species' claws could not harm one of their own. Their skin also resisted lava for short periods, and fire for long periods. They were not scent-based creatures, and he was aware the name of this species was Anaxa, with the plural being Anaxan.

Deka reached down and slashed again and again, but his claws did nothing. The former raptor raised a foot and tried to gouge Friend, but his body lacked such claws on the feet. Seeing the futility of his own attacks heated Deka's anger, and he attacked again and again. Friend lay still, seemingly impassive.

Finally Deka had exhausted himself thoroughly. He merely stood over Friend and screamed at him.

"After everything you put us through, you're going on about physics!" He tried to hold his claws as a raptor would. He just now realized he was speaking in a language he had never heard before. "You nearly destroyed the universe! Again! You killed hundreds of people and ended civilizations just to push Kylac to come to the Lake! You almost killed him to steal his control over his animal nature just to prove other universes exist! Well look at you now. You're back in a body and can't make portals. We're on equal terms again, so it's time to answer for what you've done."

Friend turned and faced him, still lying on the ground. "I'm fine. I think I'm really, finally fine. I can't open ways. I can't even move my conscious mind into the Lake. Something is blocking me, and I think it's the new physics."

Deka pounded the ground with his knuckles. "Fine? Nothing is fine! You are not *fine*! You caught a glimpse of something outside the universe, and you've been chasing it ever since! You had the ability to kill everyone in the universe just to reach it, and you tried to do it!"

Friend slowly rose to his feet. He hadn't been hurt by Deka's claws at all. "I already answered for what I did when you killed me on Reyno. I saw the universe as a reality contained inside something else. A scientific discovery. A chance to make theory real. No more spending entire years living inside theory with Rive, pondering what it might be like to live inside a gas giant or how life might evolve as a faster-than-light particle or something. I could go to one of those mysteries, so I explored it."

Kylac slowly approached them, keeping his voice quiet. "'Help me do what? Keep my mind weak so I can't think about anything but sex? Keep me docile and obedient and never leave me alone for even one breath. Never let me do anything myself? I found out what the old ways really are, and I like them. They're power.' You said that to Rive on Reyno just moments before we killed you. That didn't sound like science to me."

Friend stomped away, shouting at the sky. "This is not about instinct! Why does everyone keep saying that? No matter what a fox does, it's always instinct! Feeling irritable, he must be reverting! He's upset—he's about to revert! Don't let him go too far on his own or he might lose control! I was looking at a new discovery that changed our understanding of reality itself! I saw a glimpse of something outside the universe, and I had to touch it! It was an itch! Kylac, you saw the math, you know it's true! Someone had to leave the universe, and I wanted it to be me! I wanted it so much, but then my old ways held me back! I could've had the solution on my own if not for this thing inside me."

Deka tried to snarl at him. The most he could do was shake his reptilian muzzle while pounding the ground with his primate knuckles. "Rive kept you from becoming that thing. We chased it all over the contacted universe, and now it's in you again. It's exactly what you are. A fox acting on instinct. The people you killed could attest to that."

Friend turned back to them. "That *thing* doesn't belong in me, and Rive was no help. I saw a glimpse of the math, and something made me panic and kept me from figuring it out. If I could be rid of it, everything would be perfect, but no, something happens every time I'm close to figuring out the equation. It should be easy, but I keep failing."

Deka felt better now. He lowered his attempt at a theropod attack stance. "Now we're in another universe. You nearly destroyed everything just to come here. Was it worth it? Was it worth destroying me, Kylac, Rive—!" Deka gasped and turned. "Sonjaa!"

She lay curled up on the warm ground, shivering. Deka bounded to her and lowered himself on his knuckles. He shook her gently.

"Are you all right?"

She turned her eyes up at him. "Deka... Help... It's... I can't think. It's like the Lake."

He reached down and helped her to her hind legs. She reached around him and held herself up. They both looked around.

"Molecules," she said. "They're everywhere. I can see them. Below them are... Everywhere. They won't stop. I can't think! Make them stop! Please stop!" She hung her head and screamed.

Kylac rushed over to her and nuzzled her snout as best as he could. Even Friend turned and regarded her.

"Don't focus, Sonjaa," Deka said. "Your subconscious is gone. Your mind is accepting sensory information with no filter. Your brain will learn how to process it."

Sonjaa screamed again and dropped to the ground, curling back into the egg. "Help."

"You're an Archeon now," Deka said. "I tried to prepare you for this, but there wasn't enough time."

"I can't hear you. Everything is too loud. Too loud! I can't hear myself!"

Deka dropped to his side and curled up next to her. She held him back.

"It's supposed to happen gradually with training. We'll help you adjust."

She held Deka as she tried to shut out the universe. Friend stood over her. He hesitated a few times and then rested a hand on her shoulder.

Deka wanted to growl at him, but his vocal cords did not work that way anymore. "Our hatchlings are dead because of you. Entire civilizations gone because you had an *itch*. The sooner you accept that, the better off everyone will be."

Kylac didn't look at Friend as he nuzzled Sonjaa where she lay. "Relian canines have an instinct to get away from everyone. To be the only scent around. Friend, you've been acting on instinct since the beginning."

Friend turned and pounded the ground in fury. "This has nothing to do with instinct—I am so tired of people telling me how dangerous I am just because I'm a Relian canine! To hear it coming from another fox makes me loathe my entire species! I left Rive because he wanted me dead! When you see something outside the universe, you'll want to go there, too! That's discovery! That's science! That's what I wanted! And now we're here. It's all true.

Other universes are out there. I'm overjoyed. Just think of the possibilities. So many wonderful new places to explore. The implications it has for portal physics and our understanding of existence."

"So far away from everyone else," Kylac continued. "So far away from your raptor. 'It smells better without all those scents around. It feels so good to be myself. To do something myself. All my life, people have been telling me to be afraid of the old ways. To be afraid of what I am. To be ashamed of it. Now we're proving that we don't need to be. We can embrace our old ways and allow them to be part of us instead of letting their fear and shame turn us into something else.' You said that to me on Suum, after using portals to kill everyone upwind of us. It made you feel better. You could think more clearly about the problem without all those scents bothering you, and it only got worse from there. Listen to us, Friend. Raptors have kept us from becoming this for generations. I'm grateful for what Deka did for me. You resent what Rive did for you, and you don't care that people died."

Friend was about to turn and meet his eyes, but they heard someone approaching.

She paused at territory distance, which for this species was about four paces away. To venture into another person's territory was rude to these people. Only siblings were allowed to be so close. Even mated pairs would only come together to couple, and then they would then separate for the rest of the season.

The former Relians were family now. Brothers and sister.

"Your break is up," said the Anaxa standing at a respectable distance.

Instantly information rushed into them. Sonjaa cringed at the intrusion but the others simply became aware of it.

The Anaxan organized themselves into a hierarchy similar to primates on Earth. This species had a symbiotic relationship with a particular set of trees, and the dominant family directed the others to make the trees grow. They did not grow on their own; they required constant pruning and physical encouragement to bear fruit, the Anaxan's only food source.

This was a matriarchal society—the ability to lay eggs was more valued than the ability to produce sperm, so Deka, Kylac, and Friend had very low positions. They had taken a break from tending the trees to help Sonjaa, who had fallen ill. None of this was true until they landed here, and now it had become true retroactively.

"Beg pardon, matriarch," Kylac said, lowering his head. "Our sister is still not well. We're not sure what happened."

"Leave her with the medics and return to your tree. Your quota will not be adjusted for this time."

The Relians remembered that the extent of this species' medical knowledge consisted of convincing the afflicted they had committed a sin against the ruling family and to beg the volcanoes for forgiveness and lift the illness.

"She is sick," said Deka, lowering his head as well. "I won't leave her."

"Then your brothers must make up for both of your quotas."

Kylac and Friend knew what that would mean. It did not sound enjoyable, or even possible.

"Deka is protective of our sister," Friend said. "We will return to work without her."

Deka turned to him and tried to growl. "You do not speak for us!"

"I am the eldest."

Age was a major factor of rank for this species, and between members of the same family, it meant everything.

The matriarch looked on impassively at this apparent act of sibling rivalry. "I expect you at your tree in five."

She turned and walked back across the field. The smog from the volcanoes obscured the trees, which only grew in intense sulfur and carbon dioxide air. The trees absorbed these gasses and converted them into methane. As a reward for helping them grow, they also produced fruit.

Deka turned to Friend. "Why did you tell her that?"

Friend faced him. "We're doing what Sonjaa did when she was trapped in the Lake. We changed reality around us to give us a place in society. While we're here, we must blend in. I'm sure we'll figure out what's different about this universe soon. I promise this is a desire for knowledge and discovery. No animal instinct is controlling me."

"It seems we know everything about this species," Kylac said, "but not the universe or the planet."

Sonjaa slowly rose to her feet and hands. She spoke much louder than she needed to. "I know where the medics are. I'll get some answers from them. I'll be fine. I'm sorry about my quota. I'll make it up... later."

She hobbled away, perpendicular to the direction their matriarch had gone. Deka huffed as he watched Sonjaa leave.

"She's becoming an Archeon! I should be there!"

"Not our fault this is how society works," Friend said.

Deka tried to bare his teeth at him but this culture had no such gesture. He huffed at Friend. "We're equals again, so I won't put up with you anymore, and I don't care what your excuse is. You're a reverted fox. Satisfying your instincts is all you cared about before, and it's all you care about now. You can talk about scientific discoveries all you want, but that's what you are to me, and at the first chance I get, I *will* serve justice on behalf of our former home."

He and Kylac led the way to their tree. Friend followed seven paces behind.

2

Sonjaa hobbled across the warm dirt, steering around small plants that gave off methane. Somehow she was aware that there was oxygen in this atmosphere, a little bit of nitrogen, lots of sulfur and a noxious mix of other gasses.

She felt the molecules vibrating under her feet. She felt the electrical repulsion of the atoms between her feet and the ground, without which she would sink through to the planet's core. She felt the rumbling of the lake of lava in the distance, flames dancing and twisting on it. Though far in the distance, the composition of the fires shouted at her.

She sensed the wind blowing against her and the electrical repulsion preventing it from tearing her atoms apart. She tried to shut it out, but the technique that worked in the Lake did not seem to work here. So much information she barely knew she existed in the middle of it. The former raptor stumbled along, often forgetting she was not a theropod anymore.

Her knowledge of this species seemed to have reached a limit. She was curious about what the medics would ask her. All she really wanted was a quiet place to sleep, but she had a feeling the medics would not allow that, and neither would her mind.

She saw the tents, each made of strips of dried fruit skin stitched together with string made of roasted tree bark. One of the medics in the village saw her and bounded on his feet and knuckles to meet her.

He came up to her, keeping his head down and walking four paces abreast of her. "What is the matter, soon-to-be matriarch?"

It was a title attributed to all females in this society. Sonjaa did not take pride in it. "I am sick. I need somewhere to sleep."

"Of course, of course. My tent is this way. Follow me, soon-to-be. I must enter your territory to ascertain your illness. Do I have permission?"

Sonjaa would have loved to tell him about her illness. "Yes. Please find what's wrong."

He moved to intercept her. Sonjaa sensed she should feel threatened, but the Anaxa impulse regarding territory existed only academically. He veered closer until she was just a pace away.

Medics were trained to recognize bodily symptoms visually as well as with what little scent they could detect. He was investigating her from head to claw as she walked.

"You are extremely agitated. What were you doing when this happened?"

"Guiding the trees. My quota is so high... I can't keep up."

"Do not worry, soon-to-be. You will not have to be in service to the trees for long."

It was hard to hear him over the noise of the electrons repelling her knuckles. "What?"

The male said something. Sonjaa heard him, but the methane atoms in the sky were too loud. She shouted just to hear herself over them.

She woke up beneath a tent some time later. The medic was preparing a fruit and herb brew over a small fire. He set the cup on the dry ground within the fire and then rose to meet Sonjaa's eyes through the flames.

"You are indeed very sick. Most are agitated letting someone else into their territory, even those of the medic caste. You, however, welcomed me. Tell me, when was the last time you prayed to the fire?"

Sonjaa was listening to atoms in the fire right now, and they were shouting their temperature and composition and decay rate to her. She lay still and let their voices wash over her. She hoped she sounded normal as she replied.

"It's been more than a month. I have not had time to pray." She felt vibrations through the air that might have been her voice, but she could not hear herself speak over the sounds of the universe.

"Apparently your brothers have been dutiful in their prayers, since they are not ill." He laughed. This species laughed by pounding their knuckles on the ground. "Did you neglect your prayers simply to have medical time off?"

Sonjaa laughed weakly by knocking the dirt with one hand. "I think the fire is smart enough to know my intentions. It would not have given me what I wanted."

"Unless it knew you needed it."

"It would have given everyone the same affliction. We're all asking for rest."

"Perhaps you are intended for great things. I'm not finished communing. It told me you were about to awaken, so I stepped out to make some medicine for you."

He reached into the flames and pulled out the cup with his bare hand. He hobbled around the flame on three limbs and presented the cup. Sonjaa took it in her fingers. Her claws were so long they made gripping anything smaller than a tree branch an act of careful concentration. She raised the cup to her mouth. Sonjaa had never tasted juice from a fruit before. The closest she ever came was watching Rupi's reaction whenever she ate fruits and vegetables, enjoying these things vicariously through her fox. It went down smoothly now. The liquid was sweet and boiling hot, but her throat did not seem to mind. It soothed her body, but her mind still drowned in information. The liquid's exact temperature, the electrical blasts keeping the atoms from merging with her own, the molecules being ripped apart by the acid in her stomach—all of it interrupted the sensation of taste, and she only caught things in bursts before some other piece of information jostled to her attention.

The medic sat and faced her. "Your name is Sonjaa. Your brothers are Deka, Friend, and Kylac."

Sonjaa halted mid-swallow. "Yes. How did you know that?"

"I communed with the fire while you were ill."

Sonjaa turned to it, remembering how these people worshiped the lava and the fires it caused.

"It told me you are an intruder," continued the medic. "I'm not certain what that means. It is so rare the fire gives me such clear information. It said you came here from a distance. That you are not an Anaxa. It told me your sin is that you simply do not belong here. With that, the vision stopped. Can you elaborate?"

Sonjaa was not sure if she could trust this person. She finished drinking the liquid in the cup and met his eyes. "You wouldn't believe me."

"It has told me unbelievable things before."

She knocked the warm soil again. "What if I told you I am not from this universe, and neither are my brothers?"

"Universe?"

"This planet and everything that's beyond?"

"I do not understand. I am used to interpreting the flame, but I must admit you are more difficult."

Sonjaa laughed again. "You have not discovered portal physics yet, have you?"

"We know how the lava flows, how it obeys certain laws, but sometimes it chooses. The air burns under certain conditions."

The ground screamed at her as it continually repelled her atoms and held her aloft on its surface. Just focusing on the medic's words wore her out. She raised her voice to hear herself talk.

"I am not sick. My subconscious was torn down in the realm outside the universe. Information is hitting me, and it's very hard to handle. I've always been able to learn languages quickly, and people told me I might have potential to become an..." This language had no word for what was happening. "A master of physics. I never wanted to go that far. I was happy being able to learn languages. It's all I ever wanted to do. Now... I have no choice."

"To me, this sounds like a good thing."

Sonjaa laughed bitterly as she lay on her back. She shouted, more at the universe than the medic.

"Everything is hitting me at once! I need to learn how to handle it or I will drown in all this noise! It hurts! It's never going away! Never! I will hear it in my sleep! I'll never be able to stop it! I don't want this! I never wanted it! I was happy before!"

The fire grew taller and changed color from red to blue. The medic turned and stepped inside.

Sonjaa rolled over and glared at him. The flame seemed to dance around the medic, flickers entering his ears and nose as he breathed. The temperature had risen well above the melting point of lead. How it did not burn the tent to the ground she could not perceive.

Moments later, the fire shrank to its previous size, and the medic stepped out, not a mark on his body. Sonjaa noticed there was nothing under the fire. It stood with no fuel source.

He faced Sonjaa. "I am bewildered. The fire tells me you are speaking the truth. You have committed no sin. I am to keep you here until your brothers come to find you. It instructed me to tell the matriarchs whatever I must to keep you out of sight. Who are you? Where did you come from, and why is the fire so curious about you?"

Sonjaa was still staring at the blue flame. It burned nothing, and it remained still. Her brain took in all the information about it, and it concluded that this flame should not exist. Her medic approached and knelt down beside her.

"Please tell me more, soon-to-be. And when the fire says to, confess to a sin. Any sin. Are you prepared?"

Sonjaa could not look away from it. The pattern of its movement, the organization of its energy. Her new perception told her this was not fire. This was a life form.

3

Deka was not used to climbing trees, and yet in this reality they had carved out for themselves, it was all he did. He sat on a branch six paces in the air, gripping the leading edge and massaging it between his fingers, guiding it outwards with the motion of his palms. The branch grew in whatever direction he guided it at about a claw's reach every thirty breaths or so. When he stopped rubbing, it ceased growing.

He had been at it for quite some time, the branch extending as fast as he rubbed. He felt like a Relian canine. Deka looked up, and sure enough the foxes above him were growing their branches much faster than he was.

"I suppose you two are proud of yourselves!" he shouted.

Kylac looked down at him. He could not laugh properly, so he shook his rear side to side to simulate wagging a tail. "You raised me well!"

Friend knocked on his tree branch. His grew almost as fast as he could keep up with it, which was surprising.

"I thought you would be out of practice," Deka said. "You're better at destroying planets than rubbing your sheath."

Friend did not look down but stayed focused on his branch. "Are you really going to waste your breath provoking me now?"

"Making sure you never forget what happened."

"I'm an Archeon. I can never forget the planets I destroyed. I know the names and scents of every person I killed, plus every person who would not be born or hatched. But here... I am calm. I haven't been since the first disaster."

"This doesn't change anything. You still have to answer for what you did."

"Being banished to another universe in which I can't open spheres is fair, isn't it?"

The branch Friend guided began to sprout at the tip. Friend stopped rubbing and watched. A bud appeared on the end. It swelled to the size of his fist in only a few breaths, then to the size of his head, and then it grew to twice that size. The branch bowed from the weight, and Friend climbed backwards. The melon grew larger and larger, now half the size of Friend himself, bending the branch harder. Friend had backed away to the safety of the trunk, now standing against it. The branch snapped and careened to the ground. The melon struck the dirt. A matriarch ran to it and rolled it away from the tree and into the haze of sulfur.

Friend climbed the trunk, examining it for another bud. He found a nodule sticking out and began massaging it. It wiggled. It pushed apart from the tree, beginning a new branch.

Just after that branch fell, Kylac's snapped. Another matriarch ran over to the melon and rolled it away.

Deka was still working on his first, and he tried to rub faster.

Kylac clung to the trunk and searched for a new branch to grow. He looked out over at the volcanoes looming over them. They had not stopped erupting since climbing this tree.

They were inside one of several hundred of this type. Other Anaxan swung through theirs, doing the same thing.

Meeting food production quota was required to live in the head matriarch's territory, and their quota was thirty-one fruits a day. It used to be twenty-eight. Each tree had four Anaxan working it, and they were not even close to the speed at which the former foxes grew their branches. They would make quota in no time.

"These trees have no circulatory system," Deka said as he massaged the branch. "That's what we're doing. We're making the sap flow."

"And they are our only food source," said Friend. "They grow in the sulfur created by the volcanoes, producing methane as a byproduct. That's why we can breathe here."

"I have memories of doing this for years," Kylac said. He had yet to find a new branch to stimulate, so instead he stared out at the roaring volcanoes. "We must produce thirty-one fruits in a day, but at the end of the day, we only receive one between us. I don't remember where the excess goes. Either of you remember?"

"The lead matriarch's family perhaps," Friend said.

Deka's branch sprouted. He smacked the branch with his knuckles in triumph, then crawled back to the trunk as the fruit filled with fluid and grew to twice his size and five times his bodyweight.

"I seem to remember sacrifices to the fire," Deka said. "Something about the lead matriarch and her family communing directly with the volcanoes. It's a bit foggy. I'm not used to things being foggy."

"I love it!" Friend said. His second branch was already sprouting. "I'm just here. No unlimited knowledge of the universe. No universes in sight but just out of reach. No itching to go there. No antispheres. No portals. Just simple, normal life."

"Whatever happened to ending the universe to save it?" Kylac said.

"It still needs to be done, but without being so aware of the Lake and reality, it doesn't feel so urgent. I wonder where in the Lake we are. Can we find our way back?"

Deka's branch collapsed, the fruit fell, and Deka searched for a new bud to encourage. "I doubt it. I don't even remember being in the Lake after we left home."

"Our limited minds prevent us from understanding the journey," Friend said. "It's why we didn't create a universe of our own. Others are out there, and it proves that this process is routine. But what is its purpose? I wish Rive were here. He would love to talk about this."

"Now you miss your raptor?" said Kylac as he climbed through the branches. "You should have thought of that before you ignored him on Earth."

"We always enjoyed these things. Not just talking, living in them. I miss that so much, exploring those theoretical places with him, examining the unsolved puzzles of the universe." Friend looked out and surveyed the view. "This planet is in a primitive state. Too much volcanic activity and yet habitable. I wonder how long this phase will last, and if these life forms will remain."

Deka had found a new bud and began massaging it out of the trunk. "And you want to create a universe? You were miserable enough back home. Imagine being alone in your own universe, knowing everything that will happen."

"But it will be mine. I can start over and make life the right way. I can change things."

"Well, I'm frustrated," Kylac said. He had found a new branch and was already half a pace out with it. "Nothing makes sense here. All the variables seem logical enough, but something is missing. I can't make portals, and I don't know why."

"I'm enjoying it while it lasts."

Deka turned and looked up. "I can't even work out how large this planet is. Too much haze from the volcanoes. Maybe when our shift is up we can find a better view."

"Judging by the gravity," Kylac said, "this world must be similar in size to Rel."

"That can't be right," said Deka. "We'd be able to open spheres by now."

"Stop talking about it," Friend said. "No big thoughts of the universe. For now, life is me and this tree. My purpose is to make it grow. It makes sense. It's such an elegant feeling."

"Good," Deka said. "You can stay here forever and rub branches for the rest of your life. The three of us will find a way home."

"This will become old soon enough, but until then, I am happy."

Friend's branch had almost reached sprouting length. Deka's was halfway there.

"If we do this right," Deka said, "we can make quota early and find Sonjaa. Wait... I just remembered what happened last year. If we're too fast, the matriarchs will expect this kind of speed from us all the time."

"And they'll force the others to match our rate," Kylac said.

"They would notice if I left and the two of you somehow made quota without me." Deka pounded the tree, but not in laughter. "My mate is becoming an Archeon, and I have to stimulate trees instead!"

Friend did not seem to be listening. He guided his branch as if doing so were the solitary source of happiness.

4

The blue fire roared around the medic, swirling and flicking and entering and exiting various orifices. Sonjaa watched. Though she was aware of the composition of the flame, she also noticed something familiar. It did not move according to any physical laws. The medic stepped out of it and stood on feet and knuckles before her as the flame settled into its rest state.

"It confirms everything you have said. You are not an Anaxa? What else is there to be?"

"I don't think I can describe it. You have no other animals here? No other forms of life?"

"We have a few animals, but none of them speak. The flame tells me where you come from, there are different species who can use words. Is that right?"

"That's right. How does it speak to you?"

"We require years of training to learn how to interpret the images the fire gives us. Only the lead matriarch and her family receive it. The medics learn at her discretion, and we are not shown everything."

Sonjaa rolled to her stomach and rose up to her knuckles. "May I try?"

The medic positioned himself between her and the flame. "Soon-to-be, the fire rejects everyone who has not been trained."

"Then how do others pray?"

"Those not in the matriarch's bloodline are content with speaking to the flames which dwell in their homes, trusting their prayers are heard."

Sonjaa tapped the soil with her hand. "So your society has nobles and commoners, with clergy standing between them. We left the universe, and I still see things that remind me of Earth."

She had spoken several words in Relian and English. Her medic stood in a puzzled posture.

"Tell me something," she continued. While concentrating on this one source of energy and information, the universe seemed a little quieter. "Why are medics beneath the laborers? Shouldn't this be some special place in society, since you can commune with the flames?"

"To help others confess their sins is to expose oneself to the sins of others. Males are ideal for the task, as the sins will not enter the body and harm an egg."

"What is the most common reason someone ends up in one of these tents?" Sonjaa concentrated on the fire, letting her medic's voice become part of it.

"Many, many afflictions," he said. "Most simply forget to speak to the fire and reaffirm their respect for the matriarchs."

Concentrating on just his voice and the flame beside him helped her function.

"Why would they forget? And why should they reaffirm that?"

"Without respect for them, order is lost. When order is lost, the trees die. If males were in control, society would degenerate into one, long courtship spar. The matriarchs push us to do other things. To forget to commune is to be tempted to allow disorder to take over. My role is to convince the workers that they have sinned."

Sonjaa breathed easier. Her ears had opened up. She could hear herself think again. Finally, she existed in this universe. Everything happening inside it had become background noise.

"Convince? Why?"

"Sin disguises itself as something natural. But doing the natural-feeling thing leads to chaos, and the trees die. Quota is very important. I hope your brothers succeed in making up for it. All soon-to-be matriarchs are required to serve so they learn empathy for the workers and will not become too harsh on them later in life."

Sonjaa was about to answer him. "I'm—"

The flame swelled to twice its original size and then shrank again. The medic adjusted position and stood over her. He shouted loud enough for someone to hear three tents over.

"Soon-to-be, the flame tells me your sin is disdain for the work of growing the trees. You look forward to a time when you do not have to serve. You are a soon-to-be, but this is a grievous attitude. Those males are working to keep civilization alive, and to keep the fire favorable. To look down upon them is a sin equal to not meeting quota. If you do not repent, you may not be permitted to join the matriarchs in the future."

Outside, Sonjaa heard electrons in the dirt repelling a set of knuckles and a pair of hind feet. The weight on those atoms suggested the person outside was a matriarch.

"I understand my sin," Sonjaa announced, "but how can I repent when I do not feel remorse?"

"You shall remain here until you understand," her medic shouted back. "Pray to the fire. I will commune with it and relay its answers."

The atoms outside buzzed and hummed less, which meant the matriarch had moved away. Her medic's posture relaxed, and now he spoke quietly.

"What were you about to say?"

"Let me commune with it," Sonjaa said. "I think I can learn its language."

"I cannot allow that."

"Then let me ask the fire first. You tell me what it thinks."

He looked at the flame, then at Sonjaa. He stood up and reached an arm into it. The blaze grew and filled half the tent, changing color. The medic walked inside and promptly vanished in a swirl of blue and green. She wanted to leap in right now, but she also didn't know what she was dealing with.

The flame did not shrink, but the medic stepped out, facing Sonjaa.

"I don't believe it. It wants you to commune. Are you sure you are ready? Those who enter the fire without preparation are often never the same again."

Sonjaa rose to her feet and knuckles. The incredible noise of the atoms interacting with one another around and underneath her drowned out all other information for a few breaths, but she focused on the fire for a few breaths, allowing everything else to fade into the background. She walked straight into it.

It overtook her senses, and now the fire became the only thing she could sense. It felt so good to have only one thing screaming at her. Relief. Peace. She took a few easy breaths.

Now she felt it. Language patterns. Consciousness. It was nonlinear, similar to the Lake, with no difference between thought and speech. She had communicated like this before. The impulses sorted themselves into recognizable patterns, and everything orbited that.

Who are you? she wondered.

I am Ein, was the answer.

Are you in the Lake?

There is no lava here.

Not the lava lake. The place outside the universe, where reality exists.

Who are you? Where do you come from?

Another universe.

You know of other universes? How did you come here?

Please tell me who you are.

You are in my creation. Can you understand that?

Yes. I come from another universe. They are not my brothers. I am not an Anaxa. I am becoming an Archeon.

The word clearly meant something to the fire. The flame changed from green to violet.

Archeons. It is much too soon. I will project myself to you in a more appropriate form later. I believe you can un-

derstand. Find your companions again. I have kept you here until quitting time. Speak your medic's name. He will help you.

Ein gave her a name. The flame shrank. Sonjaa stood in the middle of it for a moment. The language patterns had vanished. Now all she could sense was the quarks and electrons. Normal flame behavior.

She stepped out. Instantly the noise of the universe crushed the tranquility of a new language. It brought her to her stomach as she became aware of the state of every collection of quarks and gluons around her. She gasped and tried to breathe and shut out the extra information, but it forced its way into her skull and jostled for attention. She heard electrical repulsion of atoms moving away from her, which meant the medic was backing up.

"You are a lead matriarch, aren't you?" he said, voice quivering. "One of her sisters come down to observe the work? I have not shown disrespect, have I?"

His voice had phased in and out with the many vibrations happening around her. Sonjaa rose to her knuckles and hobbled up to him, straining to stand upright under the weight of all the information coming down on her. Sonjaa nuzzled his snout as a raptor would. He jumped away and glared at her. Sonjaa strained to speak.

"I'm not from here. Things make a little more sense now. How long was I in there?"

"Most of the day. It is now time for the workers to receive their rations and return home."

The noise of the universe rose in volume again. Sonjaa became dizzy and she collapsed halfway to the ground from being aware of the planet's rotation. She held herself up with just one hand.

"I need to find my brothers. Thank you so much for your help. What is your name?"

He lowered his head. "I am not permitted to speak it."

She looked up and met his eyes. "Your name is Boroy."

He raised his snout and stared at her. Sonjaa heard his heart stop for a whole breath. The information had been difficult to pick out over the sound of the electrons in his blood vessels repelling the liquids and solids to keep them contained in the tubes—each fluid made a slightly different sound as it rubbed against the walls of the vessels—each solid made a different sound as it bumped and flowed along —the sheer amount of information hitting her almost made her vomit.

She had an equally difficult time focusing on him, as her eyes also took in multiple spectrums of electromagnetic energy. His muzzle seemed distorted due to the quarks in his face humming as they vibrated within their tethers.

"I am not a lead matriarch." Her voice sounded strained even to her ears. "Is there a way to leave this place? Somewhere we can go where no one will find us?"

He hesitated for several breaths before speaking. "Yes."

5

Their ration was indeed one fruit per family. The three of them rolled it across the valley, out of the fog of sulfur and into the clear air of the open plains. It was taller than they were, and weighed more than all of them combined.

"The soil must be rich in nutrients," Friend said. "Another indicator of a young planet still in its primitive state. All the nutrients are close to the surface, and untapped, which is why the trees are able to grow so fast. We are witness to an uncontacted species' early development. They may even be a lone species."

"Is this really fair?" Deka said. "I want to know why we had to grow thirty-one pieces of fruit but our share was one. Where do the other thirty go? Why don't I know this?"

"Perhaps the workers themselves are unaware," Friend answered.

"Well, as soon as we get this thing home, we are finding out!"

"How?" Kylac said. "That was a lot of work, and it was mind-numbing. We can't leave the settlement without someone noticing."

"I don't care!" Deka said. "I'm not doing that again!"

"We have no choice, Deka. This is our only food source. We're not carnivores anymore."

"There is a way out! We'll find it! Now where are we taking this thing? Why don't we just eat it here?"

Friend nudged the fruit back on course. "We have parents to feed, remember?"

"Right. Once a pair of Anaxan are allowed to have eggs, the parents are exempt from working as long as they have at least four viable hatchlings."

"So what do our parents do all day?" Kylac said.

"I don't know," said Friend. "Which means the Anaxan don't know either. But I do know they never come home until morning, which is when we have to return to the trees."

"Another question we'll answer soon!"

Deka grunted as he shoved the fruit forward. They were going uphill now, and the settlement was another thousand paces away.

"I hope Sonjaa knows where we're going."

Friend punched the fruit, laughing. "We made quota for her, so she owes us."

Dozens of Anaxan also rolled melons up the hill. Some had already made it to the top and were moving on to the village. It took the Relians a while longer to maneuver their fruit over the ridge and onto the plateau. The village was in sight. They paused to breathe.

"Deka!"

They recognized Sonjaa's voice behind them. They turned and waited for her as she hobbled across the hot, barren dirt. She held her eyes shut as she ran, and she often wobbled on her knuckles. She stopped at the bottom of the slope, straining to stay upright.

"I have help!" She sounded as if every bone in her body had shattered. "My medic... He's willing to show us a place we can... hide! Until we figure out... Come back down."

The Relians on the ridge looked at one another. Deka grunted, walked behind the fruit, and punched it back down the hill. It tumbled and bounced and rolled to a stop forty paces away. The Relians ran back down the hill and met Sonjaa.

Deka nuzzled and tried to scent her. "I'm so sorry. I should have been there while you're going through this. Are you feeling any better?"

She sank to the ground, then lifted herself back up again to make eye contact with Deka. "No, I feel like I'm going to be crushed under all this noise."

"Everything in the universe moves according to laws. Listen for those laws. Let the math emerge out of the chaos. Don't shut it out. Your mind can handle this."

She gritted her teeth as she dropped to her stomach. He helped her back up to her hands.

"We're still trying to figure this place out," Deka continued. "It doesn't make much sense. Everything seems the same, and yet I can't open a sphere."

"Never mind that." She closed her eyes and forced her limbs to bear her weight. "I think I just talked to the god of this universe."

She began running to the medic village.

"What about the fruit?" Kylac yelled.

"Forget it!" Sonjaa shouted.

"I worked hard for that! Our parents are hungry! I'm hungry!"

"We don't have parents!" Deka yelled as he caught up to Sonjaa.

Kylac huffed. He opened his mouth, took a gigantic bite, and then bounded after them. They followed Sonjaa to the village.

It was a long run back. Sonjaa paused many times, and Deka nuzzled her like a Relian while she caught her breath. Friend seemed to dislike stopping so often and kept moving.

The village appeared deserted. The medics were gone, all except one who stood at the entrance to a tent, looking around eagerly. They stopped in front of him. He met everyone's eyes, obviously much more comfortable meeting the gaze of another male.

"This is Boroy," she said, panting from mental exhaustion as well as physical. "My medic. You're not supposed to know his name though."

"All of you do not belong here," he said. "You entered my territory without trepidation. If you are discovered, you will be cast out of the settlement. There is only one place you can hide where no one will question you being here. I will take you to my quarters below."

"Thank you," Deka said. "We promise not to be around for long."

"There is no other place for you to go. Medics often hide sinners until they are ready to return to society. It is our duty to stand between them and the wrath of the matriarchs who enforce the law. I can keep all of you safe for a time."

He led the way deeper into the medic village, straight for one particular tent. A large hole filled the center, and it led underground. Boroy ran into it, and the Relians followed.

The darkness only lasted a few dozen paces, and then they passed through a barrier that resembled fire but was clearly not. The cavern opened into an enormous chamber of bubbling magma. The Archeons knew they were directly underneath the grove they had just worked.

Above them, the root systems from every tree intertwined in an elaborate branch network. Anaxan climbed up and down the roots, each holding large pieces of fruit in their crocodile snouts. The Relians observed one Anaxa on one of the lower root branches. He removed a piece of fruit from his mouth, split the membrane, and slathered his hands with it. He then massaged the fruit paste into the tree root.

One hundred and twenty-two Anaxan were doing this to all parts of the roots. Standing on the ledge, well away from the lava pool, were one hundred and twenty-two Anaxan carving pieces of fruit into sections with their claws and then leaving them in a line for the others to pick up.

Two individuals rolled a large melon from a cave tunnel. The Relians recognized them: their parents. All of the people down here were people from the village who had been permitted to have eggs.

They followed their medic along the ridge that lined the edge of the lava lake. Sonjaa shuddered and fell, clutching her head. Deka helped her up so she could keep pace with their guide. She leaned on him as she hobbled across the ridge, eyes clenched.

Off to the side, people swung from and climbed over the lattice of tree roots, smearing them with fruit paste. Others had some other, darker paste they were layering on top. About fifty paces below, the lava bubbled and churned.

Friend looked over the edge. A few Anaxan waded in the pool, swimming, bobbing, rolling fruit into the lava.

Boroy turned down a small tunnel and stopped inside a vacuole within the rock. No flame here, but the light from the lava pool made its way this far into the cave. A single piece of fruit the size of his fist lay on the stone ground waiting for him. The Relians huddled into the tight space. Sonjaa lay on her side and curled up, moaning.

Boroy took the slice of fruit and gobbled it up. When he finished, he faced them.

"The barrier you passed through earlier blanks the memory of all sinners who leave here. They remember their lesson, but not the truth."

"I understand why," Friend said. "If everyone knew their quota went back down here to fertilize the trees, they would be depressed."

"The nutrients are gone from the soil," Boroy said. "Generations ago, the matriarchs dictated everyone to dig under the trees. The magma came up, and the matriarchs communed with it. It told them how to save the trees, and we have been doing it ever since. Good growers are permitted to couple, and they are free to work down here, mixing the fruit matter with cave fungus to make it rot and fertilize the roots."

The Relians were silent for a moment. Sonjaa curled even deeper into herself, hands over her eyes and ears.

Deka turned to Friend. "I think you should stay here. Sounds like a wonderful life, breaking even and all."

Friend nudged him back. "The people who encourage the tree growth must be taught that doing so is the meaning of life. That's how I felt the whole time I was up there."

"The trees need an incredible amount of nutrients to grow," Boroy continued. "We are told they are used to ancient soil that was packed with nutrients leftover from when the land was molten. Now the soil is used up. If not for the fire directing the lead matriarch's family to organize us in this way, the trees would have died long ago, and us with them. Most growers live their entire lives ignorant of all of this. One fruit feeds a family each day. It is just enough for them to enjoy some free time, and then they must return to the grove. Worthy growers have eggs so they can do easier work as they age."

"This is easy?" Kylac said.

"Working in the heat is much easier than working in the sulfur. We do not tire as quickly. Some of us who are unfit to work become medics. It is the only way to avoid labor, but you are exposed to sin, doubt, despair, and depressing agony. People are worn out and want to stop working so they can rest. My task is to convince them to go back without explaining why. We deal with it so the matriarchs do not have to. It is a great burden, living with the knowledge of how fragile our survival is. Now that you know the truth, please tell me about where you come from."

Sonjaa uncovered her eyes and ears and looked up at him. "We are not Anaxan."

"What else can you be?" Boroy said.

The Relians exchanged glances.

6

Sonjaa hoped sleep would bring relief from the particles of the universe screaming at her for attention, but even as she slept she knew what they were saying, and they were all talking at once, never letting up, never leaving her alone. She expected it, and she dreaded it. The information had weight that crushed her. She had already been flattened as far as she thought she could bear, and now she was becoming infinitesimally thinner, the information melting her into mere noise within the noise, lost forever.

As she slept, she became aware of Relian scent. At first she shut it out as a phantom of memory, but then she realized it was a real scent in the air right now. She awoke, raised her head.

A Relian theropod stood at the entrance of Boroy's cavity, scent and scale pattern a mixture of multiple raptors she remembered.

The raptor's head tilted. "I am Ein."

She nudged Deka, which nudged Kylac, which nudged Friend. The former Relians raised their snouts and turned to the entrance. They wiggled and climbed on top of one another. Sonjaa was the first to her knuckles and squeezed out of the cavity. The theropod had backed away to the edge of the cliff overlooking the lattice of tree roots hanging over the lake of lava.

Sonjaa ran to meet the stranger, straining to see the raptor through the electromagnetic noise that clouded her vision. When they stood together, time around them slowed to a crawl, and the theropod looked them over.

"I was listening to your story. I found a bodily form you would recognize from Sonjaa's time in the flame."

Friend pushed ahead of Deka and stood beside Sonjaa. "Are you the creator of this universe?"

"Yes."

"So is it true? You were an Archeon in your universe and you figured out what the Lake is, which created this one?"

"You understand much," said the theropod, "and yet there are so many gaps in what you can grasp. This is fascinating, how you managed to create a place to exist within my equation without understanding it."

"What was it?" Friend asked. "What was it you realized that created this place? How did it happen?"

Deka smacked Friend with his hand and shoved him backwards.

"You're the fire," Sonjaa said. "The lead matriarchs commune with you. You're the one who told them to tend the trees."

The theropod turned and looked out over the lattice of roots protruding from the ceiling. The Anaxan swinging from them had been suspended in place.

"I saved them," Ein began. "These people are so fragile, and I cannot let them die. All I have to do is keep them alive for a few eons, and then the climate in this region will change enough to give rise to other sources of food for them. I chose to commune only with certain individuals because that is all they can understand for now. Eventually they will develop a more complex society. They will encounter others on this world, and then they will understand portal physics. It will all be worth it in the end."

"Meantime," Deka said, "it's pointless toil. Why not just send them food until the trees can grow again?"

The theropod turned to Deka. "I cannot do that without consequences. I must work with the atoms that already exist. This equation has rules. If I break them, I would hurt more people than I will help. This isn't the only civilization I'm preserving. I am protecting and guiding thousands of species while they are vulnerable."

"What's the goal?" Friend said. "Why bother? Do you sense anyone else is capable of leaving the universe?"

The theropod locked eyes with him again. "You are incredibly determined to understand what lies beyond your equation. I already know why, but you do not, which makes you dangerous. Your single-minded determination has already harmed so many."

"What do you call it?" Kylac said. "The place outside the universe. What is it?"

"The name would mean nothing to you. *Lake* will do. Yes, I know what it is and how it works. For the sake of the life that would evolve in your equation," he addressed Friend directly, "I hope you never understand."

Friend tried to snarl at him, but he punched the ground instead. "Please! I have been struggling with the questions for years, and if you have the answers to any of them, I beg you to help me! Will anyone else leave your universe?"

The theropod curled its hands against its chest, hiding the claws. "If I nurture the life here and change just the right variables at exactly the right moments, my equation will bear grandchildren, so to speak. Others will become capable of leaving it."

"So that *is* the goal!" Friend shouted, hopping on his knuckles. "I was right! It wasn't for nothing!"

"Can you help us find a way back home?" Deka said.

"I can tell you exactly where to go," Ein answered, "but you will not understand. The four of you cannot even understand the Lake when you are in it. I could return you to your home, but that would lead to more destruction there."

"Are there other creators where you are?" Friend said. "Can you communicate with anyone else?"

"There are others in the Lake. We know one another. We can speak across it. There are plenty of others here, too, but they do not know it. Their minds are scrambled. Only by understanding where they are can they hold themselves together. You four are not supposed to be here. Only those who gain such understanding should be able to travel between the universes.

"I know Sonjaa's memories of what happened in your reality. Antispheres are not dangerous. Mysterious, yes, but not destructive. The antispheres were only destructive because you," the theropod locked eyes with Friend, "have a destructive mind. It was a very peaceful, exploratory process for me. I didn't lose any planets trying to leave my home.

"I realize all of you are curious about the process. I did not expect to talk to anyone about it for a very long time. I hope you understand just how unusual this is, for people to travel between realities without understanding it."

"It's a privilege speaking with you," Kylac said. "I wish it had been peaceful for us."

The theropod raised its neck. "Chaos is about to touch my realm."

"What?" Deka said, trying to curl his own neck in reply.

"And order arising from it," Ein continued. "I wanted to meet the people responsible. The three of you will succeed in containing it."

"What are you talking about?" Friend said.

The theropod glared at him again. "Your mind has almost figured out my equation. As soon as it does, you will lose control."

Friend straightened up. "Why? I'm in control now! How could I lose it?"

"You cannot handle the understanding," Ein answered. "Your animal nature prevents it."

The other three were backing away, facing him. Friend remained in the center.

"I won't kill you," Ein continued. "If I do, you will cause more destruction from the Lake. I also won't stop you. Everything you are about to do has been worked into my plan. You will not cause any real harm."

Friend leaped up to him and grabbed him by the neck. "No, no, please! This isn't who I am! I want to understand the Lake! My old ways are holding me back! Everything is holding me back! Help me escape! Since I was little it's all I wanted, and then I glimpsed other universes out there and I had to see them! I had to get away! I am in control of myself! This is science so why do I panic when I glimpse the math and everything it means? Please help me!"

The theropod was as immovable as a mesa. "You possess instincts so overwhelming another species must intervene to help you control them. This is a fascinating case of co-evolution. I want to witness it."

Friend lowered himself and backed away, gazing up at Ein. "Is it possible for someone with animal instincts to understand the Lake? Does having them mean I'll never figure it out?"

"Anyone can, animal impulses or not. Some have a more difficult time than others, but there is no limit to what the mind can transcend. Let it begin."

Friend gasped and dropped to the dirt, snarling. Time sped up around them, and the theropod faded into the air. The Anaxan noticed their presence. Friend looked up at the lattice. A sphere opened on top of the nearest Anaxa climbing the tree roots. His head and a quarter of his torso disappeared as the portal snapped shut, and he teetered over and fell into the lava below.

Deka bounded up to Friend, grabbed him, and tossed him over the edge. The former fox fell snarling all the way down to the lava. The other Relians ran to the edge and observed. Several Anaxan waded in the bubbling pool. Friend hit the center. He bobbed up to the surface and floated, still thrashing and snarling. Six portals opened at once, each over one of the Anaxan in the molten rock. Their heads disappeared as the portals closed. Friend seemed to calm down for a moment, and then he thrashed again. Another sphere opened, and the lava rose into a large wave and washed him through it before closing.

Deka pounded the ground with one fist. "How did he figure it out before I did?! Kylac?!"

The former fox backed away. "I haven't found what's different yet."

"Think harder! Sonjaa, anything?"

Sonjaa struggled to remain on her feet. "N-no."

Deka raised both fists, unfolded his hands, and scratched the ground with his claws. "Think! Where did he go? How did he get there? Why doesn't this make sense?"

Ein's voice filled their ears. "He killed some of the lead matriarch's family. It will cause a good shift in treatment for the workers here. The remaining matriarchs will lessen the quota and reduce the surplus fruit for ruling family. They did not listen to me years ago when I told them they should, so Friend has made things right. I sent him elsewhere to use his destruction for a larger purpose. Now he is decreasing the population of the Itae. I dropped him in the middle of one of their mating combat rituals. He has decimated the dominant families, which will allow some of the lesser bloodlines to rise up. It will be better for everyone in the future. It is now time for you three to intervene."

A sphere opened to another planet, full of blue sky and clear water. Deka ran through the way. Kylac helped Sonjaa to her knuckles and walked her through.

7

The three Relians in Anaxa bodies stood on a much colder world. No volcanoes here, no lava, though the atmosphere was still primarily methane.

They stood on a rocky island in the middle of a pool of crystal clear water. The rock surface was smooth and flat, stained with the blood of hundreds of dismembered creatures.

These creatures had been quadrupeds. Their blood was an orange color, and their white fur was bristly and spiked, though not sharp. Most were missing heads, legs, sections of torso. Those body parts floated in the surrounding water.

The bodies had fallen as if an explosion had occurred, and they pointed toward the source of the destruction. Friend knelt in the epicenter, shaking, his scent anxiety calm for the time being.

Deka walked between the bodies. Kylac followed him. Sonjaa stayed behind and clutched her skull, her mind compressed under the weight of the different sounds coming from the air molecules around her, and the water buzzing as the atoms flowed over one another.

Deka and Kylac understood they were in no danger. They were well within Friend's scenting distance, so if he hadn't killed them by now, he never would. Their minds continued processing the variables of this universe. Something was still not right. They were clearly on a different planet, but everything felt too similar.

Five paces from Friend. They halted. Kylac stood next to Deka.

Friend thrashed, reaching out and scratching the dirt. A few dozen portals opened around them, each one spilling out body parts, blood, and entrails. Deka and Kylac heard a few dozen people drop dead in the distance.

Kylac looked at Deka. "His awareness is growing. He's learning this universe just as he learned ours. Soon he will know it as a whole, and then it will be his scenting distance."

Deka rose to his hind legs, spreading his hands. "Then we drown him before he can!"

Kylac also rose.

A sphere opened on top of Friend and quickly snapped shut, leaving empty air in his place. Ein appeared again, twice as tall as last time.

Deka dropped to his knuckles. "Why did you do that?!"

"Do not kill him in my realm. He is decimating the population of Gigee as I speak, but don't be alarmed. They are an animal species who prey on another animal species that will become intelligent in another seven hundred generations. Their numbers needed to be trimmed to allow for this to happen. His awareness has grown to fifteen thousand paces around himself, as you measure it. I have never known anyone to have this reaction to being aware of the life that is part of an equation."

"It won't stop!" Kylac shouted. "Our species has an instinctual fear of others intruding our scenting distance, and this perspective means he will soon consider the entire universe his territory! He will kill everyone because he doesn't know how to resist!"

"The three of you will stop him before he reaches that point."

"Take us to the planet he's on!" Deka yelled.

"There are no other planets. This is the only one."

"What?" Deka said. "But the numbers here... It's light years away from where we were."

"Correct."

Deka and Kylac looked at one another, and then turned back to Ein.

The tall theropod faded. "I must visit your equation when I can. It sounds like a fascinating place." Ein left empty air behind.

The former Relians stood in the middle of a serene island of death, the clear water now orange with the blood of these furred creatures.

"One planet..." Kylac said. "Light years across." He looked up at the sky. "No stars in the sky. We don't see by light. It's background radiation. Weak... Very weak."

"Kylac?"

"That's it... That's it. That's what's different! The moment of creation! The moment! It was weaker! The total mass of this universe is tiny—the moment Ein created this universe the matter did not spread out! It all came back together and formed this place! It used to be a star!"

"A star?" Deka pondered the numbers. "To form to a planet that big? Gravity would have to be incredibly weak here."

"Yes, yes! It's so weak it takes the entire mass of the universe to equal the gravity of Rel! It was a star! It decayed into this planet—didn't have enough energy to become a supernova, so it only shed its outer layers! It's perfect! Deka, the numbers are lining up! I'm starting— I'm starting to—"

Kylac hung his head. His elbows buckled under imaginary weight.

Deka's mind examined the numbers. Now that he knew what to search for, it began to make sense. The formation of this universe—the beginning, the weak inflation, the particles of Lake colliding with it, sending shockwaves through it, creating the dimples in spacetime in which energy collected and formed matter. With less mass to work with, it did not spread out very far. All the matter in the universe, only several galaxies' worth, came back together and formed a star.

The star lived, burned up its fuel, and then exploded, but instead of spreading apart, the weak explosion caused the layers to stratify. It formed a crust that trapped the heat inside. The remaining gasses collected around the cooled crust and formed an atmosphere.

The end product was a planet millions of light years across that contained close to all the matter in this universe. Different regions were like different planets, weather patterns localized to areas only a few thousand paces in diameter, driven by the primal heat still escaping from beneath the crust.

A universe of only a single planet. Deka's mind opened. Numbers rushed in. Every point in the universe became visible to Deka's mind. The spacetime fell into familiar patterns and calculable variables, just as they had back home. His mind comprehended the portal physics of this universe—just being aware of spacetime as it really existed instead of how the senses filtered it to the mind meant a conscious person could form connections between any point, allowing them to open portals, creating a community of planets linked by individuals holding these spheres open for years at a time.

And then something new occurred to him. Rising out of the patterns that comprised spacetime in this reality came extra numbers. Deka perceived the medium outside the universe, supporting reality, giving rise to the equations that made portal physics work. The equations had equations beneath them, a lower set causing a higher set to exist, both cranking away, one feeding into the other.

Deka became weak in the elbows and had a difficult time staying upright.

He had experienced the Lake firsthand. Sonjaa had shown him how to stay alive there, and he had floated across it to this reality. His mind had been taking it in the whole time, trying to analyze it. It came rushing back—now that he had a set of equations on this side figured out, his mind began automatically working out what equations needed to exist on the other side in order for those to work.

Deka collapsed. He forgot to breathe and gasped several times.

"Deka?" Kylac whispered. "No..."

New numbers stacked in his mind. A tower formed. He now realized it was possible to calculate spacetime from the Lake, which sped up the process. An antisphere formed in front of Deka as his mind pierced the barrier and explored beyond. The antisphere was about ten paces away and thirty above the ground, spinning, drawing air into it. The ground shook and began to separate.

Kylac was also on the ground, shaking. Multiple portals opened in front of him. Portals to various places in this planet's atmosphere. Kylac's awareness had expanded, and it moved faster than Friend's. He already knew the collective scents of everyone on this world. The planet became his scenting distance.

Their minds ran through the formation of this realm, from creation to star formation to decay. The terrain formed based on predicable sets of variables interacting. Deka and Kylac became aware of the planet's surface all the way around.

Life became a variable in these equations. The variables changed in predictable ways. Their cycles became the same as constants. Deka clutched his skull and curled up as the enormity of what he realized threatened to overpower him.

He became aware of the life forms that rose from this terrain, and his mind ran the numbers from the distant past into the present and then extended into the future. All of it was calculable. The numbers attacked Deka, and he gasped as he understood the universe as a whole. The antisphere spun and grew in size. The rocks shook. Sections of rock shot out of the ground and flew into the void.

Kylac had already calculated so many life forms that everything had become a mere variation of the billions of others. The life forms that emerged from these variables were the only possible results of such variables. Spheres bubbled around him, the other ends opening all over the planet, just barely missing living creatures as he fought the growing scent anxiety.

Deka stared into the antisphere he made. The Lake stared back at him. The universe existed inside of something else, and its presence created the laws of this reality. The equations were perfect, and they told him something was inside that void, but he still did not understand. Calculating the universe in this way, from an outside perspective, allowed him to touch multiple places at once. As the anti-sphere slowly inflated, he reached into spacetime and formed three connections. It was easier than ever to form portals this way. Three spheres opened at once around the antisphere. From this perspective, the Lake was not a terri-fying place. It was just where he had to go to open spheres in a hurry. He had been calculating ways from inside the universe the whole time, which had been only half the equation. Now he witnessed the whole thing—an entire tower in his mind cranking away, complex and fragile, but perfect.

The antisphere stabilized. He had been through it once and survived, so it did not feel mysterious or terrify-ing. Deka opened six more spheres around himself. His mind had already calculated those regions from the birth of the star to this precise moment, and what life forms would be there right now. He felt them staring at the spheres, wondering what they were. Deka's mind calculated the in-dividuals, their thoughts, their paths from birth to death and everything in between—obvious results from variables interacting at the beginning of creation. Life was a simple part of the equations that made up the universe.

And then there was Friend. He also had numbers—the numbers from the equation they had come from; those numbers had become part of this section of this world as if they had always been there. Deka calculated what quarks and molecules came together to form him, and it led to where he was now, and the damage he caused. Friend was in a valley seventy light years away. His awareness only ex-tended into a single light year by now. It felt good to be ahead of him. Deka closed all the spheres and stared into the emptiness that was the Lake.

"Kylac," he said, rising to his hands and feet and turn-ing to face the red and black Anaxa. "I have it, too."

Kylac answered in English as tiny portals boiled around him. "Welcome to hell!"

"It's not hell for me! Kylac, Archeons have only been working with half the numbers the whole time! We never realized there was something beneath them! Another reality! The Lake makes spacetime work! It's not chaos! Kylac, your numbers! You have numbers! I— I can—!"

Deka's mind ran Kylac's numbers from birth to death, tracing every atom that comprised him from the beginning of the universe to the present. Kylac's actions became just as predictable as those particles, and now Deka felt the connections he was pulling. He felt the primal drive of scent anxiety, and what it pushed his fox to do. Deka reached into the same points of spacetime he knew his fox would be and held the connections closed.

Kylac's ways snapped shut. The Anaxa with skin colored like a Relian canine's rolled over and stood in front of Deka. The red and blue Anaxa had just predicted where Kylac would open his spheres, and then shoved the spacetime back where it belonged.

Kylac's instincts thrashed, tried to push through. He did not become enraged physically, but his mind reached out and attacked Deka, trying to push him out of the connections he wanted to make, but Deka occupied every point he wanted to be.

He and Friend had done this on Reyno long ago, and it only resulted in a stalemate. Deka felt different. It was like a raptor's scent, but on a quantum level. Deka was here now, and Kylac's instincts reacted to that. He dropped to his elbows.

"Deka!" He swallowed. "Tame me! Keep me from hurting everyone! I can't do it myself forever!"

Deka walked up to him, helped him to his hands and feet. Kylac's mind still pushed and thrashed, searching for an opening. Deka blocked him no matter where in the universe he tried to go.

"Finally, I can help you! Kylac, I understand! I will block that fox until he can't move!"

He opened a sphere to the other side of the planet and leaped through the portal, pulling Kylac through by the hand.

Sonjaa clutched her head, picked herself up and hobbled through the field of bodies to the sphere.

8

It was a grassland, but the grass here was transparent save for black dots inside its body that absorbed carbon dioxide and released methane as a byproduct. The carbon dioxide came from the animals that roamed this land. There was no visible light here. Animals saw by way of the electromagnetic field.

Most of them were dead. Portals had been opening across the land, sweeping it clean of all living scents larger than an insect. The destruction made a ring surrounding a single creature who sat huddled into himself in the middle of this grassland. His awareness of the universe expanded. His scenting distance grew as he felt more and more creatures around him.

His mind had processed enough numbers. The equations revealed the Lake to him, and how to make a way into it, but he still did not understand it. The antisphere that opened in the sky was unstable, and it swallowed everything it touched as it expanded. It interfered with the magnetic field lines, causing the ground to shake. The reverberations would be felt for years as the planet stabilized.

His mind ran through the moment this universe came into existence and calculated the terrain as it would have developed, then the people, and then their scents. Their horrifying scents. He snuffed them out as he followed their numbers into the present, and it satisfied him until his consciousness expanded and found someone else. He worked his way around the planet. He had a long distance to go before they were all gone.

Deka and Kylac leaped through the portal just a few paces away from Friend. The Anaxa in the middle of the destruction that extended millions of paces in all directions turned to them.

"I never used to panic when in a crowd. I saw other foxes lose control of themselves around others. I was proud I wasn't like them. Why now? It happens by itself. I'm opening spheres and I'm not telling myself to. Why can't I stop? Why does it feel good? It's this *thing*. It shouldn't be in me. I don't want it. But I'm grateful I feel no reaction from the three of you. I don't want to be the only one left."

Deka punched the ground with his knuckles. He reached out with his mind, intercepted Friend's portals, and threw the spacetime back where it belonged. He reached into where Friend had broken the barrier and closed the antisphere. He anticipated where Friend would open spheres and antispheres next and blocked those ways.

Friend stood up, locking eyes with Deka. "You found the solution. I hope you're good. If there's an opening, my old ways will find it."

Deka felt Friend reaching out to random points. Deka had calculated where Friend would reach out and halted him before he could join two points of spacetime. Deka wanted to growl at him, but he howled like a primate instead.

"Stop this!"

"Deka," Kylac said. "You're dividing yourself. You're leaving openings for me to escape."

A few tiny portals opened around Friend. Body parts and pieces of skin spilled out of them. Friend did not submit to Deka's presence. Kylac's old ways, too, became bolder. They both found gaps in his blocking. Deka quickly reached out with his mind and closed the spheres before they could do more damage.

Friend's awareness now extended a quarter of the way around the planet. Tiny spheres bubbled and simmered around them. They opened onto a million locations at once, trying to snuff out a million different scents.

Kylac reached out and tried to block his ways as well. Friend flinched, locked eyes with the younger former fox.

"It will only take a moment. It'll be quiet enough for me to think. I'll have time to figure out the Lake. We both will, Kylac. I won't harm you three. I don't want to."

"This is justice!" Deka screamed.

"You're losing both of us," Kylac said.

9

Sonjaa stepped through the sphere. Friend stood on his feet and knuckles, facing Deka and Kylac. Spheres sizzled around them. They filled the field and the air, but none of them touched her. Blood shot out of some of them, making the sky drizzle red.

Portals made a distinct noise. Antispheres made an even stranger sound. It merely blended with the noises made by the other parts of reality. Death was everywhere. She had a feeling Deka and Kylac would not be able to keep up with Friend.

She focused on Friend as she struggled to stay standing. Deka had told her the universe obeyed mathematical laws. She tried to perceive them, but she did not understand how Deka could find math in all this noise—it reminded her of hatchlings shrieking for food all at different pitches and ages.

She concentrated on a particular sound coming from everyone. From the way they behaved, and what Deka had told her over the years, these were probably the quarks that comprised the atoms that made up the molecules of Friend's body. They weren't really there; just shockwaves caused by particles in the Lake bouncing off the barrier. She tried to find correlations and numbers, but it was only noise.

They sang to her. She listened to their song. She ignored the quarks and concentrated on their voice.

The universe itself had a voice, and the Lake was the source. The Lake was singing—the universe was made of reverberations. She listened to the source of the voice.

Her mind calmed. Noise gradually became music. She remembered how it had sounded normally, and what it sounded like now with portals interfering with it. The churning storm of information funneled into a sense of order. The universe wasn't shouting at her in different voices, but the same voice through numerous filters. The distortions had regular patterns—quarks made certain sounds, atoms made other sounds—all these different noises phased into and out of synchronization with one another.

Language.

The various sounds began to settle into a drone. Quickly, as Friend thrashed mentally and resisted Deka's attempts to block him, Sonjaa perceived the portals as an intrusion into this drone.

Friend made noise that interfered with it.

Kylac also made noise in the universe that tried to pierce it.

Deka was making noise in the universe that countered their voices. The sounds he made tried to restore the drone of reality.

Deka's voice felt quieter than it should be, and Sonjaa heard why. He also blocked Kylac from reverting. In the physical world, a raptor was not capable of taming two foxes at once. One raptor paired with one fox. That fox responded to one scent, the only scent that kept a fox from mindlessly living to please their animal nature. To divide one's attention was to dilute that reaction. The same thing was happening on a quantum level.

Sonjaa stood up straight and approached Friend. Spheres and antispheres simmered around them as Friend pierced reality with noise, louder than ever. Sonjaa allowed the different sounds that made up the universe to blend into a single, droning tone. The normal sound of the universe.

Sonjaa observed the noise Friend made, and how it disturbed the drone. It reminded her of the noise a reverted fox would make. Sonjaa reached out with her mind and made sounds of her own. She sent a few shockwaves at Friend. Waves that felt like they would cancel out what Friend was doing and restore reality's sound to its normal drone.

Friend turned to her. Deka and Kylac recognized the new presence and faced her as well. Sonjaa walked on her knuckles and did not let up. She understood the noise Friend had to generate to make it do what he wanted. She made identical noise and achieved the same result. She stopped making those sounds, and the drone returned. Knowing what it took to make it happen led her to what she needed to create to cancel out Friend's actions.

She made those sounds.

Friend stumbled backwards.

Sonjaa closed in. A fox had reverted, and she had helped him. She made mental vibrations from the Lake that kept the drone of reality around Friend intact. Any deviation Friend tried to make in it, she corrected. It was simple. It worked.

Friend shied away from her. He didn't even try to push Deka and Kylac now; all his energy went to fighting Sonjaa, who stood over him. The noise she made squeezed him into a smaller and smaller area of spacetime, and now she contained him in this tiny section no bigger than his physical body. He couldn't reach out and make portals at all. Sonjaa blocked all of them, and her scent was the only thing he could calculate. She was on his level, and he responded to it now. Friend curled into himself, shivering. He gradually stopped probing for a way out. The instinct to submit to a raptor took over at last.

The air calmed. The sky stopped bleeding. Deka and Kylac relaxed. Sonjaa did not. She held Friend both mentally and physically, lying snout to snout with him.

"It's all right. I'm here." She paused to breathe.

Friend's hands covered his eyes. He had returned to the womb. His voice sounded distant and strained. "How did you do that?"

Sonjaa cuddled with him. "You're safe. It won't happen again. I promise. I can keep you..."

"Sonjaa?" Friend struggled to speak.

"The universe..." she continued. "Everything blends together. That's all I have to do. Make it drone again. If you speak, I will know. I can hear it."

Friend breathed. Sonjaa sensed his mind had shrunk within the confines of his body. It did not thrash for release. Deka and Kylac breathed easier.

A new presence appeared in the field. The Relians turned to face it. It glowed in visible light, not a theropod, but it loomed twice as tall as the theropod they had seen previously, walking on five legs supporting a bulky body that resembled an insect's but with an internal skeleton.

"Well done," said Ein's voice. "This is the body I had in my home universe. It ended a long time ago. I was the only person to make it out. Lots of other people witnessed the Lake, but I alone understood it. The memories and experiences of everyone within my former home are contained in its equation. I regard it as a great responsibility to carry it with me. I thought you should see me as I really was before I send you on your way."

"To where?" Deka said.

"Anywhere but here. I warn you, Sonjaa, Friend appeared stable as an Archeon, but he makes up for it by being incredibly unstable now that he is aware of the Lake. He will revert frequently. He is still aware of the scents of everyone here, and he is not thrashing to satisfy the anxiety now, but he will soon, just as all foxes once tried to break away from their raptors in the early years of your development for the singular purpose of calming their anxiety. You will need to bring him back many times. He will submit as long as the memory of your power over him remains fresh, and then the anxiety will rise up again. Do not kill him. He will simply move his mind into the Lake. That is enough destruction in my equation. It is time for you to leave."

Kylac stumbled forward. "But... Wait! We were lucky to land here! Please don't send us away! We don't know where we'll end up, and this whole thing will start again!"

"If I let you stay, Sonjaa will fail to contain Friend within six working cycles. She is strong but inexperienced and cannot keep up with Friend yet. Best to restart the process elsewhere. May you succeed in taming his old ways there. I will inform Boroy of what happened to you and reward him for giving you shelter. It was an unexpected pleasure to meet all of you."

Ein then said something in an unfamiliar language. The Relians guessed it meant *safe travels*.

Ein's body changed into an antisphere. It inflated an instant later, and the Relians fell out of the universe. The flashes of time flicked past them rapidly, and then the travelers floated beyond it. The Lake began tearing their conscious minds apart. They reached for one another and held themselves together as they drifted away.

There it was. This universe as a whole, tiny compared to home, and the planet really did occupy the entire thing with some flecks of gasses at the outer reaches. Reality moved on without them, leaving a wake that was its past.

Kronia

I

Tanya recognized the sphere in her room from the videos she had seen on the news, so she squared her shoulders and walked through. Now she stood in an unadorned structure made of stone. Light came in through some transparent, crystal-like things hanging from the center of the ceiling. She saw the sky through them. The rest of the roof was made of jagged pieces of black stone that wrapped around to form the walls and floor.

Books lined this chamber, as well as tapes, microfiche canisters, CD cases, and various other things resting in nooks built—no, *scratched* into the stone. Other than the daylight coming through the transparent rock in the ceiling, there was no other source of light, and the walls remained in shadow. It was cool in here, which sent shivers up her spine.

Something large moved on the other side of the skylight. The body alone was the size of a city bus, and it moved like a dragon, or rather a Krone, from what few videos of Norh moving were available to watch online.

It stepped into the light, a Krone with golden scales that faded to dark green around his belly. He walked up toward her slowly, majestically, wings folded against his flanks, head low to the ground to be at her level. His red and black horns and bone ridges looked as if he had gored thousands of people in his life and never washed off the blood. Strangely, she was not afraid.

"Tanya Jayman of Seattle, Washington," he said. "Welcome to my library."

His head hovered within interview distance of her. Tanya stood still and stared. His scales were much more vibrant than in the archival videos.

"Are you... Are you Norh?"

He bared his teeth, resembling a smile, and his wings fluttered a little. "I go by Sorven now. My human side and my Krone side synchronized years ago. This is Kronia, my second homeworld. Or first, depending on my mood."

"Oh my God. Is... Am I in trouble? I exposed them, so now...?" She gulped.

The Krone lay on his stomach, still holding his head at her eye level. "I enjoy your channel. Not many people bother to go to news stations and obtain Beta tapes of the original broadcast videos. Most are content to watch what is uploaded to the net. Your analysis is impressive."

"Then it's true, isn't it?! I'm right! I'm fucking right—it's all computer animation! The government is faking the alien attacks!"

"The government isn't the one to blame. They're acting on behalf of others who wanted to use the event for a different purpose."

"Who?"

"You'll see." He rose and began to turn. "Come with me. I'll show you why I brought you here."

"Do you need me to do something? Whatever you need, whatever you want, I'll do it."

He walked toward the far end of the room. Tanya walked just behind him.

"Let me explain why I'm here first, and then you will know what to do."

She looked up as she stepped into the light. The sky was blue just like Earth's, and the stone looked like mica, but even clearer. She trotted to keep up with the Krone.

"Thirty years ago, I had an idea. Humanity is on a path to self-destruction. People felt that way during the Cold War, but the nuclear blast never happened. Everyone was too afraid to actually use the weapons. So then the Soviet Union fell, dictatorship seemed defeated, and the danger of nuclear war seemed distant. The world was poised to enter an era of relative peace.

"Then Extraterrestrial Terror Day happened, and everything changed. Nuclear threats moved to the back-burner until something exploded on American soil. They called it a destructive Relian sphere. People thought the United States was paranoid after ET-Day. They hadn't seen anything yet. The press reports on events like this every day, and they have been for years, never letting the people forget why they should be afraid of alien attacks. You've probably figured out aliens had nothing to do with it, but what if I told you it was a nuclear bomb from America's own arsenal?"

They crossed into the next room. It was full of more books and tapes and unbound documents in white boxes. The same transparent rock allowed light in through a skylight. Staircases and ladders led up to every level of the shelves built into the walls. One of the walls had a strange symbol that looked like a numeral three with elaborate arcs, dashes, dots, and points around, on, and through it.

Under the skylight, dead center inside the illuminated circle, sat a white cardboard box.

"This is for you."

Tanya stepped around the Krone and entered the light. She knelt at the box and removed the lid. She expected her face to melt off when she looked inside, but it was just full of papers. She pulled out a packet at random, Restricted Access stamped across the top.

"The contents of that box were about to be shredded," said the Krone behind her. "I was already friends with a number of people in high office, thanks to Secretary of Relian Relations CJ Rhine. One of those people saved that box for last, and he kicked it through a portal I had opened in the office. It was a great risk to his life to do that for me, but his act of treason preserved hundreds of pages detailing the real reason the United States has active military bases in nearly every country on the planet, as well as clearance to fly unmanned aircraft over any nation it pleases. Why half the nations of the world are now considered to harbor extraterrestrials. I built this library to have a place to keep documents like these."

Tanya stood and looked at him, still holding the packet.

"There's more. I'm working on the video wall. So many new channels to watch, both online and over the air."

She swallowed. "You said I would know what to do."

"Yes, I need you to start spreading this information, but not over the internet. The algorithms are already getting good at crawling for banned material. You'll need to start a religion."

"A religion?"

"May I suggest dragon worship? Something outrageous and ridiculous, but also recognizable to those who suspect something is not right in the world and extraterrestrials have nothing to do with it. You'll find the sketches and models used to create the news stories, memos between department heads regarding details of the animation, and notes from ground crews staging the explosions and soldiers."

"H... How do I start a religion?"

"I'll let you discuss that with Rive. He'll walk you through the process. In the meantime, this library is yours. Be careful with everything you touch here. It's all original, and it's old, but this region is dry and has a regular temperature, so it will remain in good shape. Borrow anything you like. Make lots of copies. Bring the originals back as soon as you can. I will know if anything is missing, and for how long. I warn you this library is for your use only. If you bring anyone else here, or if you do not return materials, you will find the way closed forever. I trust that won't happen, and your church will last a long time. I need a reliable means to return this information to the people without being automatically deleted. Rive will show you the rest. He's at the video wall. Excuse me, please. I need to visit my sister and nephew."

Sorven turned and walked back they way they had come. He disappeared into a chamber to the left. She spun back around and rummaged through the box. She skimmed a few pages. Full of revelations when taken as a whole, she was certain.

She heard claws clicking on the stone floor in front of her. She looked up and saw a grey and tan theropod walking up to her. Most of his skin was gone, and in its place was metal so smooth she saw her reflection in it, her light-colored skin standing out against the dark stone of the walls and floor. She slowly rose, holding eye contact.

"Happy to meet you," said the metal raptor.

"Oh my God. You're Rive."

He clicked his claws, bobbed his head. "The real Rive."

Tanya had seen videos of him on TV since she was a child. Every few months the press broadcast a new video of this raptor standing before a group of people in Iraq, or fleeing the scene of a troop ambush in Afghanistan. Most of the videos were just a talking head addressing listeners in Arabic, subtitles purporting to show him demanding these nations hand over their vulnerable populations for extraterrestrial predation. Tanya had examined the tapes the media used for broadcast, and looking at them in higher resolutions she concluded the Rive on the screen had been computer animated. Here he was, standing before her, the enemy of the world—the cause of all of Earth's problems and only the United States was capable of solving them by spreading its military all over the planet.

"You need to know how to start a church. Follow me."

Rive turned and walked, both metal feet clanking on the stone. Tanya didn't want to leave the box or let go of the paper for fear if she let them out of her sight they would disappear. After a moment's hesitation, she slipped the papers back in the box, replaced the lid, and ran after the metal raptor.

"So it's true?" she said, keeping pace. "It's all computer animation? All of the alien attacks—everything since two thousand? You're not really feeding on the people in the Middle East?"

He turned to her. "As Sorven reassured you, you are not crazy. There is a reason those videos are such low quality. Computer animation wasn't quite up to the quality they needed, so they made the video as grainy as possible."

They entered a large room. Television screens filled one wall instead of books and magazines, all with the audio turned up. News stations, network broadcasts, cable, satellite, English-speaking and otherwise, at least three hundred screens going at once. Rive walked to a desk against one of the empty walls, books piled on it, as well as a manila folder.

"This is where Sorven spends most of his time. Yes, he is watching all these screens at once. He's an Archeon, as all Krone are. It helps him get a feel for what's happening in the world. Even the fiction reflects what's going on, especially the commercials."

Tanya smiled. "What about the reality shows?"

Rive clicked his claws. "I enjoyed your video on that. You are correct. It is intentional. Those shows are not only cheap to produce, but designed to reinforce submission to authority. Seeking the approval of the dominant human beings, begging to please them, struggling within impossible limits they set for you, and then begging them to approve of the work you did to overcome the obstacles they created for you. It's how society works, in a nutshell, and programs such as that tell the audience it a normal thing to do—that seeking the approval of authority is their goal in life."

She rolled her eyes. "And then they complain when we need jobs."

Rive clicked his claws as he stopped at the desk. He picked up the folder and handed it to her. She took it, opened it. The first piece of paper listed all the things she needed to do to start a church, and how to disguise the information.

"I will walk you through the rest when you are ready to begin. It was actually my suggestion to let you come here. It's what I do around here, monitor the internet. My station is in the next room. You seemed the most reasonable conspiracy theorist on the net. You actually found original sources and examined them instead of just repeating what others said. That was no easy undertaking; every television station in the country had to give those tapes back to the government."

Tanya laughed. "Took me so long to find a station that still had one. I've been making those videos for years. Wondering if anyone was really watching. If anyone took them seriously. I was beginning to wonder if it was all a waste of time."

"You are certainly not alone. And here."

He turned and picked up the book on the top of the pile on the desk. He held it tenderly to his chest as he turned back to her.

"CJ Rhine was assassinated in Russia by a drone strike eleven years ago. It almost killed me, too. It is the one video of me they have that is not fake."

"It's real?"

"I don't blame you for getting that one wrong. I've seen the drone footage, and even I think it's unbelievable. I was not the target. CJ was. I did not think Russia would consider us as much of an enemy as the United States did, or that they would allow the US to fly drones over their territory and give them permission to destroy an entire town just to kill us. All the signs were there, but I missed them."

"I'm sorry."

He felt the book with one hand and spoke down to it. "I stopped blaming myself years ago. She is gone, but I saved her work."

"I read about those books. Nobody can find copies anywhere. The news keeps saying allies of the alien invaders have them, so we destroy any copies we find. Supposed to be dangerous propaganda."

"You should read it for yourself."

He handed her the book. Tanya took it from his metal hand and held it gingerly. The raptor's body stance implied letting that book out of his hands was like letting a five-year-old hold a Ming vase.

"This is the first book CJ published. It's about Crescendo. The company no longer exists, but its products do, and you will want to know what they are doing to the world's population."

His eyes were still on the book in Tanya's hands as he spoke.

"When she died, I took over her accounts, but they were bought up and her work was copyrighted. Soon the copyright spiders began crawling the net. Her books were among the first things they systematically deleted. The first test of the system, and a fitting beginning, as nobody would notice if it succeeded or failed. I saved hardcopies before that happened, and I have the books memorized in case something happens to them. I want you to read all of them."

She carefully grasped the book between her fingers. Rive looked her in the eye, but Tanya did not feel intimidated.

"Keep it hidden," he continued. "If you are caught with it, you will be arrested. Do not talk about it or read it out loud."

"I know. Some people think it's government surveillance and it was pitched to us as a way to protect ourselves from alien invaders. One of my first videos was about how it started as the entertainment companies lobbying to release programs that crawled the net and scanned for copyrighted material being used in any way."

Rive clicked his claws together. "Correct. The people wouldn't accept it, even after the Relian sphere attack. Hundreds of people sounded the alarm on government spying, but it went right through international law as a means of protecting copyright."

"Now all a company has to do is claim ownership," she continued, "and it's grounds for deletion except when downloaded through proper channels."

Rive's neck bobbed. "That's how CJ's books came to be deleted. A shell company bought the rights to her work, even though she had never registered copyright on them. It did not look like censorship, rather copyright protection. People actually sided with the corporations on this issue. A company has a right to protect its property from thieves. Not enough people foresaw the law's real purpose. When you're ready, I will let you read the others."

He passed her. Tanya turned and walked with him. Rive moved closer, hip to hip with her. He radiated heat.

"Do you know what the next phase is?" he asked.

"I think so. Right now our phones are listening to us constantly. It's supposed to make the apps more user-friendly, but I doubt it."

"Sorven found documents that show every giant internet and software company is fighting to make it legal to use your phone to listen for copyrighted material being sung, spoken, or even whistled and then charge you for it. They've already stacked the courts to rule in favor of it when it is challenged, who will say free speech does not apply to instances that may deny a company profit. It will be sold to the people as protection against alien invaders."

"Yes, yes, and hard drives! Hard drives are on their way out for the same reason!"

He wrapped an arm around her as they walked. Tanya reached up and weaved her fingers between his.

2

Tanya lay in bed, shuddering, trying not to moan too loud. The raptor between her legs had a tongue straight out of her dreams. His hands gripped her thighs as it moved against her. It was better than any dick she had taken before. He licked again. She panted and shuddered. She had come twice in the last ten minutes, and she was worn out.

Rive seemed to realize this, for he rose from her and rested his snout on her stomach. Tanya lowered her legs so they hung off the bed, looking down at him, able to see her face reflected in his metal. She would have invited the raptor up on the bed, but she did not think it would support his weight.

"I have... Never had it that good before."

He growled, but in a quiet, catlike way that reminded her of purring. "I owed you."

"For what?"

"I used an ad blocker when I watched your videos."

She laughed as she lay all the way back on the bed and stared at the ceiling. "How the hell did I end up here?"

"I'm good at the human mating calls."

"Mating calls?"

"I meant every word I said. I like your scent. We will get along very well."

"At least in bed. Wow! I just got the best blowjob of my life from the most wanted man in the world." She panted a few times, and then raised her head and looked down herself at him. "I feel like I owe you for that. You need any help?"

"I'm still teaching my metal how to make my penis work again. I'll let you know if I'm ready to try."

"You mean you don't... Oh. I'm sorry. Ouch."

He clicked his claws under the bed. "Tell me about it. Never had a reason to use it when I had one, and now that I don't..."

He sighed and then rose from her and walked around to the left side of the bed. He nuzzled her cheek. Tanya closed her legs as she rolled to her side and threw her arms around him.

"This is treason."

"Strange how in English there is only a single letter difference between treason and reason."

She pulled his head down to the bed and curled up. Rive lay on the floor, head and neck resting on the mattress, growling lowly.

"Don't get complacent," he said. "You do have a church to start."

"Yeah. An entire religion from scratch. I don't have a clue how to begin. I hope we're going to work very close."

She felt his neck up and down. The metal felt smooth, and then her hand found scales. They also felt smooth, like a snake's, but warmer.

"There are documents you should read before we begin. None of them can be online in any way. The copyright spiders will delete them, and then you might disappear."

She curled up with his head and neck tighter. "I'm a girl who loves danger."

"Then what I'm about to tell you will put you in a lot of danger. Everything you are about to read."

"I'm ready for anything."

He nuzzled one of her breasts and spoke so low she barely heard him with her ears, but through her chest. "The government is working on a new video. This time Rive will appear in Saudi Arabia. Oil refineries will be destroyed by aggressive portals, but only one video of a portal destroying something will survive. The government of that country will be accused of being soft on extraterrestrial threats. Either the US will sponsor rebels to overthrow the government and make the new one compliant with US interests, or the military will move in and install a new government overtly."

"Oh God."

"Aliens always want to attack places that happen to have oil, or lithium, or other things companies need."

She laughed. "This has to be the weirdest pillow talk I've ever had."

"I like to mix business with pleasure. It's how my mind works."

"I'd mix you with anything."

She felt the seam where the metal ended and his real flesh began. His metal felt just as alive as his real skin. Rive purred deeper.

3

Tanya sat on a folding chair in the chamber with all the televisions. Rive lay on his stomach to her left. Sorven lay on her right. Each monitor displayed a different channel. Many of them showed coverage of a single event. The US military was storming the nation of Saudi Arabia. For now, the action consisted of troop movement into the capital city of Riyadh.

The official press releases Tanya had seen showed an oil facility destroyed by "Relian spheres," as the press referred to them. The animation looked quite convincing. Despite the incredible resolution screens were capable of rendering now, the video they broadcast was grainy and unclear, but it did show a portal.

Drone surveillance of Rive in the area had surfaced at the same time. The US had reached out to the government only to be met with accusations of evidence fabrication. These accusations had been mocked in the press for weeks prior to this moment. Saudi Arabia was now portrayed as unreasonable and soft on extraterrestrial threats. Direct invasion had been the last resort, which was what Tanya watched now.

Over these last few weeks, Rive had shown her all sorts of documents that had led to this moment. Unreported by the press, diplomats from Saudi Arabia had expressed outrage that the United States was fabricating alien invasions to justify its actions around the world. They wanted to punish the United States by refusing to sell them oil. Tanya had read documents that described the CIA's attempt to encourage a coup, making sure the rebels were in debt to the US, but no rebel groups were strong enough to challenge the government. The US covertly set off bombs at multiple oil facilities in the country and created computer-animated evidence of alien invasion.

They would move in and replace the government. The oil spigots would turn on, and then the country would be flooded with outside corporations to rebuild the damage the US military had caused. It was exactly what had happened when the United States invaded Iraq in the aftermath of ET-Day.

Rive had told her the full story of what happened shortly after the Relians left Earth in the late nineties. Then in the year two thousand, the Empire State Building fell. So did the Chrysler Building. So did the Lloyds Building in London. One by one, over the course of four days, buildings collapsed all over the world, their foundations compromised, no explosions heard, no warning.

Shaky, grainy video had surfaced of what appeared to be Relian spheres opening up underneath a couple of the buildings just before they fell. Then a new video appeared which showed a metal raptor speaking in English to the people of the world, warning that more attacks would come if Earth did not yield to the will of the Relians. The raptor made demands for humans to be selected for harvest, a sacrifice of ten percent of the population of each nation per year, or more people would die. This image of Rive became the face of evil across the entire world.

A year after the attacks, video of Rive was discovered that showed the metal theropod in Iraq, coordinating with Saddam Hussein to round up his enemies of state and prepare them for export to wherever the Relians would take them. The United States invaded just a few weeks later.

Tanya had obtained original tapes of those videos for her online channel, and she had pointed out the subtle flaws in the animation of Rive and the Relian spheres. She had dedicated a year of her free time to proving the ET-Day attacks were done by the US military as an excuse to invade countries that had valuable resources, and that the government wasn't even the one pulling the strings. The citizens were left with the political mess to clean up while the profits funneled into the pockets of the corporations who moved in after the dust settled—the same corporations that sponsored the campaigns of the politicians who proposed and voted for the legislation that took the United States to war.

Now here it was again, the same event for the same reason—history repeating itself. As she focused on one screen, she saw Rive. One of the soldiers had seen him, and, in a dramatic twist, hopped off the convoy in pursuit. The angle switched to show another soldier's helmet camera as they chased the metal theropod through the city.

Tanya turned and looked at Rive. He lay with his hands together, slowly stroking his claws. She turned to the screens again, her mind drifting to everything she had investigated for her channel. Everything she had read.

Space-aliens weren't invading, but most of the United States believed they were, and that the military was keeping the people safe from invasion. Much of the world also believed it. Anyone who questioned it found themselves invaded.

All to make money. Someone was making money off these faked alien invasions, and they didn't care who died.

She thought back to something Sorven had told her: "you can tell who the real power is by looking at who you are not allowed to criticize." People were allowed to criticize the government all they wanted, but they could not say anything bad about a corporation. Free trade agreements now applied to individual citizens. Now any criticism of any company was grounds for fines or arrest because it might harm the company's reputation and thus affect sales. As a result, few people talked about this openly. Her own channel had been flagged a few times for saying such things. It was beginning, and without the burden of being called censorship.

"Damn it, Sorven," she said as the soldiers fired at the computer-animated raptor on the TV screens. "Why aren't you stopping it?"

Sorven did not look at her as he spoke. "It has to happen now. Otherwise, it will only delay the inevitable."

Tanya rested a hand on Rive's neck, watched the action for another five minutes. The soldiers lost Rive, but they caught a glimpse of a Relian sphere through which the enemy of the world supposedly retreated. The soldiers now resumed hunting down members of the regime.

"The Church of Sorven," she said.

Rive's clicked his claws. Sorven's wings fluttered.

"That's what we'll call it. We'll have a room for files like this so people can come and read them. They can watch the original videos, and we'll show them the alien threat is fake. We'll tell them the story in fiction. We can copyright it so no one will delete it. We'll use their own system against them."

Energy Landing

I

They fell through a barrier and tumbled onto grassland. Deka lay on his back. The daytime star in the sky bathed this planet in wonderful electromagnetic radiation across the entire spectrum. The atmosphere filtered out the harmful frequencies, leaving only the most useful.

His mind took in the variables, and again they made no sense. Whatever was different about this universe was not obvious. Deka enjoyed the moment of calm as the equations for the previous reality faded from his mind and left it blank to receive new ones.

After a while he became bold enough to look down his body. He had external genitals. Deka cried out—his breath caught and he choked and coughed.

"Deka, what's wrong?" said Kylac.

The former theropod gasped as he rolled over and opened his legs. "I'm a mammal!"

They were all canines, or something that resembled one. As a sense of scale, they were about as tall as they would have been as Relians, but only half the weight. Their new fur matched their former scale and fur patterns. Eyesight was weak, and their hearing worked on such a narrow range it sounded as though they were whispering to one another.

They sensed they had altered reality to give them-selves a place in this society again, and that they were re-cruits for something, but they did not remember what. They had four days before they had to be somewhere else. The four of them had left for a sabbatical of some purpose.

Their mouths had the flat teeth of an herbivore species. Friend tried to open his mouth, but it only opened about a claw's reach, just wide enough to eat plants. The grass around them resembled grasses found on many other planets in their home universe.

Sonjaa shuddered, the muscles on her face cinching up, and she shook herself to the ground, eyes clenched. Deka rolled over and stepped up to her, nuzzling her with his nose.

"Sonjaa, you did well in the last reality. Is this one any easier?"

Did she not open her eyes as she spoke through clenched teeth. "Everything's... screaming at me again. It hurts. Things sound different here."

"How did you figure out the last equation?"

"What?"

"The last reality. How did you figure it out? Did you find the relationships between the numbers that make up reality and those for the Lake?"

"Deka, I don't think like you do. I listened to the uni-verse, and it started to sound... harmony. All the sounds be-came a single tone. All I had to do was listen for... for devia-tions. That's what it sounds like to me. And that's..."

She opened her eyes, turning her head. Friend lay on his stomach, panting.

"Friend?"

She rolled over. Deka backed away and yipped at a cold nose sniffing his testicles.

Sonjaa rose to all four legs and walked up to Friend. Her hind leg seized up, making her wince. She limped the last four steps to him, dragging that leg behind her. She scented him. Her nose was so weak she could only sense that he was male.

"Are you all right?"

He met her eyes. "I have reset. No anxiety."

"Friend..." She whimpered.

The former fox leaned away. Sonjaa walked on top of him and dropped to her stomach, wrapping her paws around him. She rolled to the ground as she pulled Friend against her underside as best she could without opposable digits. Friend wiggled. Sonjaa gripped him tighter.

"I promise to help you whenever you revert. I will be there."

Friend thrashed. Sonjaa moved with him. Friend threw his body around and whipped from her grip, rolling to his paws and prancing away. He turned to Deka, hind legs buckling. Kylac was sniffing between Deka's legs.

"What are you doing?!"

Kylac looked up from behind him. "Deka's never had these before!" He returned to sniffing. "My nose is so weak here. All my senses are weak. What kind of species is this?"

"We're herbivores," Deka said.

Friend looked himself over. "We still need to escape predators."

"I hope we're not prey," said the canine with dark blue fur and a red stripe running up his muzzle and down his spine. "Does anyone know what our species name is? I can't seem to think of it."

"I don't think species here have names," said Friend, trying to scent the wind. "I keep thinking of myself as something that is not an animal. That's the only distinction. That must be what we are. A Notanimal. I feel a lot of electromagnetic energy in the air, but it's strange."

"Is that what that is?" Sonjaa clenched her eyes shut as she panted. "It didn't make this sound in the last reality. It was much, much quieter."

"Yes, it's not coming from the star."

"I'm relieved there are stars here," Kylac said.

Deka walked away from Kylac's nose. "I don't know why we're here."

"I think I do," said Friend. "We're on some sort of sabbatical, but the word has another meaning. Hunting. Surviving. Replacing."

Deka walked over to Sonjaa and nosed her ear. "Can you walk?"

She panted a few times and opened her eye. "It doesn't hurt as much as it did before. I can manage."

She slowly rolled over to her stomach and raised herself off the ground. Her right hind leg didn't function at all, and it dragged behind her as she took a few steps. Deka remained beside her, leaning on her bad side. She leaned on him and walked with her head down.

She turned to Friend, clearly expecting him to help her, but he fell back and walked with Kylac, who was trying to rub away something that had leaked from his eye socket. Sonaja set the pace.

"Why don't we know why we're here?" said Kylac. He couldn't seem to open his left eye at all now. "We made a place for ourselves in this society, so we should know everything."

"It's probably so obvious to them we don't realize what it means," Friend said. "We'll figure it out soon. Hopefully without being killed."

"Obviously we eat the grass," Deka said. "I want to know what eats us. And why we're alone out here. A species this defenseless would have to live in herds."

The grass thinned out, standing only as tall as their ankles. They came to a herd of grazing animals. At first they resembled their own species of canine, but then they noticed some of them had hind legs that did not match their upper bodies. Others had forelegs that came from a different species as well. Some had eyes that were obviously not from the same body. Others had malformed mouths and were still trying to chew.

Deka and Sonjaa walked up to one of the animals. The creature was the same size as he was, and it did not react when Deka touched it with his paw. It had short fur, and one of its forelimbs was hairless, but it did not look injured. Deka walked around it and studied it head to tail.

"I recognize these body parts. They all came from a different species."

"What do you mean?" Friend said.

"I remember something I learned in school. There are different species."

"I must not have been to school," said Kylac. "I don't remember that. I remember... There is only one species on this planet."

"No... No, that's a misconception," Deka continued. "There are other species. Scientists here distinguish them by how they are born or hatched. They begin trading body parts when they begin eating solid food."

"Trading... body parts?" said Sonjaa. "How?"

"I don't know. Obviously I went to school, so I should."

"Perhaps it's so obvious it doesn't need to be taught," said Friend.

"But the fact that there are different species of animal is not obvious," said Kylac.

The creature before them chewed the grass and swallowed and observed them, not a hint of fear in its scent.

Friend stood beside Kylac. "I remember all the animals have this type of body. Similar frame, similar bones, similar organs. Everything resembles us. It makes sense the people would assume everything was the same species, including the animals."

The creature chewed and chewed and chewed.

"Where are the insects?" Sonjaa said. "I don't hear anything. And I'm getting the feeling there are only a few hundred species of plant on this world, and all of them rely on the animals to spread them around."

The creature swallowed. It flashed into a burst of white light and disappeared. The Relians stared at the empty air. Their Archeon minds sensed a surge of electromagnetism around them. Sonjaa winced at the new surge of noises around her. Another of those grazing creatures in the distance disappeared in a flash. Multiple creatures disappeared. Half the herd had vanished.

Several breaths later, they felt a degree of pressure increase—not air pressure, rather a feeling coming from a new sense. Energy collected, settled, and then the creature returned in another flash of light. Its faint scent told them this was the same creature, but now it had new forelimbs. The arm that had been hairless was now furred, but the fur was a different length and color from the rest of the body.

Its eyes looked different, but its jaw was now misaligned. It was the same broken jaw they had seen on one of the other creatures they had passed elsewhere in the herd. The Archeons realized the creatures that had vanished had traded body parts and then returned to their places. They now resumed grazing as if nothing had happened.

The creature before them bent low and opened its mouth. The new jaw was almost immobile, so it had a difficult time eating. It bit a small clump of grass and chewed slowly, painfully. Deka rested a paw on its new forelimb. It did not react.

Sonjaa panted less, opened her eyes and raised her head. "Did anyone else hear that? It wasn't in Ein's universe."

The Relians backed away and walked onward through the field. As they traveled, they observed hundreds of animals, all of nearly identical stature and frame, grazing on the grass. The animals vanished at random moments and then reappeared with new body parts, some better, some worse.

Nobody could come up with a name for these creatures. They sensed the locals simply referred to them as animals, making them wonder if this language had different words for the different species. They followed that bad jaw around the field as it passed to six individuals.

The daytime star in the sky began to set, and they sat in the middle of this field of grazing animals. They had taken in the same information, so there was only one conclusion. The ones who ate faster flashed more often. That bad jaw prevented an animal from flashing for some time. Their minds sensed the energy in the air when an animal flashed away. Something in the plants was making them do this. Whatever was going on, it was so obvious to the people native to this universe it did not even have to be explained, hence they could not articulate it now.

"I think I remember something," Sonjaa said, dropping to her stomach and resting her head on the ground. "Sabbatical. It means to hunt... replace... evade. I think that's why... Not to eat the grass. We're here to do what they're doing."

"Trade body parts?" Deka said.

"Yes. Deka." She opened her eyes and looked at him from the ground. "Your lung. Something is wrong with it."

Deka inhaled deeply. His breath caught again. Now he remembered. "It's my left lung. It's old."

"My leg is injured. It was caught in something. That's why they sent me out here. To replace it."

The former foxes exchanged glances.

"So what's wrong with us?" Friend said.

"My eye," Kylac said, blinking some yellow fluid from it. "I can barely see. I don't know what happened to it, but I remember what's wrong with you, Friend. You have bad kidneys."

"I do?" A burst of recognition hit Friend. "You're right. How did I get these? I remember they were healthy but something happened."

"We're recruits," Deka said. "They require body parts within certain limits, or we will be kicked out."

"Well, we wouldn't want that," Kylac said. "All right. Somehow these creatures are changing into energy and trading body parts in that state. It has to do with the grass."

Friend opened his mouth and picked a piece of grass that was as long as his forearm. He rolled it around in his mouth. "Radioactive particles. I can't tell what element this is."

"Don't eat it," Kylac said. "Concentration of these particles in the stomach must trigger the flashing."

"But how?" said Friend, still licking the blade. "Radiation does not cause matter to break apart in our universe. What is different here?"

"Don't be in a hurry to figure it out," Deka said.

"This is fascinating!" Friend began chewing the blade. "Matter into energy as easily as water evaporating, and then back! What allows it to happen? Why does it not fly apart at the speed of light in all directions? What is keeping it here?"

He pushed the rest of the blade into his mouth and chewed. Sonjaa raised her head and glared at him.

"Don't do that. We don't know what will happen when we flash."

"What happens is so obvious to these people it doesn't need to be taught!" Friend reached for another blade. "I will know what to do when I'm there."

"What if you revert in that state? No telling what kind of damage you'll do."

Friend settled down, looked her in the eye. "We'll have to eventually. Grass is the only thing we eat."

Sonjaa glared at him.

"You need to replace that limb," he continued, "and I need to filter my blood. I'm dying." His minuscule tail wagged. "You wouldn't want me to die, would you?"

Deka grumbled. "If he wants to be first, let him."

Sonjaa shuddered. "If you revert in there..."

"We can't wait until we figure out the laws of this place," Friend said. "We might starve before that happens. I remember the radiation is in the water as well."

Sonjaa wanted to growl at him, but despite her canine body, her throat did not make that sound. She lay her head back down again.

"I wish we could wait until the universe settles. I need to be ready for you."

Friend grabbed another hunk of grass and chewed. The other three sat still and watched him. Friend chewed and swallowed. Chewed and swallowed.

"Anything?" Deka said.

Friend spoke with a full mouth. "I feel the radioactive particles in my stomach. They're causing some kind of disturbance in the atoms of my body. The numbers still don't make sense. I'm missing something. And this stuff tastes so good. The species on this planet can taste radioactive particles. All the life forms here are adapted to take advantage of this." He swallowed, then reached out and took another bite. "It feels so good to eat! Back home, creatures are harmed by radiation like this. It seems our bodies adapted

to concentrate the radioactive particles to trigger the—
Something's happ—"

Friend flashed. He was gone. The Relians felt energy surging around and through them. They held their breath, except Deka, who could not.

About twenty breaths later, another flash, and Friend reappeared. He lay belly-up, panting, tail-stump wagging. The Relians stood and walked over to him, even Sonjaa, all eyes on his face. He spoke in English.

"Bloody hell holy shit that was amazing!"

Everyone's tail-stumps wagged.

Sonjaa: "What happened?"

"I'm not sure how to describe it! But I have new kidneys! I'll have to piss in a few breaths because they work!"

"That's not all you got," Deka said, looking at Friend's lower half.

Friend raised his head. Both of his hind legs were swollen and misshapen, probably arthritic. He rolled over and lay on his side, his legs popping in and out of joint on the way. He moaned.

"Crap."

2

It was night, and all the animals were asleep. It was pointless to eat now, as there didn't seem to be any energy in the air. Friend lay on his side. The other Relians lay on their stomachs and faced him as he tried to explain what happened. Their new native language did not have the words to express it, and he could not speak Relain now without a throat that could growl, so he spoke English.

"The radiation in my stomach disturbed some sort of field in the atoms of my body. The radiation broke my atoms apart but not the quarks. Somehow they stayed together, but they were also spread out. When they spread out far enough, they became waves held together by... something—I don't know what—the numbers are still a mess!

"There's a whole ecosystem in that state of matter! It's... It's similar to how animals hunt one another in the physical world. They have claws and teeth and they tear bodies apart. They do that here, too, but in the energy state! Animals chase each other down, rip each other apart, but they're not trying to absorb energy. They're trying to get rid of old body parts and steal newer ones!"

"As bodies wear out," Kylac said, "the animals will get rid of their old parts. The weakest will be left with the bad parts."

"Yes, they mainly exist in the energy state, but they still need to eat as physical creatures. If they can't, they die, so it's to their advantage to have new parts! Something keeps them local to an area. Some sort of force prevents all this energy from flying off the planet and mixing with air and light. A new force that separates the different types of energy."

"So the animals evolved to be compatible between one another," Deka said. "That makes sense. It would be a survival advantage to trade parts with animals of different species."

"Yes, yes!" Friend kicked his forepaws, wincing when his hind legs moved. "I felt multiple species in there, but most of them were out of reach. All of them have interchangeable body parts! Organs, limbs, bones! Everything but the central nervous system can be changed out. Nobody tried to go for my spine. They didn't want to kill me. Just take my good legs and give me these. Ow. Help me up. Please, help me up! I have to piss! Now!"

Deka and Kylac rose to their paws and positioned themselves to lift him, but Sonjaa painfully nudged Deka and Kylac out of the way. She crawled under him and lifted his upper body off the ground. Friend maneuvered his lower body and crouched. He released a jet of dark yellow urine, moaning and wagging his tail.

"I haven't done this in days! I wish I could remember how my kidneys got this bad in the first place! Aaaaah... I lost my legs, but gained working kidneys. Good trade! Good trade. Oooohaaaaah..."

The flow didn't let up for forty breaths, Sonjaa cringing and wobbling on three legs. Friend rolled off her and plopped on his side at the edge of the puddle he'd made. He lay still for a moment. Deka and Kylac walked around and looked at the grass. Sonjaa hobbled around the puddle and stood over Friend. She nuzzled him on the snout. Friend ignored her.

"I need water," Friend said. "Lots of it. I might flash again, but this time I'll be ready."

"Any advice on how to avoid being stuck with bad legs?" Deka said as he eyed the grass.

Friend talked as if he had just climaxed. "It's just like the hunt. Yes, just like the hunt. Others are trying to invade your space at the same time as you are trying to invade theirs. They want the same thing you do, which is to be rid of nonworking parts. You move differently, senses are different... That's why we have such weak senses here. None of the action happens here. None of the competition. It all happens in the energy state. Everyone has claws and teeth there. Once you learn the impulses, you'll be hunting. You'll be fine."

"What about me?" Kylac said. "I don't hunt. I'll revert."

"You might not. There's no scent in the energy state. But if you do, your old ways might come in handy there."

Kylac shivered. His bad eye twitched and leaked more yellow goo. He shuddered and whimpered and tried to rub his face without fingers.

"Will we recognize each other?" Deka said.

"I'm not sure," Friend said. Sonjaa was still nuzzling his face. "Everything felt the same in there. Everyone trying to push their bad parts on me. I recognized different species, so maybe we can discern individuals as well. I didn't have enough time to think. It was a rush to get rid of my kidneys before someone loaded me with something worse."

The Relians fell silent. The grassland was silent. The grass itself gave off faint radiation.

Sonjaa lay on her stomach, resting her snout on Friend's shoulder. "We should sleep. They gave us another three days out here. That must mean they know it can be difficult to find body parts up to standard."

Deka turned and lay a pace away from them. Kylac remained standing. He shivered.

"We'll face it tomorrow," Deka said. "Rest your bad eye."

"I might revert in there. Reverting without a body." He trembled himself to the ground and lay next to Deka.

"I'll be waiting for you. I'll bring you back," said the blue canine.

"You better go before I do," Kylac said. "You'll need good lungs if I revert."

Friend rolled out from under Sonjaa and rose to his feet. His hind legs did not work at all, and he grunted as his joints popped and cracked and snapped. It made all the Relians cringe.

"What are you doing?" said Sonjaa.

"I am so thirsty."

Sonjaa rose to her feet, keeping weight off the bad leg. "I seem to remember someone telling us about a stream a few dozen paces downhill. I'll take you there."

"You don't have to. I can get a drink on my own."

She stepped behind him and stared at his hindquarters. She nosed his testicles out of the way and raised her neck, lifting his hind section off the ground.

Friend took a couple steps with his forepaws. Sonjaa walked him, shoulders straining under the weight. They descended the slight slope, between the sleeping animals.

Sonjaa's neck ached as Friend walked them across the field. It wasn't too far though, as she could still hear Deka and Kylac by the time she heard flowing water. She saw it through Friend's forelegs, less than a pace wide, and so shallow it would not be worth noticing if she stepped in it.

He stopped at the stream. Sonjaa shrugged him off and lay on her side next to the water. Friend lapped it rapidly, barely pausing to breathe. Sonjaa tried to ignore the pain in her hind leg as it mixed in with the pain of the universe reverberating inside her skull.

"Radioactive particles are in the water! Sonjaa, radiation does not destroy DNA in this universe, but it does destroy the bonds between atoms, and yet somehow they congeal back together as mass even after they've separated. This implies that energy behaves like mass, but what preserves the structure of the matter while it is energy? The bigger question is how matter changes to energy and back so easily. It has something to do with the radiation. I sense it's disturbing a field that preserves matter somehow. Perhaps energy is the normal state in this universe, and matter is the exception. The field preserves matter as the exception, but why would radiation disturb it? And how could animals evolve to take advantage of this? What prevents them from being energy at all—"

"Friend."

He stopped lapping the water and stared at her.

"Just be quiet for a moment."

Friend turned back to the stream. Sonjaa continued.

"One less voice yelling at me." She held her head with her paws. "Uuuuuuuh, this universe is noise and I can't shut it out! I'm worried the last one was a fluke. Everything just... fell into harmony. A nice, mellow droning sensation. What if... What if it doesn't happen like this? It's hard to imagine this place having a drone, especially when everything sounds so different."

Friend lapped the water for a few more breaths. Then he paused, lifted his muzzle from the stream.

"You're coping very well with the lack of a subconscious. It takes most Archeons years to become used to it. You have the advantage of being good at language before. You don't comprehend the numbers and equations? It's... all sound to you?"

She rolled over, faced him. "Everything gives off vibrations. In the last reality it merged into a drone. I hope it happens again. I hope it happens before you figure this place out."

"Still trying to make up for not stopping me the first time?" He began drinking again, speaking between slurps. "I thought tearing me apart and eating me on Reyno and Earth would have been enough to help you get over that."

"Friend, you need help."

He stopped drinking and turned around. "Remember what the creator of the previous universe told us? Ein was the only person to make it out. The only one. The experiences and memories of an entire universe exist within Ein. Now that home is gone, meaning Ein is the only record of that place ever existing. I witnessed the future of our home. Nobody will leave except the four of us. One of us has to understand the Lake, or our universe will spread out so far it becomes part of the Lake again, and nobody will know any of us existed."

"I didn't have to destroy any planets to get where I am. Neither did Deka."

"The work Kylac and I did prepared the two of you for this. There is a chance for all of us to understand now. We could be the only ones from our universe to join a new group of Archeons in the Lake."

While he spoke, Sonjaa rolled to her feet and hobbled up to Friend. She nuzzled him, rubbed necks with him. Friend stumbled away from her. Sonjaa tried to pursue, but Friend hopped away, wincing on his bad legs.

"Friend, I understand what you're going through," she said. "I saw Rupi revert so many times. She told me how it felt, and it moved me to mourning every time. What foxes go through. I don't have to imagine. I saw it every day. You're prone to reverting. I want to help."

Friend leaned away from her. "You are desperate for a fox."

"Aren't you lost without a raptor? Didn't you ever talk to Rive while you were on Earth?"

Friend turned to the river and took a long drink. He disappeared in a flash of light. Sonjaa caught her breath, lay back down. A few breaths later, Friend reappeared, and she raised her head. Friend stood on all fours, a much younger set of hind legs attached to him now.

"Found an unsuspecting creature. Gave her my old legs."

He turned and marched up the hill. Sonjaa rolled to her feet and stumbled after him, dragging her bad leg behind her. Friend outpaced her on purpose.

"Friend, please! Let me help you! I've been without a fox for so long. You've been without a raptor. It's like someone planned this."

"I didn't come all this way just to be attached to a raptor again. I will understand the Lake. I will know the universe as an equation, and all creatures in the universe are part of that equation, hence their actions and memories can be calculated. The equation is so large it can never be expressed entirely; it must be held in the mind at all times, like a portal calculation. That's what the universe will be to me. It will have to be me. The three of you are too hung up on the individuals inside to embrace it."

Sonjaa tried to run, but her bad leg shot pain through her whole body. She gritted her teeth and kept walking. Friend's hindquarters pulled further and further ahead. Friend kept talking.

"This raises an important question. If I hold the equation that comprises the universe in my mind, does executing the same equation again mean all the people will be the same? Could I remake the universe? Will I end up remaking myself? Fascinating to think about. I wish Rive were here."

"You can talk to me about it! As soon as the universe settles, we can talk!"

Silence. Friend was out of sight. Sonjaa limped through the field in the path Friend had made through the grass.

3

Deka was blind save for the sense of others around him. It was not sight, or feeling, or hearing, or even a sense of vibration, but magnetism. The electrons and other particles that made up his form repelled other particles, which allowed him to remain himself.

Others bumped up against him, probing him for good parts and trying to flip their parts with his. Nobody could enter Deka's space without him knowing it, but they could do a part-for-part trade. He felt every attempt at flipping body parts from the dozens of creatures bumping up against him, and his survival here just as important as survival in the physical realm.

Deka felt like a predator among predators. Primal urges swelled up—kill or be killed, protect what is yours, everyone is trying to take what is yours—because that was exactly how it worked here. Instead of using claws and teeth, they used forced electromagnetic intrusion. Waves and particles trying to trade segments, and the ultimate loser would be the one creature left with all the bad body parts.

A creature brushed against him. Deka repelled it, and as he did he felt the creature's body. It had lungs he needed. He pushed against it, climbed up it. He felt like a strand of DNA sliding up to another DNA strand and positioning equivalent pieces next to one another. He flipped parts. The creature tried to resist, but Deka's magnetism was stronger. He easily swapped the lung and then separated. The animal followed him, but another creature slid between them and latched on.

Deka wanted to return to the physical realm, but he thought he could do better, so he continued buzzing around. Animals latched onto him and probed his body, and Deka resisted their attempts to flip. He had good parts, so everyone actively pursued him. One animal tried to flip limbs with him, but Deka pushed it away. Another tried to trade hearts with him, and Deka slid further down, breaking the attempt. He positioned his energy stream alongside the animal's and flipped all four legs with the creature. He pushed it away. It collided in a parallel plane with another animal.

Deka felt himself becoming heavier. The radiation had worn off, and the field that held energy into matter came back. As if guided by instinct, he reversed course and returned to where he had been.

Deka flashed back into matter. He blinked a few times as he stood up straight. He took a deep breath. His lungs were in much better shape now, and so were his legs. He tested them, lowered himself and then raised his body. His muscles were larger and well-worked. He shook his head.

"That was incredible! I was—I was pure energy! Friend is right! They evolved to hunt in that state, not the physical! Sonjaa, you have to try it! Hunting is easy! You'll figure out how to resist others and force yourself on them. It's wonderful! I got new lungs and new legs and I barely had to try!"

Kylac trembled. Deka calmed down.

"If we do this again," Deka continued, "we must go separately. I don't think there is a way to tell the difference between individuals. Everyone is particles and waves, and they have vibrations you want or vibrations you don't want. If you don't take, you will be taken."

"Exactly someplace I do not want to be," Kylac said.

Deka looked at Sonjaa. "Your turn. Don't be afraid. You hunted on Bynadium. You'll do well."

With visible trepidation, Sonjaa reached out with her mouth and grabbed a hunk of grass. Deka sat down and watched. Kylac turned away and sat down. Friend lay on his side and closed his eyes.

Sonjaa had to eat several mouthfuls of grass before she flashed. Deka felt the electromagnetism swirling about him. His mind noticed something different about the way it behaved, but the numbers still did not make sense. Fifty breaths later, Sonjaa flashed back.

She had the bad jaw.

Sonjaa shook her head in anger. The jaw barely worked, so she could not speak. Deka tried not to laugh because it was not funny; if she couldn't eat, she would die.

Friend, however, snorted rapidly, laughing. "But your leg works."

She turned and jumped on him, knocking him over and threatening to urinate on him. Friend rolled out from her legs, still snorting.

"Don't feel bad," Deka said. "Remember it took Friend a couple tries to become good at it."

Sonjaa opened her jaw, wincing. It only opened wide enough for her to eat a single blade of grass, and her jaw only had enough strength to chew at half the rate she normally did. She couldn't growl, so she pounded the ground with her paws.

"Get ready," Kylac announced.

Deka turned around. Kylac had a mouthful of grass. Deka crouched on all four paws, ready to leap. A few breaths later, Kylac disappeared in a flash. Deka held his breath. He could now, thanks to the wonderful new lungs he had stolen from someone else. He liked these new legs as well, but he still disliked feeling so fluffy.

Kylac flashed back. Deka immediately leaped on him and pinned him down by the shoulders. Kylac's body did not give off the same scent signals, so he couldn't smell if the former Relian had reverted. Their vocal cords did not make the same noises either, so he did not sound reverted. The only way he could tell Kylac had reverted was by the erratic way his body moved. Kylac squirmed, thrashed, flailed with both sets of legs. He breathed in a way that tried to mimic snarling.

"Easy, Kylac, it's over. It's over. They're not coming for you now. Remember who you are."

Kylac placed a paw on Deka's chest and shoved him off. Deka flew backwards three whole paces, landing flat on his spine. Kylac had just rolled to his paws and stood at full height. He was huge. All four legs bulged with muscles up through the shoulders. His chest was packed with them, thick enough to collide with his forelegs and force him to stand wider, but he stood the same height as Deka. His fur was no longer a mixture of reds and blacks but a collage of greens, blues, and whites. Deka cursed in English under his breath as he tried to snarl at Kylac.

Kylac made his best snarl back and charged Deka. They collided. Kylac grabbed him and twisted him to the ground. Deka held on. He tried to flip Kylac over, but the former fox was too strong now.

Kylac had his mouth on Deka's neck but it did not open wide enough to bite Deka. This frustrated him and he flailed harder. Deka now grabbed Kylac and pulled him down. He held Kylac's head against his own. Kylac thrashed, still trying to bite and scratch. He knew he was stronger now, but he did not know how to use it without hands or a predator's jaw. He wiggled and whimpered in Deka's grip as he attacked. His paw swiped down Deka's torso, but he had no claws.

He growled and whimpered and finally collapsed on top of the former raptor. In a few breaths, Kylac came back.

"I'm never doing that again! I'm never— No!"

"You never could handle hunting," Friend said.

Kylac rolled off Deka and lay on his side, gasping.

Deka stood over Kylac. "You did well. Only in a universe where matter flashes to energy and back can a fox be bigger than a raptor."

Kylac panted a few more times. "These limbs aren't from the same species. Neither are my eyes. There are animals on this world that do fight and compete in a physical state. They also exist in the energy state."

Friend spoke from the ground. "I believe body parts like that are desirable in our culture."

"They are," Kylac said. "They're difficult to obtain because the animals are elusive."

"How did you find them? No animals in the area have body parts that large."

Kylac rolled to his stomach. "I think I panicked and went a lot farther out than I should have. Yes. That's why we came here! It's not for these creatures!" Kylac looked at the grazing animals around them. "We were supposed to go over the ridge to hunt the good creatures! Our bodies have to be up to code—it's not just the bad parts but our entire bodies!"

Deka turned to Sonjaa. She was still eating one blade of grass at a time, and she glared at Kylac. Friend had risen to his paws and stared at Kylac's eyes. Friend turned to Sonjaa.

"Get your jaw back. That was the warm-up."

Sonjaa's whole body sagged. She tried to eat faster.

4

The Relians walked through the field back the way they had come. The pickup point was just over the hill, and they had returned a day early, each of them as muscular as Kylac.

They knew those animals only as the goodanimals. They were not carnivores, but they did fight over grazing territory in the physical reality. Most animals on this world treated the plants as communal and only fought in the energy realm, but not the goodanimals. They fought in both, which made their bodies large and powerful.

It had taken them all this time to hunt the goodanimals in the energy realm, and at last their bodies were up to code. They now realized the people in their culture valued bodies like these, but their lifestyle did not maintain the musculature, or the vitality of the organs they took. Being herbivores of the communal, grazing sort, the muscles atrophied within just a few years, which meant they had to return to the wild and take new parts.

The former raptors and foxes felt bad for leaving those goodanimals their weak body parts. They would likely lose territory battles and be condemned to die without bearing young. Sonjaa was happy to have a working jaw and leg again.

The land sloped upwards for a few hundred paces before leveling off. Other people walked about in the distance. One hundred and forty-seven milling around something unfamiliar. It was only because of their time on Earth they recognized the structure.

A spaceship.

The Relians now realized their place in this society of Notanimals. They had been in the space exploration program for eighty-seven cycles. This was not their home planet, but a refueling station for their craft, as well as their bodies. This vessel wasn't even the main traveling ship. Some of the crew had been sent out to replace their body parts, and the remainder checked on the status of the mines.

People who resembled the Notanimals, but much thinner, carried crates of radioactive rock between their shoulders into the cargo hold of the ship. Another piece of the society opened up to the Relians. There were people in Notanimal society who were not good at surviving in the energy state, unable to hunt the goodanimals, which condemned them to work the mines.

Meanwhile, the Notanimals with larger physical bodies looked on and milled about. Deka turned his head and faced one of the weak Notanimals as he carried a large rock on his back. The radiation coming from it was slightly stronger compared to the amount in the grass, but it was a different element. The Relians recalled now how the elements in the plants were perfect for themselves and the animals, but not to flash something larger, like a vessel.

The Notanimal walking beside the Relians somehow balanced the rock on his back perfectly. Deka was not certain how they mined the ore without thumbs. He remembered working with one's physical body was detestable in their culture, so however they did it, it probably involved a lot of unpleasant physical manipulation.

They approached the muscular Notanimals. One in particular noticed them. He did not approach, but observed them.

"You're early," he said.

Kylac was the closest, so he spoke. In this reality, they were not related. Just four recruits who needed new body parts at the same time, so they went hunting together.

"We found good hunting sooner than we thought."

The other tipped his muzzle in approval. "Excellent. We are still waiting for a number of others to return. Enjoy leave while it lasts. Scouts found a new world past the frontier, and we will depart on schedule."

"Yes, General."

Kylac's eyes widened. He turned around and faced the others. Deka, Sonjaa, and Friend's eyes also lit up as they realized what they were.

This planet was a colony world, one of hundreds spread out over several thousand light years, all radiating from the Notanimal homeworld. Many of the animals here were transplants from there.

Notanimals created colonies on planets that had radioactive rock of a certain element. They mined the rock, transported it up to the main vessel, and refined it to just the right concentration to dissipate matter into energy.

But out in space, no force contained the energy to a certain area. It was free to scatter in all directions. By flashing the space around the mothership itself into energy, the space would move past the speed of light. The Notanimals knew the exact concentrations needed to travel certain distances, and they could control the time they flashed. They ran out of refined radiation at exactly the right moment to be where they wanted to be.

The herbivorous canines were spreading through the galaxy, always looking for new sources of fuel to exploit, new animals to hunt, new body parts to obtain. They considered exotic parts symbols of prestige. All the animals in the universe thus far had been interchangeable with their own bodies. All complex life had evolved the same type of body, so trading parts was easy.

If they found another sentient species, their first reaction was to take from them. The Notanimals were not explorers. They ate plants and treated the plants as communal property, but in the energy realm, they prowled.

The former Relians turned and watched the Notanimals carrying the ore into the ship. They weren't Notanimals. The name for these people was Underanimal, and they were in fact the natives of this planet. Unable to resist the limb- and organ-swapping inflicted upon them by the Notanimals, they were forced to mine fuel so the invaders could continue exploring the galaxy.

The Relians' hearts sank as they realized their place in society. They remembered being part of the invasion force that originally came here over twenty generations ago. The Notanimals were practically immortal so long as they could swap out their old body parts. This hunting trip had earned them another few years of life.

Kylac looked back at the male who had addressed them. He had called him General. Deka nudged the former fox, and then he led the Relians away from the ship and the other Notanimals. When they were a safe distance away, Deka sat down and stared over the grasslands. Kylac sat next to him. Sonjaa and Friend remained standing as they looked out over the land.

"What's going to happen to this universe?" Friend said. "And where is the creator? There's no evidence of intervention. Perhaps whoever made it ran the numbers forward and realized there's no way for anyone here to leave this reality. The physical laws of this universe yield people who never will discover portal physics. This implies a Superarcheon has no control over the laws their universe will have. Ein implied that the laws originate from the mindset of the creator, but obviously one has no control over that, or else one would always create a universe with laws that produce societies of people that will one day learn portal physics. Perhaps that is why the creator is not here. It's hopeless, so why bother trying? What happens after that for someone who can create universes by applying mathematics to the Lake? What kind of society do the Superarcheons have in the Lake? Is there a degree of respect for those who had a child universe that will successfully yield at least one Superarcheon, or—"

"Will you stop saying that word!" Deka snapped.

"What other word should I use?"

"Just stop. I hated it when you and Rive went on long talks like this."

"What should we do while we're here?" Sonjaa said. "The smartest thing would be to lie low until this place settles into a beautiful, predictable drone, and then we can leave. Hopefully before Friend destroys everything."

"I have to know," Deka said. "It's a given that the Underanimals of this world are incapable of competing in the energy state. Instead of finding a companion species, the invaders only find new people to dominate."

"It's the only kind of society they can yield," Friend said, "evolving from animals who were simply the best at stealing the good parts from others."

"Not true," said Sonjaa. "The locals obviously don't think that way."

"How do you figure?"

"They would have been able to fight back."

"Fight back," Deka echoed.

They fell silent for a while. The wind blew the grass.

"Stephen would have loved this place," Kylac said. He snorted. "Finally, spaceships."

"Yes," said Deka. "Spaceships. Kylac, remember those movies we watched on Earth? In every story about space colonization, there's always an empire and a group of rebels. Seems to me this place has an empire..."

"Deka! We don't belong here! Who are we to judge them? If we evolved with these laws of physics, we'd be doing the same thing."

"They just haven't met anyone who could show them life can be different. What if we did? What if that's all it takes?"

"And any change we make here could lead to the downfall of the species over time! No, Deka, let's just sit here, figure out the laws of physics, and leave. The fewer distractions the better."

Deka stood and turned around. "You can sit on your fluffy ass and watch these people suffer if you want. I'm going down to the mine."

Kylac stood and bounded after him. "Deka, we shouldn't get involved!"

"We only seem to know things that a person in this society would know, and apparently it's obvious that the locals are just not worthy. I'm challenging that assumption."

Kylac ran a few paces to catch up and then walked with him.

"All right, there's no harm in finding out who they are and what happened to them, but let's not try anything. Maybe the god of this reality is gone because the work is done and someone will learn eventually. Maybe the Notanimals will realize the Underanimals have more in common with them than they thought, and they will discover portals someday. We are from the Lake. We can change the equations and ruin whatever plan the creator had."

Deka halted and faced Kylac muzzle to muzzle. "Kylac, we were both here! We were the invaders! They weren't always that thin—we stole their bodies and made them this way! I remember hunting them in the energy realm. I remember laughing as I watched them lose to me! I remember laughing with everyone on the ship as they lost to the goodanimals we brought with us!"

"I remember it, too, but it's not real."

"Why did we create this history for ourselves? Why did we put ourselves here as an aggressor? We must have wanted ourselves to change it. That's why we're in this position. I don't think any Notanimal that's part of the empire has ever bothered to talk to one of the Underanimals. Position in society comes from how well you hunt in the energy state. I want to know what the Underanimals value. I want to know why I laughed at them."

Kylac held Deka's gaze for a moment. "It's good to hear you talk like this again."

Deka recoiled. "What?"

Kylac wagged his tail stump. "I remember a certain raptor on Kattaaka who wanted to run headlong into the forest without any thought for the insects with giant stingers full of venom that might find us. You did that all the time when we were young. Run into everything without thinking. I miss that raptor."

Deka nuzzled his former fox. "It wasn't that long ago."

"Please, let's run headlong into something I should stop you from doing. I miss those times so much."

"It always led to a great adventure." Deka turned and began walking. Kylac joined him at his side.

Friend called out to them. "You two have fun in the mines. I'm going to talk to the engineers."

Sonjaa bumped him with her head. "No, you're not."

Friend turned and walked to the ship. "I want to hear about the physical laws. It might help me."

"You're not going without me!" Sonjaa ran to catch up with him.

Friend wagged his tail. "How's the language of the universe sound to you now?"

"Still a mess, but I figured out the last one, so I'll get this one!"

They had walked halfway to the ship.

Deka and Kylac followed the line of marching, emaciated Underanimals back the way they were coming.

5

Deka and Kylac descended the slope. Artificial lights lined the wall, casting everything in harsh white that made the shadows sharp. The Underanimals walking in the other direction did not look at them. Those entering the cave alongside them kept their distance.

The tunnel ended at a shaft. A lift with a capacity of twenty people took up the center of it. The former Relians stepped on and turned around. Thirty Underanimals stood fifteen paces up the tunnel, waiting. Deka and Kylac waited for them to board, and then they realized the invaders would never share a ride with the ones they conquered. Deka raised his paw, signaling for the lowest level. The elevator unlocked and descended. The Relians remembered an Underanimal sat atop the lift, pedaling a set of gears that lowered and raised it.

They counted fifteen levels down, and then the elevator rested at the bottom of the shaft. They stepped out and pulled a cable to signal the lift was clear. It ascended, empty. Around them, Underanimals lined up for a ration of plants and tree leaves. Each person received exactly the correct ration to flash to energy and no more. The Underanimals walked to the leading walls, ate the plants, disappeared, and then reappeared moments later with a chunk of rock on their backs. They walked the chunks to a pile off to the side, and then repeated the process. The wall moved outward about half a pace in the time Deka and Kylac watched.

Deka wanted to growl. He stepped forward. "Pardon me. Somebody speak to me so I can learn your language."

Everyone stared at him. Nobody moved. Breaths went by, and then the thin canines returned to work. Deka and Kylac overheard quiet mumbling around them. Nobody had the courage to speak to them directly. The Relians heard someone approach from behind, and they turned to meet her. An Underanimal padded up to them from around the elevator shaft.

"Inspection again?" she said. "All is well, as it was three days ago. Quota is met. There are rumors it will be increased due to us exceeding it this delivery. Please tell me the rumors are false."

Deka turned all the way around and faced her directly. "Please speak in your native language. I wish to learn it."

The slightly less-emaciated Underanimal tilted her head at him. "Did I hear you correctly?"

"Yes," Kylac said. "We will not force you to speak the language of invaders."

This seemed to amuse her. She began talking. The Relians remembered it was a sign of great disrespect to speak this language in front of the invaders, so to be given permission to do so was an oddity. It gave freedom to the others around them to speak as well, as the volume in the pit rose. The language was easy enough to pick up, and after just fifty breaths, Deka and Kylac had learned all the patterns.

"You may stop," Deka said. "I know your language."

This attracted the attention of the miners. One by one they turned away from the wall and made a circle around the two Notanimals.

The elderly female before them sat down. "You decide now to learn our language? It was that easy for you, and you would not bother to learn when you first arrived?"

"I'm a different person now than when I came here last time," Deka said. "Please tell me about life before we arrived."

The miners surrounded them and sat down in the cold dirt. The hard lighting gave them the appearance of dead canines walking.

"What is the meaning of this?" she said. "Do you patronize us?"

"Not at all," said Kylac. "We've witnessed some things in our travels. We've become convinced maybe our people are not doing the right thing. They teach us we are spreading civilization to primitive cultures who need it."

"It's an assumption we want to challenge," Deka continued. "My people value being able to take the largest, most beneficial parts from the strongest animals. What did you value before we arrived?"

The miners around them wagged their tails. Everyone in the shaft was laughing at them.

"Before you arrived," said the supervisor. "There are few who remember those times. Most were born afterwards. You allow some of the older ones to have the job of keeping the others on quota. I remember the day you arrived. In fact, I remember the two of you. You landed a distance away. You made contact in the flash, but instead of sharing yourselves, you stole from us. Have you forgotten?"

"What did you expect us to do?" Kylac said.

"Before you landed, we shared memories with the animals. We shared minds with one another. We did not take from them or from one another. Then you landed. You forced your weak, decrepit organs and limbs upon us and took ours. You laughed at us when we could not resist. Then you built the mine. You forced us to extract the fuel for your ships so you can go and do this to others out there. You changed the flash from a communion activity into this."

"Then you call us unworthy!" someone in the shaft shouted.

Everyone murmured in agreement.

"We used the flash to bond with one another and with the animals," continued the supervisor. "We feared the predators who often did what you do. The animals helped us look out for them, and together we kept them away. You use the flash as predators do. You brought animals here, and they killed off the ones we used to bond with. There is nothing to commune with now."

"I want to help," Deka said.

"Let us say I believe you," she said. "It is too late."

"I will teach you how to fight back."

The miners stood silent for four breaths. Her stare hardened.

"You are serious?"

Deka took a few steps toward her. "I am disgusted by what my people are doing. I can't change their minds, but if you fought back, you could be free of this."

"One cannot learn how to fight better. One either is or is not."

"Try it," Kylac said. "You're already ahead of quota. There won't be any harm."

"Join me in the energy realm," Deka said. "I will teach you how to fight like a predator."

She considered it. Then she walked to the ration table and picked up some plants in her mouth. Deka and Kylac joined her at the table and grabbed a mouthful of plants as well. The other miners looked on in anticipation.

6

Friend and Sonjaa sat watching the Notanimals on the shuttle who examined each piece of ore as it came in, licking it, smelling it, even listening. Friend and Sonjaa remembered they were cataloging the concentration of radioactive isotopes. Each chunk was of a uniform size, but different pieces had different levels of radioactivity and had to be sorted into the different storage slots built into the floor.

Alone, each boulder had a low enough concentration of particles not to flash, but when ground up and combined with other pieces, it would produce enough to flash not just the ship and everyone inside, but the space surrounding the ship as well.

They learned from listening to casual conversation that the reason people on planets did not fly away at the speed of light was that the concentration of matter itself generated a field that contained the energy locally, or to a planet. In space, no planet held their energy down, so it could be aimed in any direction they desired.

Grinding up and combining different-sized rocks into the reactor produced a predictable amount of radiation to flash the ship for a specific period of time in a constant velocity. The engineers and scientists analyzing the rocks determined now how each piece would be used and in what combination to produce the desired travel interval.

Sonjaa sat in the middle of the shuttle, the many conversations around her hitting her at once. In the previous reality, it had overwhelmed her, but now the conversations combined with the voices of the universe.

She listened to a group of Notanimals sitting by the door in front of her, watching the line of Underanimals delivering rocks into the cargo area. They were talking about the world they had just come from. Sonjaa remembered it now. It had been an uncontacted planet, full of Underanimals just like the people of this world, and they had fallen to the domination of the invading soldiers.

"I was with six others," one female said. "We found a group of Underanimals. They were flashing with the animals, and I swear they were trading minds with them."

All six of them snorted and shook heads in laughter.

"It's not your imagination!" a male answered. "I was in the flash with them, and they all tried to flip minds with me!"

"I've claimed six worlds, and I have never had anyone try that. Even the animals don't!"

"Why would anyone flip minds with an animal?"

The group laughed again.

At the same time, Sonjaa also took in a conversation behind her. Two scientists guiding the Underanimals to specific slots in the floor to deposit their ore.

"Particle concentration is low compared to the other worlds," said one scientist.

"It will make up for the ones we picked up on the last outpost," replied the other.

"We wouldn't have these inconsistencies if they would simply mine deeper, but no, the people of this world are too scared to go any lower. They insist on expanding sideways, and we let them."

"Have to make them feel in control of something. Otherwise they won't be productive at all."

"And we have to deal with the results. Things would be so much easier if the ore were the same everywhere."

"Things would be easier if these Underanimals could be reasoned with. I hear the ones on this world used the flash to communicate with the animals. Can you imagine a bigger waste of time?"

"Sorting ore comes to mind."

Meanwhile, to her right, Friend conversed with three other scientists.

"How do you direct the ship once it is flashed?" he asked.

"Were you just born yesterday?" one scientist replied.

"No, no, I mean how do the physics work? I know how we do it, but why does it work?"

Sonjaa remembered it was a collective effort of everyone on the ship to direct their energy in one direction. When they ground up and combined the ore, the ship flashed, and then everyone aimed in the same direction. It felt different compared to being on a planet with no force keeping her localized. The people on the ship collaborated in generating their own field and controlling its direction. Their mass created a force that held her energy stream separate from everyone else's. The ship traveled with no boundary, and so long as everyone focused the field together, it would travel at maximum velocity for a specific period of time. Then the radiation would wear off, and they would halt exactly where they needed to be.

"A soldier trying to join the scientist class?" said one of the canines.

"I'm curious," Friend answered.

"Well, it starts with the five fundamental forces."

Sonjaa's eyes widened. Other conversations happened around her, and they funneled into her mind at the same time. Two people on her left were talking about the animals of this world.

"The animals on this planet were strange," he said. "They flashed, and they mated in the energy state."

"Mated?" replied a female. "I don't remember that. How?"

"They traded DNA between certain organs like we flip limbs. Before a flash, you weren't pregnant. After the flash, you were."

"Good thing we brought our animals here. Even the native wildlife needed our help."

Sonjaa's eye twitched. She took in all of these conversations at once, and they started to meld. The scientists told Friend about the equations and the five forces. She knew from Deka that there had been four forces in their home reality. This one had an extra force responsible for the ease at which matter changed to energy and back. A force that preserved matter in the flash. Friend was right. Energy was the default state here. Single atoms were unstable, but collect enough of them together and they generated a field that kept them solid. Strong radiation disturbed this field, allowing larger concentrations of atoms to flash to energy.

But the energy they flashed into was not unbound. The preservation force remained even then, which is why the atoms did not scramble when they flashed back to matter. It also explained why one remained conscious and alive even when in an energy state.

Friend busied himself perusing the formulas and the numbers, learning the equations for radiation concentration and how excess radiation disturbed the strong force and carried atoms along its waves in constant, predictable events. Sonjaa concentrated on vibrations the universe made.

The conversations around her settled into a wordless drone. So too did the universe itself. Around, inside, and underneath her, the universe had been shouting. The various voices she heard had been different from their first landing. Harmony in the noise had been difficult to find, but the multiple conversations around her had helped her funnel these different voices into a single voice, and she realized that these vibrations were not unrelated. One vibration caused another to happen, and another, and another. Tracing the sounds the universe generated from effect to cause around the entire spectrum of noise revealed congruence.

This universe had a hum. A drone. Harmony. The vibrations everything produced added up to a complete whole. Even the electromagnetism combined with the vibrations of the quarks and gluons to produce it. The tone sounded different than the previous universe, but the harmony felt the same.

She figured out what vibrations she had to produce to disturb the tone in a specific way. She remembered what portals sounded like in the previous universe, and she opened a tiny one now near the ceiling of this shuttle. It made a different noise in this reality.

She opened another one. It disturbed the tone in the same way, but from a different place.

Sonjaa took a peek into the Lake. It made a very different disturbance in the tone of the universe, and she reversed the tone she made to create it.

She realized the vibrations Friend would have to produce to make these disturbances in the drone, and she sent humming into spacetime to counter any he might make, blocking his exits.

7

They were the only two in here. Nothing else could enter their energy space, as the mine was the local area for them. Deka felt the Underanimal against him, trying to flip external limbs so she had something to show the others, but after nine flashes she had not succeeded in flipping anything on him.

Kylac had also been there, and he reported the same thing. She did not improve. Deka and Kylac had not been aware of this before—it was not common knowledge among the soldiers and perhaps not even the scientists. Strength during the hunt was not something that could be built up like a muscle, but a limitation of the neurons upon birth.

Earlier, they had gotten everyone in the mine involved at the same time. The energy realm had turned into an orgy of energy streams pushing up against each other, everyone trying to flip parts with the two invaders, who did not attack but left themselves open. The Underanimals' ability to flip parts was simply too weak.

Right now, Deka felt the supervisor trying to break through his barrier. His electrical resistance to her attempts at flipping was incredibly strong, and her resistance was weak. No matter how hard she tried, she was no stronger than when they had begun.

The flash ended, and Deka returned to the physical realm. He pawed the ground in frustration. The miners around them lay on their bellies or stood in the circle and watched.

Kylac approached Deka, speaking in the Underanimal's language. "Deka, it's time to face the evidence."

"It can't be true!"

"We know it on a subconscious level, Deka, our people. The natives of these other worlds cannot improve. In our culture, they are inferior, so they deserve a life like this."

Deka pawed the ground again.

"There's no way to improve," continued the former fox. "You can't build yourself up in the flash."

"They can't be right!" Deka shouted. It echoed up the whole shaft.

The supervisor sat down. "We have tried to condition ourselves to resist your kind, but nothing works. You did not know this before?"

"The soldiers don't know it," Kylac said. "They believe they are traveling the stars, spreading reason wherever we go. Other Underanimals are inferior because they cannot flip as we can, so they may as well be useful."

"Are you searching for your equals?" she asked.

"I do not think anyone is conscious of this goal," Kylac answered, "but we are. Intelligent life. It means life that is similar to us. They do not care about anything less."

The supervisor's ears flicked. "I hope you find it, and I hope I live to see a day when it forces you to work the mines with us."

Deka lowered his head and stared at his paws. "I'm sorry. I want to help you. I want to help everyone. Where we come from, we bring each other higher."

"I should like to see where you come from. But even if we fought back, more would come. Our existence would be defending ourselves from you. It would not be freedom. We are dead without the animals to share ourselves with. We live to survive and no more."

Deka's legs became weak and he shook himself to his stomach. "How can you say that? Don't you still want to fight back?"

"I have lived a long time. I know enough of your people to know that there is no choice. Our only hope is that one day you will meet someone who will do to you what you do to us."

Deka hid his head under his paws. Kylac spoke to her.

"If we could free you of this now, would you thank us?"

"No. Your animals will hunt us both in the physical and the flash."

Deka uncovered his eyes and erupted. "There must be other animals out there! Leave this place! Find new continents!"

"They will find us. They will make us work. We may find other animals elsewhere, or we may not."

Deka tried to snarl. "Anything has to be better than this!"

She stood up and approached the Relians. She examined them closely, scented them. "You are not the same invaders I remember. Who are you?"

Deka stood up, met her eyes. "Where I come from, I am not a mammal."

"What else is there to be?"

Deka hung his head. "I am so sorry I cannot help you. I'm also sorry you will probably forget about me when I'm gone. All of you."

He turned and walked into the elevator, head hanging. Kylac followed. He pulled the string, and the lift slowly clanked upwards. The Underanimals in the pit watched their ascent. Kylac watched them. Deka's eyes were closed. He spoke in the language of the Notanimals again.

"If I could make a portal, I'd send them all away."

"To where?"

"I don't know. Once I figure out this universe, I'll find a place they can go. Somewhere the soldiers won't look. I'll send all of them somewhere else!" He opened his eyes and looked at Kylac. "Would you?"

Two levels of the mine passed by slowly.

"Yes. All of them. Anywhere."

Nobody boarded the lift from any other level while the two of them rode it.

8

"I remember this one planet—were you there for it? No? It was full of people who believed the energy realm was bad and devoted their lives to being free of radiation. They filtered their food, they filtered their water, everything they did meant to avoid flashing."

"I didn't join the service until fifty-one sixty."

"Then you would've missed it. It was so difficult to put those people to work. We had to force flash them to swap their bodies, and then we had to make them work. Once they were used to it, they adjusted fine, but that had to be the strangest planet I've ever been on."

Sonjaa did not need to listen to their conversations anymore. Their verbal words had become the result of a long sequences of interactions between the noises that comprised the universe.

The longer she listened to the droning of the universe, the better she became at picking out the different elements that made up the sound. She focused on the sound the quarks made. Then she focused on the sounds the electrons made.

For every two vibrations, only one sound could result. For every three vibrations, only one possible disturbance in the drone happened. Every quark, every electron, every atom in the universe became a series of reactions to which there was only one response, and those gave rise to new reactions between quarks and electrons and atoms and energy waves that led to more inevitable sounds, which led to more. It was language. Every question had a single answer, and the words had to be strung in a specific way to produce both the question and the answer. String enough of them together, and reality became as predictable as a joke she had heard before.

These people became part of the vibrations that made up the universe. Their particles became the result of predicable interactions between those vibrations, which in turn arose from predictable tones that came from the Lake.

Their species as a whole became a series of predictable vibrations. Individuals became just as calculable. To produce the Notanimal she listened to now, the one standing in front of her by the door, particles in the distant past had to interact in certain ways, and that was the only way they could have behaved in order to produce her.

Friend stood to her right just a few paces away, chatting physics with the scientists. Friend had become an old joke. His particles vibrated in certain ways, so they would only be able to interact with this environment according to certain patterns. There was no other way for him to behave.

Friend spoke to the scientists about this extra force, how they had discovered it, how it worked, and how they manipulated it. Most life in the universe thus far used it to flash into energy, but it took extra effort to use it to flash something larger than oneself. When they figured out how to leave the field produced by the planet, the rest became easy.

So many new planets to visit. So much fuel to obtain. So many people to incorporate into their society. Friend would figure it out in only a few breaths. Sonjaa felt a flush of hormones realizing she had beaten the fox to it—she had only been an Archeon for a few days and she had outpaced a fox who had been one for years.

Sonjaa observed a soldier through the door force-feeding grass to one of the Underanimals who had just dropped off his chunk of ore. He himself was also eating the grass. The miner was too weak to resist the much larger soldier. Sonjaa analyzed the vibrations between the atoms, traced the interactions back in the past. This soldier needed a new heart but was too lazy to go out into the forest and hunt a goodanimal. Internal organs were not so prized among the Notanimals, so nobody would notice. In just a moment, they would flash, and the miner would be helpless to resist the organ flip.

She listened to the conversations around her. These conversations were inevitable for the species. She followed the vibrations to other planets, figured out what people must be talking about on other worlds, and it was all the same. Her awareness spread further out to still other planets. She sensed no other possible result. People who vibrated within the universe in this manner could only produce these disharmonies within it.

She wanted to snarl. Instead, she let down some of the barriers she had set up around Friend and waited.

Friend paused. His scent changed to pure panic. In his mind, the equations had locked in place, and now he became aware of the numbers everyone had. The specific sequence of mathematical interactions between quarks that produced every individual person. The primitive parts of his mind interpreted it as scent. His first reaction was to reach out with portals to silence the scents.

Portals radiated from the ship across the field. Most of them Sonjaa anticipated, and had already placed vibrations where Friend would have to open the way. He found the gaps in her barriers and made ways there instead. Spheres opened over every Notanimal's left-front leg and then snapped shut.

Everyone went down, blood shooting from their torso. Sonjaa looked at the soldiers by the door who had been talking about the horrible natives. They screamed in agony now, and it sounded so much more harmonious with the drone of the universe.

Friend mentally thrashed and tried to push through Sonjaa's barriers, but she had placed vibrations everywhere he would make a portal. She was far ahead of him, and she calculated his awareness would not catch up to her for days. The former fox looked over at her. She turned around and faced him while the scientists next to him rolled on the ground.

Friend's mind had run the numbers across the entire planet, and he was trying to snuff out every scent. His mind quickly expanded to encompass the solar system, and no matter where he went, Sonjaa already occupied that space.

The Underanimals held their ore and looked around. They backed away from the blood. The ones without ore stumbled around, wincing at the pain around them.

Sonjaa raised her voice and spoke to them in their native language. "Go home, everyone. Quota is met."

They bolted, dropping rocks and fleeing. Sonjaa strolled outside as Notanimals around her rolled in their own blood. Every soldier lay on the ground cradling their leaking shoulder.

Sonjaa felt Friend standing next to her. His mind had already run the other side of the equations to calculate the Lake. His old ways thrashed and tried to open antispheres, but Sonjaa blocked him from leaving this reality.

"When did you figure it out?" Friend asked.

"Not long ago. The universe is much easier to understand if I think of it as language."

Deka and Kylac crested the ridge. Sonjaa stood taller. Friend huddled into himself as Sonjaa stomped any attempt he made at creating ways over anyone else.

"Sonjaa?" Deka called, looking at the people in agony around himself.

"Friend, he's missing the equations for the last force, and the ones that link it to the strong force. You'll be better at explaining it."

Deka and Kylac carefully stepped around the moaning bodies as they approached the ship's cargo ramp.

9

Deka and Kylac understood how this universe worked. The equations at the beginning ran forward, producing predictable interactions between atoms from then to the present and into the future. Every person became a result of those interactions, making individuals and civilizations easy to calculate.

The invading Notanimals had a culture of dominance —they were the only ones in the universe to have it. They would never meet another race to challenge them. Every Underanimal they encountered on every planet would succumb to their will, and their civilization would perpetuate itself in an endless expansion across the galaxy, exploring for the sake of finding new planets to exploit so they could travel farther and farther.

The people they subjugated could not build themselves up and resist. Everyone in this universe was either good at hunting in the energy realm, or they weren't. Anyone who did not do well while flashed was condemned to work in the mines, fetching the ore needed to fuel or build Notanimal ships. They had no choice, or they would be forced to flip organs with a goodanimal that needed new lungs, or new kidneys. Other soldiers would flip lungs and joints and force them into submission. It was the only future possible with people like this.

Deka, Kylac, Sonjaa, and Friend lay on the ridge overlooking the grassland. Most of the Notanimals had bled out breaths ago and now lay motionless on the ground. The Underanimals from the mines had come up to see what happened. They stared at the Relians but dared not approach.

All four of them understood this universe. They could leave now and Friend would only have harmed the invaders down here.

They knew the math. They had run the numbers, and Sonjaa had changed a few vibrations in the din of reality to be sure of it herself. All species here did not have these instincts. Without the Notanimals, the universe really would be at peace, and it would stay that way until the end. A few would leave this planet in time, but when they made contact they would commune with the life they found, cooperate with it, become one with it. They would not subjugate it. When they eventually met life they could not flash with, they would have a new culture to understand, and they would discover portal physics. And then, at the end of these interactions between vibrations—the end result of the equations—emerged three holes. People would leave the universe.

Deka turned and looked at Kylac. The former fox looked back, reeling internally from being so aware of every life form in the universe. Even now as Deka blocked him, Kylac thrashed and tried to snuff out a few scents to relieve the anxiety. Friend also itched to break out of the barriers Sonjaa had set up around him.

They had the same facts. They had reached the same conclusion. In the scope of all reality, by the numbers, more people would suffer if the Notanimals continued to exist than if they were dead.

The foxes itched to act on this knowledge. They attempted to open spheres on top of Notanimals across the entire universe, but the raptors held back, sensing something else in the projections. The Notanimals only had to be absent, not dead—the others only needed a head start start so they could outnumber the Notanimals and be ready for them—able to counter this conquering mindset with co-operation in the physical as well as the energy state.

Deka took down the barrier over the heads of some of the population of Notanimals across the universe. Sonjaa let down the counter-vibrations she held over Friend. The former foxes opened thousands of spheres at once. It rained blood. Deka and Sonjaa observed the former foxes next to them. This was relief, satisfying their desire to snuff out the scents in their territory, but only the people who knew how to build ships and leave their planet; the raptors limited their foxes to them.

The grassland filled with their blood. The Underanimal miners behind them looked on in awe. The foxes satisfied their instinctual drive, snuffing out the invaders on other planets, other colonies, other refueling outposts.

They ran out of people, so now the raptors sent the ones offworld back where they had come from. There was enough room for everyone. They would adjust to the entire invading force appearing on their home planet with no way to leave.

The portals stopped sizzling around them, and the former foxes snuggled up to their raptors. Friend nuzzled Sonjaa, licking her snout, begging her to let him do more. Kylac also licked Deka's snout.

Deka rose to all four paws and turned around, Kylac still licking his muzzle. The Underanimals stayed thirty paces away. In the crowd, he found the elder supervisor from the pit.

"They will never bother you again. Leave this place and travel north. You will find your animals. You are no match for the ones the invaders brought with them, but you can learn to take them out physically. I promise. You are free now. We sent them back to a pre -exploration state, and they are now confined to their homeworld for the next hundred or so generations. It will give you and everyone else time to establish space-traveling societies of your own. Societies that will not dominate but will share themselves with others. When the Notanimals eventually do figure out how to leave their homeworld again, there will be more of you than them. You will be able to push them back."

She stepped forward. "Who are you?"

Deka did not waste time explaining it. She would not understand. Nobody ever would. He opened an antisphere. Sonjaa stood up. Friend was still licking her muzzle, pleading her to let him continue. Kylac had gained control of himself, and he stood normally, still shuddering from scent anxiety.

Deka turned, walked against Kylac, and led him through the antisphere. Sonjaa and Friend followed. Once in the Lake, they held one another and prepared for whatever lay beyond.

Friend expressed that now they knew how a Superarcheon thought.

Deka berated him for using that word again.

As the universe drifted away from them, Deka declared they would never do that again. The math may have been sound, but they still did not have the right to do that to someone else's universe.

Friend laughed.

They exited the region where this reality resided. Kylac and Friend calmed down as they lost the equation that defined it. Scent anxiety faded, and now the nothingness of the Lake began to swallow them. They saw where this reality was going, and the future looked much brighter with the Notanimals confined to their homeworld.

Toledo

The Church of Sorven was the only religion whose followers knew it to be total bullshit. Even the most devout believers knew it was designed to be a smokescreen in front of the computers that listened to their every word, and the real reward of the faith was to gain access to the Egg Room.

Brett walked down the stairs to that very room right now, flanked by two escorts dressed in yellow and green robes. Each wore a dragon mask, combining styles from cultures around the world. Nobody knew exactly when they would be allowed to know the truth behind their faith, but everyone had their day eventually if one showed signs of understanding.

At the bottom of the steps, his escorts stopped at a door. It was locked with an old-fashioned doorknob that required a physical key, no internet connection, a puzzling sight for most people these days. The Egg Room was also said to have lead within its walls, preventing any cell phone signals from entering or leaving.

He surrendered his cellular phone to one escort as the other unlocked the door. Brett followed, and then they were locked inside this room.

His escort looked at him and nodded to the monitor on the table in the center of the room. Tapes lay on it, along with a tape player that was more than a century old. He marveled at the objects resting on the shelves lining the walls: real books, real paper documents, other tapes, compact discs in jewel cases made out of plastic, a testament to a time he had only read about, when oil had been so plentiful plastic was used for frivolous, disposable products. The covers were faded, which meant they were real relics from the past. He stood before the ancient tape player and inserted the first cassette.

The monitor flickered. The face of the late Tanya Jayman, founder of the Church of Sorven, greeted him.

"If you are watching this tape, it means you have shown you understand the story of Sorven, the first dragon. You've heard us tell how Sorven visited us during the last Ice Age and tried to steer society along the right path but left when he discovered humans could not be led. You have heard the preaching of his second coming, during the early twenty-first century, when he spoke to me in a vision and gave me the five great truths, along with the nine great questions, and that our goal in life is to seek answers to those questions to achieve a higher state of mind. By now you know that things are not what they seem. Several famous people died in my lifetime, and yet as I am making this recording, they were making public appearances. Nobody can ever attest to seeing them in person, but they are all over the news. Your first suspicion is correct. It happened in my lifetime, and while everyone noticed, few understood what it meant. Play these tapes. I'm afraid there is no way to prove they are not fake anymore. I trust you will be able to see tell the difference between something that is real and computer-generated imagery. Between a real voice and a computer mimicking it."

The Egg Room was so named because people came here to emerge from their shells and learn the truth of the world in which they lived. Now this room was his for any topic he wanted to pursue. He immediately went to a shelf labeled "entertainment" and flipped through the tapes and discs. He found what he wanted.

He turned to his escort, who waited by the door, arms folded, stance neutral. Brett did not know who was under the mask and robe.

He slipped the tape into the machine. An episode of *The Simpsons* began playing within a letterbox subtitled with the year nineteen eighty-nine. The animation was so sketchy, not like the smooth animations produced today. The voices sounded exactly the same as they did today.

The screen switched to a different episode and new copyright of just a few decades ago. The voices sounded identical. The animation was silky. Computer-generated. It was the same episode as before, but remade with the new technology.

Since Brett had been a child, he sensed something was wrong. Relians were to blame for every problem in the world, and the United States was the only nation qualified to fix everything. It seemed too convenient.

Entertainment had first caught his attention. Books, television, internet shows, movies—everything was essentially the same. Movies shared entire ten-minute blocks of dialogue. Same for television; two shows he watched shared camera angles and dialogue exchanges for minutes at a time. Same for books; he had noticed entire pages of text nearly identical.

The Simpsons was proof of it happening. The animated series had been on since before he was born, and yet all the voices were identical. It had become variations of the same thirty plots, augmented by allusions to other forms of entertainment.

The tape moved on to show Michael Jackson in the late nineteen eighties, and then Jackson apparently alive and moving about today, still singing before supposedly live audiences.

The tape showed computer models of the concerts taking place, showed the software that had created the audience, the models used to animate the King of Pop, the software used to create the news reporters who supposedly covered the event.

The singer's voice sounded the same as it had over a century ago. He even looked the same year after year after year. Nobody noticed, it seemed, because they did not have time to notice.

The actors on television were not real. None of the news anchors or even ordinary people appearing on it were real. The news was computer animated. Movies were computer animated. All footage that was supposed to be archival was computer animated. All of it looked perfect unless one could compare them side by side.

Brett ejected the tape and flipped through the documents in that section. He skimmed through a pamphlet printed by the Church that summarized the contents of the shelf, how the country came to this.

Sometime in the early twenty-first or late twenty-second century, computer-animation became so good it was impossible to tell apart from reality. Hollywood took full advantage of it by bringing dead celebrities back for new movies.

Computers also became good at recreating their voices. Singers and dancers came back for new albums. At first, everyone knew they were just recreations, but as the companies produced more and more of it, the new generation could not tell the difference, and they simply expected entertainment to be created in this manner, not by people, but by machine. The companies had become so large and had so many investors to please they could not do anything besides what had already been profitable, which was why they brought back the moneymakers of the past. All of them.

The entire cast of *The Simpsons* had returned for new seasons, and nobody seemed to notice they had been dead for years. The show had been running for almost a century. This had become standard for all media.

Humans were not needed to do performance capture for these new hyper-realistic, computer-generated films. The computer was so good at mimicking human behavior that algorithms rendered their performances in real time. The models spoke their lines perfectly, gestured at exactly the right moments, looked and acted so close to the real thing. It was, in fact, the final iteration of a video game engine. The interactive media of yesteryear had been the ancestors of today's entertainment: completely algorithmic, no programming needed, no animators, no human intervention.

Authors had come back from the dead as well. Michael Crichton had been releasing new books for decades, his stories variations of the same set of core themes. Screenplays, novels, songs, short stories, magazine articles, news articles—all of it created by computer.

The algorithms had years of data to determine exactly what would sell, and computers generated material to fill that demand. Formulas determined how many minutes of sex should be in it, what angles would appeal the most to a given audience, how many minutes of what type of suspense would resonate, what plot twist would be most acceptable, and so forth.

The pamphlet ended with a list of tapes and documents to read for proof of these assertions. Brett wished he could be in here for the rest of the year.

He slid the pamphlet back onto the shelf. Another was labeled "government." He stepped up to that one and pulled out the summary pamphlet. It outlined how the world went from warring tribes, to kingdoms, to empires, to democracies, and then finally to corporations. The transition from rule by the government to rule by the economy had been so gradual nobody had noticed. Now it had been retconned. These tapes were all that were left of real archives.

All public services had been privatized decades ago. The State had been split into hundreds of disconnected companies. Government had become a global, scripted theatrical drama written entirely by computer and broadcast in pieces on the net and over the air. People still voted, but they were unaware their votes only affected which CGI model advanced and which faded away. People assumed the government was ruining their lives, but all the decisions happened in corporate boardrooms.

Literacy was down, finding no profit in an educated, comfortable population. Entire cities had seen water shortages for years, and whole regions of the country endured periods of the day when power was out—deliberate, coordinated shortages to manipulate prices in certain regions to extract the most profit. These companies were already in the process of merging into giant conglomerations that answered only to the wealthy families who owned shares.

Another shelf had "technology" written on it. Its pamphlet explained that the internet was once comprised of millions of individual pages hosted on many different servers. The internet had become consolidated into only a handful websites controlled by three major companies operating under seventy different names, most of which were behind paywalls.

As bandwidth became cheaper and faster, downloads became as obsolete as magnetic tape. The end result was there was no such thing as a download. All information was stored on central servers and accessed on demand. Everything from music, to video games, to movies, to word processing programs was stored on remote servers and flashed to the user's screen.

Hard drives did not exist on home computers anymore. Physical storage was a thing of the past. No computer or cell phone accepted its input. All computers were constantly connected to the internet, and people paid to access movies, books, television shows, internet archives, and even their personal files.

Under the heading of "why," Brett read it happened due to consumer demand, so the companies claimed, as did the history archives on the internet. But this room contained tapes of old news footage and court testimony in which people claimed the companies themselves pushed the change on people in order to force copyright protection onto them.

Their desire was an internet without piracy, and an internet without theft must be an internet without downloads. Home computers were now incapable of storing any information at all, and this was sold to the consumer as a convenience, as home computers could be made even smaller than they already were. They had so little processing power because all they had to do was fetch images from the net. All the processing technology went to the central servers that ran the programs and streamed the media. Consumers did not pay to own music, movies, books, or apps anymore. They paid for permission to access them. Punishment for crime no longer consisted of fines or jail time, but denial of access to their personal files for periods of time.

Brett had been told all the changes in the country had been to protect people against extraterrestrial invasion, but these tapes and documents showed how large companies wanted more profit, and the people who ran them changed society itself to get it. History as a whole was not a story of the blind leading the blind, but conscious decisions by powerful people for the sake of personal gain.

Another summary pamphlet on the "medicine" shelf outlined something else he had been curious about for years: how pharmacists became replaced by vending machines. Brett was only a child when it happened. He remembered hearing it was because of safety, but he had always wondered.

The pamphlet stated retailers and large companies tried to do it as far back as the nineteen nineties, but they did not succeed until late in the next century. It took them so long because nobody trusted a machine with medical advice at the time. It had only been a matter of time before people felt comfortable letting computers tell them what medicine to take.

Doctors didn't write prescriptions anymore. Computers now recommend pills. Machines dispensed them. Doctors were only needed for the most invasive medical procedures, but machines had begun to perform many of those before Brett was born.

The pamphlet went on to describe a time in the distant past when the doctor was the most respected person in the community, not to mention the most valuable character in a story. Now the profession had been converted into an assembly-line task, obeying computer systems that told them what needed to be done. Computers and robots had turned every skilled job into such a task. Medicine had been one of the last to be automated.

Brett remembered the broadcasts: first the press reported some huge news story about a child killed by following bad advice from a pharmacist. The press then obsessed over it, asking questions, suggesting it had always been a widespread problem, but only now had anyone begun to pay attention.

Second, politicians cited these news stories to justify legislation in the interest of public safety.

Third, the bill to legalize and replace pharmacists with machines passed by an overwhelming majority. Nobody voted against it for fear of being labeled anti-safety.

Now he read that the press and the government had been computer animated long before that happened. The whole thing had been a scripted event to convince people this was necessary. Now pharmacies were vending machines, cutting costs for the business and increasing profits. Drug-related injuries had only increased over the following decades.

His escort stepped away from the wall, and spoke from behind her mask. "Your time is up for now."

He turned to her. "Already?"

"The algorithms will flag you if you have not moved or spoken for too long."

"I just started."

"What have you learned so far?"

Brett sighed as he slid the pamphlet back onto the shelf. "I exist to make money for someone else."

She unfolded her arms and gestured to the door. "You have hatched. If you speak of it to others, allude only to the Church sermons. As a registered member, you will not be charged royalties for quoting Church literature, or flagged for quoting material that is supposed to be deleted."

Brett walked around the table.

"You are now in possession of a great burden," she continued. "The burden of being awake. Sorven is a real Krone watching over Earth, making sure people do not forget the truth. Carry this burden with you. Bear it well. Sorven may need us someday."

His escort unlocked the door. Brett walked out, taking his phone from the other escort at the door. As he ascended the stairs, he looked forward to when he could return to read the many books on the wall. That would be a multi-day commitment, and he would have to save up the vacation time for a few years. He had noticed books by CJ Rhine in there. Documents on paper from a time long ago.

He left the Church of Sorven. He looked no different, acted no different, sounded no different, but he had emerged from the egg a new person.

As he passed a digital movie poster, he paused to look at it. A sensor detected the proximity of his phone, which informed him that a small royalty had been deducted from his account. It then thanked him for enjoying this poster and supporting the artist who had created it, but Brett knew no artist had created that. An algorithm had made it, a variation on a single composition, fine-tuned for maximum audience response.

Brett walked on. A song played on the radio from a driverless automobile. His phone informed him a royalty had been deducted from his account and thanked him for enjoying the music. The expenses from just walking down the street every day were enough to keep him bonded to a job. Now he understood why.

His work perpetuated a system designed to keep him busy and obedient. Knowing all of this made him more miserable, and now he understood why the Church existed. The more people like him there were, the harder it would be for the system to continue.

Screens hanging from every building all over the city switched the commercials they played based on whoever was in the vicinity. Brett observed how the screens changed for each pedestrian as they walked down the street, how they read crowds, averaged out their tastes, and played the advertisements that would resonate with the majority of them.

Brett's custom advertising tended to be for chiropractor services, as statistically people with his occupation developed back problems. Most people lived in this personalized bubble of advertising, never noticing their world seemed perfectly suited to their needs, but Brett had noticed, now more than ever.

All at once, they switched to a news broadcast. The anchor was computer generated, but her voice and actions seemed so natural even Brett forgot she was not a real person. She announced to the nation that Rive had been spotted in South Africa and had opened a Relian sphere on top of one of the oil synthesis plants.

Brett refrained from smiling, lest the facial recognition algorithms flag him for suspicious behavior, which might trigger them to deny him access to his music or streaming series for a few days.

He recalled a sermon the Church had given last month, a parable about how the great dragon Sorven thwarted a plan by the evil Quagliols to destroy the field of plants in a southern continent whose growth allowed the world to continue rotating.

Brett had figured out what it had meant and thought it was such a clever way to warn him something was about to happen. He obediently watched the breaking news, cheering with the rest of the people as at long last, after decades of trying to steal the vulnerable populations of numerous countries around the planet which just happened to have the natural resources corporations needed to be profitable and thus required the US military to occupy them for the protection of the human race, the military gunned down Rive.

Immediately after the broadcast ended, a commercial played offering the image of Rive's lifeless, metallic, dinosaur muzzle for sale as their cell phone background. Brett purchased it dutifully, along with everyone else in the city.

Particle Landing

I

Sonjaa had no eyes to open or close. She lay on her belly, watching the dots swirl, bouncing off things in the distance, forming the outlines of her surroundings.

She tried to blink, which confirmed she did not have eyes. As she rose to her hind legs, she realized she had more than one set of them. From the way her body made her feel, Sonjaa had a thorax between her abdomen and head.

The quarks made different noises compared to both realities she had been to before. The electrons in the dirt repelling her body also made different vibrations against her molecules. The black dots suspended in front of her created prominent vibrations as they bounced off things, a brand new sound that had not existed in the previous realities. Reality sounded loud and messy. She let it flow through her and into the background while her mind figured out how each vibration fit into the droning sound that made up the universe. It was coming easier now.

She searched for her fellow Relians, but all she could see were black dots suspended on top of solid white. She reached up with a clawed hand and swiped her fingers through them. Some of them reacted like air and swirled around, but they did not knock into other black dots and disturb them.

The points of blackness swirled on their own like dust, seemingly independent of the wind. The dots drifted to her left. A million at the level of her feet bounced off the ground, and the surface became visible. Those specks collided with a body lying nearby. She discerned the form as the black dots bounced off it, outlining its surface in points of blackness.

"Kylac?"

The body moved, disturbing the specks above it, heaving some of them upwards. Many disappeared under the surface of his body. Most of the particles bunched up as he moved against them, coloring his body in black. He stopped moving and stood upright. The particles swirled without him, and some of his outline disappeared into the white background.

"Sonjaa? Is that you?"

"Where did we land?"

She began to see details as the points bounced off them. Kylac's new body had an insect-like appearance. The skin texture looked bumpy and rigid, and his jaw had pincers. More dots swirled around in contrast to the direction of the wind, and now Sonjaa saw wings folded along Kylac's back. His body had three segments. Four legs comprised the abdomen. The thorax had a pair of arms that ended in claws similar to a raptor's, but on four digits.

Two more bodies rose from the white ground. They compressed the dots, making a temporary insect-shaped shell that floated off their exoskeletons and dissipated into the air again when they stopped moving.

No one had eyes.

The other three played with the dots in the air, which reacted to most of their movements. Kylac tried to catch a handful of them, and he succeeded in collecting a bunch between his palms, but the particles drifted through his hands and into the air a moment later.

Deka tried to sniff them. The particles entered his nose and then emerged from the back of his head.

Friend was feeling his arms. His fingers appeared to grasp solid, formless white. Sonjaa only saw the movement where the dots bounced off him. He brushed the specks from his arm. They flew off and twirled through the air again.

Kylac tried to scent the area, but he did not seem to have a sense of smell either. They all had pincers in their mouths. They all had wings. Friend tested his, unfolding them, buzzing them. They made waves in the air, weaker waves among the particles.

"Any ideas?" Sonjaa said.

"I think I know what these are," Friend said. "They're neutrinos."

Sonjaa remembered them talking about these things before. Rive had described them as crumbs. Little pieces of atoms leftover from the decay of neutrons and protons. In their universe, they were infinitesimally light. Billions of them passed through the body every breath unnoticed, as they almost never interacted with larger particles. They had made unchanging whining sounds in the previous realities. Here, they made all sorts of crackling noises.

"We're seeing neutrinos?" she asked.

Deka waved his hand in front of his face, watching how it became visible against the compressed points of blackness on the leading side, invisible on the other, and how they flipped back and forth. "I think he's right."

"Neutrinos are more interactive in this reality," Friend said, "and it seems this species evolved to see them. And only them."

Kylac stood, face upturned. "Look."

The daytime star in the sky appeared black against pure whiteness. A stream of particles outlined its edges.

Sonjaa figured the stream surrounded the entire star, but she could not see it head-on.

Around them, the landscape appeared featureless white everywhere except surfaces off which the particles bounced. Trees stood in the distance. The particles bounced off a slice of white, revealing a large outcropping of rocks. Other large insects landed and crawled into caves between the rocks.

"I know who we are," she said. "We're defenders."

"What are we defending?" Deka said.

"The king. Yes, in this society a male controls the entire colony and—"

"No..." breathed Kylac.

Deka and Friend looked at one another. They had realized at the same time they were part of an evolved insect colony. A civilization of thousands lived below them. The king secreted special hormones, the only thing their olfactory nerves detected, and whatever that chemical told them to do, they did it. It made them part of society, devoted to a mindless task as one of a group working for the common good. As defenders, they had considerable freedom to move about, but as soon as they returned to the colony and inhaled the chemical again, their purpose in life would be renewed and unquestionable.

Sonjaa turned and looked at them. "I'm not going anywhere near that scent."

"I don't sense anything is holding us here," said Deka. "Let's leave before we have no choice."

Deka unfolded his wings and took off. Sonjaa unfolded hers and buzzed. Lifting herself off the ground felt strange but perfectly natural. She followed Deka. The former foxes flew behind her.

The farther out she looked, the thinner the dots became. Sonjaa expected them to form a kind of atmospheric perspective, like water vapor making the distance seem hazy, but the dots disappeared into the whiteness as distance increased, all except the things they bounced off of. She could make out the black sight of half-trees far away, visible only halfway because the solar wind drove the particles in a prevailing direction.

Animals scurried and hopped around below, leaving a wake of empty whiteness behind them. Many swaths of land were invisible, and the animals appeared to stand on solid nothing for dozens of paces before they moved to a part of the ground with particles bouncing off it.

Deka began a descent, and Sonjaa followed him all the way to the ground. They landed in a clearing far away from the colony. Kylac and Friend touched down immediately after, stumbling to a stop and folding their wings.

Half-trees and half-rocks were everywhere. Behind them appeared to be nothing, although some of the neutrinos passed through those surfaces and emerged out the other side, highlighting the leeward end of everything in a weaker outline. The species had special words for these things, parallel descriptions to light and shadow in the languages of their home universe.

Sonjaa's new anatomy did not allow her to sit, so she lay on the ground with her upper body erect. "Let's... Let's just sit here this time. Don't get involved. Sit and take in the view."

Kylac lay his abdomen on the ground. "Rest. It sounds so good."

Deka went down next, the ground seeming to reach up and cradle his body with the way he disturbed the black points. They lay in a triangle, facing one another.

Friend walked among them. "That was quite a decision we made in that last reality. Four hundred and thirty-one million seven hundred thousand and fourteen people."

Deka swiveled his head in the former fox's direction. "I feel weird, too, but we did that universe a favor. The Notanimals would have kept everyone down, and nobody would have discovered portals. Sending them back to their homeworld means others will have time to figure out ways to defend themselves."

Friend's wings buzzed against his flanks, the closest gesture he could make to show laughter. "Oh, I know we did the right thing. Each universe has one equation. We knew the same numbers and we reached the same conclusion. Four hundred million lives were worth destroying for the sake of several trillion over the lifetime of the universe. Puts my fifty-six planets in perspective, doesn't it?"

"Friend—"

"No, Deka, you listen! Sonjaa, Kylac." He turned his whole body around, facing each of them as he spoke. "The three of you, along with Rive, killed me over two million six hundred and forty-two thousand lives because I had the courage to admit that fifty-six planets were worth losing to understand the Lake. I knew the numbers. I calculated the life of the universe, and I determined someone needed to get out. If someone doesn't understand the Lake, our home will be doomed to die just as that energy universe would have, as if it never existed. Preserving the memory of our home was worth three million lives if it means the universe as a whole will not be forgotten."

Sonjaa wished she could close her eyes. She wished Deka would stop him, but the memory of the previous reality's predictable vibrations had already faded from memory, and now the weight of what they had done felt heavy in her skull.

"Now here we are," continued the former fox, parts of his body periodically vanishing as neutrinos bounced off and emerged from it. "Making decisions on behalf of billions! It's different when you understand the universe in this way, isn't it? Now you know what it's like to know all of reality as an equation. Life is part of that, and you declared a few million numbers irrelevant compared to the solution."

Deka: "What we decided was—"

"I caused disasters that ended the lives of a few million people, and it was worth it! Now the four of us caused a bigger disaster to save trillions more, and you can't blame your old ways for it! You, Deka, and you, Sonjaa, allowed me and Kylac to destroy millions of people. You know you did the right thing. If you believe that, then you now understand what I did in our reality."

Deka turned his head away from Friend. Kylac faced Deka. Sonjaa stared at the ground.

"Kylac," Friend continued, "on Reyno you told me you would never think of life that way, but do you feel guilty now? The math was perfect. We did the right thing!"

Kylac rose to his legs. "Don't you dare compare what you did back home to what we did to the Notanimals! You didn't know the math when you started destroying planets, and you sure didn't know it when you forced me to understand, so don't try to tell us you were on some quest to save the universe the whole time! You saw the universe as a whole, you stopped caring about the people in it! You killed hundreds of people around us because you needed space to think! That wasn't math, that was canine instinct!"

"The disasters were worth it if it meant someone left the universe! You made the same choice back there!"

Now Deka stood. "Did you hear yourself back in Ein's reality? You were lying there killing everyone around you! You said you couldn't stop yourself from opening portals over them, and it felt good! We made a choice based on the direction the equation was going, you used portals to calm your scent anxiety! That's what this is all about, Friend! You're a reverted fox trying to clear his territory! Only difference is you know how to use portals to do it!"

Friend: "And notice who did the killing, and who sent the people who posed no threat back to their planet. Why was that, Deka? And you, Sonjaa, why?"

Sonjaa did not seem to have a single muscle in her face anymore. The urge to close her eyes was so strong. Being unable to act on it made her itch inside.

"It made sense at the time," she said, "but now that the drone of that universe is out of my head... I can't remember."

Everyone took a few breaths, observed the particled landscape vanishing and appearing in the neutrino wind. The particles silently drifted and blew and wavered around and over them.

"Impressive how fast it happened," Friend continued. "I was afraid of it, too. Believe it or not, I was terrified of the destruction I caused until I realized what the math implied. Something outside the universe. Other universes out there. A way to reach them. On Reyno, I confirmed I was right. I could leave this universe. I wanted to so badly, but my old ways held me back. It was agony, being so close to understanding. I realized someone *had* to leave or it would all be for nothing. That was my goal. It's because I did all of it first that you followed so quickly. Doesn't matter if I reverted or not. The math was just as sound in our universe as it was in theirs."

Sonjaa stared at the ground, watching the particles make it visible and then invisible when they drifted away.

Friend turned around. "Yes, Deka, we're equals again. So stop telling me I'm just a fox mindlessly appeasing his scent anxiety. I've heard it all my life. I don't need it from you, too. This has nothing to do with me. This is math."

He left the triangle and walked into the wind. Kylac looked at the former raptors a couple times before deciding to follow.

Sonjaa wished she could close her eyes.

2

Walking through the particles was strange. They did not clump together against Kylac's face and obscure his vision. No matter how many of them gathered in one place, he still saw though them. He followed the wake Friend left in the particles, matching his pace just a few strides behind him.

"Where are you going?"

"Anywhere. I need to think, and I don't need raptors around telling me I'm dangerous. I left the universe and I *still* have to listen to it!"

"Wait." The older insect did not slow down. Kylac wondered why he didn't fly. "I understand now. The larger goal, the sense that this is bigger than any civilization. I knew it before, too."

Friend turned around. His insect anatomy made walking backwards as easy as walking forwards. "You should have merged with me in the Lake! We wouldn't be here if you had just gone along with my idea!"

"You weren't even sure what would happen. It might've made things worse."

Friend picked up speed.

Kylac ran faster to keep up. "We have untamed old ways. We did the right thing pulling you out here. I agree with you. This means something, and we need to understand it. You could get past this if you'd let someone help you."

"We don't need to be tamed! We proved we didn't need raptors back home. I've always been able to tame myself. I just need to keep trying."

"I can't believe you think nothing was wrong the whole time you forced me to learn about the Lake. You weren't in control, and neither was I."

Friend turned back around. "We were free, Kylac. The equations kept us from reverting until you started blocking me."

"We lived to satisfy our scent anxiety. I knew it was happening. I stopped you from going further."

"If I'd had more time, I would have figured it out, and I could've left the universe on my own. I thought you'd want to join me once you learned what I learned. I thought all foxes felt the same way I did. You were so close to Deka I figured you must have wanted to get away as badly as I did and I couldn't be the only one, but I was wrong about that. You crawled back to your raptor, and that told me it had to be me who understood the Lake. Being exposed to different equations might be just what I need to figure this out, and if it weren't for my old ways distracting me, I might be there by now! I should be there! I am better than this, so why do I keep...?"

After a few paces, Kylac interjected. "Keep what, Friend?"

The other insect slowed to a stop. Kylac stood just a pace away from him, staring at his back. He waited for Friend to speak. After standing in silence for several breaths, Kylac continued.

"In Ein's reality you said you weren't in control. Portals just opened on their own, and killing the people around you felt good. Do you finally understand?"

Friend's entire body sagged. "This isn't me. It's something else. I severed it back home but it wasn't enough. It chased me. It found me. It held me back. It's still holding me."

"That's what the old ways feel like. Deka stopped me from becoming that monster. Sonjaa stopped you."

"I don't need a raptor! I didn't leave the universe just to do this again!"

Kylac approached, rested a hand on Friend's arm. "I think we're on the same side. We need to understand this. But you know what you are without a raptor now. We won't get there with untamed instincts. Sonjaa can help you. She's done it twice already. If you let her, we'll figure it out together. It will be like old times, before the disasters."

Friend turned to look at Kylac. The dots began drifting back the way they had come.

Kylac laughed by shaking his wings and twitching his pincers. "Deka and I lived with you and Rive in a few of your theoretical realities. My favorite was the singularity."

Friend's wings twitched. "Rive and I always liked that one. It was fun, letting someone else in. Imagining life that might exist inside of one."

"You talked to Rive for entire days about how physics would become so distorted life could only exist as pure thought. I enjoyed sharing that with the two of you. Deka liked it as well. You and Rive had a unique bond."

"I was happy then. I was in control. Stable. That's who I am. What I become when I get close to the answer... It's not me."

"Do you even remember what you said on Ein's planet?"

"I remember what I said, but I don't remember why."

"'I never used to panic when in a crowd.' What came next?"

Friend panted a few times before speaking. "'I saw other foxes lose control of themselves around others. I was proud I wasn't like them.' You've made your point."

"'Why now? It happens by itself. I'm opening spheres and I'm not telling myself to. Why can't I stop? Why does it feel good?' Those were your words."

"I know what I said. That was someone else. I've been in control since Vico."

Friend stood in silence for quite a while. Kylac waited.

"Or..." Friend stammered. "Or I thought I've been in control."

"Can you at least admit you have old ways?"

After a considerable time standing in the particle wind, Friend replied. "While you were on Earth, I separated my old ways from my higher mind so I could concentrate on the Lake. I looked them in the eye, and they chased me. They *hunted* me. Those months I spent outside the universe, I was prey. Helpless. Terrified. Running in the open, day and night. I didn't need sleep or food, and it didn't matter where in the universe I hid. They caught me. I didn't die on Reyno. I died whenever my old ways found me. I could feel myself becoming something else. I kept them on a leash, let them play on other planets, and I watched them panic. All I could think was... This isn't me. That thing down there killing entire villages can't be me, and yet we were connected. Kylac, I am the only fox who has ever met his instincts. Those few months, being attacked and eaten by my own animal nature again and again —dying over and over, trying to escape this thing. That's why I needed you. I was desperate. I... I needed..."

Kylac fluttered his wings. "We can figure this out together. Our raptors will keep us from panicking."

"I should be able to do this. I shouldn't need..."

"Denying the truth won't help."

The dots were drifting back the way they had come, all of them, as if obeying a command to return home. Kylac turned around and faced where they were going. All the neutrinos moved in the same direction, uniformly spaced out, colliding with objects, floating around them, continuing their migration.

Friend stood next to Kylac, observing. The dots blended into white in the distance, but the direction remained consistent. The neutrinos suddenly had somewhere to go. They followed the migrating particles.

3

Deka felt weird lying on a solid white surface. It was invisible for entire breaths until a neutrino popped out of it, or bounced away, or rolled along it. Deka's mind took in their movements and parsed the numbers. They had to be neutrinos, but they did not behave the way he expected.

He looked over at the other insect. "Sonjaa—"

"I don't want to talk about it!" She turned away. "I don't want to think about what we did. It made sense then, but now? *Shit.*"

Deka fluttered his wings. "I was going to ask if you'd thought about what I said on Mero."

She looked up, wings twitching. "About trying to be married?"

Deka rubbed the claws on his hands together, simulating a Relian smile. "You did save my life on Labccr. It's only fair I offer myself in return."

"Deka, I don't know." She took a deep breath. "It still doesn't feel right. I like you, but once the kill was gone and you filled me, that was it. I don't know what we are now."

Deka grumbled. "We've been together for a long time. I still like having you here. Even while we were in the Morton household and there was nothing to hunt." He laughed again. "I thought I might have to hold you back from killing them a few times."

"You almost did." Her wings twitched. "Funny. We never coupled the whole time we were in that house. Or while we chased Friend's old ways."

"Never wanted to. Did you?"

She thought for a moment, observed the dots. "Once. Right after I thought I killed Jeff. That felt so good I was hoping you'd mount me."

Deka laughed. Sonjaa's wings laughed at first, and then she rubbed her talons together. It had been so long since either had shared predator humor.

"I might've asked you anyway," Sonjaa continued, "if not for that dinner party."

"That was a bad evening. Thankfully we got to hunt on Beslos."

"I was glad to hunt again, and the killsex was perfect. Made me feel alive. I forgot the disasters ever happened. Then we chased Friend's old ways. The kills we made were some of the least satisfying. It was amusing, though, you letting me feed Kylac."

"I was hoping you wouldn't take it as pity. You never took me away from him. Kylac likes you. You could hunt for him, too, if you wanted. There were so many things I wanted to say, but I couldn't because Friend was listening. You always smelled good after a kill, but scent isn't everything. Other cultures mate for life. We could try that. Have you ever considered you don't need a fox? That you're not less of a raptor without one?"

Sonjaa looked at the ground, wings twitching. "Beslos was difficult. Rupi and I lived there for a while."

Deka scratched the dirt with a talon. "I wanted to show Jeff something big, and I like hunting other predators. Seemed like a good choice."

"Don't be sorry. I was glad to hunt again. One time I took a hit from a Sikor. Slashed me with her claws. All I can remember is Rupi licking my wound. She slept against it, keeping it warm. That was agony but she helped me through it. That's what I needed. Someone to hold me while I got through the pain. She wanted to be close all the time, and I always felt proud of her for that. Her instincts demanded she push me away, but she wanted me there. I never tired of feeling her fur against me. It's what I miss most about her."

Deka laughed. "Makes me wish I had fur. Maybe next landing."

She turned to him. "I know it'll never be the same, and I like you..." She looked in all directions, wings unfolding. "Oh, *fuck* it. Deka, did we really know?"

He sighed. "We absolutely did the right thing."

"It made sense then, but now?"

"That's what scares me."

"Friend is right. When I was in the Lake, watching him destroy world after world, all I wanted to do was stop him. And now I think maybe it was worth it after all."

"Discovering the Lake... It shouldn't have happened that way, but it did, and it may not happen to anyone else, ever."

"But we still did the right thing stopping him."

"Friend admitted it on Earth. He would have overpowered Kylac and then satisfied his scent anxiety just to understand this. He cleared whole planets so he could think. He would have done it to the whole universe."

Sonjaa tapped the ground, observing her insect forelimbs. "Now we have two foxes who are capable of doing that when they figure out the equation that makes up the universe. I understand it. I can hear the echoes producing sounds in the universe. I know what it's like to be aware of so many people at once. It scares *me*. How do we help them? How did the ancient raptors figure out how to transfer their scent anxiety into something else? Can we do that now?"

"We'll have to."

"Going from scent anxiety to sexual relief was an obvious progression."

"The raptors of ancient times had a large population of foxes to work with. The ones who calmed down when they coupled with everyone around them stayed with the raptors. The ones who didn't ended up dead when they tried to fight other foxes as their territory shrank. We can't pick and choose. It's just these two."

"What if we already figured it out?" she said, raising her upper body higher. "I think I remember why I let Friend kill the Notanimals. They feel pleasure when they calm their anxiety. We can't stop them from doing it altogether, but if we used it for a purpose."

Deka rolled upright and faced Sonjaa. "Balancing the equation. We used their old ways to steer the development of the universe. We can condition them to derive pleasure from that instead of wiping out the whole thing. That's why we did it! That's how it will work out here!"

"Deka... Have we appointed ourselves qualified to make these choices?"

"We *are* qualified. Friend is right about that. We have become the disaster now, but we can control it. We don't have to let them destroy anyone, just do whatever is necessary to direct the universe until someone can leave it. With enough conditioning, we won't need to block them. Our foxes will acclimate to the feeling of the universe being in balance, and their old ways will be under control."

Sonjaa looked down at the ground. "This is terrifying, Deka. We're talking about deciding who lives and who dies. On Earth, that is the definition of evil."

"Friend said so himself: we are where the gods would be. We know the equations, and we know what happens if we change the variables. If we don't, our foxes will destroy everything."

"I know it's going to feel a lot different when I figure this place out, but right now, I don't think anyone should have... the..."

The particles began to migrate in one direction. Their sudden uniformity in motion and spacing caught their attention immediately. Sonjaa stood up. Deka also rose to his feet and watched.

Moments later, Kylac and Friend returned. Their proximity showed they had a new understanding.

"This is familiar," Kylac said.

All the animals around them ran against the flow of black dots. Deka wanted to go with them, but something urged him to follow the particles. Kylac joined him at his side, with Sonjaa and Friend behind them.

Friend caught up to Sonjaa and kept pace with her. "I... I have old ways. And I also admit that I can't... seem to control them on my own. We're on the same side now, am I right?"

Deka took a breath. "Yes. I understand what you wanted. I want to work this out, too. It may be the only chance our universe has."

Sonjaa finished. "If we do this, we do it as a Relian pair."

Friend's voice sounded strained. "I want to do it myself. I've been trying since the first disaster, and I'm no better. I lost control on our first landing. I was about to lose control in the Energy realm. I am tired of becoming someone else when I approach the solution. I." Friend stammered. "It has distracted me, and I... I... I need... I... I can't sever it, and now... It's still holding me back."

Sonjaa touched flanks with Friend as they followed the particles. "Deka and I have an idea for how to help you. Once we figure that out, we can work on the Lake."

Friend seemed reluctant to let her touch him. "I am used to thinking of myself as stable. But about Ein's universe. I don't know why I said any of that. I don't remember why I wanted everyone around me dead. I was only barely aware of opening portals over people as my sense of awareness of the equation spread. The more of it I sensed, the farther out the spheres opened, and I just felt better. I keep thinking I can control it, but maybe I am getting nowhere. You have done very well with no training. I've never known anyone to adapt so quickly to losing their subconscious. You beat me to understanding the universe last time, and you prevented me from becoming that thing on Ein's planet. If you can help me control this, I'd be grateful."

Sonjaa twitched her pincers, rubbed necks with Friend. The former fox leaned away. Sonjaa leaned into him, walking flank to flank. He shied away. Sonjaa leaned again, and this time Friend walked with her.

Deka and Kylac twitched their wings, exchanging glances.

They walked with the particle migration. It seemed to be speeding up. The dots moved faster against their backs. They disappeared into the white distance.

4

The wind blew perpendicular to the flow of neutrinos. The Relians followed them farther and farther out. Something inside them told them this was exactly what they were supposed to do, even though all the other animals and large insects flew, hopped, and ran in the other direction.

The flow appeared denser now, like walking through a solid that did not resist them in any way. After about a hundred paces, there were no neutrinos in the air. The world had become white from horizon to horizon. Within the whiteness, they heard a faint buzzing. The Relians felt an urge to stand their ground and flash their claws at the nothingness.

Friend sounded breathless. "No neutrinos. It should not be possible, but if they are more interactive in this reality, then there would be fewer of them."

"Where did they go?" Deka said. "And why are we standing here?"

"Get ready for a fight," Sonjaa said. "I think I remember now. This is what we are supposed to guard against. Them."

Friend: "Who?"

The buzzing noise became much louder, filling the whiteness. Their Archeon sense of hearing told them seven hundred sets of wings were coming closer to them. The Relians spread their wings and rose ten paces into the air. They hovered and waited.

"I remember something," Deka said.

He found a muscle he didn't know he had, attached to a gland in his abdomen that housed several dozen mildly radioactive pellets. Deka squeezed that muscle. The particles went through filters and tubes, and out of his mouth came a stream of neutrinos. Millions of them flew in a straight line for twenty paces and then fanned out into a cone. The cone enveloped ten insects. These insects were only half the size of the Relians in their current bodies but twice as hungry.

Knowledge came to them: these beetle-like things were similar to locusts on Earth, but they ate the flesh of animals and insects. The swarm was vast, though they only saw this tiny slice of it. Whiteness cloaked the rest. The particles Deka emitted orbited the insects a few times and then funneled into tubes sticking out the tops of their heads.

This was how they hunted. They absorbed the neutrinos for hundreds of paces around themselves, robbing everyone of their sight, hunting by hearing and an advanced sense of smell.

It was the only advantage the beetles had. Otherwise they were defenseless, which meant the four Relians could easily take out enough of the swarm to divert it from their colony.

Friend, Sonjaa, and Kylac found their new muscle and squeezed it. The four of them emitted a stream of neutrinos that revealed the approaching swarm for hundreds of paces. As insects, they would have relied on this exclusively. As Archeons, they knew how to use the rest of their senses to track the beetles.

The neutrinos swirled into the swarm and vanished. The Relians charged, claws out and ready. Deka's primitive sense of hearing told him exactly where an insect was, and his claws crunched straight through its skull. It bled neutrinos, which bounced off nearby beetles and then fell into their tubes.

An insect landed on Sonjaa's back and tried to bite her wings off. She spun around and slashed sideways. Invisible blood and visible neutrinos spilled out of its abdomen.

Friend and Kylac flew back-to-back, launching neutrinos around them, revealing the swarm of beetles as they closed in. The former foxes stabbed wherever neutrinos bounced. They felt blood and guts spilling all over them, but the black particles were all they could see.

The swarm enveloped them. All of the insects in it came to help their fallen, and now the four Relians flew as a single insect, covering one another's back, disturbing the swarm from inside it, killing anything they could reach.

They did not bother to launch neutrinos at the beetles, which kept their own bodies hidden. The fight now happened in total whiteness. The only neutrinos came from the broken bodies of those they had killed. Hundreds of them lined the ground by now, still emitting a stream from their own glands that absorbed the massless particles.

The beetles did not know how to handle this threat. They were used to defenders giving away their position in a stream of particles. Now four defenders had taken out half the swarm in no time.

Their ears picked up something else. A second wave approaching behind the first. Seven thousand beetles.

Their first instinct was to return to the colony, leaving scent trails along the walls and ground for more help. They flew higher and buzzed over the first swarm toward the colony.

Friend snarled, sinking lower in the air. Sonjaa saw him drop and followed, Deka and Kylac immediately behind her. Friend descended all the way to the white ground, his invisible body lying on its side, convulsing. Sound was the only way to locate him, and Sonjaa landed next to him. Deka and Kylac landed off to the side.

A portal appeared in front of Friend, invisible at first, and then neutrinos began spilling out of it in all directions. They collided with the Relians and cast one side of them in black light. The particles became caught in the flow and vanished into the pursuing beetles.

Friend thrashed and cried. Eight more portals opened, spilling out more neutrinos. The insects were only a few dozen paces away, swallowing all the neutrinos that emerged from the spheres.

Friend snarled, and the air sizzled with portals. Insects dropped from the sky and landed in a burst of black particles. The initial swarm had now become a pile of cracked bodies on the ground. The particles they released migrated toward the larger swarm.

Sonjaa lowered her invisible head to Friend's. "What is it? What's different?"

Friend strained to speak. Sonjaa heard him laughing.

"You want to be tamed, remember! It's the only way to figure this out!"

Friend growled as he opened a hundred portals at once. They flashed around them, coughing particles that became swept up in the stronger migration into the swarm. Bodies fell from those portals, insect parts crunching on the ground underneath them.

"Atoms. The density. It's higher here. Everything is closer."

Sonjaa turned to where she heard Deka standing. "What?"

"Neutrinos back home don't interact with much because there is so much space between atoms. If there is less space, they would interact a lot more."

"I don't think in atoms!" Sonjaa shouted.

Deka sounded dreamy now. "Everything is the same except the spaces between the atoms. That would mean... Could that be the only difference?"

Friend's limbs moved as if gripping prey. Another thousand portals opened, spilling out pieces of beetle, but also burrowing mammals, animals fleeing the approaching swarm, and other insects who had taken refuge in trees or underground.

Deka turned to Kylac. Sonjaa heard him pushing spacetime back in its place. Deka held Kylac down mentally. Sonjaa's mind took in reality, examining the vibrations. Everything was the same, but closer. She thought how that would affect the voices of the things shouting at her.

The force that held atoms at a distance was only the beginning. The particles inside the protons and neutrons, the quarks, also had a great deal of empty space between them. In this reality, those particles remained much closer together, and yet they worked essentially the same as they did back home. The change balanced out perfectly.

The Lake always spoke the same language. Its echoes through the many realities felt different because of the different media it filtered through. Her mind separated the vibrations. She examined how they felt compared to the previous realities.

She realized how the drone should sound with this change. The individual vibrations began to fit together into a uniform background noise. Portals and antispheres became disturbances in it.

She felt Friend reaching into spacetime, disrupting the drone of reality over several million creatures. Sonjaa intercepted him, restoring the universe to its usual hum.

Kylac lay on the ground, looking up at Deka, begging him to give him relief from his anxiety.

Deka and Sonjaa exchanged glances. There were no neutrinos to see by, but Sonjaa's numbers meant she would have to stand in one particular place, looking at Deka, thinking a certain thing.

To Sonjaa, the noise of the universe arranged itself in specific ways, and the vibrations that comprised Deka had to be arranged in a specific way right now, so he would be staring at her, thinking of only one thing.

The noise had settled into order. Sonjaa interpreted it as language. Deka interpreted it as an equation; Friend and Kylac were as much a part of it as these other insects. Their numbers—their noise—meant they would behave in a specific way, right at this moment, or none of the previous calculations and reverberations would have happened.

Friend rose to his abdomen, looking up at Sonjaa. He mentally begged her to release him. The anxiety was too much—he hated losing control every time he got this far with the math so he had to calm it. Sonjaa bent low.

"Our plan is for your mind to adjust to the limits we set for you, and you will feel anxiety only in the presence of an imbalance in the universe."

"We make the judgment," Deka said to Kylac at the same time. "We *are* qualified. Life is part of the equation, and we will teach you to balance those equations. Can you calculate what that swarm's part is?"

Kylac nodded. Friend nodded as well. They knew the swarm was the only thing on this planet keeping the other life forms down. If this species were allowed to exist, the inhabitants would die off, and the planet would also die. But without this species, several other species of insect would be free to rise up. They would become conscious, and in time they would join the contacted universe in this reality.

They sensed a contacted universe here. Hundreds of Archeons across this reality, and a dead end at the conclusion of the equation. Without this species of insect, holes would punch through the universe and into the Lake. Someone would leave this reality eventually, and one of them would be a descendant of the intelligent insects from this world.

None of it would happen if the beetles existed.

The former raptors understood the valuable opportunity. The former foxes recognized what was about to happen. It would be agony, but they would endure if it would help them control their animal impulses.

The raptors opened up the spacetime over the approaching swarm. The two foxes eagerly opened spheres into those areas and killed the beetles. The air became still. The neutrinos spewed from the bodies, returning vision to the land.

The foxes breathed easier, and then they panicked again as their minds became aware of people across the universe. It wasn't enough; they wanted to destroy them all.

They calculated Sonjaa would maintain control over Friend for years.

Friend stood up and begged Sonjaa to let him destroy the rest. Kylac clung to Deka, also making the same plea.

"Not yet," Deka said. "You need to get used to deriving relief from balancing the equation. Destruction for a constructive purpose instead of merely satisfying scent anxiety."

"I don't want to be tamed!" Friend yelled at Sonjaa. "I shouldn't need this! I shouldn't need a raptor holding me down! I can end this now!"

Sonjaa felt him thrashing. She blocked his every attempt to break out of his confines.

Kylac also tried to break out. Deka counteracted him at every turn.

"We can wait in the Lake," Deka said. "Sonjaa and I will block you there. Time will move faster."

An antisphere opened. No neutrinos came out of it, but neutrinos did gravitate toward it and vanish.

The Relians prepared to shed their physical bodies and release their conscious minds. Deka gathered his fox. Sonjaa raised Friend off the ground, and they walked through.

5

Two years felt like mere days in the Lake when they swam ahead of the universe and waited for it to catch up to them. Sonjaa and Deka succeeded in containing Friend and Kylac, even out here. Their thrashing never ceased. Now that Deka contained him, Kylac let himself go, thrashing and crying out—trying to act on the impulse was relief in and of itself. The raptors imagined this is how primitive foxes must have acted centuries ago, when raptors first realized how to convert their scent anxiety into sexual desire.

Deka and Sonjaa had allowed their foxes to suffer the scent anxiety for a while, and then opened more spacetime over the beetles. Their foxes felt relief destroying part of a species because they sensed the equation nudging closer to that point where the universe would develop holes in it leading to the Lake, evidence that people would leave it.

Sonjaa and Deka dropped the barriers over more of the beetles. Kylac and Friend sent spheres and antispheres over three million of them across the planet. The equation became much more balanced now, but still not quite where it needed to be. Deka and Sonjaa blocked their foxes from opening more spheres. The relief of changing the numbers to be closer to the desired result made them feel good for a moment. Then the anxiety rose up again, and the raptors blocked their foxes.

Kylac and Friend knew what the raptors were doing, and they hoped it worked. Conditioning their minds to panic only when the equation felt unbalanced, and then to derive pleasure from adjusting it so people would leave it in the end. Channeling their territorial aggression into sex wouldn't work anymore, but this might achieve the same result.

Friend thought it felt good to be limited. He still wanted to break out with all his might, but he did feel a difference now.

Kylac also felt better. Still panicked, being so aware of the life in the universe feeling so close to him, but a balanced equation felt like relief. Destroying the whole equation would not. For the first time since Friend had pushed him to understand reality on this scale, he felt good about it.

They begged their raptors not to stop.

They still had a few more years before Sonjaa lost control of Friend. Deka and Sonjaa waited another year before letting their foxes destroy more beetles.

Kronia

I

John halted mid-step. The library appeared exactly as the Church teaching described it. He never doubted it was real, but to see it in person made it real.

He saw six dragons walking about. A couple of them turned to him and scented him from a distance. They plodded on without a word. For a brief moment, John did not feel welcome here.

He heard something behind him and turned around. The portal he had come through had vanished, and a Krone stood in its place, head down to his eye level, teeth bared in an imitation of a human smile.

"Jonathan Crosworth, welcome to the library."

John suddenly had the energy to run laps around the sun. "What do you need me to do, Sorven?"

"The Church needs a new leader for the western US branch. I think you'll do just fine."

"I would be honored."

"You've watched all the tapes, read the documents. Was there ever any doubt as to if they had been faked?"

"Many times. Computers create everything else. Why not those?"

"I have something to help with that, and your first act will be to present it to the congregation."

The Krone turned and crossed the room. John kept pace beside him, head held high, carrying himself with a sense of duty.

"Have you had a chance to review the newest documents we've preserved?" said the Krone.

"No. If I take a day off, I risk being fired."

"I wish I had another way to distribute this information, but digital copies are too easy for algorithms to detect. You should read the documents on farming."

"Are farmers real? They're on the news all the time, but I've never met one."

"Farms don't exist anymore. Neither do farmers. Corporations own the land and hire temps to work it. Commercials still show archetypal farmers working hard day and night to grow our food, but it doesn't happen that way. Feudalism has returned, but now faceless corporations are the new nobility, and hiding behind them are the new landowners. Soon farms won't exist at all. Food will be chemically created in factories."

"I wouldn't be aware of it if not for the Church."

"There's a lot of new information that's still working its way to the members. As leader of the western US branch, you will not need a job. Your concern is protecting this information from the wrong hands and making sure it ends up in the right hands. Rive is handling the Church funding. There are new documents on pollution and agriculture I want you to read as soon as possible. Have you noticed all the advertisements for medical treatments?"

"Yes. Cancer treatment, lung failure treatment, digestive disorders, and on and on. Pills, surgery, lots of transplant commercials."

They passed a video wall. A Krone with bright white scales accented with flecks of red and pink lay in front of it. Some of the channels on television and across the internet were in other languages. The Krone under the transparent section of ceiling did not pay attention to him, and John walked on to the next room.

"Citizens are urged to become organ donors," Sorven replied. "There is a new market for bodily organs, artificial, genetically grown, and transplanted. Selling one's DNA for medical purposes has become big business."

"The ultimate act of desperation. I never wanted to do it. I don't want them to clone my organs so they can sell them to others. They'll only give me one year's worth of salary for it."

"Very good. You know how the market makes you poor while enriching those on the receiving end. That hasn't changed, but the rest of the world has changed so much since I began watching. With the scarcity of oil, industry resorted to synthesizing it. Oil is more important than people, as it always has been, but now it's worse. Industry pollutes as much as it wants, anywhere it pleases, and nobody knows about it because the news is computer animated. Reality is what people see on the internet, not what they experience, all because someone decided cellular phones and automobiles were more essential than human health. It's not just pollution either. Plenty of other things contribute to this carcinogen world. The companies that bought Crescendo, for example."

"I read CJ Rhine's book on that. She wrote it over a century ago, and it's all still true."

"Regrettably, yes."

"I know," said John. "Three companies control all agriculture. Each has its own line of patented plants and cattle and chickens and everything else. They pretend to compete."

"The oceans are a plastic soup," the Krone continued. "The chemicals are in every person and animal. The body absorbs them continuously. The human body is a wreck, and nobody will admit artificial chemicals are the cause.

Microbes evolved in this toxic environment to eat the plastic, but the waste they excrete is just as bad."

John nodded as Sorven spoke. "Thanks to the documents the Church preserved, we know this was part of their business plan: hope a microbe evolves that will devour plastic and solve the pollution problem."

"They evolved, but that just gave these companies an excuse to continue hurting people. 'Evolution is the answer.' It's still an ad slogan for industry as a whole. Cancer is as common as a cold. Everyone has asthma. Digestive problems. So many medical problems hospitals and doctors compete for business. You had three tumors removed just last month."

"Third time in six years."

"Our documents show business leaders believe they are doing a good thing, revealing which humans can adapt to this world and which can't. They believe they are advancing the human race through evolution to the stimuli they create. The rich never expose their families to these chemicals. They never put themselves in this genetic lottery to decide who is worthy and who is not. It has always been this way, to one extent or another."

In another chamber, they passed a Krone with jet black scales watching a video wall. He had no ridges or horns on his head, and his wings were in tatters. An old Krone. All of the channels depicted people in sub-Saharan Africa in various languages. A black woman climbed up the ladder in this room. She pulled down a pack of documents. She noticed them and waved to John. He waved back. The Krone in the center of the room regarded them but did not move. John walked with Sorven through the library.

The Krone continued: "Some say money represents man's intellect and ingenuity, but it actually represents the instinct to be the dominant monkey in the group. That is the cause of all of this."

While he spoke, they had passed through two more large rooms, each with a Krone in it watching a wall of screens. Another human sat at a desk in one of them, reading through a stack of documents. He had an obvious tumor on his neck.

Sorven turned to John and imitated another human smile. "You are surprised to see so many Krone here?"

"Yes, actually."

"My little project caught the attention of my people. They were curious what I built, why I was in here all the time and why the entire contacted universe was talking about me being out and about so often. Most of the Krone are here. Each one is patron to a particular nation. Some nations have several regions within it. I'm over the United States. It's where my human side is from, so I'm nostalgic for it, though I also help out with the Philippines."

"So the sermons on patron dragons were symbolism, too," John said. "I wondered if it was real."

In the next chamber, all the stations on the monitors were in American-accented English. A box rested on the floor under the skylight where Sorven would lie down and watch the screens. John walked up to the box. Sorven remained in the shadow that ringed the walls of the chamber.

The box moved. Something scratched the cardboard from the inside.

John hesitated. When the box settled, he knelt down and opened the lid. A Krone hatchling about the size of a Golden Retriever turned its head up to him. It had silver and yellow scales. It croaked at him. John looked back at Sorven, mouth agape.

"The first Krone to hatch in more than a century. We have been abandoning our children in the ruins of the Lost for too long. We decided it's time for a change. The Church shall raise this eggling. All who see her will know that the Krone are real, and so are the documents and tapes. This information must be preserved to keep the spark of life in humanity. Now that the world is united under a single economy and people are at the mercy of decisions made in shareholder meetings, it's more important than ever that some people remember the past as it actually was. This library is yours. Come and go as you please but do not bring anyone with you, and return materials quickly. If you abuse this privilege, the portal will close, and I will choose another Church leader."

"I will not abuse this privilege, Sorven."

"And take good care of that eggling while she's in your possession. Krone infants are capable of growing up without a parent's care, but we don't want this one to be raised that way. She will be a child of Earth. Rive will fill you in on the details, and he will also give you the newest documents you are to adapt for the Church. You will need a lot of time coming up with sermons based on them that won't trigger the copyright spiders."

John felt like he could make the sun stop in the sky. "I will not let you down."

Sorven spread his wings, smiling like a Krone this time. He walked into the light and lay in front of the video wall. A couple hundred news broadcasts and internet shows hit him all at once, none of which had real people behind them.

John had read that internet shows had once been independently produced, but now the large entertainment companies had bought out the independent producers and replaced them with computer animation. All criticism was computer generated. All programs about people talking about ordinary life. All convention reports. Conventions themselves. None of it existed except as animation produced automatically by a nearly-perfect video game engine. All produced to give the illusion of independence. Their audio was not that loud, but to John it sounded like a jumble of noise.

Sorven's shoulder rested right up against him. John didn't know what to do now, so he sat between the Krone and the hatchling in the box and watched the screens. He stroked the hatchling's head. The baby Krone stopped squawking and leaned into his hand.

"Where is Rive?" John asked.

"He's in Shenzhen, on his honeymoon. Rive has been helping the people in the region organize for years."

John waited for Sorven to elaborate, but the Krone did not, so he stroked the hatchling while he watched the video wall.

2

The metal liquefied and found the most pleasing form within these confines. Rive was now buried to the hilt in her, and she shuddered underneath him. Rive withdrew slowly and then pushed back in. Xiu leaned farther over and gasped. Rive held her around her stomach, nuzzled her face with the side of his muzzle, and thrust again, faster. Her scent became stronger as she panted. Rive inhaled it, licking the air to get more of it.

In the back of his mind, the Multitude took in all the new sensations. Rive had taught it how to reform his penis. He had tried it extensively before today, and he had deliberately waited until they were married before letting Xiu know he was ready.

He could not physically ejaculate or produce lube from his slit, but all the sensations were there, and he had even taught his metal to form his penis to accommodate wherever it was. It had just formed into what Rive determined to be the ideal shape and size for Xiu, and judging by how she reacted, it was a success.

The metal was alight with activity as it took in the new sensations. Reproduction was as alien to it as the concept of heat, and Rive hoped it wasn't too much. He had communed with it almost every day to prepare it for life in reality, so this had been the next logical step.

As a bonus, it also meant he could satisfy this itch he had felt for decades.

Xiu came as Rive thrust. He had made sure his metal knew that was important when forming his penis again. Rive sensed it was a bit too much, so he told the metal to re-form slightly so every thrust wouldn't send her over the edge. The next few minutes were much calmer, but no less intense.

She reached around, held him around the head. Rive enjoyed this more than anything. Even when he lacked a penis, he had taken pleasure in the subtle gestures humans displayed when they took their guard down. He especially liked the gesture that showed Xiu wanted him closer—that being inside of her didn't feel close enough.

She was tired, so Rive decided to wrap it up. He told the metal to reform and he sped up. Every thrust brushed her sensitive point, and she came again. Now Rive let himself go. He didn't ejaculate, but the metal sent the appropriate signals to his brain, and his metallic penis pulsed.

He knelt on top of her and withdrew. Xiu rested on her hands and knees and panted. She raised herself, turned around. Rive looked down at himself to see what he looked like now. It was nothing close to how a raptor's penis should look, but it worked. She opened her mouth to speak.

Rive shut down and collapsed on the floor.

The Multitude's reality enveloped him. Rive's mind interpreted it as an Earth city with no ground. The buildings formed a three-dimensional matrix, and each one exerted its own gravity. Rive stood on one edifice, looking up at the cubes that formed the city.

You must be kidding! Rive shouted into the distance.

Millions of points of light flew from the buildings and congregated around him. They gave off vibrations of confusion. Pleasure was also as foreign to them as pain; they had no idea what to think of feeling both at the same time.

I told you that's what it felt like! I showed you what rubbing my slit did!

The Multitude vibrated at him. It felt even more intense with another person; all the senses worked together to stimulate the mind—scent, sight, touch, hearing—they could not interpret it all.

The points of light flashed separately and then in cascading patterns. They collectively said they did not wish to repeat that experience.

If you want to join the universe, you'll have to get used to biological urges!

It felt too much like pain. They did not want to deal with biology in this way. Thoughts were acceptable, but the tactile sensations remained confusing.

Rive allowed his mind to shed the points of reference so he could take in reality as they understood it.

3

Rive opened his eyes. Xiu sat at the desk in the other corner, dressed in jeans and a loose shirt. He could see the typewriter from here. She was working on a list of demands for the corporate entities that ran the city. Having already written about a ban on child labor and multiple seats for the workers at the corporate board meetings, Xiu was now on the part about pollutants in the air and water and mandatory measures to clean up the messes the companies had caused, or work would stop again.

At the same time she was speaking on the radio to someone about the protests going on downtown. Local police had changed position in reaction to which financial buildings and statues and monuments the protesters threatened, and she was directing leaders to other symbols of oppression around town. Law enforcement couldn't protect all of them at once, so she took advantage of that from her vantage point.

Months ago Rive had supplied her with copies of documents recovered by the Church, but Xiu was not associated with it so nobody could connect the protests with the Church. More and more people in the area were becoming aware of what the companies were doing to them, and the information was having an impact.

Xiu didn't use her phone or her online accounts. Analog signals and paper was how the strikers had to operate.

Rive waited until she pushed the microphone away before raising his head, moving a leg. She heard the floor creak and turned to him, smiling.

"I was just about to ask what it was like for you and then you fainted! You've been out for two hours."

Rive growled, spread his legs and arms. "Sorry about that. My metal was overwhelmed. Shouldn't happen again."

She continued typing. "Was it good for them, too?"

"They're still learning the difference between pain and pleasure."

"Where do you even begin with that?"

"That's why it took me decades to explain sex to them. Just as long to teach them how to make my middle claw work."

"It was worth the wait. Were you a stud before you lost your skin?"

Rive clicked his claws. "Just the opposite. When I was with my fox, I never let myself feel anything like this. I thought I had to devote myself to him. That if I didn't, he'd revert. It never happened, but... I still felt that way."

Xiu laughed as she wrote another paragraph. "Haven't you been teaching your metal for over two hundred years? It took them this long to understand sex?"

"They have been teaching me about their reality as well, and I still do not understand. It makes me frustrated. I'm an Archeon. I have never encountered anything difficult to understand before, not a language, not a civilization, but the Multitude. They keep me humble."

"So you're working against the entities that replaced the governments of the world, teaching an alien species how reality works, calculating a portal to send an entire mountain range halfway across the galaxy, and somehow you have time for me."

Rive stretched out. "Plenty of hours in the day." He growled again. "Did I miss anything while I was out?"

"All the signs are there. It's happening soon. I want our demands finished and distributed so we establish cause and effect. The algorithms will blame extraterrestrials and justify everything. The people need to know what's about to happ—"

Rive turned to the door. She had heard it, too. Footsteps coming up the stairs. Rive completed the equation for the second portal he kept ready just in case this happened. A sphere to the library on Kronia opened on the other side of the room, Sorven and a man he had not met before visible through it.

"They're coming," Rive said, rising to his feet. "Go."

She shoved her chair aside and crossed the room. "Absolutely not! I've been reading about this for months. I'm not leaving you on our wedding night!"

"Xiu, please!"

She stood beside him, holding him around the shoulders. "It's not a drone strike. I'll be fine."

Rive reluctantly let the portal close as the door burst open. Two soldiers in dark uniforms stood before them, guns drawn, fingers on the triggers. Rive stood up straight, leaning on his wife as he turned to the two men.

"Guys, hello! Took you long enough to find me."

The soldiers opened fire. Bullets chopped Rive, slicing his skin, bouncing off the metal and ricocheting off the walls. Xiu did not flinch as the bullets flew. The metal raptor stood still and took the shots. He had already told his metal to shut off his pain receptors.

These were not bullets. His metal informed him the projectiles had injected him with something, and it contained DNA from the Gaow plant. Another fast glance at the raw information his metal fed him confirmed it was bacteria that feasted on flesh, modified to feast on Relian and only that.

The soldiers stopped firing and stood ready.

Rive laughed with his voice. "I hid in China because I knew the industry here would never allow a drone strike with so much factory equipment around. I read about this operation in the works months ago, but I couldn't find any details about the new weapon."

As he spoke, his metal told him it could kill and remove the bacteria, but he would lose some flesh in the meantime. It had isolated his central nervous system to keep him alive until then.

"So... Let's find out how well it works. Hope the shareholders are watching."

Rive stood in an open position. He did not feel the pain as the bacteria ate his body from the inside, but the feeling of something happening reached his brain. He raised his arm. Six bullets had struck him there, and foam emerged from the holes, as well as noxious fumes as they ate skin, bones, and ligaments.

He held up his arm for the cameras attached to the men. The skin bubbled and puffed like a balloon. Rive reached around with his metal hand and tore the skin off.

The bacteria had multiplied into large, green masses inside his arm. The flesh quickly disappeared, and the colonies excreted black liquid as waste. Some of it dripped to the floor as his arm sizzled. The same thing happened to his remaining leg. He didn't strip the flesh from it, but tar dripped from the four bullet holes as gasses leaked out.

The theropod stood still and let the metal isolate the colonies. In a minute, one of them had eaten the flesh on his arm through. Rive told the metal to detach it. His arm wiggled and then fell free and clattered to the ground in a smoking, noxious mass. Seconds later, it detached the parts of his leg as well. Rive felt hollowed out. The metal spread open at his chest, exposing his body cavity, and a succession of liquefied organs spilled from it. Xiu stood firm, watching the soldiers instead of what was happening to her husband.

The metal sent him images of his body as it reformed the missing pieces of his limbs. The metal had spread itself out so far it had to leave parts of him hollow just to remake his limbs. He still had enough flesh making electricity to keep the Multitude active.

Rive cleared his throat and stood straight before the soldiers, folding his claws.

Xiu removed her arm from Rive and dove for the papers on the desk.

"Listen to me. Businessmen are actively trying to end the world. We have evidence."

She stood before the soldiers and held the packet out.

"You probably think you're working for the government of the United States, and you really do believe there's an alien invasion coming that will bring disease to Earth. These papers prove there is no government. You work for a company owned by the industries behind what is about to happen here. You will ask why anyone would want to do this. The answer will always be for money. People began rioting when they read this. This isn't an alien attack. Human beings have been planning it for years."

The soldier in front took the packet and ran down the stairs, the other following. Xiu sighed in relief and turned to Rive. The metal was beginning to reform the other half of his missing lung. Rive heard the soldiers leaving the building.

He sat next to the bed and shuddered. Xiu knelt beside him, rubbing his snout. This attack had been the test. The biological weapon had been modified to feast only on human flesh, and in the coming weeks it would be released in multiple cities all over China. Video of Relians invading those same cities would surface, and computer-generated experts would claim extraterrestrials had brought disease with them.

Parallel to this, the working people had organized resistance to the working conditions and pollution. They had grown tired of being used as the world's factory, just as the people of the Middle East had grown weary of being used as the world's oil synthesis plant, and the people of southern Asia had grown weary of being used as the world's seamstresses, and so on around the world.

Dissidence had spread throughout the country, and some corporate owners had begun to fear the strikes and the riots would kick industry out altogether. This bacteria would decrease the population, disrupt the protests, and make the people even more desperate for work.

It would also give the corporate entities an excuse to deploy their private mercenaries and force people back to work at gunpoint. The media in both countries would point out that work can continue as normal, and nobody would ask why the press reported on it from this angle, as if that was the most important takeaway.

"Business with pleasure," Xiu said as she felt his muzzle. "Your favorite."

Rive reached out and rubbed her fingers. "The next time will be even better. I promise."

He leaned forward and mouthed her neck. She played his fingers in return.

Confluence Landing

I

The city below bustled with nighttime activity. Bipedal lizards walked up and down the blackstone streets, which absorbed heat from the daytime star in the sky and held onto it until nightfall, when the cold air stimulated the mineral to release the heat gradually. The streets felt like daylight through the feet, which meant the city remained active even at night.

The avenues were wide enough for four Krone-sized creatures to walk abreast. A quadruped lizard about as large as a one strolled between the buildings right now. The other reptiles driving autocarts treated him as part of the traffic.

The vehicles had a pair of minerals inside them that discharged electricity in large bursts from one rock to the other until eventually the number of electrons equalized and the minerals needed to be replaced.

Streetlights made of fragments from lightrock lined the road. Lightrock emitted visible light when broken. Gemists regulated the rate of emission by combining elements in precise quantities so the resulting compound didn't burn out all at once. The rocks in the lamps and in the autocarts lasted years before they began to dim.

Although there appeared to be multiple species down there scurrying about, they were all actually the same species, just different ages. After hatching, the tiny lizards had loose skin and walked on all fours. They remained this way for a few years, growing gradually into their epidermis until they entered the next phase. They shed their skin, retreated to a special room, grew to three times their previous size, then emerged as adolescents. They remained this way for another eleven years or so before shedding their skins and growing again.

This continued throughout their lives until they reached the size of the Krone-like creature that now walked through the streets as part of autocart traffic, an elderly reptile, now only able to live in the outer districts. Many did not live long enough to reach that phase, but those who did enjoyed the freedom of flight and the simplicity of construction.

The elderly raised the buildings, repaved the roads, and repaired the tall structures. The young did the more nimble work of combining elements into minerals, carving those minerals into useful shapes, researching new combinations, selling and distributing domestic and industrial blends, and so forth.

They called themselves the Hegesh. Each age group also had a name. The small hatchlings were Legesh. The next size lizards were Migesh, and so forth up to the largest lizards known as Hegesho. Nine phases in total, each named after a digit in their number system, which was also base nine.

Kylac pulled his head in and shut the window. It was not made of glass, but a special combination of elements forming a mineral cut into thin sheets that held in heat while letting light pass through.

Kylac's tight scales had the same red and black pattern of his fur when he had been a Relian canine, now with a dewlap hanging from his chin.

He turned and leaned against the wall, which was also made of some kind of stone-like compound that held in heat. The vibrations the atoms gave off felt unlike anything he had sensed before. The numbers meant the atoms inside contained two hundred and six protons and neutrons. Enormous atoms, and yet they weren't radioactive.

Sonjaa sat across the room at a terminal built into the wall. Her scales also matched her former pattern. Like Kylac, she was in the third phase of life.

The terminal functioned similar to the computer systems on Earth, but it had not been manufactured so much as mixed. Gemists had perfected a method to combine several elements into a mineral that could be whittled down to form paths for electrons to flow. The processor was also an artificial combination of elements carved and calibrated to respond to electron flow.

Deka and Friend had scale patterns that matched their former colors as Relians. They held tablet computers in their hands, reading the media this world generated. They had only been here one day and already they had a feel for this culture.

"I like this place," Kylac said. "And being a reptile again is fun."

"We're cold-blooded," Sonjaa said. "Don't forget that inconvenient reality. We'd slow to a standstill if the temperature dropped ten degrees."

"That's what I admire about it."

He turned to the blackstone in the center of the room. It emitted the heat it had absorbed during the day. Every room in this flat had one stone in it, each precisely mixed from several different elements and then carved to meet the need of that particular room. Specific angles resulted in different levels of output and retention. This one had steep angles meant for large output over a relatively short time. The other stones in the sleeping room had fewer cuts for more gradual output.

"Atoms in this universe are so stable," Friend said. "I'm beginning to wonder if there is radiation at all."

"There has to be," Sonjaa said. "Stars still burn."

"And they burn much hotter and produce different elements. Everything here is big. Back home, elements above lead were too large to remain stable, so they radiated particles and energy until they reached a more stable form. Here, nothing seems to decay."

"I know," Sonjaa said. "The vibrations have much more variety. In other realities, I had the feeling elements became too loud, so they shook themselves apart. Not this place. The periodic table has over six hundred elements."

Deka looked up from his tablet. "Six hundred? Where are you?"

"This is a library terminal. Collected knowledge of the entire culture is here for anyone to read. Most of the elements are described in terms of the minerals and gemstones they combine to form. They seem to be the most common compounds, both in nature and in manufacturing. There's a lot of talk of cutting and shaping minerals and stones for specific needs. Gemist isn't just a career. It's common knowledge."

"I love this place!" Kylac bounded to the window and peered outside again.

"We've been to realities with periodic tables stable into the two-hundreds," Friend said. "I'm more concerned with the mystery of how we give ourselves a place. Every reality we visit, we cast ourselves as something within the society. Sonjaa did it when she first visited the Lake, and we do it, too. The most logical thing to do would be to set ourselves down somewhere quiet and out of the way so we have nothing to distract us, but we never do. We always end up in the middle of where we must be to change things, but how? Are we conscious of it on some level we have yet to discover?"

"I think we are," Sonjaa said, still reading the screen. "Why else would it keep happening?"

"Think back on our time in the energy realm."

"Which one?" Kylac said.

"The first one, with the Notanimals. Deka and Sonjaa allowed us to destroy certain members of that species and relocate the rest because they knew the equation needed balancing, but in the next reality they did not remember why they let us do it ourselves. Later, it made sense, and they've been using it that way ever since. It implies a subconscious at work."

Deka looked up from his tablet again and stared at him. "What if we don't black out when we leave a universe and float through the Lake?"

Sonjaa turned away from the terminal and looked at Friend. "We'd remember something, wouldn't we?"

Kylac turned from the window. "Are you talking about a new subconscious?"

"Not a new one," Friend answered, "but something that has always been there. Once we learn how to tear it down, we will understand the Lake. We will be able to control how we change reality around us when we enter a new equation, if we chose."

Sonjaa turned back to the terminal. "Reality always seems to alter in just the right way for us to find something that needs to be fixed. It can't be luck. Maybe we *are* in control and don't realize it."

"I'm sure of it. After all the realities we've been to, one would think we would know how it works by now, but it may yet take more time."

"I'm in no hurry," Deka said. "Now that the two of you are ignoring the people and focusing your anxiety on the imbalance, this has been fun."

"This won't be fun," Kylac said. "I just remembered what we do for a living. We're assistants to experimental Gemists."

Everyone looked up. They remembered, too.

"Exactly!" Friend shouted. "This is what I mean! We never cast ourselves in the important roles of society, rather as observers of those important roles so we may understand what is wrong. We could have been experimental Gemists, but instead our job is to assist them in whatever they are doing. There must be something our second subconscious wants us to see."

"I don't know what they're doing," Deka said, "so it must not be obvious to someone in this society."

Sonjaa rose from the seat. "Given that everyone here knows about minerals and elements, whatever they're doing must be special."

Kylac looked out the window. "If we can, I think we should stay a while. Long enough to be an Hegesho. I miss Norh and Stephen. All the places we've been, we have never been a creature that size. I wonder what it's like."

Deka clapped his hands together, laughter for the people in this phase.

"What's so funny?" Kylac said.

"My first thought was you just wanted to have a Krone cock inside you again."

Kylac clapped once. "There was a time..."

"Sometimes I miss the fox who found excuses to have sex with everyone, as if he needed any." He turned to Friend. "You, too."

Friend clapped slowly in weak laughter. "I don't miss being that kind of canine. I think of it now as a temporary solution, channeling our instincts into sexual desire until we were ready for something else. Perhaps we were always ready to advance but a certain species of theropod held us back."

Kylac clapped. "I miss walking around halfway out of my sheath all the time. I used to enjoy that most of all. Mind being so aware of the universe, keeping portals open across multiple planets and keeping the body satisfied at the same time. It kept me grounded."

Friend yawned. "Someday Relian canines won't have that reputation anymore. We'll be known for this instead."

The multi-faced hunk of crystal built into the wall vibrated. It kept time on its own with only two tiny fragments of energystone inside. It vibrated seventeen times, which meant one hour until midnight. They reported for work at the sixth vibration, and their bodies needed five vibrations of sleep. Deka and Friend set the tablets on the table and rose to their hind legs. They retired to the far room and lay on the slab of blackrock, cut to release heat in just the right amount to induce sleep.

The Hegesh slept communally. Flats never housed fewer than four people, and they never had more than three rooms. Lizards of the first four phases often changed living quarters several times a week, moving in and out on a whim as needs required and personal associations ebbed and flowed. Since the Hegesh did not become sexually active until the fifth phase, they had no reason not to.

Sonjaa curled up with Friend. Deka and Kylac lay together. The gentle heat from the stone soothed them to sleep.

2

Two lizards in the second phase carried a piece of crystal into a chamber, element three hundred and six.

At the same time, two lizards in the fourth phase carried a chunk of element six hundred and one to a chamber built into the center of a different room.

In the control room looking down on the third chamber between the first two, behind several layers of transparent mineral with a hardness greater than that of diamond, six Gemists in the fourth and fifth phases looked on. Nine technicians, all in their second or third phase, sat at terminals.

Friend's station monitored a row of sensors aimed at the sample of element five hundred and sixty-eight, a metallic element that became liquid at temperatures below the freezing point of water. Beside him, Sonjaa's monitored a glass tube of element three hundred and forty-two, an inert gas which existed in no other state.

The other stations monitored general settings and controlled the rate of reaction. Everyone had their instructions for this experiment. It was routine, just more data, but all of it combined was sure to produce useful results.

The Gemist gave the signal. One of the lizards pressed the button to begin the reaction. Both side chambers vacuum-pulled the two elements from their tubes into acceleration rings below ground. Their velocities reached critical points. Magnets diverted them into the same ring and they smashed together in the central chamber.

Friend's sensors lit up. He remembered now he had been here since the beginning, so this did not surprise him. The air inside the chamber became plasma. The metallic element became plasma as well.

Sonjaa's sensors also pinged as the gas became plasma. It expanded rapidly and then broke the test tube. The elements mixed within the central chamber. Electric sparks surged everywhere, and the pressure increased, though there was no apparent cause.

Moments later, the atmosphere in the central chamber calmed. The elements separated and returned to their natural states. Element five-six-eight precipitated out of the air and became solid again, coating the walls and floor.

Friend had fine-tuned the sensors to detect the moment the element changed states, but no matter how well he adjusted them, he had yet to detect the moment of transition. He turned to Sonjaa. She turned to him. Her dewlap puffed slightly, indicating fear. Friend's twitched as well in agreement.

One of the Gemists picked up a crystal on the desk and spoke into it. "Cleanup crew, you are clear to enter." She set the crystal on the desk and watched through the window. "Preliminary."

The lizard sitting on Friend's left answered. "Reaction sustained four percent longer compared to previous cutting."

A lizard in the second phase spoke next. "Temperature unchanged. Pressure unchanged."

"Very good," the Gemist replied. "Non-control reactions?"

That was Friend's station. "Still no transition data."

Sonjaa spoke next. "No reading."

"Curious," said the other Gemist. "I'm beginning to wonder if there is a transition."

"Everything points to it," replied one of the others. "We have the best sensors available. The lack of observable transition implies there simply is none."

"Which has even bigger implications." He turned and walked through the control room. "Recalibrate. Enter next cutting as planned."

The Gemists exited down the hall, leaving the technicians to comb through the data. Friend and Sonjaa looked at one another, both trying to keep their dewlaps from swelling. The sensors could not detect the transition, but the Relians had.

Those two elements in the chamber did not have a plasma state. Under no circumstances would they be able to exist as a molten, electrified gas hot enough to rival a star, and yet they had just become plasma in the presence of a collision between elements three-zero-six and six-zero-one. There had been no transition. The elements simply were plasma, as if they had always been. The force had not come from the collision of the elements themselves but from something that happened after the collision.

Sonjaa interpreted it as the universe speaking in a different language. The vibrations had been different, the quarks that made up the atoms hummed in different voices. As one set of vibrations collided with the other, they drowned out the pulsations of this universe, and new voices had filled the chamber.

Friend interpreted the event as different numbers emitting from the test chamber. They apparently stopped at the test chamber, but Friend sensed pieces of those equations beyond the chamber as well.

Both understood what their Archeon senses told them: there was no transition between the two because the new vibrations and the new numbers meant there simply had been no other state for the atoms to exist for those few moments.

The Gemists thought they had discovered an element combination that converted all forms of matter into plasma and were trying to understand why it occurred and what applications it could have. They had done hundreds of these experiments with different concentrations at the atomic level and at the mineral level. The results had been remarkably consistent.

They read the logs.

In front of the collision chamber, the door opened and four lizards between the second and fourth phases entered. They wore protective clothing, a combination of element four-two-zero and two-forty-seven, which formed an artificial mineral that made an excellent filter allowing only oxygen and nitrogen through while also insulating the wearer.

Deka wore one of those suits into the chamber, holding a hose connected to a backpack. The metallic element covered the room from floor to ceiling. Deka switched on his hose, as did the rest of the cleanup crew. The gas projected in a narrow cone, and as the temperature dropped, the metal liquefied and flowed down the walls and floor. They guided it to the center of the chamber and built it up into a ball. In moments, it solidified again, and the four lizards picked it up and carried it out of the room.

It didn't feel the same as it had when he had brought it into this room. The atoms were not as comfortable being so heavy. Deka sensed beta decay, but it felt different from what he remembered of home. To someone without an Archeon sense of reality, the difference would be imperceptible.

They carried the spheroid to an isolated chamber where they stored all their experiments. Different rooms branched off the main hallway, each sealed by a thick door. This storage facility housed radioactive material leftover from these experiments. They had not been radioactive until after the collision.

Deka remembered in the early years of this discovery people had not worn protective clothing, and then they became sick. The Hegesh knew something was different, but radiation was not known to science, so they did not understand it yet.

Most of the elements and compounds in these rooms only gave off alpha and beta particles, but a few of them produced gamma radiation. Deka surveyed the chambers as they carried this hunk of metal into isolation. The windows blocked all the radiation, but inside, each test was rapidly decaying into other elements.

They reached this experiment's holding cell and set it inside. After sealing the door, Deka followed his crew back to the receiving bay and awaited the next samples.

Below ground, Kylac sat at a workstation, studying an uncarved piece of element three hundred and six the size of his fingertip. The instructions on his terminal told him to cleave the mineral into a piece with twenty-one point six degree facings. The previous collision had called for twenty-one point eight degrees.

He remembered they had focused on this narrow range of angles for almost half a year. Cleaving the minerals to such fine degrees had been tedious, but the results were best like this. Retroactively, his job had been to isolate individual atoms for collision, but the results were even better when more atoms were involved, which was not how things usually worked. His job had changed to carving the element in mineral form within the thirty degree range, and the sustained reaction time had been only forty breaths at the most. The twenty-degree range sustained reactions for five times that length.

Kylac knew in another room someone was busy carving element six hundred and one to the new specification. They would try every angle until they found the exact combination to produce the longest reaction.

He slipped on his magnifying goggles, picked up his chisel and hammer, both only about five times the width of one of his former Relian hairs, both made of several different elements that combined to form a substance hard enough to cut this mineral, and made his first tap. This heavy metal felt incredible. Kylac could spend the whole day just touching it. Heavy and yet stable. Violent reactions at both the atomic and mineral levels. The physics that allowed this should be obvious, but he had yet to figure out how this universe worked.

He cleaved it at exactly the required angle. Around him, others cleaved their minerals, too.

3

"This is not a chemical reaction," Deka said.

They sat and stood in their usual places around the main room of their flat. Deka and Friend had tablets in their hands, reading the current events. Sonjaa sat in front of the terminal, facing into the room. Kylac leaned against the window, watching the Hegesho construct an apartment building a few streets down.

Friend: "It's not the elements that change into plasma. The laws of physics change."

Sonjaa: "From the data Friend and I read, the Gemists think this could be a new technique to create metal alloys. Change both elements into plasma, let them mix, the reaction yields a new combination, one that wouldn't have been feasible with conventional methods."

"And they're aware of the side effects!" Deka looked up from his tablet. "They know it makes the resulting metals unstable somehow! They have a whole warehouse full of radioactive experiments!"

"They don't know what radiation is," Friend said. "I can't find a single radioactive element in their periodic table."

Deka continued. "Something is wrong in that test chamber. The collision of those two elements alters the laws of physics, and then they reset after so long, but not completely. The walls and windows are unstable as well."

Sonjaa sighed, dewlap puffing slightly. "They've been doing these experiments for years. Even they aren't sure what's happening, but they have calibrated the collisions for maximum duration. Right now their goal is for the samples to become stable over the long term."

Deka: "One of us should find a way to access the records for experiment monitoring. I'll be too busy cleaning up. Kylac, do you think you can break away to go down there?"

Outside the window, one of the Hegesho hoisted a three-story section of wall in his claws and placed it on the foundation. He leveled it and held it still while the foundation solidified.

"I wonder how Stephen and Norh are doing," Kylac said to the window. "Sorven... How long have we been gone?"

"Ky—"

"Yes, I think I can access the logs. I may be able to talk to people who run tests on those samples. And I wonder if Rive moved that mountain range to Neben yet."

Friend looked up from his tablet. "You're homesick?" He clapped once. "We're on a journey to save our universe from oblivion, and you're preoccupied with a couple people we left behind."

"They were good people."

Friend shook his head. "I believe once we understand the Lake we'll become capable of recalling the equation that comprised each universe we have been to. This is another aspect of the second subconscious. I suspect we do remember those equations, but our minds are not capable of handling them yet, so it has set up a barrier in front of them for now. When we succeed in tearing down this second subconscious, we will find another layer of awareness behind it, a *Lakemind*. One that remembers everything we do in the Lake, and everyone in each universe, as if personally."

Kylac still spoke to the windowpane. "You actually want to figure out the equation? That really is enough for you?"

"You have experienced it dozens of times," Friend replied. "When we figure out the equation for each universe, we know everyone all at once, past, present, and into the future."

Kylac turned away from the window and met Friend's eyes. "I dread it. Every breath brings me closer to figuring out the equation."

Friend clapped again. "Why the sudden interest in ignoring this new perspective? You should be happy. We have raptors over us to keep us from panicking. This is everything you wished we had done back home."

Kylac blinked a few times before responding. "Let's live here for a while. Just... Live. We can experience life as an Hegesh. Get to know our neighbors. Meet our old schoolmates."

Friend: "Is that all you want to do?"

"I'm so tired of this. Every day I'm waiting to figure it out. Waiting to revert. Feels like every three days or so I panic. I'm tired of the dread." He looked out the window again. "I don't understand how you can want to get closer to it."

Deka stood and moved to the window, touching hips with his former fox, trading heat, a bonding gesture among the Hegesh.

Friend answered. "I want to be close, but the anxiety distracts me. I'm determined to make it to the other side."

"I know how the Krone feel." Kylac observed the Hegesho. Two of them carried an entire floor of the apartment complex and then set it on top of the walls they had raised. "Unable to be part of anyone's life. But the Hegesho... They're larger than everyone and yet they still have a place in society. Why can't we? Why do we have to move on after we fix the equation? Aren't we stable enough to stay in one place for a while?"

Friend huffed. "And do what? Collision experiments for the rest of our lives?"

Kylac: "Get to know people. You don't miss that?"

"Absolutely not. Rive kept pushing me to be with others. I never liked it much, even without sex involved. This is so much better."

Sonjaa clapped. "Does this mean you like me more than Rive?"

"You're better at dealing with a reverted fox than he was. It's been a big help."

She leaned over and nuzzled him on the neck. Friend did not react. She nuzzled him harder. Friend huffed and bumped noses with her. Sonjaa continued nuzzling him while impassively Friend read the tablet.

Kylac felt the windowpane with his reptilian fingers. "So we just keep drifting across the Lake until one of us figures it out? How long will that take?"

Deka ran his fingers down Kylac's back, imitating the gesture of grooming fur with his claws. "We're still diverting your instincts. Maybe when we're sure you and Friend won't panic and try to break out, we can stay somewhere for a while. I've been enjoying the journey, now that we're not fighting the two of you all the time."

"Deka." Kylac turned to him. "As soon as I learn the equations of this universe, it's all over. I'll revert. What if understanding the Lake will mean more of this? It doesn't sound like a happy ending at all."

"Who knows what kind of society the Superarcheons have in the Lake."

Deka glared at him. "Friend..."

The older lizard clapped. "You have yet to come up with a better word."

Kylac looked out the window again, placing both hands on it as the giant lizards built the apartment. "When you figure out the equation for this reality, don't tell me. I really don't want to know."

"Knowledge is always better than ignorance," Friend said.

"I never wanted this. Back home I built a subconscious to keep myself from feeling this way. The dread. Perpetually feeling like everything is leading up to scent anxiety, and then it happens and I have to live with it for hours, days, entire years. Now it's back. I have no choice but to live in it. I don't think we could go home even if we knew the way."

"Why would you want to go home?" Friend asked. "We left the universe. That was the goal. I'm glad to leave it all behind. So much easier to think out here."

Kylac sighed. "That's the important part, isn't it? Space to think. It's all you seem to care about."

Deka held Kylac around the waist. "Is it at least getting easier? Directing your anxiety at the imbalance instead of the scents of the people. Is it helping?"

"I suppose, compared to Reyno. And Earth. I don't know who I am, Deka. I'm depressed and moody. The whole time we were on Earth. Every planet we visited chasing Friend's old ways. I miss being happy. I was happiest when could meet people and live in other cultures and learn how to make portals. I miss watching you hunt. My life now is waiting to revert."

Deka rubbed Kylac's dewlap, another bonding gesture in their culture.

"I see that spark in you when you recognize the imbalance in the universe and you let me guide you to fix it. It's like going back to when we were little. How often you used to revert. Whenever I brought you back how you'd walk around, out of your sheath all day, eager to find someone to be with."

Kylac leaned on him as he watched the building rise two more floors.

"I wish we could go back. Those years feel more real to me than anything since."

"We're getting there."

Deka watched the Hegesho with him.

4

Kylac finished cutting his piece of element four-eighty-five. He removed his goggles and leaned back. As he hoped, he had made quota before half the working day expired. He stood and walked to the fifth-phase supervisor, who was three times Kylac's height and mass. It would not be long before the lizard retired from this sort of work and began to do the physical tasks in the city, relocating his living space to be with others his age, in structures to his scale.

The lizard saw Kylac had finished his work for the day and allowed him to leave. Kylac walked out of the carving area, clapping quietly to himself, thinking if only Stephen could see this society. Stephen's supervisor would have found more work for him to do and then increased the quota others had to meet in the future.

The lightrock in the ceiling gave off a pleasant glow on the mineral floors, which gave off heat that kept his body moving fast, as well as his mind.

He turned a few corners and then found the area where Deka worked. The team was taking the samples others made and placing them into the chamber. The former fox walked onward to the warehouse.

The rocks and metals and liquids and gasses behind the sealed doors did not seem to belong here. Everything in this whole universe felt so heavy and yet so stable, and to know these products now existed in a state of decay made Kylac uneasy.

One tiny room had several canisters of nitrogen in it. They had become plasma in the chamber, calmed back into nitrogen, and now emitted faint radiation. He calculated it would decay into helium and then into hydrogen, and then the hydrogen itself would break apart. They had never been to a universe where nitrogen was unstable. It was wrong both mathematically and empirically.

Walking up to the next containment chamber, he saw a small chunk of pure gold resting on a stand behind the door. Kylac had never seen radioactive gold before. His Archeon senses told him it would decay down through the remainder of the periodical table until it reached hydrogen, and then it would simply dissipate. The Gemists thought they could find a stable result for practical use, but Kylac did not believe it would happen.

"Did you need something?" said a voice.

Kylac hoped someone would notice him and give him an opening to ask questions. He turned and met the eyes of a lizard in the third phase. She had black scales with swirls of blue and lavender mixed in.

"I'm Kylac. I'm with the cutters. I finished early, so I wanted to see what happens to my work."

She clapped her hands. "Would you like to see the numbers for the gold sample? I'm Glea. I'm on the team that monitors these samples."

"Yes, please. Do you have access to any of the others?"

"All of them."

"I want to read them, if I may."

"Of course, come with me. I'm about to begin taking readings on element four-thirty-two. It's in the process of decaying into what we think is uranium, but an unstable form."

She began walking down the hall. Kylac sensed the elements and compounds in the chambers they passed, all of them in the relatively rapid process of decay. Some of them gave off radiation so intense Kylac would have sworn it went beyond gamma rays.

Just a few breaths later, he wore a protective suit and stood in the same room as element four-thirty-two. Glea and two other phase-two lizards held atomic sensors that detected the composition of the atoms and what they were doing as a group. The readings confirmed what his Archeon senses told him: it had been element four-thirty-two yesterday, and right before his eyes it became uranium.

He remembered uranium in this reality was so stable they used it to build these isolation walls, among other types of metal. Watching it emit radiation was so fascinating to these people they could not contain their excitement. Kylac's dewlap puffed under his suit. What these people considered a fantastic chemical transformation was in fact the total breakdown of the laws of physics within these atoms.

The numbers still did not add up. From everything Kylac had observed, this uranium should be as stable as iron, and yet it was on a journey to hydrogen, and then to nothing at all.

They left the chamber and decontaminated their suits. In the lab, the team sat down at terminals to compare the readings. Kylac joined Glea at hers. Months of data showed the slow decay from one element into another.

She showed him logs that documented the regression of element six-forty-four all the way down to hydrogen. It had descended through six decay phases, each one documented. She replayed video they took of the moment it transitioned from solid lead into liquid mercury. It remained in a liquid state for a few weeks before evaporating into helium. Then it became hydrogen. Then it became nothing. Kylac watched the whole series of videos, Glea clapping the whole time; it made her so happy to be on the leading edge of science.

She noticed his dewlap swelling. "Why are you nervous?"

Kylac looked around. "I wish I could say. Something... Something about this makes me uneasy. I heard how people get sick when they are near these experiments."

"It is a little unsettling, but we will understand it. Just think how we could use this! If we can figure out a way to halt the decay, we can create our own elements. Mining elements and refining ore will be a thing of the past."

Kylac held his tongue and stood up. "I hope I live to see that day. I should go home. I promised my flatmates I'd tell them what I learned."

He was about to walk away, but his feet did not move.

"Or... Would you like come back with me and tell them?"

"Are they curious about what we do?"

"They all work here in different departments. They're interested in the end results of the experiments. We don't get to hear about them. Can you bring some of these logs?"

"I'd be happy to tell them more about what happens after the experiments."

"I'll take you there. It's just a few streets over."

They walked hip to hip together. Kylac enjoyed the heat she gave off. It had been so long since he had touched someone besides a Relian.

They walked home as the daytime star set in the sky. The street felt so warm. Kylac talked about how he grew up in the area and heard about the experiments going on in this building. He liked cutting gems and studying the elements and how they interacted and could be combined into minerals and rocks for good use, but he did not want to pursue one of the usual jobs. He wanted to be part of the next generation. Not mining, but experimenting on the elements that made the minerals that held their civilization up. Not chemistry, but merging the elements in whole new ways.

Glea had the same desire. Her parents sold household and commercial gems, and they wanted her to take over the business. As a hatchling she had wanted to make the gems and minerals they sold. Quickly she realized combining the elements into minerals was laborious and dirty, so she pursued her interest in the elements themselves. That led her here, to a place where heavy elements decayed into lighter ones by way of some unknown process. She wanted to be part of the research that found a good use for it.

They crossed several streets talking about this, walking with their hips touching. Kylac remembered it was a common bonding gesture, trading heat with another reptile. It's what they did in their phase, as their reproductive organs would not switch on until the fifth phase.

Kylac led her up to his flat and opened the door. Friend, Sonjaa, and Deka were already home. He had interrupted their conversation about the day's experiments.

"Hi, everyone," Kylac said. "This is Glea. She works in the warehouse, and she promised to tell us all about those decaying elements."

For the first time since leaving the lab, she separated from him. She held her tablet out and connected a cable to the tablets Deka and Friend held. A moment later, they were full of logs and videos. Sonjaa joined them at the chairs.

Glea showed them videos of elements and compounds decaying from solids to gasses and finally to nothing over the course of several weeks, months, or years. She showed them logs of raw data that confirmed the composition of the atoms, and the experiments that yielded those samples. Friend and Sonjaa were eager to crosscheck those results.

Sonjaa: "Has anyone noticed correlation between the decay of the atom and the elements they yield?"

"The Gemists are still working on that," Glea replied. "There does seem to be mathematical consistency between the energy emitted and the weight of the atom, as well as the elements it decays into. I didn't bring those tables with me. I didn't think you were interested in the math."

"We're interested in everything," Deka said, scrolling through charts of raw numbers. To Glea, it seemed as if he simply glazed over the numbers, but Deka was reading and memorizing everything.

Glea clapped. "Who are all of you? I've never met anyone who was interested in the technical side of what's going on. Most people are curious about the idea of elements decaying, but nobody wants to look at the numbers."

Sonjaa looked over Friend's shoulder as he scrolled through the charts. "You might say we're a little overqualified for this work."

"If you want, I can come back tomorrow and bring the math in progress."

"Yes, please," Deka said.

Glea clapped. "It's so new it hasn't even made it to the library system yet."

Kylac stood up and walked away from Deka's chair. He held Glea. "Great. Now, no more work. Let's go somewhere."

"Now? But there's so much more to look at."

"A bite to eat," Kylac said. "I am so hungry."

Glea held Kylac back, giving him as much heat as her body took from his. "Normally I eat with my flatmates but I'd be glad to share some time with all of you instead."

The other Relians began to rise. Kylac walked to the door.

"We'll be home later. It's so nice to get to know some-one new and do something other than figuring out the equation, isn't it?"

He led her out the door and closed it. She faced him, puzzled.

"We're not all going?"

"No, just the two of us. It'll be fun."

"Just the... two?"

Kylac remembered it was unusual for anyone to do anything in groups of less than four. Kylac replied in a voice loud enough to hear through the door.

"We come from a place where people tend to do things in pairs. I've been living with them for years."

She stared at him, then she clapped. "All right. What place is that?"

"Enough about me! Enough about atoms! Where did you go to school? Where is your flat? How do you know your flatmates? I want to meet them!"

This sounded much more usual. She walked against his hip again.

"Oh, when I moved to this city I didn't know anyone. It was an awful couple of days until I met them at a conven-tion."

Kylac had no knowledge of a convention. He liked reaching the edge of the reality-altering knowledge he al-ways had when they entered a new universe. She told him about it as they reached the street level. The heat of the blackstone felt icy compared to the heat they traded.

5

Kylac woke in a strange room. Glea lay behind him, arm around his waist, hip pushed tight against his tail. Ky-lac's slit was touching a strange reptile. He was used to hav-ing a weak sense of smell, but his sense of touch was quite acute. Glea was the most familiar heat source. The other three had been strangers until last night.

Aoc, the lizard he spooned now, had lived in this city his whole life, but he had left school to work in the respected field of mineral extraction. Kylac had not known about it until Aoc told him, how clean they were because they used combinations of other elements to liquefy the ore and separate it into its various components.

Unlike mines in most other worlds, these were places people wanted to work because it was such a fascinating process. Many elements had counterelements that made them easy to extract and refine. The Hegesho dug for the ones that could not be mined in such clean ways, as their physical strength suited them to the task.

The other two had actually hatched from the same egg, and as a result they shared a special bond nobody else seemed to have. Kylac had been unaware of this until they told him about the mental connection. It sounded psychic.

Kylac had stayed up far too late listening to Glea's flatmates. He never wanted them to stop talking. He tried to shut the numbers of the universe out and simply listen. He didn't want to go to work. He wanted to travel the city and share sleeping space with every reptile, hearing their stories.

The crystal vibrated on the plate. The Hegesh uncurled from one another and rose from the stone one by one. Kylac felt cold without them, and he reached out for Aoc. Glea rose from behind him. Kylac was the last person on the blackstone bed.

"Don't go," he said. "Please don't go."

Everyone clapped. They thought he was joking about the lack of heat.

"Time for work," Glea said. "I'll talk to the Gemists and ask if they'll let me have the math they're working on.

It's supposed to explain the decay of these atoms. Brand new equations."

"Tell them if you want, but please don't tell me."

"I thought you wanted to know."

"I don't want to figure it out. If I do, I'll lose this."

She looked puzzled. She sat down on the blackstone and held his shoulder. "Lose what?"

Kylac rolled over, wrapped his arms around her. "Being close to someone. Connecting with them."

"You have that all the time. Your flatmates are nice."

"It's not that. Sometimes I miss the old bonding."

"What are you talking about?"

The others had left the flat and were on the way to eat. They would gobble down a couple unintelligent mammals and then go to work. Glea should have left with them, and her body language suggested she wanted to.

"Would you believe me if I told you I wasn't always an Hegesh and I used to be a mammal?"

She blinked at him a few times. "You used to be food?"

Kylac clapped. "Not one of the Loica. Just... a mammal."

"What other kind is there?"

Kylac clapped again and then yanked her down to the blackstone slab, curling up with her and closing his eyes. She embraced him back.

He felt like a fox again. The kind of fox he had been before Friend forced him to understand the Lake. The fox he had been before the disaster, when everything was just fine. He had Deka, he had portals across the contacted universe, he had sex with everyone he met.

He never reverted.

Never lived in fear of his old ways rising up.

Glea held him, pushed her hips against his, rubbing against his slit. Kylac tried moving his hips the way he remembered. He tried again, breathing as he remembered, trying to make blood flow to his groin. She breathed with him.

Kylac opened his eyes. He remembered something from school. One of the other phase one lizards asked the teacher about something called "early bloomers." The teacher wouldn't comment on it much, only that some lizards feel the reproductive urge while still in phase two or three. He wondered.

It opened up a world of possibilities Kylac had not considered. A chance to explore this. An opportunity for two outsiders to help them work through a need they could not satisfy. Kylac wanted to help her. It was easier for females to deal with this than males, and he remembered hearing about many males who felt hormones early. They had no way to act on it, so they lashed out. Most spent an entire phase in hiding until their bodies caught up to their minds.

Glea rolled away from Kylac and stood up straight. Her dewlap had puffed. Kylac reached out to her. He was just about to confess but she ran out the door and down the hall.

"We can still catch up," her faded voice just barely reached Kylac's ears.

Kylac rose from the bed. He never wanted to let go of her. She had a secret, and Kylac wanted to know for sure if he was right. All the clues added up, but there was still room for doubt, and he had not felt this in as long as he could remember. He could help her experience everything she wanted to feel, without the shame associated with it in this culture. He ran out the door and caught up to her flatmates on the street.

As they tore apart and gulped down pieces of rodent from a vendor, he prompted them for more stories of the mines and what being twins was like. Glea spoke more about her former home and how her mother was now in the ninth phase, a fully-grown Hegesho.

Kylac wanted to know how the elderly lived, every detail, how it was possible to keep in touch with them, what sort of relationship a ninth phase could have with their children and grandchildren. About then, it was time to report to the lab.

Kylac did not want to cut stones and prepare samples for experiments. He wanted to share a blackstone bed with every lizard in this city. He wanted to know them all by name, and he wanted to be part of their lives.

Glea practically had to drag him to the lab a few streets over. When their hips separated, Kylac felt so much colder, despite the heat from the blackstone warming his body through his feet.

He carved his gems and prepared the day's samples in record time, then he walked down the hall to the containment warehouse. He almost entered, but he realized if he went in, he would expose his mind to more of the laws of physics, and the more he did, the faster he would figure out the laws of this universe.

The faster he would revert.

Kylac clapped, turned down the hall, up to the next level, and marched out the front door. The city greeted him. The light from the daytime star baked his scales, and it felt so good. The city bustled with people of all phases. He picked a direction and let his feet take him somewhere.

6

Kylac stumbled through the door. Deka leaped from his chair and bounded across the room.

"Where have you been?!"

He embraced his fox, trying to wrap his neck around the red and black lizard. Kylac noticed Glea standing by the window, holding a tablet. Friend and Sonjaa shared a tablet and were looking up at him.

Deka released him. "You've been gone three days! I've been looking everywhere!"

Kylac clapped. "I discovered Lozic!"

Information came to them: Lozic was fermented Loica blood.

Kylac dangled from Deka's arms. "I slept with everyone in the whole *fucking* city!"

The English word confused Glea. Deka guided him to his chair and plopped Kylac in it. The former fox's eyes wouldn't focus, and his speech slurred. He gripped Deka by the shoulders and pulled him down, snout to snout, speaking a mixture of English, Relian, and Neben.

"Deka! This is real! This! I want it back! I miss sex. I miss meeting people! I miss them knowing who I am! Remember on Lesa I had a line of people waiting to fuck me! That was real! Deka! Deka! Deka! Don't let me see the universe again! Let's go back to the way things were. I want to be a fox again! Let me be a fox again! Please let me be a stable fox!"

He had pulled Deka into his lap. Kylac's eyes rolled to the back of his head and he reclined in the chair, still holding the blue lizard in a strong grip.

"I spent three days doing what I used to do. Sleeping with everyone I wanted to. Three different flats. Sixteen people... Almost makes up for the f... that my cock doesn't work! For this species, it's enough just to share heat. I don't want to leave! I want to be an Hegesho! Deka, let's stay! Let me stay so I can be a fox again! I want to sleep with people again, please... Please... Deka... please..."

His eyes closed and he went limp. Deka unwrapped Kylac's fingers from his shoulders and straightened up.

Glea stood hip to hip with Deka, clapping. "I'm impressed he made it back to your flat."

Deka rubbed his shoulder.

"We must ensure he goes to work tomorrow," Friend said. "They'll terminate him if he misses another day."

Kylac jerked awake, glaring at Deka and shouting in Relian. "No, no, I'm not going back! If I go... I don't want to know the laws of physics! I'll revert! Deka, I'll revert I hate reverting I hate calculating people I want to be a fox again Deka please don't let me revert! No no no no no I want it back! I want it to be real again! This is real, Deka, this is real—I want to feel real I wa—"

Kylac heaved. Deka picked him up and carried him to the restroom. He propped Kylac over the lavatory. A few heaves later, Kylac vomited. Deka spoke to him in Relian, as best as he could approximate with the mouth and vocal cords of this species.

"Kylac, Glea's been giving us the equations for atomic decay. It's not supposed to happen in this universe at all. Every number says it does not happen. Something is wrong. The universe itself could be on the edge of disaster. You have to come back to work."

"No-o." He vomited again.

"The numbers still make no sense in the context of this universe. We don't know what's happening. We should have figured out the laws by now, but we're missing something important."

Kylac heaved. Only acid came up. It slipped down the lavatory and into the pipe system that led underground. The pipes were made of element five-sixty-six, which had the unique property of killing the bacteria in their bodies, rendering their waste sterile.

Kylac's dewlap swelled to a bright red. "Deka. Please. I love it here. This is the life I want. I was happy before Friend forced me to learn about the Lake. I was happy. No antispheres. No life is the same as math. No scent anxiety calmed by... fixing the whole fucking universe. I'm tired of thinking so... big. I want to be happy again. I want you to run down the path on Kattaaka again. Grab an electric crystal on Neben. You weren't afraid of anything. I want to do the big thinking for you. I felt useful. Now... We used to be happy. Those times are gone aren't they? They're never coming back."

He heaved again. Nothing came out. He hung from Deka's arms, coughing.

"Kylac... I'm so sorry."

Kylac heaved. This species expressed sorrow by making a raspy wheeze. He made that sound now, tongue hanging out, eyes closed, over and over.

"I know you miss the old days," Deka said over his fox's wheezing. "I do, too. Things were simple. Make portals, meet people. I've been enjoying this, Kylac. I really have, and I thought you were, too. It really does feel like we've gone back to our youth. You used to revert all the time, and I watched you grow into a fox comfortable in crowds of hundreds of people. I was so proud of you for overcoming your instincts, and watching you progress again is like the old days. You were a desperate fox on Reyno, and you climbed out of it. You faced what the Lake is and you overcame it. I don't dread when you revert because I know you'll do the right thing."

Kylac heaved while Deka spoke, but nothing happened. "It's not the same. It's not the same. I'm not the same. I hate reverting. I hate that I'm reverting again. I remember being young and prone to it and I never wanted to go through... again. It was over! I was stable! Now everything leads up to it! It's just like when we chased the antifox. Every day is just one more day closer to losing control of myself and I have to do it over and over. I hate this!"

Deka rubbed Kylac's dewlap with his muzzle. "We're helping so many people. I barely have to block you anymore. I know it doesn't feel the same now, but you have come so far. It probably doesn't feel that way, but you are getting your old self back, better than before. If you keep going, you won't revert at all. We had to earn those good years. We're on the way to earning them again. You're almost there."

"I can't—I can't—I ca-a-a-a-ah!"

He vomited again. Deka held him tighter until the wave passed. Kylac coughed his mouth clear.

"I miss sex... I miss when it calmed me down. I miss it when I reverted, and you being there was all it took to bring me back! Now... I revert, the whole universe is at risk! This can't be right... This can't... This can't..."

He coughed, dry-heaved a few times. Nothing happened, and he trailed off and hung his head. Deka hoisted him upright and walked him to the sleeping room. Kylac was already asleep. Deka set him down on the blackstone and then returned to the common room. His own dewlap had puffed partway. Glea stared at him from the doorway. Her eyes stopped Deka in his tracks.

"What was that? I studied ancient languages, and that wasn't any of them."

"Those were three languages," Friend replied. "None of them are spoken in this universe. Or rather the odds of them being identical to a language spoken somewhere in this reality are so small they are practically zero."

"Friend," Sonjaa began.

"There's no reason to lie to her. Glea will never believe anything we say to cover for *that*, so let's move on. Something is wrong in your equation, and we think the experiments are the cause."

Glea's dewlap puffed a little "The cause of what?"

Deka sighed. He walked to the window. "This is complicated, but you will understand."

7

Kylac woke long before the crystal vibrated. He blinked a few times. His head hurt. His body ached. His mind vacuumed up information about reality. Four people touched him as the blackstone gave off wonderful heat.

Kylac untangled himself from the arms and legs of his former raptor and crawled from the room, keeping his eyes shut as he felt his way to the lavatory. He climbed up to the faucet and took a long drink.

A hand on his shoulder. He recognized the touch as Glea's. Kylac swallowed again and again, barely pausing to breathe. Finally he felt able to talk. He pulled himself all the way up, turning around.

"You meant what you said?" Glea asked. "You really were a mammal and you came from a place where people did things in pairs?"

Kylac clapped weakly. He stumbled out of the lavatory and into the common room, plopping down in Friend's chair, catching his breath. Glea stood at the door to the lavatory, looking at him.

"They said something is wrong here," she continued, "and it's probably because of what we're doing in the lab."

"I don't want to care."

"What do you mean?"

"Glea, I want to enjoy this while it lasts. Once my brain figures out how this place works, I won't have to get to know anybody. I will know everything about everyone, and then I will revert. Right now, this is all I want. To deal with normal things. Even this. Ow."

"How can you not care? If something is wrong, we need to know about it."

"We'll know soon enough. After I figure it out, good-bye happiness. Forget discovery or spending time with any-body. Glea... Tell me more about you. Please."

"About me? That's hardly important—tell me about where *you've* been! What's it like to be from another universe? You know what this radiation is, and it's common where you come from? You need to talk to the Gemists about it."

Kylac clapped. "Tell me about you. Talk to me."

"My life is boring! You've been to other universes! You've been other species! Were you anything like the Loica?"

Kylac clapped again, turned away. "I'll tell you a story if you tell me one about you."

She stepped out of the door and sat in Sonjaa's chair, facing Kylac. "All right. What story do you want?"

"You told me a while ago that you ate your sisters. Why?"

She told him she had hatched along with sixteen other eggs in the nest. Her mother was absent for this time, and the hatchlings grew in isolation for several weeks without a parent's care. The weakest members of the clutch became food for the strongest.

Kylac did not remember this, so it was not common knowledge among the Hegesh that they allowed their hatchlings, the Legesh, to devour one another.

Glea remembered eating three of her sisters. She remembered defending herself from her brothers and sisters. Their parents returned and separated the young, and the survivors received enough food to live.

"That's an experience I've never known," Kylac said.

"Tell me about a time when you were a mammal. Do you remember nursing on your mother?"

"We don't remember that far back. Not consciously. My first strong memory is actually of Deka. Our parents brought us together with the others our age. I played with all the other raptors and foxes, but something drew me to Deka. From the moment I smelled him, I didn't want to leave his side. I didn't know why back then, but... We got along so well. From then on, we went everywhere together, all over the contacted universe. I pushed him to go places. I pulled him to planets with good hunting. Then one day he met a sentient aquatic species, and he started pulling me to places that had other aquatics. He went on a quest to meet them all, to experience a life he could never have. I enjoyed watching him. It was during one of those visits I reverted for the first time. I remember Deka brought down his first kill. The first one he made entirely on his own, not the first one ever. Others wanted to share the kill. Suddenly all the scents of people around me made me panic. I attacked them. Did they tell you about reverting?"

"They mentioned it. Something about animal instincts."

"My species has a primal drive to keep other scents away. The urge is so strong we become violent. Certain things trigger it. For a while, it seemed everything did. Deka helped me come back so many times when we were young. Now... Something new makes me revert. It's even more overwhelming than before. It's so terrifying I gave up being an Archeon so I would never have to feel it again. Then we chased Friend's old ways from planet to planet. I had to take down my subconscious and remember it all over again to stop them. I wanted to die. I was ready to let the old ways take me so Deka would have to kill me. I didn't want to live like that anymore. I missed being happy so much I was ready to give in to my instincts just to feel joy one last time. Now here I am. As soon as I figure out this universe, I will feel it. Deka helps me use it for a greater good, but it is still a nightmare. Every waking moment in between is dread. Waiting for it. Waiting for it to find me."

Glea shook her head. "I'm afraid I don't understand any of this. I want to. It's all so hard to believe."

"We'll prove it soon enough. Yes... Soon."

"They told me about radiation, but I don't understand it. How can atoms decay? Why would they?"

"Glea, let's do another. Tell me... Are you an early bloomer?"

Her dewlap swelled rapidly. "Oh, I get that question a lot. No, no, I'm not one of them. I just enjoy heat a little too much sometimes."

Kylac shook his tail, which beat against the chair and the floor.

"What was that?"

"This is how my kind laughs."

"You have a different way of laughing?"

"Glea, you can tell me. If you want someone, I could help. I've done it many times before."

"Kylac, I will tell you anything about me if you talk to the Gemists about radiation. If it's common where you come from, you could explain everything."

Kylac clapped slowly a few times, looking at her, seeing a person instead of a piece of an equation.

"The better topic is why they don't seem to decay here," he said, "and why they've started. Let's go to the lab. I can explain it better there."

"We're not due there for another vibration."

"We'll get a head start."

They rose and walked down the stairs. The streets were empty this early in the morning, so they reached the lab in no time at all. On the way, she elaborated more on her memory of surviving the clutch, and what role her parents had in raising the survivors, now only six. Kylac wondered aloud what psychological consequences an experience such as that would have on a population.

They entered the lab complex and headed down the steps to the lower levels and into the warehouse where the Gemists housed the results of the experiments. Kylac wanted to show her the sample of element six-forty-two, the heaviest element they knew. It decayed the fastest. It was so dangerous its containment room had no window, so they had to rely on remote sensors to monitor its regression.

They stood at the doorway now. Glea placed her hand on the control panel by the door, which activated the screen. It showed a perfectly ordinary-looking hunk of metal. The image looked distorted due to the intense energy it emitted.

"Did anybody die handling this?" Kylac said.

"No. By the time we ran this experiment, we already knew the danger."

"I'm surprised those suits protected the workers. Did they?"

"They fell ill later, but eventually recovered. I am told they still deal with the health effects. We have not done another experiment with elements this heavy again, and we won't until we are sure the results will become stable."

"It's giving off radiation beyond what I've seen in any universe. Stronger than gamma rays."

"But why?"

"We're still not sure. I wish we didn't have to figure it out. I want to get to know you instead. I want to know your flatmates. I want to explore and live other cultures. It's what me and Deka did. Years at a time. We went to Rel more frequently after we became Archeons and he met Sonjaa and Rupi. It was fun watching him have sex after a kill. Things were so simple then. So easy."

While Kylac rambled, she walked away from the control panel and stepped to the next chamber. The screen automatically turned off.

"Do elements decay into hydrogen where you come from?"

Kylac caught up to her, hip touching hers, one arm around her back, one of her arms around his.

"No. They decay to lead. That's where atoms stabilize."

"Lead? That's as high as your periodic table goes?"

"For stable elements. Everything above that decays, but slowly, over hundreds or thousands of years. Sometimes longer."

"That's... unbelievable! I'd love to see the math that describes it. Do you have it?"

They walked down the hall, toward the main lab. They passed sample after sample, some more lethal than others, but all on a rapid decline to hydrogen.

"That is why we believe something is wrong. Atoms are supposed to find a stable resting point. The atoms that come out of that experiment do not. They decay completely."

"The Gemists will be here shortly."

"They won't believe me."

"You know the equations for decay! You can fill in the gaps in their knowledge. They'll believe you then."

"I know how decay works where I come from. I'm not sure what's happening here."

They walked into their lab, where they analyzed and processed the data they collected.

"You should still talk to them."

Kylac fell into a chair in front of one of the terminals.

"Come with me. If we're lucky, we'll catch them before the experiments begin!"

Kylac leaned back and closed his eyes. "I'll wait here. Wake me if you find one."

She left the room, clapping.

Kylac dozed off listening to the sounds of lab. He heard the chamber crew picking up the first sample.

Sounds of lifting. Doors opening. Kylac thought about what he had said on Labccr. Begging Deka to kill him after Friend's old ways were dead because he wanted to let the old ways take him. His animal mind. The last form of happiness still open to him. He had meant it. Taking down the barrier he had set up between himself and what he saw in the new equations that described the Lake had been so painful he yearned for the simple feeling of satisfying his most basic urge. The barrier was still down, and as soon as he figured out the laws of this universe, he would see the Lake again, making the equation that was this universe possible, and then he would feel it again for as long as it took to correct whatever imbalance it had. Waiting for the nightmare to begin. Relief when it was over only to leave and suffer scent anxiety again.

Life had become the nightmare.

Kylac bolted out of the chair and ran down the hall. Deka and the crew wore protective suits as they carried a large chunk of heavy crystal, specially carved for this experiment. They loaded it into the first tube, closed the door, and left to receive the next sample.

They loaded tube two. The main chamber opened. Kylac ran to it and climbed inside the vacuum tube. The crew loaded the test samples into the chamber, the next two they would attempt to merge in the plasma state. Kylac watched Deka as he helped them position the materials.

Kylac's head reeled. It was either this or live the rest of his life perpetually on the edge of scent anxiety.

They finished loading the test chamber. They walked out and closed the door behind them. The lights switched off. The door sealed. The vacuum tubes in the other chambers turned on. Acceleration began.

Kylac climbed down and stood below where the two minerals would collide, facing the camera positioned outside the window. He shouted loud enough for it to hear him.

"Sorry, Deka, but I can't do this anymore. I was miserable on our trip to Labccr, and things have only gotten worse. I'll never be happy again, and I don't want to live like this. I hope Friend finds what he wants."

Kylac saw through the windows to the control room. The Gemists were in complete panic up there, calling everyone, trying to shut down the experiment. A few breaths later, the two elements collided, the air became plasma, and Kylac's body along with it.

8

Kylac expected there to be nothing afterwards. Instead he felt the ripples of the Lake against his skin, and he cursed in every language he could think of.

He drifted away from the location of the test chamber as the crew ran inside, cleaning up, searching for any signs of Kylac.

He drifted further away. Kylac cursed himself again. He was on his way out of the universe, and even that would not be an escape. He would land in another universe alone. The thought of reverting alone terrified him more than before, and yet he could not seem to move now.

The Lake squeezed him, spreading him in multiple directions. Kylac remembered what Sonjaa said, how he needed an anchor to hold himself together. He stopped resisting. He drifted away as the Lake pulled him apart. It felt like the happiness that was always out of reach but his hyper-awareness kept him from feeling.

He exited the universe. The whole thing appeared to him now. The galaxies and the planets. He could almost see the people moving about within it.

And then he noticed another presence. A second blob of reality riding inside of the first. It did not resemble anything he had encountered before. All he saw in this second equation was gas and plasma, the only two states of matter that could exist there.

His consciousness focused on where he had just come from. A hole in the first reality, and the second reality bleeding into the first from a point located precisely over the test chamber. Kylac adjusted his perception to the universe's path across the Lake. That hole flowed with both realities. They had been traveling on top of one another since their creation, possibly the result of two people from the same universe understanding the Lake at the same time.

Kylac looked the other way, where the universes pointed. He calculated where they would end up. The equations locked in place, and they intersected in the worst possible way.

He focused on the test chamber. His particles of consciousness drew together. Kylac sensed an imbalance greater than he had ever experienced before. He was about to revert, and out here he would be free to open portals anywhere he wanted.

He focused on Deka, the blue lizard kneeling on the ground, making wheezing noises, dewlap swollen bright red, visible even through his suit. One of the cleanup crew held him, trying to comfort him through their suits as Deka cried "he was my fox" in Relian over and over.

Kylac was already giving in to scent anxiety, and without Deka's help people might die. He gathered some photons and formed a projection of his canine body, complete with missing ear. He let his consciousness flow into it, down through the barrier between the Lake and reality, and fell all the way inside.

The fox knelt on the floor of the test chamber. The crew turned to him, mouths agape, dewlaps swelling. They had never seen a canine before, let alone a mammal this large. Kylac ran to Deka. The blue lizard climbed to his feet, the other Hegesh still holding him. The fox grabbed Deka by the helmet and shook him. Tiny spheres opened and closed around them as Kylac resisted his growing scent anxiety.

"It's not just one universe! There are two universes here! Two different sets of laws! Everything is stable in this one, but in the second, only two states of matter exist! Plasma and gas!"

The crew herded around him.

"What are you?"

"Where did you come from?"

Kylac shook Deka harder and panted. "Ignore the radiation! It's not part of this universe! Deka, hurry!"

Kylac felt nauseated, and he dropped to his hands and knees. The portals around him opened faster as his awareness expanded to encompass the solar system. Deka had done an excellent job diverting his scent anxiety to something else. He didn't hate the collective scents of everyone in this reality. Now he hated this imbalance. He wanted to kill it, but he had not worked out the entire equation yet, and he still had to work out the second universe.

Deka held him by the shoulders. He looked at the crew and then pulled Kylac out the door. They ran to the decontamination room. Deka slammed the button, and the spray showered them in dense water that captured any particles carrying radiation. Kylac was merely a projection, so the water didn't touch him at all. As soon as the spray finished, Deka removed his helmet.

"What makes atoms so stable?"

The canine did not let go of him even as Deka took off his suit. The hole in this reality had become the scent his anxiety focused on. He had to kill it, but he didn't know how. The spheres around him opened and closed in panic. Kylac kept the other ends in the upper atmosphere as he panted through gritted teeth.

"The weak force here is very weak! There are radioactive elements, but they're so rare and so heavy they decay instantly! They... won't find them for thousands of years! They're not supposed to—! This isn't... to happen!" Kylac screamed, holding Deka tighter as the dryers kicked on and blew hot, sterile air on his scales. Kylac's fur did not puff. "Deka!" He shrieked again as the presence of the imbalance closed in and surrounded him.

The dryers turned off. The doors opened. Deka stepped into the changing room and ripped off the rest of his clothing. Kylac could practically hear him thinking. Breaths later, Kylac felt Deka where he wanted to open spheres. He blocked him, pushed Kylac inward until he existed only inside this projection, unable to reach into space-time or beyond. Kylac felt much calmer with Deka nearby.

He dropped to his hands and knees and breathed. The looming presence of the leaking hole in the universe filled him with rage. Deka held him mentally, and now physically as he brought him to his feet.

"Who are you?" asked an unfamiliar voice.

They looked at the other side of the changing room. Every Gemist from the control room stood before them, dewlaps swollen.

Upstairs, the technicians shouted data from the sensors. Sonjaa and Friend lowered their heads as they poured over the numbers. They incorporated the information around them, and it began to form a complete whole.

Friend recognized it. His sensors had picked up something new as Kylac's molecules became plasma. It had detected the moment he became nonliving, when his atoms left the universe, and with that came the solution.

Friend gritted his teeth and held the side of his chair. He stared at a hole in the universe, and it made him angry.

"Sonjaa." He reached out and held her shoulder with his other hand. "Two universes! The instability of the experiments doesn't belong in this reality! It's coming from different physical laws interacting with this one!"

She held his hand. "I'm right behind you."

Friend panted through his teeth. He looked out the window and tried to snarl at the hole in the universe. He could not believe he did not sense it before. His mind ignored the collective scents of the life forms and focused all the rage on this hole. It was closed now, but the pieces of equation it left behind tainted the test chamber. Friend felt them everywhere, not just in the chamber and the warehouse, but permeating the entire building, and some numbers had leaked out into the city.

As he became aware of the stain this imbalance left, his scent anxiety expanded to include those parts as well. He snarled at all of them, but it came out as a wheeze. His dewlap swelled and reddened.

"Separate the vibrations, Sonjaa!" He gripped her harder. "Two different drones, one intruding into the other!"

Sonjaa held him by the shoulders and lifted him from his seat. The rest of the technicians were too busy shouting over each other to notice them, so they ran out the door and down the stairs to the main level. The entire building was in a frenzy, lizards running down the halls to the lower level to see what had happened. Nobody noticed Sonjaa or Friend as they retreated into a deserted office.

Friend collapsed to his hands and knees, panting through his teeth. Tiny portals opened around the office, all leading to the test chamber. This imbalance was in his territory. He had to destroy it, but he could not, which enraged him.

A few breaths later, Sonjaa stood over him mentally and returned the spacetime to its comfortable background hum. Friend held her and breathed easier. She shielded him from the ability to calm his scent anxiety, and he relaxed and waited for permission to act on it. The thing still loomed in scenting distance, but as his mind expanded to encompass more and more of the universe he did not care how many people he became aware of.

Sonjaa shoved Friend back into the womb, and he felt powerless to do anything about it. He yielded. The anxiety calmed. He looked her in the eye, still holding her. Sonjaa held him tighter. She licked his snout. Friend did not return the gesture. She did it again, harder this time. Now Friend licked her back. She felt like a raptor again.

A sphere appeared in the office. She rose to her feet and led Friend through it back to their flat. It closed behind them.

Downstairs, Deka shouted to be heard over the cries and questions coming from the Gemists and other lizards.

The Gemists and probably every Hegesh in the building had packed themselves into the changing room and the adjacent hallway. Deka shouted so everyone could hear them, though he sensed it was pointless. His mind still worked on both sets of equations, and preliminary results told him nothing he said now would alter the course of the universe.

"Your universe travels on top of a second universe with different physical laws. The two elements you combine break the barrier between them, and the laws of physics bleed into one another."

Kylac resumed where Deka left off. "You think the effects are confined to the test chamber, but those effects are beginning to destabilize atoms in the whole building and even across the city! Eventually the new laws of physics will cause every atom on this planet to decay into nothing. Life on this world will end."

Deka finished. "The contaminated particles will spread to the rest of the universe, ending it prematurely."

Bedlam resumed as the lizards talked at once. Deka and Kylac caught every word, and nobody even understood what it meant for there to be a second universe. The people on this world had yet to even comprehend there were other planets besides their own. Most were more interested in the giant canine standing among them, asking how he could speak.

Deka and Kylac exchanged glances. Deka made the way behind them. It opened into their flat.

Kylac calculated exactly where Glea would be, and he looked straight at her. He gestured for her to come with them. She pushed her way through the crowd. Kylac reached into it and pulled her from it. Before the others realized what had happened, Kylac led her through the sphere right behind Deka, and the portal closed.

9

They had three-quarters of a vibration before anyone thought to look for them here, so they took their usual places in the common room and discussed their options. Normally there would be no need to discuss anything, as they all knew the same equation, and it always led to one inevitable conclusion, but the addition of a second universe made everything more complicated.

They did not know the laws of this second reality and could not observe it directly. The only thing they had to go on was how its laws affected physics here. They had never calculated something like this before. Their minds cranked away at it.

"Can we stop it?" Deka asked.

"No," said Friend. "The damage is done. The collision of elements three-oh-six and six-oh-one created a hole in the barrier between reality and the Lake. Because another universe happens to exist on top of this one, it broke that barrier as well. The instability has spread across the city—it will not stop even if we halt the experiments now."

"We can remove the contamination," Kylac said.

"Including the people?" said Sonjaa. "It's too late for that. Unstable particles have traveled on the wind. The entire planet has been affected. When they discover portal physics, they will carry the particles offworld."

"The effects will spread," Deka said. "Eventually every atom in the equation will decay into quarks that can't bond. It will dissipate billions of years before it should. Every breath we waste here shortens the life of this reality by ten years."

Glea stood at the front door, leaning on the frame. "Are you—?"

Kylac interrupted her. "No, we have not decided to do anything yet. There are holes in this universe, or there will be if we manage to prevent it from decaying. It won't happen if the decay leaves this planet."

Glea's dewlap puffed slightly. "Kylac, I—"

Kylac did not face her. "You're about to say scientists have not proven there are other worlds yet, but just take it for granted that yours is not the only one."

"What's supposed to happen," Deka continued, "is this planet exists as is for generations until you discover the Loica are intelligent. Experiments in elements stop, and you devote your time to understanding a companion species. Learning to understand another species leads you and the Loica to discover portal physics and join the contacted universe."

"This hole in reality..." Friend said, gritting his teeth. Sonjaa held him down from making aggressive portals. "It should not happen! It doesn't matter if we seal it. We can remove all of both elements from the universe, and it won't stop the decay!"

Glea opened her mouth.

Kylac spoke for her. "How do we know this? It's what I told you about, Glea. Deka channeled my scent anxiety into hatred for imbalances in the universe. I have reverted.

It's a nightmare of anxiety—this urge to kill everything around me. Deka is holding me down so I can think. We're consciously directing this urge toward things in the equation that are preventing people from understanding the Lake. I'm compelled to fix this. We can calculate a single atom's journey from the beginning of the universe to the end. Clumps of atoms are no different—they've even more predictable. Just like you."

She opened her mouth again.

Kylac turned to the window, holding his canine muzzle between his hands. "Now you're going to say that's unbelievable please tell me more and I will tell you more and you will say oh there is so much more we don't know and I will refuse to tell you more because time is wasting and we need to figure this out now and you will say there is no choice and I will agree there is no choice."

"The planet must be eliminated," Friend said. "If we also remove all of element six-oh-one that currently exists, the universe will survive long enough for several people to leave it."

Kylac turned from the window to meet Glea's eyes. "Glea, you are about to be appalled at the suggestion. If I explain it to you in less sterile terms, you will agree it is the only way."

She glared at him. She opened her mouth again.

"I already know what you're going to say!" Kylac shouted. "There's nothing you can say that I haven't heard! Glea... I'm sorry. This is what I meant. I wanted to get to know you. Now life is part of the equation—you are part of the equation! It's all you are now! I know everything you will ever say or do! I know about how you tried to mate with a phase five in the previous city. I know your urge to have eggs. It's premature, and you wonder if you're an early bloomer, but you've never told anyone because you were hoping to meet a phase three who also felt the same way. I wanted to be that person. I could've been."

Glea's dewlap swelled all the way.

Kylac's tail wagged, and he turned around and pounded the window.

"I am reverted. Whenever I figure out the equation, this happens. I'm anxious, and fixing the equation is all I can think about. It's better than wanting to kill everyone in scenting distance, but this is miserable! It's all I do! Land, live for a few days preparing to revert, and then start all over again! The people are just things to be fixed!"

Friend stared at him. "You actually like what Deka did to you? You enjoyed being obsessed wish sex? This is what having knowledge of the Lake means. Our satisfaction doesn't come from getting to know people but understanding the equation."

"Still just numbers to you."

Kylac did not turn from the window. He tried to watch the Hegesho constructing the apartment building, but now he could calculate their every move into the future. He didn't need to watch. He knew the people who would live in there, and he knew exactly how it felt to be an Hegesho. The experiences of every person in reality had become obvious results from the moment this universe came into existence.

Kylac calculated Glea would cross the room and stand hip-to-hip with him. She did. Kylac's fur was merely a projection, so it didn't react. It didn't feel soft. Kylac adjusted his projection to be closer to his former body, and now his fur reacted to her touch.

"Glea, if we left now without changing anything, you would become a Gemist. You would never find a stable result of the reaction, so you would abandon the experiments. Eventually you would discover a new compound that replaced the energystones with something more efficient. You would not live to witness the moment your species met its companion."

Glea spoke as the giant lizards raised the walls on the next level of the building. "You can eliminate just the contaminated particles, including the ones in the people. You don't have to destroy the planet."

Friend leaned back in his chair. "The contamination has already spread into the oceans. If we wait just one generation, it will reach the mantle. We may as well eliminate it now."

"No!" Kylac shouted, turning to the room. "We just got here! I'm not leaving these people! We can't save the world, but we can save them."

"That will take—"

"Friend, I know the easiest solution!"

"For the sake of the equation—"

Kylac tried to snarl at him. "I meant what I said years ago. I will never enjoy thinking of life this way. Yes, Friend, I like what Deka did *for* me. He kept me from falling into my animal ways. Sex wasn't a waste of time because it allowed me to live. I miss living. I'm working on the math. I know we can do it. We can move them into the Lake, give them new bodies, alter reality around them so they fit into a new society. We can even store their old memories for them to discover later."

"That would take a long time," Deka said.

"We have nothing but time."

"All you want to do is fuck everyone," Friend said. "Can't do it physically, so you want to make us move them. If not for Glea, you wouldn't feel guilty about the loss of one planet compared to an entire universe."

"They're worth saving! I'm working on it now. I hope all of you are, too."

Everyone was silent for a while. Kylac held Glea. He shared heat with her. It didn't feel good anymore, just vibrations of molecules.

"Please speak to me," Kylac said.

She gulped, making her swollen dewlap wag. "I would have taken my secret to the dust."

"You wouldn't have. Next year, you would have found several other early bloomers, and you would have confided in them."

"You should be thinking of that gigantic hole in the universe!" Friend yelled. "I can't think of anything else!"

"Sonjaa tamed you well," Deka said.

Friend huffed. "Tamed. I need taming. I need..."

Sonjaa: "I agree with Kylac. We've had it easy on all the previous landings. Remove one species of animal, one planet, ten planets... This time we have intelligent cultures to worry about. It wouldn't be right to remove the planet without moving the people somewhere else. We can move them to other cultures. It will take a while, but it can be done. As far as the people know, our changes will extend into the past."

Deka clapped. "We've been moving on too quickly. I think we've all lost perspective. Let's stay a while and get to know these people. We'll find appropriate places for every single person. Does that sound good, Kylac?"

His fox's tail wagged.

"Will you do this now?" Glea asked.

"Soon," Kylac said.

She reached out and felt Kylac's neck. He had no dewlap, but the gesture was just as meaningful. "How will I know? What will happen to us?"

Kylac felt her neck in reply. "I'll move you personally. I'll leave your memories intact. You'll remember living two lives."

She leaned on him, looking out the window. Kylac held her back. "So you do still feel something even now."

"There's no logical reason not to just destroy the planet and move on to the next universe before Friend or I break free. I'm doing this because I want to feel something for you. For the Hegesh. Do you have a preference for what you want to be in the next life?"

"You al—"

"Yes, I already know, but please say it anyway. I want to listen. It reminds me of when I was stable and happy and I knew hundreds of people on as many worlds."

Glea thought for a while as she felt the fur on Kylac's back. "If there is a species out there close to this one, the one you used to be, I think that's what I want."

Kylac comprehended the numbers from the beginning of the universe until now, considering how the reactions then would create life. "There are several. I can think of one in particular you'd be happy as. You will be unique in that you will remember the difference between life now and life as a mammal. It will be a good place to be an early bloomer. You will not be shunned for it, and you will even give birth multiple times. Plus you can teach the people about chemistry and the periodic table."

"I... I think I'd like that."

"You definitely will."

Kylac retracted his projection and vanished. The three Relians stood up. Sonjaa opened an antisphere, and they disappeared through it one by one. It closed just as the Gemists and the entire lab walked through the door to their flat. Glea clapped her hands.

"Never forget those Hegesh. They have just saved us all."

Antispheres opened over all the people in the building, and they vanished. Glea stood alone looking out the window. Antispheres opened across the entire city, snatching up people hundreds at a time. In less than a vibration, she stood alone in the city.

Glea walked down the stairs and stood on the empty street. Quiet was an alien concept to her. Isolation as well.

The buildings vanished inside antispheres. The ground disappeared. The city vanished in a cascade of black spheres, leaving her suspended over a hole in the ground that went down to the core of the planet. The unimaginable distance overwhelmed her.

The core vanished. Chunks of the planet also disappeared. Knowledge entered her mind, and she understood her world as a whole, even the parts she did not observe. It had been gutted like a Loica, leaving only a few fragments where the invasive laws of physics had not yet touched.

She was the last person on the planet. The last cluster of contaminated particles.

10

Glea knelt on her hands and knees, weight on her back, a pair of furred arms around her. The male on top of her had just climaxed. Others had lined up to be next. A rare event indeed when a female remained in heat all year and yet was not receptive. Males lined up to be with her. She looked down at herself, at her green fur.

She felt her face. Her muzzle was long and pointed and ended at a cold nose. Fur covered her body. A strange sensation overcame her, and she quickly realized it was heat. It came from her own body, not from the outside. Her body made its own heat.

She wanted to get up and find a mirror, but now the scents of the males in the room overwhelmed her. The one behind her had tied her, and he filled her full of more heat.

She remembered growing up in this community. She remembered these people, having known them since she was young. For a fraction of a breath, she remembered being in a city full of reptiles, but now all of that submerged, and this new reality replaced it.

A quarter-vibration later, the male separated from her and climbed off, and another replaced him. She wanted more. People like her had very high status in their society, she remembered. Soon the king would summon her to the royal city.

Knowledge came to her. Knowledge she would not have naturally. While she would live with other canines who were also in heat all the time and would be expected to attend to the king's needs whenever required, she would have access to unlimited resources in the royal city in the meantime. This species' knowledge of science extended to alchemy, but she could show them element combinations they had yet to dream of.

The sanitation minerals alone would save countless lives and change society. Her knowledge would impress the royal family so much they would give Glea her own laboratory to pursue these experiments. She would recruit more and more people into this emerging field, and her name would echo through the ages as the person who brought their species into a modern era. This pursuit of knowledge would allow another species to rise to sentience, and that would lead to the discovery of portal physics in a few hundred generations.

Now she knew what she looked like. Her race had a name: the Sepp. Covered head to toe in blue or green fur, they resembled the species Kylac used to be. Right now they lived in warring nations united under several royal bloodlines, but that would change soon, partially thanks to her and the knowledge she would pass on to them.

She climaxed again as the male tied her.

Life in the court would mean she could satisfy this feeling that had been inside her for many years. Now her body allowed her to act on it whenever she wanted.

She noticed someone in the corner of the room, a canine with red and black fur, white underbelly, pointed muzzle, round pupils. She smiled as she recognized Kylac. He wagged his tail.

Conversation entered her mind. The Relians had spread the other Hegesh and even the Loica out across multiple worlds. They could not make room for all of them here, as it would have overwhelmed the planet with people.

Kylac told her to tell the story of the Hegesh. Never forget what happened. Others lived on this world, too, and she would recognize them. Eventually other species on other planets who told those same stories will meet, and they will realize they correlate. They will remember what happened.

She promised. She had the feeling that Kylac was happy. He had fixed the hole in the universe, steered reality back on course to a good end. He felt just like the male behind her, enjoying climax as he watched the results of what he had done.

She had helped him find his way to make this enjoyable. Friend preferred the simple solutions: removing a species, removing a planet, removing an element, and then the universe fell into the holes they made and veered to a better ending.

Kylac had yearned to connect with the people more, using individuals for more intricate solutions. Setting people down in the right place, multiple wheels in motion, watching them work together to achieve a personal solution. Right now he sensed all the people they had placed on other planets, and he watched them change the numbers for multiple species. Hundreds of them. People whose lives they improved as a result. Species who would discover portal physics sooner thanks to them. Then those changes created yet more changes. Now even more people would make it out before the end. The collective scents of the universe no longer disturbed him so long as they all worked together to achieve this greater goal.

Friend, too, watched from the Lake, also satisfied to witness what they had done. He disliked the delayed gratification, but Sonjaa had held him back and forced him to join Kylac in using the Hegesh to create smaller solutions and watch them add up to a larger change in the calculated future. Now Deka and Sonjaa did not have to hold them down, but they still had to leave. Friend would eventually become aware of the scents again and break out of Sonjaa's control. Kylac, too, was at risk of reverting if they remained here too long. They had to move on to continue their conditioning.

Glea thanked him for telling her, and for giving her what she had always wanted plus the chance to continue her work as a Gemist. She promised to preserve the story. Kylac's tail wagged. They would never meet again, but Kylac knew her future, and it would be better here than it would have been on her former homeworld.

She looked forward to meeting others who knew the story of the Hegesh.

The red canine vanished into the wooden wall. The male behind her was still tied. Glea climaxed again and again. She couldn't wait to meet the king, and she was already planning the layout for her lab in the royal city.

San Diego

I

Stephanie sat on the couch watching the news over the net. As a devout churchgoer, she knew of a time when the internet had been full of people who made their own shows and produced their own videos. History specials called it the dark days of the internet, when piracy was rampant and profits suffered at the hands of thieves. Now thanks to the copyright spiders and the visors that parsed every word and fined or shut down people for criticizing any movie, TV show, or corporation, the internet had become entirely corporate-owned. Nothing but official channels for official entertainment, all of it computer-generated.

The news program was about the military. None of the footage was real. The real military men were not nearly as muscular and handsome as this computer-animated farce portrayed them. The women in the military were not supermodels, and they never came home to cheering cities of Americans thankful for defending the world from the threat of extraterrestrial invasion. She knew from the Church that people who signed up for the military never came home.

Stephanie rose to her feet. Her left leg was slightly longer than her right. She was not wearing her compensating brace, so she limped to the refrigerator. She had a tumor in her left breast she could not afford to have removed at the moment, the bank having turned her down for another loan on the grounds she was already in too much debt from the previous tumors the hospital extracted, and the computerized visor over her face correcting her eyesight, and the corrective brace for her leg, and the corrective brace for her fingers to make them the same length, and so many other things she needed to make her body function just to be employable.

She wore her corrective visor now, which is how she received this newsfeed. These visors had replaced cellphones many years ago, as well as home computers and tablets for most tasks. She had to pay a subscription fee for the service, but since she could not afford it, hers was subsidized by Augmentads. If she looked at an object in the real world the computer recognized, it displayed advertisements over her vision for pizza, or a movie, or a series, and so on. The visors were connected to the internet at all times, tracking her movements and targeting her with ads throughout the day, listening to her speak, deducting her for mentioning or listening to copyrighted material while building a database of her words to target her with specific advertising.

She was glad she made enough money to pay for the Augmentad tier of service on her visor, as people who could not afford it at all were are required to speak advertisements to people they met in exchange for free vision correction. These scripts popped up over one's field of vision, with a quota alert right next to it, warning the person that if they did not meet weekly quota, their vision would be shut off. They were not allowed to tell these people their words were corporate sponsored, so it still felt like natural conversation. Stephanie would never have known about this if not for the Church.

It sounded suspicious, how many of her family members mentioned brand name products and services at awkward moments—how many strangers walked up to her on the street and started telling her about this product, or that series, or that movie, all of which she had expressed passing interest in over the previous days or weeks.

Her life was full of targeted commercials for braces and surgeries and bank loans. Her newsfeed recommended articles and commentary on the state of the human body. Birth defects have always been around, they said, and everything happening now was no different than in previous centuries. Medicine has just become better at dealing with these problems.

Stephanie had seen the tapes. She had read real histories of her country and the world. She had seen old photographs of real people, not computer altered to make them look like the people of the present day. She knew it was not natural; these changes had been caused by chemicals infiltrating the ecosystem. Chemicals and waste runoff from the manufacturing of the technology that made modern society possible had become so ubiquitous in the environment they affected unborn children by the millions, and this was simply accepted as a fact of life. Contamination interfered with the development of eyes, so vision was universally poor. People were routinely born with limbs not the same length, skulls out of shape, joints not aligned, and so on. Compensating for these had become big business, and people like Stephanie worked their whole lives just to afford the attachments and devices that allowed them to be "employable."

Organ failure was so common her visor could recognize the symptoms automatically, summon an ambulance, and apply for a treatment loan within seconds. She knew from the Church sermons that it wasn't a natural or routine event. Produce and meat no longer existed; food was chemically synthesized to be patented, and the body simply wasn't designed to handle so many calories in such high concentrations. The pancreas was the first thing to wear out by age thirteen, sometimes earlier, secreting enough insulin to handle carbohydrates in excess of eighty times what humankind evolved to handle. The liver often went next, processing so many concentrated fats and residual chemicals it simply gave out by age twenty-eight. This combined with all the artificial substances added to the food damaged the body over time to produce the modern human. Stephanie finally understood why everyone's body required routine monitoring to keep hormones balanced.

With great difficulty, she poured herself a glass of wine. Carefully taking the glass between her short fingers, she returned to the couch and sat down. The computer-animated military, full of handsome soldiers with limbs and muscles all of employable length and size, had successfully restored a deposed ruler of some foreign nation to his position.

The reports over the last few weeks had claimed the usurper had allied with extraterrestrials, who gave him military aid and helped him seize power. Stephanie had listened to the sermons, and she understood what Sorven was trying to tell the people of Earth: that person had not seized power, but had been elected by people trying to form a classic-style government and wanted to kick out the companies that were creating the pollution that was causing all of these health problems.

Shortly after this, video had surfaced of Relians gathering in the country. Computer-animated footage showed hordes raptors and foxes fighting the military, and the brave men and women standing firm and pushing them back to rescue the nation from an oppressive alien regime which would have required the country to sacrifice one million citizens per year as livestock for their predatory needs.

Stephanie knew the truth. She had friends who had gone into the military because it promised a cure for all their ailments. The only way to be cured, instead of compelled to buy attachments and compensators, was to sign one's life away to the armed forces.

Everyone needed a leg extension. Everyone needed an optical visor, as glasses weren't enough anymore. The military had technology that could repair the eyes themselves, but that wouldn't make industry much money. The definition of living in luxury had fallen to simply being what employable had been three hundred years ago.

Stephanie had read the documents that showed the companies knew the effects these chemicals had in the ecosystem, and on the human body, but by now they didn't even need to maintain the appearance of caring. People had to live with the effects while the wealthy who owned these companies lived in artificial cities under geodesic domes in the middle of the ocean, shielded from the pollution from birth until death.

Something else was going on, too. The news reports had changed. Overnight, the media now portrayed the military with superpowers. Soldiers no longer needed to sleep. Neither did they need guns to liberate people from tyranny. They stalked the enemy like predators. Their senses were sharp, like that of an animal. They had become unstoppable agents of freedom.

Stephanie wanted to know why, and she hoped Sorven would reveal it to the Church.

2

The pews sat fifty other parishioners. Nobody spoke to one another. Hardly anyone spoke in public anymore. Anything said would be used against them by computer algorithms. Watching the real archives of how society used to be was surreal because people were so loud back then.

At seven o'clock, the lights dimmed and the screen over the stage lit up. She could have watched this on her visor from anywhere, but it looked better if the advertising computers logged her as physically in Church.

Albert Lantam wore his symbolic yellow robes. One of his hands was malformed due to exposure to toxic chemicals in baby food, which Church documents alone had brought to light years ago. He wore a compensator to allow his fingers to grasp things. His right eye was also too large for his skull, and the cumbersome visor over his face produced a lot of heat while it corrected his vision. She wondered if he had to look at Augmentads all day, or if he could afford the ad-free subscription.

He was computer animated, too. All religious institutions had been bought out by the corpocracy decades ago, and as far as the algorithms knew, the Church of Sorven had been as well. Nobody realized it was creating its own content because the systems were supposed to be fully automated. Someone in the Church—likely Sorven himself—had managed to insert its own code into the servers to hide this from view.

The real Albert Lantam lived in Minnesota. Stephanie had met him in person. He looked exactly the same as this computer-animated model.

"Good evening, followers of Sorven and seekers to the answers of the nine great questions. I have an exciting story for you tonight, one Sorven himself revealed to me in a dream the other week. It has taken me this long to transcribe it from the dream language into something I can relate to others. It begins with a man. This man has arms of different length. One of his ears is larger than the other. One of his feet is missing. He has a bone spur on the sole of his only foot. He isn't unlike you or me.

"He wishes to serve his country, but the military can't use him because he can barely walk, let alone work to provide for himself and his family. So he prays to Sorven to heal his limbs and restore his body so he can help his country preserve freedom around the world.

"Now I know what you're thinking. Why would this man's prayers be answered when yours are not? To that, I all can say is that Sorven works in mysterious ways. Sorven is not human, so his way of deciding how to make things right does not always make sense to us. For whatever reason, this man received an answer, but not a miraculous one.

"Sorven sent him five vials full of liquid. The first was labeled 'dinosaur brains.' The second, 'lizard blood.' The third, 'dog essence.' The fourth, 'predator plant.' The last had no label.

"This man acted in faith and drank each vile one after the other. After drinking of the first, the man's senses became sharper, and his ears returned to an employable size. After drinking the second vial, his foot was restored so he was able to walk better than ever. After drinking the third vial, he experienced an aggressive drive to achieve like he had never experienced before. After the fourth, he discovered he no longer craved food as he once did. After the last vial, he did not feel any different, but now he was ready to join the military and fight to protect the world from the alien threat that has loomed over our planet for three centuries.

"He joined, and was so admired and in demand that he was not allowed to return home. He wished to, but he was needed elsewhere, so it filled him with joy to defend the world.

"It was an act of faith. An act of faith. These vials stand for what we can accomplish if we work hard enough to earn it. Faith represents our work, and the vials are the rewards we will receive for being faithful to our lives."

Stephanie barely listened to him for the next ten minutes. She wanted to smile, but a camera might have been watching and the servers would flag her for acting suspiciously and possibly restrict access to her paid music or movies for a few hours, days, or even weeks.

The meaning was obvious to anyone who knew the Church: there had been experiments in human genetic research, and they had finally paid off. The same technology used to splice genes into plants was finally being used on humans, and the source genes were from Relians.

The vials represented raptor and fox DNA. The military would restore one's limbs and senses all right, but they would also insert raptor musculature into the body. They would enhance the nose to detect scents, which gave a person strong instincts to kill. The military channeled that into killing the enemy, and the raptor DNA allowed them to track down the enemy by scent and hearing and move in for the kill swiftly.

The enraged soldiers could never come home. Nobody was allowed to see them like this. Stephanie hoped footage existed of what those people looked like on the battlefield. She wondered if they were mentally unstable and that was also why they never returned home. Soldiers hadn't been allowed to return in years, so she guessed this had been happening for a long time.

Albert Lantam finished the symbolic interpretation of Sorven's vision and now switched back to the sermon itself.

"The vision also expressed a lot of pride. Sorven feels that he caused this. By visiting us at such a crucial stage in our development, he created what is happening, and he is happy with what he sees. This is what happens when dragons visit Earth. It's a wonderful thing, and he admires it, and the brave people who undergo such a transformation."

When he said a vision expressed something, not Sorven, he meant the opposite. Supersoldiers roamed the world, ensuring those nations did not rise up and try to become more than a labor class, or a farming class, or an oil-synthesizing class. Now that the soldiers had the instincts of a fox combined with speed and agility of a theropod, the exploitation could continue. Sorven felt guilty that all of this happened because he had brought Relians to Earth.

Lantam continued with another vision, this one far less interesting and mostly nonsense to throw off the algorithms.

3

Stephanie sat in the Egg Room, reading copies of emails and automated transcripts of phone conversations between people high in the corporate hierarchy. She thought about the dozens of job opportunities she missed by being here instead of on the road, and she would have to pull another overnight to make up for it, but this was always worth it. Without her time here, she would never have known what employment had become.

Employment did not exist anymore as history described. There were no formal agreements between employee and employer. Instead, employment had been broken down into odd jobs that displayed on her visor in real time, and she replied to each offer whenever she wanted. Though it had, as archives claimed, freed the worker from the rigid structure of the working day, it had also placed every worker in constant competition for these jobs, turning everything into a temporary position and a race against everyone in the region to fill the simplest tasks, pushing wages to the bottom.

Stephanie had been told that, in theory, this could have given people more free time, but because employment was always precarious and the future always uncertain, Stephanie could never make plans more than a few days out. Her workday consisted of riding around the city in her self-driving car for fourteen hours a day chasing blips on her visor, hoping to beat twenty other people to each opportunity.

Her map locator would report her as being at Church right now. In the Egg Room, she wore a special visor, a hacked model that corrected vision without a subscription or an internet connection. It never left this room.

Her escort sat in the room with her, as always, dressed in yellow and green robes. Her right limb was missing halfway to the elbow due to chemical exposure in the womb. She wore her dragon mask over her visor.

The documents recounted candid evaluations of the soldiers, mostly field reports emailed to government officials around the world. Earlier, she had watched footage of the soldiers in action. Their limbs were misshapen and twisted into something between a theropod and a canine, but they still had human skin. Their faces were that of a dog's, and they were constantly in an enraged state. Some of them were quite insane. They had been trained to kill any and all scents in an area except those of fellow enhanced soldiers. It was all some of them could think about. They were even more effective than unmanned aircraft because they worked in large groups to take out concealed targets.

Soldiers had been permanently deployed to international bases long before the alien DNA was introduced to prevent them from telling the real story of what the companies were doing overseas. It was still called the United States military, but citizens of each nation also thought they were signing up for their own military. The Armed Forces did not belong to a nation, but to a cooperative owned by the largest businesses that produced the very chemicals and products that kept the people of the world in compensators.

This cooperative really did have the means to cure all chemically-induced defects of the human body, but soldiers never received that. The documents showed the generals feared soldiers would defect if they had bodies able to do so. One could not hide from the soldiers that they were not liberating people from extraterrestrial invasions, but protecting businessmen from the wrath of entire populations. The conversation revealed in the documents showed the Relian DNA was added to ensure soldiers could never fit into society again.

"Is there a solution?" Stephanie asked, looking up from the pile of documents and books and discs.

"Only Sorven knows that," said her escort from behind the mask.

They were free to speak here. No algorithms listening to them in this room.

Stephanie slammed the papers down on the table. "They are poisoning us so they can live easy! Now they're changing our DNA! They already own everything! What is the point of doing any of this?! What's Sorven waiting for?! Why doesn't he end it?"

"I don't know, but the real solution is beyond even him. You've seen the archives of Rive speaking to the US Senate in the nineteen-nineties. Humanity has no companion species to help us tame our animal instincts. Our society is little more than humans living to satisfy their primal drives. The dominance instinct in particular has been growing out of control for generations. Peaceful societies which emphasized nurture and tolerance have been swallowed up by it, leaving only this. We are the victims of this exaggerated animal instinct to oppress and conquer. If Sorven intervenes, the cycle will only repeat."

"I want to do something! What is the point of knowing it if I can't?"

"Is it better to live in ignorance and be happy, or to have knowledge and be miserable?"

"I'm tired of being miserable! I'm tired of sermons! I want to fight!"

"What would you do?"

"We still have guns! If all the Church members acted at once, we could do some damage! We could make them run!"

"They have drones. They have genetically-modified soldiers with uncontrollable scent anxiety. We can't do anything without our visors, and the algorithms will figure out it's all Church members. Then it will be over. The knowledge will die with us."

"I can't stand this anymore! I want to be a human being!"

"That is the reason thousands of mass shootings happen every year. No matter what they do, they can't improve their lives. They were told to go into debt to buy compensators so they would become desirable to employers. They were told to go into debt to educate themselves so someone would want to hire them. They found no work. The hope of social mobility has been monetized. They're sick but they can't afford treatment. People can't take control of their lives. Machines and computers do all of the tasks that require skill, and yet we are still expected to prove ourselves useful. Eventually people realize there's nothing they can do about it. They lash out the only way they have left, and the people in charge don't see it as a problem. It decreases the surplus population. Our corporate monarchs see themselves as the real human beings. There are ways to channel this anger."

Stephanie clenched her jaw. "What can I do?"

Ether Landing

I

After visiting so many universes, Sonjaa had begun to think of each as a slight variation of just a few variables at the beginning that resulted in enormous differences by the time she arrived. This was the first reality she had been to that sounded nothing like a mere deviation.

The electrons did not vibrate at constant rates, but in pulses.

The quarks did not make uniform crackling sounds in her Archeon sense of reality, but vibrated in variable pulses.

Probably as a result of this, it was the first reality she had been to that did not have planets.

Space did not exist. Electromagnetic waves bent and curved through this substance. Gravity did not seem to be a factor in this reality, though the force still hummed in the background.

Sonjaa floated in the fluid, neither sinking nor rising. There was no up or down. Her sense of orientation did not exist anymore. They had not landed on a planet, but at a hub for portals in the contacted universe. Creatures of all shapes and sizes swam around, under, over, and through hundreds of portals arranged in a spherical grid thousands of paces in diameter.

Friend floated next to her, taking in the sight. Light did not exist in this reality, rather they saw by vibrations produced in the ether, and they also had special glands in their skulls that produced sonar-like waves.

The portals gave off certain vibrations. People gave off others. Everything produced compressional waves, even the electromagnetic energy. It wasn't unlike the Lake, but things still moved in linear paths here, so the environment felt relaxing instead of threatening.

Sonjaa turned to Friend. The former fox had taken the form of a Plin, who were some sort of aquatic species: long, streamlined, smooth fins, jagged teeth. Somewhere between a dolphin, an eel, and a shark. Sonjaa had the same type of body.

"I don't think there are any stars here," Friend said. "They couldn't form in gravity so weak, but atoms still collect into molecules, and this universe apparently does not need stars to create the heavy elements. I still feel electromagnetic energy in the ether, but it doesn't behave the same way."

"Odd name you've chosen for this. It's not the word any of the people use."

"They don't have a word for this substance, but it reminds me of the old theory in some primitive cultures back in our reality. The idea that light needs a medium through which to travel, just as sound does. A physical substance to carry the information. They could not comprehend at the time that space itself is not empty and is such a medium."

"Here, it's true. Electromagnetism is a compressional wave."

Friend turned away from the hub and directed the vibrations from his speech bladder at her instead of into the ether in general. "How does it sound to you?"

"We've been to so many places, but they were all variations of the same hum. This... It doesn't sound like all the others. Nothing is constant. Everything exists in pulses. What about you? What are you getting out of this?"

"I'm not certain what to make of it. It's exotic."

"Think I'll figure it out first?"

Friend laughed. "You are ahead of me by four."

She laughed, smacked him with a fin.

"Sonjaa, I am impressed by how well you've done as an Archeon. I did not expect you to excel at it."

"Why is that?"

"Because I vaguely remember your numbers back home. You were never meant to have this. You were adept at languages, not portal physics."

"Deka told me that a long time ago. He thought I got this only because I ended up in the Lake and the future changed the past."

"And you've managed to keep me from panicking ever since."

"It worked out," she said. "Back on Rel, you wanted to talk to me about this idea that time equals motion. Motion within something. The universe must exist somewhere for this to happen. And then you opened the first antisphere that swallowed me and all of Rel. Now I'm your raptor. Maybe someone planned this just so they could laugh about it."

"Yes, I'm someone's fox again. I revert, you react, and somehow... I respond. It's a fascinating sensation."

She looked at him sideways. "Sensation?"

"Yes. I panic, you overpower me, and I feel this other impulse. That I need to yield. I never felt this with Rive. Whatever is happening, it's not me. It's not who I am."

Sonjaa flicked her fin and floated right up against him. "This *is* you, Friend. Everyone has base instincts. Some more so than others. That's why we have companion species. That's why I'm here. I can tell whenever it rises up in you. Raptors help their foxes tame this part of themselves."

"Rive never felt it for me."

"It's in there. He brought back reverted foxes after the disasters."

"That was marvelous to watch, thinking back on it. He became something else after the metal remade his body. I became something else, too." Friend looked around, drifting away from her. "I've been thinking back on all the things I said before. What I told Kylac. Things I said to Rive while all of that was happening. I don't remember why I said any of it. I remember wanting to leave the universe so badly, but it felt like discovery. Reverting is supposed to be a loss of control, but I remember being in control the whole time. Was I? You were right to kill me on Reyno, but even then everything made sense. I needed to think, all those scents were making me anxious, the math showed they weren't real, so just get rid of the extra variables. You showed me there was another way. There had to be. Everything was logical, but why did I say that? Why did I do all of that? I don't know anymore. If I'm not sharing theoretical realities with Rive, who am I?"

Sonjaa swam and rubbed against his flank again. "You have come so far. This really is like watching you grow up. Same for Kylac. It's like starting over, helping young foxes learn how to control the monster inside of themselves."

She turned back to the hub. The creatures swimming around were so used to having no sense of up or down. Sonjaa heard the vibrations of Deka and Kylac in their midst, diving through one portal, emerging from another, swimming upside down into another and then emerging sideways from yet another.

"That you're even saying these things means you have progressed," she continued. "You can admit you have instincts that need to be tamed. You are so much better now.

And this time you're channeling your old ways into some-thing good."

"Much more productive than sex."

"Any progress on understanding the Lake yet?"

"Not yet. I wish I could think about it for longer. Even after fixing the equations, I start to panic when I get too close to a solution."

"We'll stay here as long as we can."

"When I work it out, I wish to return home. We need to check for an imbalance in our own universe. Maybe if we make a few changes, more people will leave."

Sonjaa rubbed snouts with him. "If you had said that before, I would have said absolutely not. But if you figured it out today, I think I would trust you with our home."

Friend flicked a fin and drifted away from Sonjaa. "I want to see the equation again. I had it when I was there, and it bothers me I can't remember it now. I want to know if anything I did changed it. Was there an imbalance the whole time? Perhaps I was reacting to it, which would ex-plain everything I did and all those things I said."

Sonjaa floated up against him again, rubbing snouts. "Don't deflect. You did all of that before you understood the equation."

He flicked his fins and drifted away, placing a claw's reach between them. "There must be a cause."

"Keep thinking about what you said on Reyno. That's your cause."

"It doesn't feel like me. I couldn't have said any of those things. But I did."

"You still have a long way to go before I trust you to be in a universe alone. No rush. I like this place. I don't want to leave for a while."

Friend turned to the hub as well, but directed his voice in a narrow cone at Sonjaa.

"This universe is so dense. It's as if space itself has congealed."

"It had to. The sounds everything else produce shake it so much it can't exist in any other state."

Sonjaa looked to her right. A wheel-like plant floated a few paces from her. It had evolved a root system that fanned out for fifty paces, absorbing any nutrients the compressional waves careening through the universe brought to it. It had no leaves, as starlight did not exist, rather this species had an open, trunk-like center that took in ether waves, funneled them through special organs, and used them to generate electricity to drive life processes. Dozens of those plants hung suspended in the distance. Thousands of similar species existed in the contacted universe.

She turned to the hub again. Deka and Kylac were swimming through it, between the portals and the people, straight for them. They, too, were shark-dolphin-eels.

Sonjaa called to them. "Were we right?"

Deka sent a narrow wave toward her. "We found a few more of them. They form the center of every cluster."

Kylac continued. "They're the source of the waves."

Sonjaa wagged a fin and turned herself around. Behind them in the distance, an antisphere the size of a star loomed, continually sending pulses through the ether.

"So it's what we thought," Friend said in a wide broadcast so Sonjaa could hear. "That's why this universe doesn't need gravity. These antispheres create the disturbances that stir the atoms."

Deka and Kylac halted in front of them. They sent waves from their speech bladders just strong enough to reach their group.

"This is the most incredible reality we've landed in!" Deka began. "All the same parts needed to move efficiently inside a fluid, but we live in space itself! And—and—"

Deka did this every time they landed as aquatics. The life that had fascinated him so much as a child was now his—the depths, the places he could never reach, the entirely new perspective on reality, all of it now his to experience, and he could freely interact with the people on their terms. He could swim at the crushing depths and not be harmed, be underwater and never have to come up for air, make the subsonic pulses and communicate directly with them. Everything he ever imagined.

"We aren't bound to an ocean here!" Deka continued, swimming and rolling about. "They aren't bound to an ocean! People here don't look up at dry land and wonder what lies beyond! There are no limits—everyone is free to move about the clusters—they swam to other clusters before they ever discovered portals! Everyone is an aquatic species—just imagine being able to swim from Rel to Movar, and that's how we met everyone! That was how we'd make—it's startling to think how it would have impacted their—just think about..."

Deka was looking at himself, experimenting with his fins, experiencing his new sense of orientation, squeezing his vocal bladder. It was all so new and yet so familiar.

Friend sent waves of amusement at Sonjaa. He whispered that Deka had never outgrown his childhood fascination with the lives aquatics had under the oceans and rivers across the contacted universe, and it was satisfying to watch him live it. Sonjaa returned the waves of delight. As many times as it had happened, it had not become old yet.

She gazed at the antisphere while Deka got the excitement out of his system. A blob of deep blackness the size of a star hovering in the ether generating wind through the fluid that comprised the universe. Sonjaa felt the prevailing waves it generated against her scales.

Finally, it seemed Deka had finished being amazed. He settled and began speaking in complete sentences again.

"I'm trying to imagine the beginning of this universe," Sonjaa said, projecting her voice behind her. "Everything inflated, space congealed, atoms sitting at rest."

Friend continued. "They would have stayed that way forever. Everything evenly spaced out, uniform, unchanging."

"Nobody knows where they came from, or even what they are," Kylac continued. "Everyone says they've always been there."

"And they don't do anything but make pulses through the ether," Deka finished, still dreamy and breathless.

"Pulses that happened to be responsible for pushing atoms together," Friend said. "All the plants rely on these waves for feeding, so they must have been there for a very long time."

"Could they be natural?" Sonjaa said, turning from the antisphere and facing the other three. "Things sound so different here I wouldn't be surprised if space is compressed so much the Lake leaks through on its own."

"Anything is possible," Friend said. "Does anyone know what our role is? I can't seem to recall what place we've created for ourselves."

"I do," Kylac said. "We're frontier explorers."

Friend perked up. "That's it! We are due through one particular sphere shortly to explore a new region of ether just discovered."

Sonjaa just now remembered. "Where the ether ends..."

The other three turned to her. They remembered, too.

2

They had to swim through five portals to reach the frontier. Each cluster had an antisphere in its center, a dark star sitting in the middle of a solar system, but instead of gravity pulling matter into orbits which then collected into planets, the antisphere sent pulses through the ether. Over time, these pulses pushed the suspended atoms together, and clusters of atoms formed around the antispheres. Some clusters eventually blew apart in the prevailing wind. Others evolved life forms that held the matter together, forming the foundation for more complex life.

The clusters they swam through to reach their destination revealed the breadth of possibilities in this reality. The Lake was very much part of their lives here, but nobody knew what the antispheres were, or why they pulsed. Nobody knew what the ether was made of and why waves traveled through it. The answers were not obvious to the inhabitants of this reality, so the Relians remained mystified.

The four dove through the last portal, emerging in a cluster held together by a species of plants. The web-like roots extended thousands of paces, absorbing most of the vibrations from the star-sized antisphere.

The interlocking web of tree roots was the size of a Dyson Sphere, with the antisphere at the center, pulsing, pushing, stirring. Various small creatures also swam around in these roots, eating them. Others migrated through the ether, harvesting the organic molecules dispersed throughout. Plants secreted waste products, the animals ate them, the plants absorbed their waste products, and thus the cluster remained in balance, loosely woven together, lightly stirred by the vibrations that made it through. A peaceful shelter from the empty ether beyond.

The Relians moved away from the center, diving over and under roots and trunks and pushing animals out of the way. This particular cluster had a special situation in the known universe. As the branches thinned out, they came to the edge.

Other Plin had gathered here, fellow explorers and researchers, including a few Archeons from other clusters. Multiple people resembled types of fish. A few others resembled jellyfish, but they had brains and other organs, all visible through their transparent but hardened skin. The former Relians joined the group. Everyone floated in front of the edge, staring at the ether.

It appeared to be a wall in front of them. The ether that made up spacetime in this reality seemed to fold upwards, around, and over them into a denser form. The vibrations emitted by the antisphere behind them reflected off this wall and back at them. There appeared to be nothing beyond it.

Sonjaa remembered she had volunteered to go again today, and a couple jellyfish-like creatures pulsed up to her and began tying a rope made of softened tree roots around her torso. They looped one rope in front of her dorsal and pelvic fins, and then a second rope over the first. They swam away forty-five degrees apart, pulling the other ends, and then tied them around tree roots.

"Great," she muttered loud enough for only their group to hear. "My only safety is a rope."

"Do you remember what's beyond?" Friend said.

"I don't know, but I think it's obvious."

"Good luck out there," Deka said. "We'll listen to the others."

Friend's fins flicked, making him roll side to side slightly, a gesture of agitation. "I don't like this."

Sonjaa flicked one fin at him and then turned to the wall. She inhaled a big gulp of ether, sucking in the thin oxygen and nitrogen, and darted forward. Her body began to pry apart. Particles of conscious energy surrounded her, replacing the ether, and she recognized the universe moving about her as it traveled through the Lake.

She heard vibrations as they bounced off reality. The echo they produced sounded a lot different from other realities she had witnessed. The universe itself sounded dense and thick from here.

Her body wasn't entirely gone. It had merely been loosened just enough to allow her mind to perceive what lay beyond the ether, but she still felt the ropes touching her assortment of molecules.

Just as she had begun to get her bearings and observe the universe from the border, the ether enveloped her again and her mind condensed back into a brain. She floated exactly where she had been before, but the ropes had been stretched taut. Nobody else had moved from their positions.

Now she remembered. The wall was moving and yet it did not appear to be from this side of it. Only when one crossed to the other side could one perceive it. What Sonjaa had just experienced had been the ether catching up to her.

She swam back to the others. Her Archeon senses told her the ropes that held her were slightly less dense now, and her own body had also been changed by the experience. The Archeons for this cluster only allowed people to swim as far as the ropes allowed. Too far and they feared the body would dissipate. They had lost several volunteers to the void beyond the ether in the early days of this discovery. The ropes kept people at a safe distance to return, but a person could only make so many trips in a lifetime before too much of the body dissolved. Sonjaa had made two trips, and she only had five more before her limit.

Friend swam up beside her, touching her fin with his. "What happened?"

"It's the Lake," she whispered back.

Friend began untying the ropes from her.

"Friend, this is the leading edge of spacetime. We're watching the universe expanding."

"I hear some of the Archeons talking about it. They know that much."

"It's where the ether meets the Lake. I wasn't all the way outside."

"That would explain how so many others have come back."

"These people know about the Lake already! They're trying to explore it!"

3

Deka and Kylac swam behind the line of people at the universe's edge, listening to everything. Some of the things they heard jogged new memories of this reality.

The people of this equation had been exposed to the Lake before they were sentient. They knew something lay beyond the universe before they understood other clusters existed. Many had taken dives into the antispheres at the center of their clusters. All they knew then was that people who entered one never returned, but here, at this particular cluster, a place existed which allowed a person to leave the universe and then come back.

The Archeons knew the universe was expanding, and they also knew the ether itself was not flowing, but stretching. It gave the illusion of the ether catching up to a person who had entered the wall.

The current theory stated that the universe should be moving at the speed of a compressional wave, but since it did not, it must be much older than expected, possibly close to dying.

Deka and Kylac had done the math and concluded no universe could have enough mass to overcome the lack of containment in the Lake. All of them spread out and dissipated over time. This wall should be moving so fast there would be no way to catch up to it and thus no way to bear witness to the edge of the universe.

But here it was, and it had become a popular attraction in the contacted universe. The Archeons had concluded it was safe for everyone to take a trip to the edge and then come back with minimal effects on the body.

Kylac sent a narrow wave to Deka. "Could this be the imbalance?"

"I'm not sure."

Deka faced the wall. Someone had just been tied to the roots on this side. This dolphin-octopus swam to the wall. Moments later, she emerged, the ropes tight. Deka and Kylac had been aware of the ether stretching.

"I'm even less sure what we can do about it," the former raptor continued.

"Maybe it's the antispheres," Kylac offered. "How can they exist naturally? Something must be wrong here."

"If it's wrong, then all life in this universe depends on it staying wrong."

Kylac turned to the wall, sending speech vibrations backwards at Deka. "This seems a little beyond us."

"It is interesting. Everyone has known about the Lake for generations but they still don't understand it. They understand portals, so recognizing the two sets of equations are related should be an obvious leap."

"That must be where they're going. There can't be anything else on the other side."

"Could we have landed in time to witness someone leaving the universe?"

"The odds of that..."

"Think what that would mean! They could answer our questions! We might—"

Deka did not have a sense of smell in this reality, so it caught him off guard when he picked up a familiar scent. He turned in the direction it came from. He stared at a particular creature facing the edge of the universe, twice as large as Deka, a jellyfish with armor covering most of its body. Their armor plating grew from the tree systems in their native cluster, which discarded their scales as they grew. The jellyfish collected and assembled them into a protective dome around their fragile bodies. Deka remembered them as the Agl species.

"Wait here," he said to Kylac, and then swam to the jellyfish floating a few dozen paces from the edge.

The Agl did not have genders. They reproduced by cloning themselves and setting the polyps free. Their unprotected DNA changed and mutated as they swam aimlessly. Most died, but a few good mutations survived to maturity, genetically dissimilar from the parent.

He approached the Agl, taking care to avoid the tentacles. The Agl had control of their venom, so if a tentacle brushed against him, he wouldn't be stung, but it was still polite to avoid them.

Deka only picked up the echo of his sonar off this Agl, as well as the echo of the prevailing vibrations from the antisphere. The scent signal was gone, but Deka didn't doubt himself.

"Pardon me," Deka said.

The Agl turned to him, one vibration-sensing organ peeking through a circular slit in the armor. Their "eye" could move to any part of their bulb they wanted. It sent a voice vibration back to him.

"Yes?"

"Does the name..." Deka hesitated. He wasn't used to acting on subconscious knowledge like this. "Does the name Chreeb mean anything to you?"

The Agl floated in place, eye still fixed on Deka. "No."

Deka remembered he could pronounce his real name now. "What about—" Deka made ultrasonic sounds. He hadn't been able to say this name before, but now it came easily with a speech bladder.

The Agl did not move. "You are Deka, aren't you? I've seen you here a few times. Your mate has taken a liking to the beyond."

Deka remembered he had met this person before. Its name was Geden.

"I'm giving another demonstration later," the Agl continued. "It's meant for Archeons, but all are welcome."

Deka's fins hung, and the subtle waves coming from the antisphere in the distance nudged him. "We'll be there."

"Good. Remember Sonjaa's limit. Wouldn't want her to fall off the edge of the universe."

Deka swam backwards and then turned around. Kylac met him halfway. Deka reached out and grabbed Kylac's head with his fins, trying to make direct contact so his voice wouldn't have to travel through the ether.

"That's Chreeb!"

"What? Chr—"

"I caught his scent! It's him!"

"He doesn't have a scent."

"Kylac... I'm... I'm an aquatic now! I can—I can finally..."

Kylac separated himself from Deka and floated just above Deka's level to look at the Agl. "Deka, I remember this person. Geden teaches other Archeons about... Oh. We'll have to be there now."

Deka sucked ether so fast his body had no time to extract oxygen. He ran out of breath. Kylac tried to hold him, rubbed his back with a fin, and Deka gradually breathed again.

4

Deka remembered when he and Kylac last traveled to Ixcy. It had been one of the first planets they visited after the disaster. He had been worried about everything at the time, but Chreeb especially.

The fish had fallen unconscious, and he never woke up. His body remained active, but the brain activity was gone. Deka remembered spending days in that tree, standing in the water, holding Chreeb and talking to him, hoping his voice would bring him back. Deka and Kylac hadn't known then what was happening, but now everything made sense.

Deka recalled the conversations they'd had over the years. Life under the ocean, life in all the different oceans. He had made many close friends among the aquatics, but he and Chreeb had connected. Chreeb had taken Deka on a few swims as far down as the raptor could go on a single breath. Deka wished he could return the favor, but the best he could do was make portals to places on dry land he wished the fish to see. Life on the land was a life Chreeb could never experience, and Deka had done his best to help the fish experience it. Learning to understand one another's perspective had given Deka a glimpse of how life must have been when raptors first realized foxes were sentient. It had been a feeling Deka cherished even before the disaster took Chreeb's life.

The armored jellyfish pulsed and floated in the middle of a loose sphere of several hundred people. It sent strong waves to everyone in the audience, lecturing as loud as it could.

"...as I have said for years, I am convinced what we experience at the leading edge is in fact the same thing that lies at the center of every cluster. Somehow pieces of the realm beyond the ether rest within our universe as well, sending pulses through it, creating the disturbances that pushed atoms together. It is not merely where the universe ends. It is in fact where the universe resides."

Deka couldn't believe he was hearing the ultrasonic voice of Chreeb. He didn't know how, but that voice sounded exactly as he remembered during the few brief times he heard Chreeb's real voice under the water. He usually only heard it as the tree trunks channeled and amplified the voice into tones within a Relian's hearing range.

"As most of you know by now, I believe I am the only one in the contacted universe who can create ways into this realm. I have been working on one for some time, and I am ready to demonstrate."

It paused for a moment, and then an antisphere appeared next to it. The audience sent long waves of awe through the ether. The antisphere sent pulses in return, the exact same pulses that the star-sized spheres sent out. Deka remembered Geden once said it had been aware of this realm for its whole life and finally figured out how to make portals into it. Now Deka wondered if that's what Geden really believed.

"Those of you who have been through the wall will recognize the similarities between this sphere and what we glimpse beyond the edge of the universe. I am still trying to explain to the Archeons how the math works, but I admit I am at a loss..."

Deka swam backwards and left the congregation. Kylac followed, stopped next to him. Sonjaa and Friend huddled behind them.

"We have to get Geden alone," Deka whispered.

"What will you say?" Kylac said.

"Are you sure that's Chreeb?" Sonjaa said. "I don't get any sense of that from it."

"It *is* him! What if— What if, somehow, Chreeb held himself together in the Lake? What if he found an anchor, too, but drifted away from the universe and landed here, altering reality to give himself a place?"

"And we just happen to land here?" Kylac said.

"We've been there for so many events... Friend, what if you're right? What if we're in control of where we go in the Lake behind a new subconscious? What if I brought us to this equation because I knew Chreeb came here?"

Deka turned around, looked through the crowd at the jellyfish still lecturing.

"Geden is the only person who can make portals into the Lake," the former raptor continued. "He remembers. He knows what happened to him subconsciously, but he believes his own altered reality just as Sonjaa did. I helped her remember. Maybe I can help him."

Deka listened to Geden for a moment. "...only a conscious mind can exist outside the universe, but I have yet to understand why or how."

"That implies we have been living two lives," Friend began. "One life in the Lake and another in reality. What must go on in the Lake while we're there? Are we deliberately picking which realities to visit?"

"That's unsettling," Sonjaa said. "We're making decisions and living an entire life we can't remember."

"What will happen when we jog Geden's memory?" Kylac said, turning to watch the lecture again.

Deka flicked his fins from side to side, shaking in anticipation.

Geden's lecture changed to the mathematical theory behind the antisphere he had just opened. Gradually the audience dwindled down to less than half of what it had been, just the Archeons now and those who enjoyed numbers as well as theory. The former Relians floated in place, flicking their fins to stay still against the prevailing waves.

Geden now began describing to the Archeons some of the math it sensed in the Lake, and the group approached

Geden directly with questions. The jellyfish could not answer most of them. Right away Deka perceived the gaps in its knowledge. Geden opened these ways because of the latent memories of where it had been, not because it knew anything about it. It did not know this, so it justified the knowledge retroactively as having felt this place since being a polyp.

The Archeons in attendance still tried to tease more information out of Geden, as they always did, but nothing helped. They promised to try again next time, and gradually the audience dispersed.

Geden noticed the former Relians were the only ones here. It directed a loud voice at them.

"Are the four of you really that interested in the physics, or is it just Sonjaa?"

Deka wiggled his tail and swam up to Geden. "We are all Archeons."

"You never mentioned that before. Which ways do you maintain?"

"None here, yet, but soon we will figure out this place and how it links mathematically to the realm beyond the ether."

No language in this universe had a word for *lake*, as water did not exist in large bodies. Deka had reached Geden. He lowered his voice.

"Chreeb... I told you the story of the time Kylac took me to a planet that had no liquid water. None at all. Never had water on it. The people there had evolved at the bottom of liquid methane oceans. They breathed the methane and gave off oxygen as waste, and they live their whole lives at the bottom of frigid pools of methane. It rains methane on that world—a planet alien to both of us, but it had one little place where oxygen-breathers could survive. All the oxygen the locals exhale bubbles out of the water from time to time and..."

Deka tried to read Geden's body language. From the way its tentacles waggled in the breeze, Geden was confused. Deka switched tactics.

"Geden. Chreeb, why do you know so much about the realm beyond? As far as you know, you've felt it since you were a polyp, but why? Why you? Has it ever occurred to you that you know it so well because you were there?"

Geden hung in place for a few beats. "Deka, what is this about?"

Deka felt someone swimming up closer from behind. The waves in the ether felt like Friend. Deka spoke before Friend could pull him away.

"You were in that tree, unconscious. I stayed by your side for three whole days talking to you, trying to help you come back. You told me a story about when you explored a cave in the bottom of the ocean and went even further down than you had before."

Geden flicked its tentacles and backed away slightly.

"You told me about a planet where the water was so deep it became a gel. You wished you could share that with me! You described it to me so well I felt as if I had done it myself. You were always so good at that... I tried to be just as good at telling you what being on a desert planet was like. I..."

Geden tilted its head and began to pulse away, revealing the vulnerable bulb beneath the armor shell.

Friend spoke up. "A disaster happened in your former home. An antisphere similar to the one you just made touched thousands of portals on Rel, ripping the minds of many Archeons into the realm beyond. Some managed to hold onto themselves."

The jellyfish stopped pulsing. It hung in the breeze. Deka resumed where Friend left off.

"It pulled part of me away, too. It took away my ability to hold a portal open for longer than a few breaths. Made it painful to hold an equation in my mind for too long. That's the part of me I lost. You... You lost so much more."

Geden held still a few paces away. Deka swam closer.

"The entire contacted universe suffered. The disaster killed many Archeons. Some had no way to establish their portals again. Kylac and I were the only two Archeons who could make offworld spheres at all. We saved many civilizations from ending. Some only barely."

Geden pivoted, peered at him through its armor. It hung in silence for a while, then sent a narrow wave at all four of them. "I've seen things like that in my dreams. I've never told anyone. How do you know?"

Deka said his real name, the one he could pronounce now. "...you remember these things. You remember the pain and confusion but you don't understand it. What happened?"

It pulsed back toward them for a few paces, and then stopped.

"One dream I remember... I... was surrounded by the realm beyond the wall. But the ether did not catch up to me. So many images hit me at once. More than I could handle. I took them all in as I tried to understand where I was. It only made things worse. And I felt others nearby. I heard their voices, so I clung to them. Everything began to drift away."

Deka swam up to Geden, touched a tentacle with a fin. "It wasn't a dream."

"Is that possible?"

"You were in the realm beyond the ether. That's where we came from, too."

"No one has ever come back. That's why we only allow people to cross a certain distance at the edge."

"You did come back. You created a place for yourself to exist in this reality. Chreeb, you told me you wondered what it would be like to be a jellyfish. You told me some of your closest friends on other worlds were jellies. That's why you took this form."

Geden let go of itself, letting the breeze blow it around. Deka held Geden steady as it sent out vibrations of confusion and pain.

"I... I don't think about these nightmares."

"They weren't dreams!"

The breeze blew both of them sideways and spun them in a little circle. Deka saw the other three watching from a distance. He quickly sent Friend a narrow wave in thanks.

"Deka..." Geden began. "They were screaming in agony as I held them! They never stopped! They were confused... So was I. Holding everyone together became my goal. And then—and then... the universe vanished."

"What happened then?"

Geden wiggled free of Deka and pulsed half a pace away. It reached with all its arms and felt the armor. It pushed the armor off its bulb and held it to the side in a few tentacles. The former Relians stared. Agl never did this in front of anybody, especially carnivorous fish, a leftover of survival instinct.

The jellyfish stared at Deka, its eye now free to move all around its bulb. The transparent skin revealed its organs from brain to stomach. It was only one cell thick. Still gripping its armor, it pulsed up to Deka. It felt him with an arm. Deka reached up with a fin and touched Geden's bulb. The skin puckered inward. If Deka pushed too hard, he would push straight through, and the fluid that comprised Geden's circulatory system would leak out. Geden's eye swirled all around the bulb and finally settled on Deka.

"The last thing I remember before everything fell away was someone talking to me. A hand on my back. Something about trees that sprouted... underwater. Watching it happen."

"That was the first story I told you! Chreeb, I was there for your last moments!"

"I heard a voice when reality went dark. Very faint. I always wake up... just as I'm hearing it."

Geden had wrapped some of its tentacles around Deka and was holding him against his bulb.

"You woke up here," said the former raptor.

"In the dreams there is no ether. No... There was an ether, but it wasn't as thick."

"Water. Liquid. You lived in it. Maybe that's why you came here. It was an entire universe made of liquid. You could explore it the way you always wanted."

"Your voice. I remember now. You were in my dream. It was real? Deka... Where was I? What happened?"

Suddenly Geden unwrapped the former raptor and pulsed upwards, all nine tentacles raised.

"Water!" Geden now spoke in the aquatic language of Ixcy. "Entire planets covered in it. Empty space. The trees, birds, oceans—the water tasted different everywhere I went. I remember. You... You liked hearing about that."

Deka called him by his name on Ixcy, excited he could speak Chreeb's language now.

"You called me Chreeb," he said. "Birds... The birds called me that. You could speak their language. You understood mine through the trees but couldn't speak it back. I understood the bird's language! The trees. The birds. I was an Archeon in the ocean! An ocean! Every ocean! Deka!"

He let go of his armor and pulsed through the gel. He embraced the former raptor with all nine arms, wrapping him tight and pulling him up against his naked bulb. Deka could not grip him back, and the arms squeezed him so hard he feared being speared with venom.

5

Deka followed Chreeb through several portals, finally emerging in one cluster that had no trees growing in an elaborate lattice. Deka's Archeon senses told him space itself was under a lot more pressure here than in the rest of the universe. He did not know of this place, and quickly he realized why Chreeb had led him here.

The extra pressure forced the ether into an even thicker substance. A jelly. Nothing drifted here. Everything hung in place. Most of the atoms hung separately in an environment that made forming molecules difficult. Only a few single-celled organisms had evolved in the ether surrounding the antisphere, but enough oxygen floated here to support visitors who wished to experience one of the wonders of the universe: a cluster that had failed because the ether was too thick.

Deka had a difficult time swimming through it. He laughed. Chreeb sent laughter back to him.

"I can't believe this!" Chreeb said. "We're swimming together! Where did you learn to swim?"

"We created a place for ourselves in this universe, too."

"You, Kylac, Sonjaa, and Friend. Where is Rive?"

"It's a long story."

"Tell me in a moment. We're almost there."

Deka bored his way through the thick ether. Pulses from the antisphere moved through him but did not disturb any of the atoms. The emptiness was eerie yet beautiful. Chreeb could be here only because he was wearing armor, otherwise the pressure exerted by the gel would have crushed him.

A few dozen more paces, and Chreeb stopped and pivoted toward the antisphere. Deka caught up, suspended himself next to him. The ether gripped him so tight he felt he would never be able to move again, but he calculated with enough effort he could break free.

"Why this spot?" Deka said.

"I'm surprised you don't know this place. The density of the ether is a variable, and it's cyclic."

"It gets thicker?"

"Wait a few breaths. I remember I used to come here as a medusa. It was such a dangerous place and... And I... I didn't come here when I was young. I wasn't a child in this universe, was I?"

"All of your memories of this place are retroactive. Can you remember when you arrived?"

Chreeb stared at the antisphere in the far distance as it bathed this cluster in pulses. "It must have been the first time I woke up from the nightmare. That would have been... Twenty-four years ago in Ixcy years."

"So we've been gone at least that long."

"How long have you been here?"

"Two days."

Chreeb grabbed his armor with a tentacle and he rotated the eyehole to face Deka. "That's strange. I remember you so clearly for years. Sonjaa had been afraid of crossing the edge of the universe, and then she finally did it, and now she wants to do it all the time. None of that happened?"

"It can be confusing, even for us."

"And you're a Plin. You made yourself into a fish! Have you ever been one before, in any of the other places?"

"A few times, but always in water. This is the only equation I've been to where creatures live in space itself."

"Here it comes."

Deka felt a wave approaching. He adjusted himself to be comfortable, and the wave swept over him. The ether thickened and squeezed Deka, now taking on the consistency of ice, but still warm.

Deka laughed, tried to budge, but the ether resisted him. He laughed again. Chreeb laughed with him.

"Chreeb, I wish I could hug you!"

"I am glad I can embrace you at last. We talked for so long about doing things like this."

"Is this what it was like in that ocean back home?"

"This is even better!"

"How long does it last?"

"Only a few breaths."

"Does it ever become too dense?"

"Not that I have ever felt."

"Why don't more people come here?"

"It's barren and empty. Oxygen is thin. There's nothing to replenish it. Every breath we take here deprives someone in the future from seeing this."

"Oh... That's disappointing."

"I have to show you another place. This one has more life. Will your fox be all right alone for a while longer?"

"He's not alone. He's with Sonjaa and Friend."

"Sonjaa is Friend's raptor now, and she's an Archeon? How did that happen?"

"I'll tell you on the way. This is fine for now. The ether is loosening. What's going on here?"

"It's the realm beyond. I believe it's exerting pressure on this universe, squeezing spacetime into a fluid. It's particularly strong in this region."

Moments later the ether released them, and they swam freely again. Chreeb led the way back to the portal, Deka following in the thick wake he left behind.

"All right, Deka, we have a long swim ahead of us. I have to know. What happened to me, and what are you doing here?"

"So much happened after you left Ixcy."

6

People dove into the leading edge of the universe. They remained there for a moment and then they emerged, the ropes tight. It was the only way to tell this area of space was stretching out. The three former Relians floated and watched within the trees.

"How many times in a lifetime can you witness the universe expanding?" Friend said, twitching in excitement.

"Finally, something that impresses you," Kylac said.

"Of course from a physics standpoint it's nothing special, but to be able to go somewhere and see the leading edge... To be able to dive in for a few breaths and then come back. We have never witnessed anything like it before out of all the realities we've been to."

Sonjaa laughed, turned from the edge, and faced Friend. "Finally, something that impresses you."

"It is unique. Not only is it accessible due to space itself being habitable in this reality, but it is traveling so slowly we can watch it. All the different permutations of physical laws. What is causing this? Sonjaa, how does it sound to you?"

She laughed again. "You try describing how the universe sounds! If you could, you wouldn't need math! But this is incredible. Even more incredible that we meet someone we know out here. I remember Deka spending days in those trees talking to Chreeb."

"He missed one of your cycles that way," Kylac said, laughing with his vocal bladder.

"I know! I went to see him just to find out what mattered more, and he stayed in the tree instead!"

Friend laughed. "You never told me about that!"

Kylac turned to face the other former fox. "He wanted eggs. Sonjaa wanted eggs. They agreed to have a clutch on her heat, but then Deka got to talking to Chreeb, her cycle came, and instead of taking a few breaths to be with her, he ignored her!"

Friend laughed.

"How could I compete with a fish?" Sonjaa said, loud enough for them to hear. "I was ready, and he just stayed in that tree. I slept there, trying to fill the place with my scent, but he kept talking."

"When did he come out?" Friend said.

"Two whole days after my cycle passed! I yelled at him for that. Deka, what happened? I thought you wanted eggs! And he said he didn't want to interrupt Chreeb. We had to wait until my next cycle. Then we... We lost them in the disaster."

"Yes, I know your loss," Friend said. "I recall everyone we lost in the disaster. It will be worth it."

Sonjaa glared at him for a moment. Her eyes did not blink, and right now she wished she could clench her eyes shut and dig her killing claws into the dirt. A few vibrations in the universe had found harmony in Sonjaa's mind. The rest began to harmonize around them.

A few moments later, Kylac spoke. "With Deka able to swim with Chreeb now, we may grow old here. Forget missing a cycle—Deka could miss entire years being an aquatic creature free to swim about in space itself. It's a life both could only imagine, but especially Deka."

"Now that we found him," Friend said, "what do we do? Can we take him with us?"

"Could there be others?" Sonjaa said. "He said he managed to hold himself together, so maybe other Archeons did the same thing without realizing it."

"If Friend is right, we will steer ourselves there if we find someone. I wonder who else could have made it out intact."

"And was able to hold together through the Lake," Friend continued. "I've felt many particles out there, but they're not coherent. That still eludes me. What are the particles that make up consciousness? They must be interchangeable somehow, and yet when contained make up an entire person. What laws govern their behavior? If we could stay in one place long enough, perhaps we would have time to figure it out. Sonjaa, do you think I'm ready to remain here for longer than you can contain me? I think I've done well keeping myself under control after the imbalance is gone."

"Let's hear what Chreeb has to say about this equation. Maybe he can tell us something new about the Lake. I'd like to stay if we can."

"It will still be a wonderful place even after I can calculate it."

Sonjaa rubbed his fin. Friend flicked his fin and drifted slightly away from her. A prevailing wave hit him, and it pushed him against her. Sonjaa rubbed snouts with him. Friend steered himself away again.

New vibrations emerged from the ether. Sonjaa heard all the forces changing pitch and wobbling around before righting themselves and finding their old pulsing tones again, as if the new sound had tried to blow them out like standing flames.

Sonjaa turned to face the origin of the noise. A pair of paws were pushing against the ether. A muzzle appeared between them, mouth open. It moaned, the ether itself carrying its voice.

"Friend..." Sonjaa said.

"It's not me."

The vibrations it produced told Sonjaa this thing was not trapped in the ether, but behind it. Something was in the Lake, pushing against the ether, trying to break in. It resembled a Droden from the planet Hithe.

Kylac swam forward a pace and let the ether slow him to a stop. "Is that... Barul?"

The hairless, bipedal canine continued pushing on the ether, screaming. Everyone at the edge had turned away and come to look at the source of the new vibrations. The three former Relians swam closer to the outline of one of the first Archeons killed by the disaster.

Another set of vibrations hit them from behind. The ether bent and distorted into a shape resembling a Bellows from Lesa. Next to that, another distortion appeared, a Geleen, roaring and reaching into the ether. More figures appeared, all stretching their arms in Friend's direction.

The leading edge of the universe vibrated in a single voice. Figures emerged from it, flying straight into the ether. Living antispheres. Dozens of them. Most consisted of indiscernible limbs and formless faces, but others were more complete. The former Relians recognized multiple species from their home reality, bipedal mammals and reptiles—creatures that could not exist here. Their shrieks and roars merged into a single sound that blew out the laws of physics ahead of them. The ether dissipated into spacetime, swirled around, and then reformed behind the group as they passed.

The crowd scattered. The living antispheres ignored them and ran through the ether straight for Friend. Sonjaa spun around, intentionally slapping both Friend and Kylac with her tailfin, and then swam for the trees as the army of antispheres advanced.

"Close the portals!" Sonjaa shouted, hoping some Archeons heard her over the noise of the invading figures. "Close the portals!"

Friend and Kylac caught up to her as they weaved through the branches in the cluster. It was only a couple thousand paces thick to the other side, and then a few million paces to the antisphere at the center of the cluster.

The voices of the invaders found harmony, and they now screamed for one thing.

7

Each cluster had what the people of this reality called a primary plant, which described the plant life that provided shelter for the cluster and allowed animals to evolve. Sometimes it was a species of bacteria, but most of the time it was vine- or treelike life form.

The trees reproduced in different ways. Some used the animals to transmit their seeds. Some broke sections of themselves off and sent them adrift to find a new place to begin growing. Some did not reproduce, but were in fact a single organism that perpetually grew and grew, often shedding old branches, which the wildlife ate.

Deka and Chreeb floated in a cluster where the trees reproduced by casting seed pods into the ether. They remained just inside the web of branches, looking out over the frontier. Thousands of pods drifted out there. Most would remain dormant indefinitely, but a few would find areas with a high concentration of carbon dioxide, which would erode the pod casing, and the plant would sprout.

One pod in the distance split open. The seedling used its stored nutrients to begin rapid growth. Six tiny branches shot out and extended forty paces, forming a wheel-like structure. It captured as much carbon dioxide as possible as the breeze from the antisphere pushed molecules in its direction.

It began to give off oxygen as a byproduct and drifted with others on the frontier. Animals and bacteria would eventually find their way over there and begin to live nearby, which would create new carbon dioxide pockets for seeds to sprout.

Deka turned to the jellyfish. He had removed his armor and hung it on a nearby branch. Deka now looked at the naked bulb and every internal organ.

"Almost the same as watching trees sprout at the bottom of the ocean."

Chreeb's eye moved to look at Deka.

"I wish you could've seen them. It's a rare event. Even more rare when someone is there to watch the vine rise to the surface. This is just as good. No planets. No stars. Space is breathable. I am relieved Ixcy did not die without me. Thank you, Deka, for helping them."

"They would've been fine without us. I knew they would be. I came to find out if you were all right. It was one of the first stops we made."

"All because Friend discovered the realm beyond the ether. The *Lake*." He had used his native language on Ixcy to speak the word. "The realm is so peaceful here. It gives life to everything, but it destroyed entire worlds back home. It's hard to imagine."

"It took you from me, it took Sonjaa from me for a long time. It almost took Rive. We lost so many worlds to it. Millions of people. Kylac and I did everything we could to stop Friend from ever doing it again, and now we've come to agree with him on a few things. Someone has to leave the universe. Someone must understand the Lake so our reality won't be forgotten when it dissipates."

"Taming your foxes in a whole new way. I..." Chreeb emitted incoherent vibrations. "I... I-umm-mm-ms-s—"

Chreeb's tentacles began flailing, brushing against Deka, knocking him away. Something appeared to be growing behind the jellyfish.

"Em-ma-rrhh-eelll-sss-eeehhhhhh—"

He began to spin around, about to bump into a branch; Deka darted behind Chreeb and positioned himself between his bulb and the tree. Limbs flailing and bulb undulating, his body tried to move in all directions at once.

Something appeared in the ether surrounding Chreeb. The ether puckered and heaved outwards. Deka recalled the antifox back in his home universe. Chreeb's entire body swelled. One of his arms ballooned to the size of Deka's body, then it contracted, seemed to fall into itself like a singularity, and his arm sank into the ether and vanished. Deka held him as hard as he could with fins.

"Chreeb!"

The jellyfish undulated and took Deka up. Down. Sideways. Arms flailing and vocal bladder sending out random noise. He slammed Deka into one branch. Then another. He slammed into one so hard it snapped against Deka's body. With every sudden change in direction, Deka flicked his tailfin to steer them so he would collide with the tree instead of Chreeb.

The Agl's body continued swelling and puckering. A lump grew out of his back, separated, formed the image of a face and paws trying to push through, and then fell backwards into the ether.

The jellyfish pivoted and pulsed down into another branch. Deka held his bulb, flicked his pelvic fin. They spun around just enough for Deka to take the impact. Chreeb pulsed again, pushing Deka harder into the branch. Deka held on, felt the prevailing breeze and the new echoes it produced.

Part of the bulb puckered. A feline head emerged from it, stared at Deka's eye, and roared at him. It then fell back into the ether, and Chreeb lost part of his bulb. Fluid did not leak out but became sucked up as another distortion of ether grew from his body. It stretched and strained until it formed an antisphere in the shape of a Ninelegs from Kattaaka. It stood on Chreeb's bulb, its lower abdomen still part of him. It stretched and reached out and then broke away, skittering around the ether as if it were solid ground, and then dove in.

Chreeb shouted incoherently. Deka recognized the patterns in the mumbles. Voices of some of the Archeons who had died in the first disaster.

He recognized the Archeon from Be'ohn emerging from one of Chreeb's tentacles right now. Chreeb was mumbling in her voice, mourning the loss of her planet. A moment later, the antisphere broke off and ran a few paces into the ether before vanishing into it.

Chreeb seemed to calm down for an instant, and his voice returned. "Deka... What's ha-a-a-ppening?"

Deka held him tight in case he suddenly accelerated into another tree. "You said you found others in the Lake! Others who were screaming out in pain! You brought them with you!"

The jellyfish moaned as an arm emerged from his bulb.

"You held yourself together by merging with all of them! They're waking up and they're breaking free! Where are they going?"

"Friend... It's all I can think about. Friend."

"Fr..."

Chreeb must have realized it at the same time, for his remaining arms went limp and drifted in the breeze.

"In my dream, all I wanted to know was why. What happened? Why was I in pain? You told me. You told them."

The antisphere shaped like an arm morphed into a reptilian head and then sank into the fluidic spacetime, taking more of Chreeb's body with it. He had only four limbs. More than half of his bulb and bodily organs were missing, and yet he did not leak fluid.

His bulb could no longer undulate. Deka released him, grabbed an arm in his mouth, and pulled him out of the trees and into the thin air beyond. Deka faced his eye.

"I didn't get all of everyone," Chreeb pulsed. "Just pieces... Pieces of people who were in pain. People like me. Drifting in the realm."

His body swelled, another antisphere emerged from his bulb, broke off, and swam away. Three more distortions puckered underneath his body. Deka rested a fin on his bulb.

"I drew them to me," Chreeb continued. "I pulled them close. It made us feel better."

Deka rotated. He held himself next to him and lay a fin over what was left of his bulb.

"You held them so close they became you. They're still aware of who they were."

Two tentacle-arms wrapped around Deka. Another antisphere climbed out of him, taking the vague shape of an avian the size of a Relian theropod. It flew into the ether. Chreeb's body shrank a little.

"Deka, I can't remember Ixcy. All I can remember is... The ether. And you. The stories you told me."

The arms wrapped around Deka tighter. Deka cried.

8

The portals were still open, but Sonjaa noticed a few of them had closed after some of the horde had collided with them. Sonjaa took Friend and Kylac through a few of them, but it didn't matter where she went. The living antispheres simply poured out of the nearest antisphere and dove for them, chopping through everything they touched. One antifox had been enough to cause disaster across their universe. A group of them would slice up enough trees to destabilize life in entire clusters.

Sonjaa had managed to outrun them for some time, but now they didn't need antispheres to enter the universe. They had figured out they could punch through on their own, and now they popped out of nowhere all around them, reaching out for them.

She swam through the web of finned branches, darting under and over. Antispheres in the shape of various creatures from back home emerged around them, cutting up trees, reaching out for them in pursuit. She felt Friend's and Kylac's vibrations behind her as they kept up.

Sonjaa heard the distortions they made in the universe. These gave her something new to listen to, just how different they sounded compared to the normal echoes of physics. This was the Lake itself coming to meet them, and those laws of physics were the same everywhere. How it sounded from inside this universe helped her find harmony.

An antisphere in the shape of a reptile snout opened in front of her. Sonjaa dove down. Friend and Kylac followed, staying just a few paces behind her. She did not want to risk them touching any more portals, so she steered them in the direction of the back edge of this cluster.

She took the most meandering path through the trees she could, giving herself more time to find harmony in this place, hoping they wouldn't anticipate where she was going. The irregular pulses generated by the quarks and gluons began to fall into a pattern, and they settled into a drone which caused other vibrations in this reality to make their pulses. Now she understood why this universe sounded so different.

The antispheres existed here because this reality had a weak structure. The Lake pushed as hard on this universe as it did on all the others, but because it was weak to resist this pressure, the Lake squeezed reality into a gel-like form, which slowed its expansion. The squeezing meant atoms joined easier and gravity fell into the Lake rather than distending the ether. The universe became harmonious. Sonjaa closed off the ether immediately around their group, which held the horde back.

They emerged from the trees and stared at the antisphere that formed the center of this cluster. It pulsed. Sonjaa now heard how the pulsing affected the laws of physics across the universe.

The living antispheres had lined up in a semi-sphere before them. Half-bodies, whole bodies, heads, limbs with no torso but still arranged as if a body were there. Dozens of species. Hundreds of people. Sonjaa recognized them. They had been with her when the first disaster happened.

Now she remembered something. A presence in the Lake shortly after she had fallen in. She remembered this someone vacuuming up the terrified, confused particles, becoming huge and then fading away.

Sonjaa felt people poking at the closed spacetime behind her. The hoard had surrounded them, bumping up against the barrier that enclosed her and the former foxes. Kylac and Friend swam up next to her and stared out at the antispheres, visible only when the large one in the distance pulsed.

Sonjaa noticed all the child-shaped antispheres, some of them shaped like Relian theropods. There was no way to know if they were her chicks.

"Friend," Sonjaa said. "I believe you have something to say to them."

He flicked a fin and faced her. "What?!"

"Don't you recognize them? These are the people who died in the first disaster. They want to know why, and they want to hear it from you."

Friend turned. The horde waited at the barrier Sonjaa had set up. The former fox swam a little ways forward.

"Everyone! The disaster was tragic and painful. It hurt me as much as it hurt you. But I want all of you to know that we are on the verge of discovery! We are on a quest to understand the Lake and save our universe from dissipating with no one to remember it. Your deaths will not be for nothing. I promise."

Sonjaa growled with her vocal bladder. She dropped the barrier between them and Friend. They closed in faster than he could flee.

9

Chreeb had been whittled down to little more than a few pieces of arm and internal organs with a couple hemispheres of bulb covering them. Somehow they functioned without connecting in reality. They must have connected in the realm beyond. Deka looked straight into Chreeb's eye. Nothing had broken off of him in thirty breaths, so he figured this was all that remained of the former Archeon from Ixcy, the only particles of himself he had held onto when the disaster tore his mind from his body.

"They took everything. Except my memories of this place. Those are mine."

Deka could barely speak his vocal bladder pulsated in grief so much. "I'm... I'm so sorry."

"I'm glad. This is all I can remember. It's a wonderful place. I was only alive because I absorbed so many others. It was enough to form a complete person. This ... all that's left of me now. They need peace. I need it."

The Plin righted them and began swimming back toward the portal to the main hub for this cluster.

"Deka?"

"I'm taking you to the wall! We'll leave the universe! I can absorb your particles. Maybe there will be enough for you to be conscious."

Chreeb barely had strength. His tentacles were slipping off Deka. The former raptor tried to hold with a fin as he entered the branches.

"We'll be like Stephen and Norh," Deka continued. "I'll carry you with me. I promise!"

"I'm not here right now. I feel the nightmare taking me again but this time... I'm not afraid."

They entered the branches. The portal was so far away, and then they still had other spheres to go through before they could reach the wall.

Deka felt half a tentacle-arm squeeze him. "Thank you for finding me. Thank you for giving us answers. Peace..."

That had been all his strength. The tentacle slipped off. Deka reversed and swam down to catch him, but the jellyfish was falling away faster than the laws of physics seemed to allow. He was dissipating.

"Happy to share a swim with you at last. To watch the trees sprout... To swim in space... with no limits. An endless ocean. It's what I always wanted."

The faster Deka swam, the further away Chreeb fell. "It's been the best day of my life," he shouted.

"Tell Friend I forgive him. I hope the others forgive him, too. Tell Sonjaa not to let you miss her next heat." Chreeb laughed. "I'm spreading out."

Distance had become so distorted Deka gave up swimming toward him. He let the ether halt him as the jellyfish faded. "You can start over! Collect around me—you don't have to let go!"

Chreeb had already dissolved.

Distance had returned. The branches were mere paces away. A pulse from the antisphere nudged Deka backwards. He let the waves push him wherever they wanted.

10

They flew at Friend all at once. As a group, they ripped Friend's body apart one piece at a time. Some touched his skull, and Sonjaa heard his conscious mind spilling into the Lake. Antispheres touched, crossed, absorbed one another, slicing Friend into thousands of pieces.

Kylac held his breath as he looked on. The horde had fallen into itself, and Friend was no more. Sonjaa laughed. Kylac glared at her.

She opened an antisphere and swam through as she separated her mind from her body. She emerged in the Lake and perceived the particles of the disaster victims. They had scattered themselves across the Lake when they converged on the former fox, as she had hoped.

Friend's particles were among them, moving fast. His were easy to identify. Sonjaa swam toward one, collected it, moved to another. She parted the silent Lake particles that once made up the victims of the first disaster and recollected only the ones that screamed.

As she collected more and more of him, Friend clung to her. He had still not figured out the universe, so he was helpless here. As she swam to another clump of Friend's conscious mind, he sent a few waves at her.

Friend asked if Sonjaa had done that on purpose.

Sonjaa told him he deserved that. He needed to feel the pain for himself.

She reached another particle and it reattached to Friend. Sonjaa held him together, and now Friend exerted his own force to hold his particles in place. Sonjaa could tell that it still hurt.

She continued: that was how it felt to be ripped apart and enter the Lake screaming. People suffered for that larger goal. Sonjaa told him never to forget that—and not dismiss the loss of her hatchlings as no big deal or look his victims in the eye and preach to them about the good of the universe. They suffered even more than he did because they had given their lives for it, so show some humility.

Friend did not make any waves for some time. Sonjaa homed in on the last particle and adjusted her nonlinear course to intercept. Finally, Friend made a wave.

He told her he knew it hurt, and that he was sorry for the loss of her clutch. Sonjaa sensed Friend still meant that the loss was nothing compared to the fate of the universe.

She didn't remember Friend being so indifferent to the feelings of others before.

Friend expressed that all of this had been for science. All of it served a greater purpose. Why should anyone be angry about that?

Sonjaa expressed Friend still had a ways to go before she would trust him with their home universe.

Friend replied he hadn't reverted, so what was she holding him back from doing this time?

She collected the last piece of Friend, and now they rested while they traveled with the universe, watching the flashes of time go by. They noticed particles of consciousness entering reality, streaming into the brains of newborns. Other particles streamed out of the brains of the dying, becoming part of the Lake again.

Some of those particles felt familiar. Sonjaa and Friend adjusted their perceptions to one particular cluster. Deka appeared to be drifting from the spot where particles had emerged.

Sonjaa projected herself as a Relian theropod down to reality. Friend followed, projecting himself as a Relian canine, missing his tail. They materialized near Deka.

Sonjaa opened a sphere for Kylac, and the former fox swam through it, facing her. "Are they gone?"

"The victims of the first disaster got their revenge," she said, standing on the ether as though it were solid. "It tore them apart. They can't form again."

Kylac laughed. "And now you're five ahead of Friend."

The older fox sank half a pace. "This time it feels like a loss."

Deka drifted limply, vocal bladder so exhausted from grief he could not cry anymore.

Kylac swam up to him. Sonjaa walked on the ether, and they nudged him with their noses. Nobody spoke for thirty pulses. Finally, Deka sent a weak wave to everyone.

"I held him as he died. This time he heard me. He heard me."

Kylac touched Deka's fin. Sonjaa bumped him with her nose. Friend turned and gazed at the antisphere in the distance as it sent life-giving waves through the ether.

Neben

I

"Sheryl."

She turned around and faced the metal raptor approaching her. "Yes, Rive?"

His feet clanked on the stone floor. She wondered why he didn't wear pads or something to cut down on the noise. She also wondered why his skin was still shiny and grey when he could mimic the appearance of real scales.

"I have finished something I want you to start distributing."

Rive walked behind the Krone lying in the middle of the chamber and stood at the edge of the cone of light. He was holding a book, and it looked brand new, which meant he had just printed and bound it.

Sheryl slid the packet of documents back onto the shelf and climbed down the ladder. She walked on her leg compensator to the light on this side of the Krone. Sorven lay in the middle of the room, under the skylight, watching the screens. She had become very good over the years at tuning out the noise coming from the video wall and simply going about her research. She stood just outside the cone of light coming from the ceiling. She took the book from his metal hands.

"What is it?"

"Three hundred and twenty-two years ago, a woman named Lucy Schrifton came here and wrote an autobiography. It chronicled all the things she saw, people she'd met, and what was happening to the human race."

"Lucy Schrif... Wasn't she one of the women the Relians took to the stars?"

"Yes. I wanted to wait until the humans offworld had diverged from the humans of Earth before releasing it."

Sheryl flipped through it. "For a book about life offworld, it's very thin."

Rive rubbed his claws, chuckling. "Lucy was a lawyer. She was exceptionally good at getting to the point. I'm making more copies, and I'm working on translations."

Sheryl looked up from the book and met his eyes. She had been told time and time again that asking questions would not be grounds for punishment. She had to ask. It had been burning in her for years and now the topic had come up, exactly what she had been waiting for.

"I will read it, but Rive... Why hasn't it happened again? Why don't the Relians rescue more people from Earth?"

Rive's neck curled back as he stood straighter. "The population has steadied at about twenty-seven thousand. Almost every pair of Relians has a human. The original group was lucky humans happened to trigger the same instinct raptors have for foxes. Otherwise no human would have been able to leave."

Sheryl clutched the book, tried not to raise her voice. "Aren't I worthy? Isn't everyone in the Church?"

Rive's stance changed. She recognized it as a mournful posture. He closed the gap, standing halfway out of the light and resting his hand on one of hers. She let him weave two of his metal claws between her trembling fingers.

"I know you're jealous," he said. "Everyone is, so I will tell you the same thing I tell every Church leader. We can't rescue everyone. There isn't enough room in the contacted universe for the entire human race. You have untamed instincts. If we took everyone off Earth, the same thing that is happening there would happen on other planets."

Sheryl gritted her teeth.

"You may say it," Rive said. "It is no secret."

Sheryl stopped shivering as she shouted. "You let us rot on Earth while heaven is just a few steps away! Why does the Church exist if not to find worthy people?"

Her words echoed even over the din of the video wall. She looked past Rive at the Krone. Sorven still watched the screens.

"Every Church leader asks these questions," Rive said as Sheryl met his eyes again. "Everyone in the Church asks, as well. You are no more worthy than anyone else. You are doing a great service for the human race, but this does not give you special favor with us. Nobody has it. There are ten billion people on the planet. This is more than forty times the total population of all sentient species in the contacted universe combined. There is no room for all of you."

"What about just the Church? Only a couple million of us worldwide. What do we have to do to be worthy?"

"There is nothing anyone can do." Rive rubbed her fingers gently. "The people who left Earth did not deserve it either."

"You said as long as our needs are met, there won't be a reason for anyone to fight. Wouldn't the contacted universe be the answer?"

"You'll find the answer in the book."

He lowered his hand from hers. Sheryl held his gaze.

"I can't stand to see people suffering," Sheryl said. "How can you sit here and watch it? Are you going to do anything about it, or is it just entertainment to all of you? What is the point of preserving these documents if you're just going to dangle paradise out of reach and laugh at us for hoping salvation is coming?"

Sorven spoke without taking his eyes from the monitors. "We never promised salvation. Only human religions do that."

Rive turned halfway around and looked at the Krone. Sheryl raised her eyes.

"We promised not to let information vanish," he continued. "We promised to keep the people of Earth informed of what was really happening."

Sheryl wrung the book in her hands and threw it to the floor. "Get off your ass and do something about it! We're ready to help!"

Sorven still did not turn away from the screens. "We cannot rescue everyone, and your next question will be why the Krone don't descend upon Earth and end this. You are not the first to ask. It would not be a solution. We would have to crush the human spirit to keep the dominance instinct from oppressing others. We don't want a race of submissive pets. If we were to destroy the corporate entities that own the world without installing ourselves in their place, the entire planet would descend into a regressive age deeper than ever before. The cycle would start again. It always does. As soon as the oppressed have a taste of power, they become what they fought to bring down, and in a few centuries you would have the same society we see now."

"Then why did you bother forming the Church? What are you waiting for?"

"For the people to become angry enough. A catastrophe will happen, and when the Church is all that is left, the Krone will be able to come in, and the people will welcome us."

"What catastrophe? Nothing is happening!"

Rive turned to Sheryl. "From your point of view, it looks as if nothing is happening, but we have a perspective that is much longer than a single human lifespan. The changes are more obvious from this point of view. We are trying to pass on that perspective to others. The owners of your society will cause the disaster. It is brewing."

"How?"

"You have already read about it," said the Krone. Rive and Sheryl both turned to him. "The corporations of the world are stockpiling biological and nuclear weapons. Genetic engineering has made even the common cold fatal. There's enough to wipe out the entire human race in a matter of months. They tell the people these weapons are for defense against extraterrestrial invasion, but they are actually meant to quell mass rebellion."

"And you're going to let it happen! Billions of people will die and you're just going to sit there and sun yourself in the glow of the nuclear blasts!"

Sorven's shoulder muscles flexed, and he rose from his belly. He spread his wings all the way out, but she did not get the feeling he was amused. Sorven turned to her and took one step. His forepaw rumbled through the chamber and shook the ceiling.

Sheryl had seen him do little but lie in that spot for years, so she had forgotten how large he was. He stood six times her height. This time he did not lower his neck to be closer to her eye level.

"If I could save everyone, I would!" he roared as he took another step toward her.

Rive picked up the book and backed away in the other direction. She almost took a step backwards, but despite Sorven's voice, she did not sense she was in danger.

"This is the burden of knowledge, Sheryl!" he continued, voice rattling the plastic cases on the shelf.

He walked toward her, one step at a time, craning his neck even higher.

"I carry even more knowledge with me, and the pain that comes with it! That is what it means to be Krone! To know so much but unable to change it! To be immune to everything and watch everyone else fall! I was human once, and I take no pleasure in watching what is happening to my home!"

The dragon closed in. Sheryl stood firm, clenching her fists in fury. The Krone stopped about ten meters away.

"You want us to fly down and end it all! You want us to bring humanity to its knees and rescue everyone! We would be worse than any dictator in history! We would be demons! We would inhabit your nightmares!"

The muscles in his body flexed in a cascade from his chest down to his tail. Sheryl wondered how he stayed in such good shape despite doing nothing but watching screens all day. She gazed upwards.

Sorven roared, spreading his wings. He raised his paw, held his claws up, backlit by the skylight.

"Creatures of hell who would force the human race to submit! It would be a never-ending reign of terror! That's what we would have to be to ensure no person rises up and dares oppress another! We would have to become the oppressors! We would slaughter anyone who tried to defeat us! We would crush—" He brought his hand down on the stone. The room shook. "—anyone who dared to cooperate against us! Nothing can hurt us! We can survive anywhere! You would not be able to stop us, so you would either submit! Or die!"

Somehow he crossed the distance between them in the blink of an eye, his claws poised over her skull. They were easily as long as her body. His voice was by her left ear.

"Is this what you want for the people of Earth?"

She unclenched her fists as she whispered. "Yes." She took a breath through her nose. "It has to be better."

The hand rested before her. Sorven lowered his head to her eye level and folded his wings against his back.

"I became that very monster once on an uncontacted planet. That's what it took to make the people understand. That is what the Krone will never be. We will not force ourselves on anyone. We will not oppress. We will not dominate. Using oppression to end oppression never works. The only way to end the cycle is to let it destroy itself. That is what the Church will bring about. The information we preserve will allow it to reach its inevitable conclusion, one humans have avoided for generations thanks to the victor writing history."

Sheryl stood firm and held his gaze. She did not blink. Sorven turned around and walked under the light.

"I am glad you expressed your frustration. Every Church leader goes through this, and I have given that performance to each one of them. Every person needs to see the alternative. Read Lucy's book. It will give you comfort."

He lay on his stomach in front of the video wall, casting a shadow in the shifting glow of the computer-animated news and fictional programming. Rive clanked across the chamber again. Sheryl stepped away from the wall and waited.

He held the book out to her. Sheryl took it from his hands. Rive bobbed his neck at her then turned and walked to the next chamber. Sheryl opened it.

2

Vae and Tema chose me to leave Earth. We spent some time watching the Tava chew on bones. It's all they eat. They're not hunters. Predators are everywhere, all from off-world. The Tava socialize with them now. Their instinct is to hide and wait for predators to make kills. Their companion race looks like kangaroos with feathers. The Savex actu-

ally are predators, and it looks so weird to me to see a kangaroo with sharp teeth. Predators who helped their much larger companion race learn how to overcome their fear of predators. We must have lived there for months, just being among them, hearing their history, the stories they told, not to mention being among the predators and prey from the contacted universe.

Eventually we left, and the first place Vae and Tema took me was someplace they promised to show me. I forget the planet's name. A species of male that lays eggs. I got to watch them do it. They were eager to demonstrate. One hell of a biology lesson. So much of a lesson it made me laugh. Tema asked me why I was laughing. I remember telling her I didn't know. Nothing was funny, but at the same time it was. Once I got used to it, I felt bad for laughing. Their eggs were delicious.

It was around then I realized I hadn't taken any medications.

...

I thought I would be bored without television. It turned out I just needed to learn how to appreciate other forms of entertainment. Vae and Tema showed me one notable way Relians stay entertained. They will sit on a hill, close their eyes, and take in all the scents the wind brings them. They enjoy doing this on hills with lots of people upwind. They can sit there for hours just taking in all the scents that come their way. They narrate for me. So much they learn just taking in scents. Sometimes entire life stories are on the wind, and I felt I was missing out on most of the worlds we visit. Through them, I learned to experience senses beyond my comprehension. It became my goal in life.

...

When Rive brought me here to write these words, he asked me if there was anything he could get me. Anything from Earth I wanted to experience again. The first thing that came to mind was pizza. I knew it would make me sick, but I still wanted it. Rive brought me one slice. Plain cheese. The smell alone was all I needed. I could only eat a few bites before my stomach ached, but it was worth it. The ultimate comfort food. For me, that's home in a single whiff.

...

My lack of fur severely limited where I could go, but we found a solution. Several species out there shed their fur in a similar way reptiles did. Normally they bury these pelts so predators wouldn't find their scents. This time they donated them to the offworld humans. They lasted years, and while often a burden, keeping track of the damn thing, it opened up lots of new places to visit.

Hundreds of planets within walking distance. Hundreds of different cultures. Until I learned some languages, it seemed everyone was just lazing around, taking breaks to eat. All of it looked so animalistic to me.

When you're in an environment where your native language is dead and you're surrounded by so many different cultures, something switches on. Some sort of innate ability to absorb everything in your surroundings. You become a child again. A sponge soaking up information. When I learned the language, I realized they weren't just animals. They knew history, philosophy, mathematics, anatomy, medicine. None of it was something you had to go to school to hear about. All of that was the ocean of culture they lived in all the time, similar to how movies and television was the ocean my culture swam in. Bible stories used to be that ocean, too. Once I could swim, I absorbed it.

3

Rive knelt on a building inside a cave. Boq, Neben's avian Archeon, stood beside him. Rive had told her years ago this moment would arrive in her lifetime, so she had been preparing for it.

The cave was dry, and the Dekanites lay strewn about, their glow having faded days ago. They had been carving the caverns higher and wider for centuries, and just the other year they had connected the last one. Neben now had a vast underground network of chambers and tunnels large enough for a mountain range and an ocean.

When Rive first began working on the calculations, he had also worked out how long it would take. The complexity and enormity of the task had overwhelmed him, but the Multitude had no concept of time, or a lifespan. It took years for Rive to tell the Multitude this was not something he should have been able to do. It involved a non-spherical portal so large and complex it would take more than a lifetime to calculate, but it could be done. The metal had given him that lifespan.

Sorven stood on the ground, neck even with the roof of the stone structure, wings fluttering from time to time in anticipation.

The regional Church leaders from all over Earth stood in attendance. Some were already thinking about how to turn this into a sermon.

Boq had set up portals around the caverns so Nebens and offworlders all over the world could watch as Rive brought a species back to life.

The crystalline Eich in the pools on the desert surface looked through eagerly. Some remained in their traditional canine shape. Others had taken the form of either a pangolin-like mammal or an avian of this world. A few others shifted to other shapes they preferred. They traded bolts of lightning.

The Selts and the Zjr also waited and watched. The Zjr could barely stand on their own anymore, even from birth.

People from all over the contacted universe had come to witness this.

The Multitude buzzed in Rive's mind. They had been waiting for this moment for centuries, had observed Rive making the calculations one cubic pace at a time, and in the meantime he had learned to understand the reality in which they were trapped. The real universe. It had taken Rive centuries to learn how they comprehended the realm they created for themselves to inhabit, in which the alteration of reality itself was communication. It had taken the Multitude an equally long time to understand the needs and actions of biological creatures. It had been painfully slow, full of missteps and misunderstandings, but in the end they were ready to rejoin the mountain range and bring back a full report.

Rive began opening the portal. A point of darkness opened halfway up to the ceiling and began spreading out. Rive followed the equations. He had not had to calculate a portal that required his full concentration since he was an apprentice, but a portal of uneven shape spread out over such a long range required so much of his brainpower he could not think about anything else.

The portal spread. At first it looked like liquid suspended in the air, but as it stretched, it began to resemble solid metal. The portal spread laterally through the caverns, growing vertically in a calculated, controlled manner.

Rive had never calculated a portal larger than a Krone before, and never a non-spherical one at that. There had been no reason to until now. Watching the math come to life in the real world made him proud. His metal observed it happening, and it gave off warm vibrations in his mind as it greeted their people.

The tear in spacetime ripped halfway around the planet and expanded vertically. The inside of the metallic mountain range reached upwards. Rive had calculated long ago how high the caves needed to be, so the emerging mountain range filled the caverns precisely. The edge of the portal began to wrap around the contours of the jagged metal, peaks brushing against the ceiling of the cave system.

The contacted universe observed the mountain range emerging underneath Neben. The base now touched the bottom of the cave system, carving into it in some places, but resting nicely in others.

Sorven's wings fanned out. Boq's feathers puffed. Nebens on the other side of the portals stomped in the sand and splashed the water as they watched. The Selts cradled their feeble canines, most too sick to look at what was happening.

Rive clenched his fists. Executing an equation this long was a strain unlike anything he had felt before. His head began to hurt. The metal comforted him. The equation rushed toward completion.

The edges of the mountain range came through. Rive had calculated the exact contours centuries ago, and now the portal matched them precisely.

Rive collapsed to his side. He shuddered as the equation seemed to take on a life of its own, tearing at his mind, clawing its way out and taking everything Rive had to keep it focused and orderly.

In a few more breaths, he had wrapped the mountain range inside a portal. He closed it. The portal snapped shut. The metal mountain range stood in the cavern, reaching hundreds of paces high and several thousand long. The portals throughout the cave system now looked over underground mountain peaks.

Rive rested on the stone as everyone cheered. It began to rain.

4

About two years after we left Earth, James and Beth wanted to have a child. Beth's pregnancy was under lots of supervision. The Selts took personal charge of the humans for this. They studied every aspect. They taught others so next time anyone in the contacted universe could intervene if necessary.

Beth went to Selta to give birth. I think half the contacted universe showed up to witness the first human born offworld. Multiple couples had children after that, and raising a child in this environment was surreal. My only frame of reference was drawings and movies about the Middle Ages, but life isn't like that. Nobody is living in filth, struggling to survive. Why would they; all the basic needs of survival are met, raising children is not a struggle to them, neither was it an obligation.

James liked being a father so much he and Beth started caring for other children of the contacted universe, learning about all the different needs they have. Just recently I saw them with a Yimidrin infant. Birth is quite rare among their kind—the women become aggressive during the mating cycle, but at the same time the men are too big for them, so the entire species usually shies away from heterosexual contact with their own species—so for them to let someone else watch a child is truly a demonstration of trust.

One of the strangest things was watching predator species caring for human babies. Beth could leave her child with anyone from any planet. Herbivores trust their children alone with carnivores, and nobody is hurt. If a child is lost, most people can smell who it belongs to and find them in a crowd. Usually it's not needed. So many children are raised by the entire contacted universe. Makes me wonder what happened to us that we don't do that. In many ways, we used to. Then we let things get too large. The individual mattered less and less. We thought it was progress.

I have lived long enough to meet those children's children. They are with raptors and foxes as well. The raptors are raising the children past the age of six. Their parents are barely involved, fox, human, and raptor alike. I've never seen anything like it before, someone so young somehow disciplining someone else. It's as if the raptors hatch knowing how to be good brothers and sisters, mothers and fathers.

I realized years ago what I was seeing: different species maturing at different rates. Raptors mature much faster than humans, so a six-year-old has the maturity of a thirty-year-old, and yet is still a child. Foxes age at a different rate compared to humans as well. A six-year-old has the mental maturity of a teenager, but the body of a grade-schooler. I did not expect having to unlearn the normal frames of reference regarding age. They do not apply to nonhumans. Though very young, the raptors handled responsibility I would normally have only trusted to someone in their thirties.

I've watched young foxes revert to their old ways, and the raptors know how to bring them back. It isn't something they need to be taught. They do the same thing for the human children, though their old ways are more subtle. I never would have recognized it before, but now it's so obvious. The dominance instinct in particular. The primate drive to keep others down so one can rise to the top. Other primal drives like hoarding and staking territory. The raptors redirected these early and often.

Everything the raptors do for their foxes, they do for their humans as well. Now the children are adults, and I hardly recognize them as human. Really, what is the human race when we are not fighting each other for dominance or struggling to get out of someone else's control? What are we?

I could barely comprehend what I was seeing. Speaking to these young men and women was like speaking to extraterrestrials. I still laugh about that. Relians make sense. The birds of Neben make sense. The snakes and canines of Hithe make sense. But members of my own species? I don't understand them at all, and this is a good thing.

...

I asked Vae what happens if a raptor dies. Who takes care of the fox, and now the human? It is rare, but it can happen, and if it does, there is no shortage of raptors willing to help a lone fox, even if it means hunting for two.

Foxes know who they will get along with by scent. Raptors know this, too, so matches happen automatically. A raptor will do the same for a human, if necessary. So far it hasn't happened, but it might someday, if Vae dies before I do.

Vae is becoming too old to hunt for us. I am not worried. I have seen the elderly in other species. The younger ones allow them to eat from the kills they make. Why not? There is plenty to go around, and the young ones know that will be them someday, so it is important to allow the elderly to eat.

I am approaching the end of my life. So is Vae. So is Tema. I have lived a good, healthy life. I have seen things humans haven't even imagined. I have seen things we have imagined, and they are real. I regret absolutely nothing, and I wish to leave this behind for future generations on Earth to know that we are okay. Humanity lives on, and I have seen a glimpse of what it will become.

The raptors have helped us become better, just as they do for their foxes. The end result, I have to admit, is a good thing. No one is fighting each other. No one is keeping anyone else down. No one is drawing borders and sneering at people on the other side. The raptors know this kind of be-

havior will end up tearing the contacted universe apart if left unchecked.

Vae recognizes it in me, too. Multiple times I wanted to do something, and she nudged me to do something else. I listened because my reward has always been a new species I can live among. A new place I can live. New stories to find. New oceans of information to absorb. I realize I was reverting, so to speak. Humans revert all the time. It's less violent than foxes, but raptors recognize it for what it is. I suppose this means I, too, have become extraterrestrial, and my fellow Earthlings would not recognize me as human either.

5

Boq had filled the caverns with water. As it rose, elections began to flow through the mountain. The Multitude was coming back to life. Rive watched from an oasis on the surface, the same as everyone in the contacted universe.

From the outside, there was no way to tell if they were awake. When the caves had flooded, Rive stood up and walked to the portal Boq had made especially for him. Sorven lay in the sand and watched.

Rive stepped through. The crushing pressure of the water on top of him did not affect his metal at all. The metal over his face stretched to cover his eyes, and he walked blindly up to the mountains. He lay a hand on it. His metal fused with the mountain range. The metal shut him down, promising not to take long.

6

I didn't hear about what happened to Sraad and Heze until we met on Tavax. C-Corn exposure. Rive told everyone what was happening, and he updated me on how it's being used now. It scares me, knowing the planet is being filled with substances that hurt people, but it continues because someone is making money. It was once my job to defend such companies, offering settlements to keep people quiet so nobody would see a bigger picture. I feel bad I was part of it, but I needed money, too, so I never thought of a bigger picture either. That's how money makes the world go 'round. Maybe what I'm writing now will make up for it.

They still have scars from the reaction that stuff gave them. Sraad has red patches of bad scales all over her. Shedding her skin is quite painful now. Heze has areas on her face and arms where fur doesn't grow. Both have breathing problems. It hurts to see. I feel horrible for the people on Earth who will have to live with the consequences of this. I'm sure it will only get worse with time, but stock price will go up, so all is well as far as the big-shots are concerned.

Their human, Jessica, seems to enjoy the impossible places. Places where she can stare at a world's sun and not go blind. Places where there is no solid land but floating islands of squishy plant life. She's been studying the math the Archeons use to describe the motion of the planets and the stars and the atoms and molecules in our bodies. Somehow she swims in this ocean of information, and she understands it. She's no Archeon, but she actually enjoys living in the numbers. Several times she tried to explain to me how you can see the numbers affecting us in everyday life. For a while, I think I understood, too.

...

It took Nipe several years to work through the trauma those bastards on Earth inflicted on her. People forced her to revert by making her fight dogs, all to create a tape of a reverted fox for the press to use to make people afraid of Relians. Since then Nipe has had trouble being around other canines. *She reverted more frequently. Being around human scent sometimes triggered it.*

Ekal deliberately took her to places where lots of canines were around, and Nipe had to exert physical effort to be among them. Gradually she recovered from the experience. She can be around other canines again. She can even be around the scents of other humans without feeling anxious.

Veronica opened up even more after leaving Earth. Fell in love with several people on multiple planets, only one of whom was human. She had a daughter. For the most part, the Relians raised the child. The parents were there, of course. We, the offworld humans, were part of our children's lives, but not to the extent one would expect. The contacted universe raised them. We had to be somewhat distant so we wouldn't raise them in Earth's ways. None of those worked out here.

...

I've asked other raptors and foxes what they thought of Earth. I was beginning to think they disliked being there. That nothing struck them as interesting and they'd only remember what happened to Nipe and that would be their opinion of the human race. Turns out Relians did enjoy some aspects of human cultures.

Our relationships with domestic animals, in particular. Dogs, cats, livestock, horses, snakes, monitor lizards, parakeets, iguanas. Relians who witnessed humans around animals had lots of good things to say. Dogs and cats didn't treat the Relians any different from other humans. That doesn't surprise me.

Beekeeping fascinated them, how mankind figured out how honeybee hives worked before recorded history. Amusing to hear about how they participated.

Martial arts. Several foxes and raptors enjoyed watching it, and they even tried learning. They said it was so interesting to see self-defense without teeth or claws, and to experience it helped them identify with a species that has no such natural weapons. One Relian pair managed to make yellow belt while on Earth. I missed the broadcast of them in a tournament, demonstrating how they adapted the moves to their anatomy. They even sparred with humans, some of whom were black belts. I forget which style. I hear Rive sent them back to Earth for a few weeks to finish a rank. Their green belts are hanging in a cave on Tavax. They still demonstrate.

The USA only saw footage of the reverted fox. I don't think anyone aired the martial arts tournament. Rive showed it to me the other day. I would have paid money to see black belts spar with a raptor and a fox. Or a raptor in custom-made beekeeping clothes.

Wine-making. Spirits. Alcohol in general. It didn't seem to affect Relians, and yet so many of them enjoyed learning about it. One fox earned a Sommelier certificate, and she never tasted anything. Scent alone is all she needed to evaluate wine. Sort of defeated the purpose, but it put the human sense of taste and smell into perspective for everyone around her.

Calligraphy was another standout. Several Relians really liked handwriting as art, since Relian has no written language. Other planets have writing, but it seems human cultures around the world have particularly impressive traditions. I hear there's a growing movement to give Relian an official written language, using various human styles as inspiration.

Was a relief to hear so many cultures on Earth had a positive impact on them. We really are good people. Just a few things holding us back.

7

Rive switched back on. His metal had separated from the mountain range, so now he turned and walked back through the portal. The pressure eased as he exited the cave and stood on the desert sand. His metal uncovered his eyes, and Rive clicked his claws.

"They know everything that happened. They understand. Some wish to remain in the mountain, but some wish to become metal explorers. They will help the Zjr."

As he spoke, parts of the mountain liquefied and broke off. The pieces formed crude limbs and stood at the portals, waiting.

A Selt helped her Zjr to his feet and then walked him to the portal. The closest metal explorer observed. The Zjr only had one working eye, and his spine was so weak he could only hold his head up for a breath before he had to rest it.

He was one of the young ones. The old ones, who had been alive since before Deka, Kylac, and Sonjaa were last seen, were in even worse shape. Rive turned and observed the salvation of two species. He had been alive long enough to watch the Selts struggle to keep the Zjr alive, but disease and genetic drift had finally outpaced even what the Selts could do. The Zjr had been dying for years; the Selts had merely kept them alive long enough for the Multitude to save them.

The Zjr reached out. The metal explorer on the other side of the portal reached through and touched the Zjr's paw. It became liquid and flowed up the Zjr's arm, over his head, and into his body. Rive had given them the biological information on them. They knew what a Zjr was supposed to be and how to correct the defects.

Flesh that could not be saved fell off. The metal ejected bone too weak to keep. Unneeded blood also spilled out as the metal worked through this canine's body. A few breaths later, the Zjr lay still on the ground, what little healthy flesh he had fused to flexible metal. He raised his neck, strong and healthy enough to do so now.

The Selts cheered. The female who had led this male to the portal nuzzled him. He nuzzled her back.

Rive held his claws together. More metal explorers waited by the portal. More Zjr gathered around portals, waiting for salvation.

The metal raptor sat in the sand. Sorven strolled up, lay beside him, lowering his head to be at Rive's eye level.

"Feel better?"

"Yes, so much better, as does the metal."

"It's a bold step they're taking, becoming part of the universe the way your metal did."

"There is so much to experience. Even knowing what the consequences would be, they still want it for themselves."

Sorven's wings wiggled on his back, and he smiled with his mouth. "Sounds familiar."

Rive smiled with his face as well.

"So what will happen to you?" Sorven said. "How long can they keep your brain working?"

Rive looked out over the Zjr as they became metal explorers. Some of the Selts chattered amongst themselves. They grieved how they could no longer save their companion species, but seeing them healthy again made them so happy. The Selts had long ago expanded their medical practices to the entire contacted universe. They had lost their companion species, but now they were free to help others, and the Zjr were free to live as well.

"They have no reason to. I kept my promise. What happens now is extra. Just like you."

Sorven's wings fluttered. "I told you. My body won't let me die until I scratch one last thing off the bucket list."

"I hope I live for that, too." Rive clicked his claws.

Sorven swung his neck over and nuzzled Rive on the cheek. "Haven't seen much of you in a few decades. Where have you been?"

"Brazil. Australia. Multiple places around the contacted universe."

"Harass any members of the Morton family dynasty lately?"

"Not them specifically, but I've appeared in some parlors, mostly just to scare people out of certain choices."

Sorven laughed again, bumped Rive on the flank with his head. "I'm not surprised seeing this mountain range. I'm not surprised the Zjr agreed to become cyborgs. What still surprises me is you as a lady's man and a predator. I remember when you hatched. If you were human, I'd have called you the biggest nerd ever. Now here you are. Indulging a vendetta."

Rive clicked his claws. "It took most of my natural life to discover who I am. I never once thought of Friend as holding me back, but now I understand we held each other back. I didn't want a fox. He didn't want a raptor. But... it's what we had to do. We were both so desperate to try to be what the other needed we became someone else. When I met Crystal... For the first time in my life, I felt something for someone. And when I lost her, I felt something I never imagined being able to experience. Those first decades exploring the emotions of anger. An incredible time. I never desired her physically when she was alive, but after she was gone, it was all I could think about."

"And you haven't stopped since." Sorven leaned close to Rive's ear. "Revenge is the origin of every supervillain, and even a few superheroes. Half of Shakespeare wouldn't exist without it."

Rive shooed him away. He looked up at him, clicking his claws. "All the people responsible for her death are gone. I made their lives hell just keeping her work in circulation."

"You were like Banquo's ghost to the Morton family, if he never left the table. Not to mention the hundred or so others who funded that tape."

"Tracking all of them down and holding them responsible was a satisfying experience unlike any other."

"Watching you become a supervillain was so entertaining. It was like a living comic book."

"A boring one. I never killed a single person."

"Wish I could have participated more. Many days I wish I were human again if only to be part of things like this. But I've settled for influencing it instead. Thank you so much for all you do for the Church. I couldn't have done any of this without you."

"Thank you for introducing me to Earth."

"Your life as a supervillain has plenty of sex to make up for the lack of violence."

Rive rubbed his claws. "With Friend around, I never let myself experience it. I'd been told for so long if I left my fox he might revert, and I was so scared of that I didn't let myself do anything else. Without Relian society... Exploring that side of me has been fascinating. I have enjoyed becoming someone else. Becoming the person I was meant to be. Without a fox. I often wonder who Friend was supposed to be. Without me."

Sorven exposed his teeth in a human-like grin. "I think we met the real Friend many times."

Rive nodded like a human in reply. "All those years we were together, and I never realized it. There were signs. Nothing added up until the end."

"You know, Rive, even before I shared this body with a human mind, I disliked how Archeons insisted they have no subconscious. I always found it arrogant because when it came to the workings of the universe it was true, but somehow they still have a subconscious when it comes to their own ordinary lives. They miss the obvious no matter how aware of reality they are. The Krone did. Relians did. The people of Uiv did. The disaster made them aware of problems they'd been ignoring for a long time."

Rive rubbed his claws. "It has been a privilege, living long enough to witness Relian society changing because of our story."

"The Selts have been caring for the Zjr for so long they assumed they couldn't do anything else. Relian reptiles have been taming their foxes in one specific way for so many generations they never planned for what would happen when foxes were ready for other ways. I'm happy to witness everyone finding new identities. The disasters showed the contacted universe that the species pairing doesn't have to be rigid and permanent."

Rive stood and began walking to the portal that led to Kronia. "I'm going to Japan."

Sorven looked over his shoulder, wings waving. "For what?"

"Sushi. I'm celebrating the end of a multi-century portal calculation."

"By eating plastic-infused, genetically-modified, patented fish at your favorite restaurant?"

"Even better. I'll stop at Palc to catch fish myself and bring them to Earth. I'll give the place something no human alive has ever tasted before and never will again. Something clean and real and not owned by anyone."

"Very good. Give them a truly alien experience."

Rive disappeared through the portal, laughing with his hands and his voice.

Sorven laughed with his wings and his voice as he turned and settled into the sand. He watched the Multitude join the contacted universe, saving the Zjr from extinction and relieving the Selts of the burden of keeping their companion species alive. Their society would never be the same, and the change would be good.

8

Malcolm asked me to tell the world that despite living like a caveman with no obvious comforts, this life has been better than he ever imagined. He observed most of the comforts of home were meant to distract us so we believed our lives are happy and we would keep working.

He, Ratash and Irus have been together as long as I've been with my raptor and fox, as if they were made for each other. Malcolm speaks six languages and is proficient at another dozen or so. Without all the distractions, he remembers more. He learned more in one year out in the contacted universe than he learned in twelve years of school. It's so much different when the ocean of popular culture isn't just fluff.

Malcolm told me there was once a time when he was happy doing factory work fifty to sixty hours a week. That he heard about office jobs and he was proud to have avoided sitting at a desk all day dealing with gossip and carpal tunnel syndrome. Now he can't remember why he thought that. In his own words, "the thing to be proud of was no work at all. I didn't see that until it become an option."

That is the point of living now. To experience things. To get out and live. Malcolm did. He's practically a comparative historian now. He knows so much about the history of other planets. He's probably up to all of them by now. Every single world in the contacted universe, even the worlds that were lost in the disasters. He can recite them, draw parallels. He wanted to know them, and it became his life's goal. From what he told me of growing up, school robbed him of learning as a source of joy. He found it again offworld.

I watched Irus revert once. It happened for no apparent reason. First thing he did after Ratash brought him back was fuck Malcolm. It was surreal. After spending time with my own fox, I've come to appreciate what they go through. Animal impulses just under the surface, threatening to break through at any moment. It's not something they can simply resist or ignore. It's different for them. It took me a lifetime to understand how.

You would think people as sexually obsessed as those three that's all they would have room in their brains for. Old stereotype, I suppose. Ratash has become a physician. All his knowledge of mammal anatomy had to be of use somehow. Everyone learns medicine to some extent, thanks to those oceans of culture that are useful instead of distracting, but Ratash in particular took to it. People call him a reptile Selt, and they have been on that world for quite a while, learning about anatomy and disease and other things that affect other species. I'm told the Selts never used to share this knowledge, keeping it for the Zjr, but since the disaster they have opened up.

Ratash can take a Yimidrin all the way to the hilt. I've seen him do it. Sometimes he draws a crowd. Everyone else is scared of them, as they hang down to their ankles, but Ratash is quite popular on that world. He has my respect, certainly.

Irus and Tema got close. So close the six of us got together and we liked the idea of raising a fox child. Irus became a father, and Tema had a daughter.

Watching Irus around his daughter was like watching someone else switch on. After seeing him panic when other scents were nearby, watching him become attentive and doting made me smile. Foxes can smell paternity, and they have an instinct to be close to their pregnant mates and children until grown, and then scent anxiety takes over again and everyone separates. Nobody has to do that anymore. We've stayed in touch since Tema's daughter found a raptor and the contacted universe raised them the rest of the way.

I like Malcolm. He enjoyed helping raise Irus's daughter while we were together. Watching his raptor cuddle-fuck him times a day is always fun. They're old men now and they're still going. He didn't teach any aliens how to love. They already knew that. They had to teach him.

9

I am now seventy-four years old, according to Rive and Sorven. I have not been sick since I left Earth. I have not lost any sleep. I have never been hungry or cold. I've been uncomfortable and I've hurt myself, but in terms of what we think of as a side-effect of aging, I've experienced none of it. It's not true what we've been told, that as the body ages, we just have to live with more and more pain and it never stops.

Pain is caused by us doing things over long periods of time the body was not supposed to do. The stress of keeping up makes us more vulnerable to disease. It changes our body chemistry, which means things break down faster. Age does change the body, but not like it does on Earth.

I am healthy. So are Vae and Tema. We have been together this whole time, and I still marvel that I have never become tired of their company. There are places I have not been. Things to do. People to meet. Oceans of culture to swim in. Senses I don't have to experience. I became an artist, creating scent sculptures, texture sculptures, electromagnetic statues, trying to experience senses and perspectives I do not have. I wouldn't trade any of this for life on a couch watching movies wishing I could be Indiana Jones fighting Nazis, or Ripley battling aliens.

I have heard that after I left, people mourned us for giving up our freedom. My raptor has kept me free all this time. She has pushed me to do things I otherwise would not have. She has kept me from doing things I should not. I lost way more freedom at my job every day. I thought I was free until

I met Vae and Tema. I thought I was free until I left Earth. If I could talk to God and make one request, it would be for everyone on the planet to be rescued.

But it's not that simple. Humans need help. Step one is admitting we have something inside us that needs taming. Everyone in the contacted universe does. They have a companion race to help them see it. That's the real rescue.

10

Sheryl closed the book and reclined in her chair. Sorven lay in his usual place watching the monitors. Dozens of Krone throughout the library were doing the same thing, observing just as many nations.

She thought about the archive footage of Rive speaking to senator Sattle shortly after the Relians left Earth with their humans. Aliens told humanity exactly what was wrong, and nobody listened. The result has been giant corporations releasing propaganda telling the people going to work is a virtue and it is freedom.

It was dominance. An out of control animal impulse to reproduce. Nothing more.

A few individuals left Earth, their animal nature had been tamed, and the result was peace.

Could it be scaled up to include everyone on Earth?

Sheryl concluded it was not possible. Scaling everything up was the reason Earth was in such shape.

The first step was to convince the people there was a problem in the first place. The individuals who first left Earth understood. Convincing the entire planet was an entirely different dilemma.

She smiled as she pondered things looked hopeless, but eventually the people's minds could be changed. The animal nature that was pushing humans to do this to others could be diverted into something beneficial. First humanity as a whole had to understand itself from an outside point of view. It had to see itself as creatures acting on animal impulses that needed to be tamed if it hoped to progress beyond these impulses.

She could see it now, the direction the Krone wanted to take everyone. It would happen. Eventually, humanity would understand.

Sheryl picked up a notebook and began writing.

Left Landing

I

"So..." Left Sonjaa muttered. "Are you ready?"

A tiny voice in her head, audible as if she spoke the words herself, answered. *I'm on Tumelo. Nobody else is around.*

"It's been so long since we could share a moment like this."

Far too long.

"We need to do it more often. Why can't we make quiet moments more often so we can be together?"

You're a Left. I'm a Right. We're not supposed to agree on anything.

"I wish we would."

She sat on the edge of a cliff along with thirty-four other Ekesta and more than sixty offworlders. She looked down on the clouds and waited for the Atokos, sparing a moment to admire the planet in the sky.

Do you see them? said her Right half.

"They haven't shown up yet."

Soon. Are you sure you can send me clearer images? You've been telling me about them so long I feel like I've already seen them. It still makes me wonder why they can fly but you can't.

"My species traded flight for articulate fingers."

Other species fly and they have fingers. Why don't you?

Left Sonjaa laughed. "Well I didn't pick how I evolved."

Sonjaa's Right half was a quadruped, a mammal, and knowing her Left half was a flightless bird fascinated her. Left Sonjaa sent her some direct images of the Atokos, trying to be as vivid as possible; by the time the images reached her other half, they would be faded, but she had been experimenting with techniques to concentrate and send clearer images. She wanted to try something she had only ever done accidentally before. Left Sonjaa believed she could duplicate those moments at will. Tonight was the test.

If I could fly, I would join the Atokos and shape the clouds! Everyone would admire me!

"Except the Atokos. They wouldn't know what to do with you."

They would try to outsculpt me!

Sonjaa opened her mouth, but the first Atoko ascended through the clouds and flapped in place, interrupting her thought. These lizards were fifty times her size. Their wings were in tatters, yet they still flew. Their bones grew outside their bodies, holding their skin and muscles in place from the outside.

"I see one. A male. White and green scales, and his bones are bright yellow." She sent her moving images.

Oh, I can see that! You're right; it's so much clearer in motion.

"A few females have flown up from the surface. They're waiting for him. He just flew to a cloud bank and... He's circling it. He's pushing the air inward. The cloud is puckering inward. He's made a spiral out of it."

The crowd of onlookers cheered. The Atoko did not regard them. These creatures were animals, and their courtship ritual was so touching people came to watch from planets all over the contacted universe.

"Several males are now here. Even more females. The males have chosen one cloud each. One is circling his. Another cut his in half and is flying between and around the halves. Another... He... He's shaped the cloud into a globe. More males have flown in. One with green bones. White bones. Orange and white. More females, too. Everyone has taken a part of the sky. The other males saw the sphere and they're trying to make their own. White bones is... He's making two at once. The way he has to fly to make it happen. It's adorable. Spheres. Everyone's trying to make them. Red bones has three of them going at once."

Sonjaa laughed.

"One male made a crude cube. Now everyone wants to do better. One is flapping in place as hard as he can, pushing the air hard against one side of the cloud. He flew to the other side and pushed it together. They're flying so fast to keep up. They finish one side, the other sides begin spreading out. Are you seeing all of this? I'm projecting as hard as I can."

Yes, I can see it. How can something so big be so nimble?

"She's... She's flying towards... The red one. He made three globes. Oh, look at them. They locked talons. They're flying together! No, don't go below the clouds, oh!"

He must have been good at spheres.

"Three at once and spaced evenly apart. The lead female chose him. Another made a choice. She picked the one with blue bones. They're flying together. They went below the clouds. A few more males appeared. They're shaping the clouds again. Some are still trying to make cubes. Most are still struggling to hold them together. Yellow bones has made one. It's about as perfect as he can... Someone is flying towards him." Left Sonjaa laughed. "The females are fighting over him! They really want this one. The dominant one had to shove the others under the clouds to remind them of their place. She's now flying up to yellow bones. They locked talons. They're falling through the clouds."

Go, yellow!

"I'd go with anyone who could make a cube out of clouds."

That explains your last affair.

Sonjaa laughed. "His voice just happened to match the mating call of my race. I couldn't stop myself. You'd do the same."

Probably.

Sonjaa looked away from the cloudline and up into the sky. She felt her Right half somewhere among those stars. As many planets as they had been to in the contacted universe, they had yet to meet. Right Sonjaa often wondered if there was more than one portal network. There had to be; the universe was larger than a single galactic cluster, so Right Sonjaa could easily be hundreds of galaxies away—an unthinkable distance. Finding one's other half was a theme that occupied many stories and songs. For most, it was an impossible goal, but there were tales of people succeeding.

She turned back to the flying reptiles.

"One group has moved on from spheres. Now they're competing to make the best straight line. Five new males are here. One new female. They still seem determined to make cubes... One of the new males isn't in on the trend. He's trying to sculpt the clouds into uniform waves. Black bones is trying to take two straight lines and twist them into one another.

I want him.

"So do I, if he succeeds. On second thought... I think I'll take green bones. He broke away and just made a cone out of his clouds. Black bones just took two straight pieces of cloud he sculpted and twisted them together. Order is gone! They're fighting over this one!"

The female Atokos had the same color bones, so they were much harder to tell apart and Left Sonjaa lost track of the action for a while. Finally they settled again, and the courtship display continued.

The Atokos recreated all the basic shapes. Sometimes they showed their prowess in flight by sculpting recognizable things that existed on the ground, like trees and certain rock formations. Sometimes they sculpted other animals.

Her Right side marveled at the moving images she was receiving. Several times she said they were still faint, but the movement helped fill in the gaps.

Left Sonjaa wondered if the animals had other halves as well, and how they dealt with them. What was it like for the animals to have a counterpart elsewhere in the universe, constantly aware of what they said, sensations and memories occasionally passing between them. She presumed it was no different from how conscious beings handled it, but she often wondered if they were confused, hearing voices that came from nowhere. The Ekest did not figure out what was happening until they discovered portal physics. Knowing there was an entire universe out there meant only one thing: everyone possessed pieces of quantum particles that linked them with another being no matter where they were.

Left and Right felt a compulsion to meet. Always a tugging, a yearning to go out and find one's other half. Left Sonjaa thought about that as she listened to her other half marvel at what she was seeing. The courtship continued until night fell, and then everyone fell asleep. Sonjaa remembered the ones who had chosen mates would stay together until the eggs hatched and then they would meet again for another contest of cloud-shaping, though pairs who had mated the previous season were far more likely to choose one another again, provided his cloud-sculpting skills were still up to her standards.

The daytime star set. Now paired off for the mating season, the giant reptiles descended below the clouds. The crowd of offworlders filed toward the portal that led back to the hub.

That was wonderful. Moving images are so much easier to see than still ones. I'll have to show you a few places next.

Left Sonjaa suddenly couldn't stand being apart from her Right half. Though she could hear her counterpart no matter where she was, tonight the thought of allowing the usual chatter of daily life to come between them would only increase the distance from each other. This was the closest she had ever felt to her other half. She wished she had an idea where she could be. If there was a second contacted universe, there had to be a third and a fourth. Would it ever be possible to find each other?

"I'm hungry. I can send you images of that next."

I can't stay here all night. I have people who are expecting me.

Her Right half had always been more flighty. "Please. We don't have to end this now."

Silence for several degrees. Finally her other half answered.

All right. I'll wait a little longer.

"I'll go to Medel! Very good nuts there! I know just what I want to share with you!"

Her Right half was a carnivore, so the idea of eating nuts and fruit fascinated her. Left Sonjaa had sent her images of it before, but only recently did she have a good grasp on how to send moving images and sounds to her counterpart. She hoped to try taste sensations this time.

She stepped through the way to the hub and scanned the portals. She found the sphere and began walking through the crowd. She passed dozens of people walking on two legs, four, six, three, and some had no legs at all but slithered along the ground. Everyone's attention focused inward. They looked ahead, but not at anyone while they spoke to their own counterparts elsewhere in the universe. Occasionally they addressed someone here, but attention was always diverted to the voice in their mind.

Left Sonjaa walked through the portal to Medel and emerged in a tropical climate.

"I see a tree. There's a nut about a quarter of the way up. I'm going for it."

The people of Medel were mammals who climbed the trees for these same nuts. Sonjaa's wings ended in articulate fingers instead of feathers, making her suited to climb the trees as well. This adaptation had grounded her species, and sometimes she resented being a flightless bird, but that nut the size of her head hanging from the tree looked tasty.

She began climbing. As she did, she focused her mind and sent the images across the quantum connection to her Right side. She grabbed branches with her feathered fingers and pulled herself up the trunk.

I can see the branches! I can feel my hands holding the branches!

It was working better than Left Sonjaa expected.

How are you doing this? How do I send feelings this strong?

Left Sonjaa's talons wrapped around the branches easily. They were a leftover from when her kind had lived in the trees. Now they functioned flat for walking on the ground. Her body had a compact, almost theropod stature. Most species evolved from reptiles into avians, but her species went the other way. People in the contacted universe often commented that in a few hundred generations, Ekesta would lose their feathers and become full reptiles if they continued to live like this. Sonjaa liked the idea.

She reached up and twisted the nut free, dropping it to the ground. Sonjaa spread her arms and jumped. Her wings would not let her take flight but they did slow her fall, so she landed gently beside it.

Left Sonjaa covered her nut with a wing, felt its surface with her fingers. Her beak was designed to crack open the hard shells. In fact, her species' beak was the strongest in the contacted universe. She could break the bones of an Atoko if she wanted. Breaking things with her beak was a source of pleasure for her, and it was one reason the Ekesta traveled the contacted universe, always in search of tough nuts or fruit to crack. Everything in her wanted to break it open, but she waited to hear if these sensations were reaching her counterpart.

I feel like I'm behind your eyes and in your hands. I want you to feel how I hunt, too. Can you teach me how you're doing this?

"I don't know if I can. A few days ago I just started doing it. I twist the sensations up as tight as I can and send them to you."

I wish I could do this for you, too!

Left Sonjaa opened her beak and clamped down on the nut. Her jaw muscles flexed, puckered out as they worked hard. She felt a crack. Feeling something crack in her beak always felt good. She squeezed harder. The nut shattered, and the meat spilled into her mouth.

Mmmmmmm...

She dug into the center and devoured the fleshy pulp. She wished her Right side could send equally strong signals. She desperately searched for a way to explain how she was doing this. It happened in flashes frequently when they were young, but now Left Sonjaa confirmed she could do it deliberately.

When she had eaten her fill, she relaxed and roosted a few steps away.

That was satisfying.

"We should work on this while you're alone. Concentrate. Take your senses and twist them in your mind. Send them to me. Find something to eat or touch and force it through."

I don't know what you mean.

"Take me on a hunt! Sometimes I can feel what you're doing when you're hunting something. If we figure out which parts come through on their own, maybe you can grip how to control it."

Silence for a while. Left Sonjaa's stomach growled. She stood and found a small rock and swallowed it. The impulse satisfied, she began walking back to the hub.

I can't. I promised Holo I would meet his family today. They just molted, so now is the time.

Left expected it. Every time she felt like she had caught her Right half, she slipped away. Her other half was a mammal who seemed to want to fly more than Left Sonjaa did.

I'm up here. ... No, I'm alone. ... Quality time with my other half. ... I know, but she insists on sharing moments like these. You should try it sometime. Take some time to be alone with your Left. ... I know that, but it's so much different when you do the same things together at the same time, eat at the same time. It really does feel like she's there.

Her Right half was talking to someone else, wherever she was. Sonjaa listened. Every person had this going on all the time. Most of the day, they tuned it out and went on with their separate lives. Sometimes voice didn't transmit at all, but most of the time everyone was privy to whatever their other half said.

Everyone had many close friends here on the Left side, but their relationship to their counterpart was far more intimate. Sonjaa long had the feeling that her intimacy with her Right side was stronger than most, crossing the line to outright yearning to be with her. The urge had only strengthened with age.

She picked up on the sleepiness coming from her Right side. Sonjaa settled onto the branch and closed her eyes.

2

It happened every time two Ekesta met on a planet. They always stayed together, and this attracted others and still others until finally a flock had gathered. The vestigial behavior was a leftover from the days when they migrated to escape winters.

Left Sonjaa sat in a tree gnawing on a seed casing. It split with great effort. The shell pieces fell to the ground, and she chewed the meat. Twenty other Ekesta sat in adjacent branches and trees, also gnawing on seeds.

"I feel the water," said someone above her. "It's cold. How can you like cold water? ... I'm eating something, and I think it wakes me up just fine."

A male in the next tree also spoke. "I don't like him. She doesn't sound like a good match for you. ... I don't care how preened she is."

Everyone around her was speaking to their other half. Sonjaa listened to hers. Right Sonjaa was not a member of a herd species, but her kind did form close bonds with individuals. Holo's parents were here.

Hi, it's so good to meet you at last! ... We've been together for almost a year. We didn't want to tell you in case we changed our minds. ... I wasn't here yesterday because my other half wanted to watch the Atoko with me.

Left Sonjaa could not hear what her Right half was hearing. The signals were not strong enough. She wanted to listen. She wanted to feel where Right Sonjaa was standing. She remembered growing up with that voice in her mind. Left Sonjaa remembered comforting her during storms on her world. Ekesta still hid from the rain, even when a portal was nearby. Storms were the worst. Thanks to her other half, Left Sonjaa learned how to ignore the instinct to huddle under leaves and wait for the rain to pass.

Offworlders walked underneath her as she chewed the meat of the seed.

Right Sonjaa did not seem to share Left's eagerness to be intimate. All Left wanted to do was share sensations, but Right had been courting a male named Holo for a long time, and now Left listened to everything she told his parents.

She had never heard Holo's voice, only what her other half said to him. She had felt how he made her feel, and Sonjaa wished to feel that for herself, but she had yet to find anyone. She often wondered if her Right half had received the urge to take a partner and bear young, leaving the Left half forever alone with a yearning she could never satisfy.

An opaque sphere opened on top of the head of the avian in the next tree. A moment later, the sphere closed, and the Ekest fell off the branch, blood spraying from the neck. Blood dripped from the next branch up, then a headless Ekest dropped to the ground.

Left Sonjaa heard screaming inside her skull, and the voice did not match her Right half. This voice sounded male, and it was not howling in pain. She felt lightheaded, and then a moment later she was falling. At first she thought she was falling to the ground, but then she realized there did not seem to be a ground. Her perception of reality faded, and now she felt voices around her. She felt jostling around her. The voices were not heard so much as felt, unable to reach out, unable to touch anything, unable to stop themselves from spreading out.

She felt it, too. Spreading, her sense of self fading.

Then she felt screaming coming from within. This voice was familiar. It was her Right half. Sonjaa pulled herself toward the feeling, following the yearning and grief. She wasn't certain how she moved herself about now. This felt familiar, like the dreams she had had all her life about being in some strange place she could not see but somehow still sensed.

She moved against the flow of the particles. She dodged particles that bounced off some sort of barrier. Through that barrier, she felt Right Sonjaa. She reached into the barrier. It resisted her. Knowledge seemed to come to her: she could not enter this place without a physical body, so she would have to gather particles. Suddenly she became aware of trillions of unused molecules, already assembled and ready, that she could use. She would only need a body for a moment.

She found the echoes of her old body, including her head, which had only been transported a pace away. She sent it to where the screaming was coming from, reattaching the head, not enough to survive for longer than a few breaths, but that was all she needed.

She saw again. She saw the real world. Her senses returned to her, and she saw a quadruped with both feathers and fur. The fur formed the main covering of the body, and the feathers curved through it like rivers carving her over and around.

"Right?" she croaked.

"Left?"

Just as Left hoped she would do, Right Sonjaa bounded to her and placed a paw on her face. As soon as Right atoms touched Left, they slid into one another. Left Sonjaa reached out to her counterpart. Right reached back. When fur touched feather, they were pulled into one another, molecules merging as everything else faded away.

3

Sonjaa lay on a smooth surface. Her body did not feel like her own, but her mind did. She gasped and leaped to her feet as she looked down her flanks and chest. She was a raptor. A Relian reptile.

Beneath her feet was a translucent plane resembling glass. It felt solid, but the texture did not match its appearance. She rubbed a foot back and forth. It was not slippery.

Blackness filled the sky. The faded image of a planet took up half the horizon. Within this planet danced an infinite amount of movement. It took Sonjaa a moment to realize she was watching the inhabitants. More than that: she was watching the molecules that comprised the planet. She focused on one particular area, at the vast collections of atoms surrounding an empty space where Sonjaa had been, telling their other halves what had happened and that it was all true: when Left and Right meet, it creates a whole new person, and they ascend to a higher plane. An Archeon happened to be in the vicinity when the merging took place, and she confirmed it. All of it. She had been aware of Left and Right atoms merging, and now to conserve mass and energy the resulting particles entered a new plane of existence.

Sonjaa rolled to her feet and took a step. The planet vanished from view. Her heart stopped and she held her breath. Her Archeon senses told her she had just moved three light years away. She took a step back, and the planet came into view. She listened to that Archeon speak, but she did not say anything else Sonjaa hadn't already heard from her time in this universe.

She took two steps, moving two light years distant from the planet. Blackness surrounded her. Only the flat sheet of glass separated her from it and created a horizon. It appeared dimly lit, as well as her body, with no obvious light source.

Shaking, Sonjaa knelt and held her head between her hands. Her memories of this universe extended forty years. The first thing she remembered actually happening to her occurred nineteen years ago.

"Nineteen years," she whispered.

Her Archeon senses told her she was not really speaking. Blackness did not surround her. She was not a Relian reptile. Her mind had projected a familiar reality on top of wherever she was. She did not know how to comprehend it, so this is how she perceived it.

"Nineteen years."

Their retroactive history creating a place for themselves in society had been so good she had believed it, and she had been living it this whole time, without Friend, or Deka and Kylac. Sonjaa shivered at the thought of losing so much time. She turned and looked at the spot she had to stand for the planet to be in view again. Surrounded by blackness made her cringe; if she left this spot, there might be nothing else out there, and then she could be lost forever.

She did not seem to be hungry, and though she was inhaling, she took in no air. Air did not exist here. The senses did not exist here. Everything she felt was projection. She dreaded to know what was happening. Her Archeon sense of reality told her this place was pulsing and shattering. Her mind comprehended the sounds of the universe as something breaking, but she could not tell what was broken.

Sonjaa took another look at the spot she had to be. Hoping distance remained consistent here, she stood up and marched six steps in no particular direction. She moved half a light year away with one step, two light years with the next, five hundred paces with the next, and the next three took her to a different galaxy with each one.

Sonjaa backed up those same six steps and then the two previous. The planet came into view again, along with the comforting feeling of familiar activity. Reassured this place behaved consistently and she could return to this spot whenever she wished, she picked another direction.

Stars flew by as she walked, giving off light and heat. One red star filled the entire horizon, even visible through the ground. She had never seen a star up close like this without being blinded or fearing radiation. She watched it swirl and churn for a moment, wishing to see it smaller. As she thought it, the star shrank until it was the size of her head. She blinked. The star rotated and flickered, flinging off a wave of plasma. She wanted to see inside it. The star moved toward her and expanded, swallowing her. Now she watched the atoms dance inside. She was aware of the heat and radiation, but none of it actually touched her. She felt warm. She felt light. Projecting these feelings onto the star kept her grounded.

Stepping away, the red star vanished, replaced by a field of white stars. She comprehended the inside of a neb-ula, and she watched hydrogen and helium collect into clumps. She reached out and tried to touch them, but her atoms passed right through, which sounded bizarre to her Archeon sense of the universe. She was in a Right section of the galaxy. Nothing but Right atoms. Leftright atoms did not affect Left or Right atoms by themselves.

Her straight-line march across the glass plane took her in a twisting, broken path around the universe. Still the molecules and atoms popped and crackled from every-where along the glass.

She paused at a solar system. Remaining still on the glass plane, she moved her mind around the system and found each planet. Several gas giants, some asteroids. No life.

She walked away from this system and ended up thirty light years distant. Sonjaa had yet to discern a pattern for navigating like this. She was vaguely aware that she was not really a physical person here but a collection of Leftright particles roaming the universe. Her particles sounded strange compared to Left or Right alone, but she could not place why. Somehow her particles held together without needing a rigid structure.

Sonjaa wandered, seeing lots and lots of empty space. Gradually she realized she was seeing less of it, and every step seemed to take her to a planet, or a star, or something that filled the blackness around her.

She understood her mind was filtering out the emptiness. Somehow she had learned not to leap to empty areas with each step but to seek out only the strong gravity wells. She wasn't used to doing something subconsciously.

One step: a planet filled the horizon.

Next step: another planet half a light year away

Next step: a black hole at the center of that galaxy. Sonjaa was tempted to peek inside, but she thought better of it and stepped away.

Her very next step showed her a nebula. She sat down and observed, remembering her time in the Lake during the disasters, watching Deka and Kylac on their private world, trying to go down and meet them but unable to break through, and meanwhile the sights and sounds and actions of every person in the universe flowed into her mind. It had taken all her strength to remember who she was. Now here she was again, better prepared for it this time.

"Friend," she said. "He killed me. He reverted. He's killing people right now."

She remembered where she had been killed. Her mind had taken in enough of this plane to get a sense of its shape.

Order had begun to emerge out of the chaos in her movement, and she had built a partial map of most of the universe this way. She thought she knew how to return to the spot where her Left side had died. She picked a direction and began running. Planets and galaxies and stars and black holes and asteroids sped around her. She took in the activities of trillions of atoms on them, millions of people both part of a contacted universe as well as lone species.

This reality had six separate contacted universes in six separate areas of spacetime, three Right, three Left. The universe had room for hundreds of additional portal networks, and if they ever met...

Sonjaa turned, following spacetime in this new way. Her movements around reality were not random at all, and she turned and began to run, passing hundreds of worlds.

She slowed to a stop as a green planet filled the sky, and the activity of the atoms made her hands sag. Only one sentient life form existed on this planet, and he sat in the middle of an ocean of blood he himself had made after exterminating the life. Sonjaa sank to her knees, shaking in grief and rage. She pulled in with her mind, and Left Friend sat before her, clutching his skull. He wasn't a canine here, but a marsupial resembling an opossum on Earth.

"Friend," She reached out to him, tried to touch him. Her claws passed through him.

Friend gasped and began pacing, feet splashing in the blood. Sonjaa recognized the body language. He was so far gone he had forgotten how to speak. He only comprehended scents, and he had just calmed the urge.

Sonjaa wanted to embrace him. She had been living alone for nineteen years, her Right half the only company she ever wanted. She had forgotten all about Friend. Her fox was suffering, and she could not reach him.

They had helped so many realities find balance again. Friend had shown great progress. If he figured out the laws of a universe first, he restrained himself until Sonjaa caught up. If Sonjaa figured it out first, he gladly let her contain him so he could direct his rage away from the people and toward the imbalance in the universe. Changing the equation in a way that allowed people to leave it later calmed Friend's instincts, and Sonjaa had helped him create this connection.

It had been every bit as satisfying as growing up with Rupi. Her fox needed a raptor's help badly. Whenever her fox had reverted, Sonjaa guided her fox and prevented her from falling into that chasm of scent anxiety, so watching Friend go from trying to destroy every scent he could reach with a portal to using his mind to set the universe on a better course had filled her with joy.

Now Friend was pacing in an ocean of blood, still reaching out with his mind, scenting distance expanding with his understanding of the equation. Eventually he would reach other planets and begin exterminating them.

She tried to touch him again, but she only passed through. Sonjaa clawed the air, hitting the glass ground. Her fox needed her, but she could not help. She did not feel exhausted or out of breath, but she paused, bent at the knees and eye level with the pacing opossum.

She rolled over and lay on the glass. All her efforts to help her fox, all the work she had done, the relationship they had forged all these years... Nothing had worked. Friend was exterminating another planet, pacing in rage at the scents in his territory.

Sonjaa wanted to cry for the loss of life—she was angry at Friend for taking his anxiety out on people again—she hated herself for failing to be a better raptor for her fox— she wanted to reach him desperately and keep him from harming anyone else ever again.

The emotions mixed into a single roar as she jumped to her feet and ran away. More galaxies and planets and stars flew by. Sonjaa's map of the universe became more complete. She did not feel physically tired, but when the feeling passed, she slid to a stop and slashed her claws at a black hole consuming a neutron star within a nebula. The entire universe at her clawtips and she couldn't touch any of it.

More shattering sounds around her. They seemed louder than before. Less like shattering and more like repeated noises. She began to discern patterns in the noise. It was coming from the glass itself.

She stood. She heard footsteps behind her, and she turned. She saw nothing, but something was definitely standing five paces away.

"Who are you?"

A disembodied voice answered her. "Good, you can sense me now. You are progressing very fast. I've been watching you since you arrived. My name is Lio. I saw your Left and Right halves meet. I'm an Archeon."

Sonjaa looked around. "You... I heard you talking to people about how we arrive at a higher plane when Left and Right merge."

"We are slowly teaching people about it. Archeons have an easier time finding their other halves than others of course, though not everyone does. Often there is no way to find each other, even being mentally linked on a quantum level. I found my other half over two centuries ago."

"Then... Then how were you there? How did the people see you?"

"It is an advanced technique. Those of us who have found our other halves can split them again whenever we choose. I go back from time to time. Can you see me yet?"

"No."

"It will come in time. Are you an Archeon or an apprentice?"

Sonjaa did not know which story to tell Lio. She thought for a moment before deciding to be completely truthful. "My name is Sonjaa. I am an Archeon, but I didn't have any ways yet. I was only just beginning. Is anyone else here?"

"Oh, people surround you. There are millions of us here. Distance does not work the same in the Leftright plane as it does elsewhere. You just haven't learned how to perceive us yet."

Sonjaa swallowed, held her hands apart, curled her neck, a submissive posture. "I need help. Something bad is happening. There's a f— Someone is out there. He's reverted to what we call the old ways. His species goes into a panic when scents are nearby, and he will not stop until everything around him is either dead or wounded. Both halves might be killing people with portals, and when he becomes aware of how this universe works, he will kill everyone. Can you help me reach him?"

The voice was silent for a few beats.

"Lio?"

Only the gently rotating proto-stars answered her.

"Lio!"

Moments later, Sonjaa felt a presence next to her. "Sorry. I just asked around. Follow me."

Sonjaa felt the presence moving away. She followed in its wake. It made no audible sounds, and Sonjaa tried to force it to make footsteps, or a trail in the glass plane, but neither worked.

Planets and moons and stars and colliding galaxies passed by. A few of them were inhabited, and in brief flashes she saw what everyone on that planet was doing. Inhabited worlds passed by so fast Sonjaa only caught a glimpse of everything going on. A green and blue planet came into view. It had one continent in the middle of its vast ocean. Sonjaa comprehended only a single sentient life form, and her hands sagged in grief.

She saw Right Friend. He had a body that looked like a cross between a rodent and canine. He, too, paced and snarled in all directions. A view of a second planet appeared, and she saw Left Friend superimposed onto the landscape right next to his Left counterpart. A single mind shared between two bodies eighty-five million light years apart.

Sonjaa felt Lio's presence next to her. "You know this person?"

She stared at both halves of Friend. "He is my fox."

"What?"

"My fox. Left Friend killed me, but I found my other half and brought myself back to meet her."

"I don't—"

Sonjaa turned to the direction the voice was coming from. "I don't have enough time to explain! I'm the only one who can stop him from doing this to other planets! He will find a way off those worlds, and if they meet, they will come here and kill us all!"

Stunned silence. The creatures projected on the planets paced back and forth, growling in their own ways.

"Where am I?" Sonjaa shouted. "How does the universe work?"

No reply for several breaths. Sonjaa growled and stabbed the glass plane with her killing claw.

"The universe! How does it work? I need to figure it out before he does more damage!"

"I don't understand what you're asking," Lio said.

Sonjaa stabbed the ground again. She wondered what it really looked like to them, what her molecules were doing. "The universe has a sound! Right now all the pieces are screaming at me. Something sounds broken. How do they fit together?"

She felt a change with Right Friend. The rodent-canine was no longer projected on the planet. Only nonsentient life forms lived on it now. Lio's voice became panicked.

"How did he—? Where did he go? Sonjaa, what's happening? Everyone is looking for him!"

"There's nothing you can do to stop him! Help me figure this place out!"

"Please help me understand what you mean."

Sonjaa growled at herself. "There are two others who are like me. Deka and Kylac. Do those names mean anything to anyone?"

Silence for a moment. Then Lio spoke again. "Nobody has heard those names."

Sonjaa calmed her breathing. "It's all right. It's all right. Maybe they don't call themselves by those names here. Maybe nobody's met them. Maybe Kylac hasn't reverted. All right. Let me think."

"Sonjaa, I must help the others find this person. We can warn others to evacuate the worlds he goes to, if they're contacted."

"No, please stay and help me. Tell me about this place. The faster I understand where I am, the sooner I can stop him."

Silence again.

"Lio, trust me, I am the only one who can! Where am I? What happened to me?"

The two planets moved away. Sonjaa had the feeling she was being led somewhere.

4

"This region consists entirely of Right atoms. Each one of them has a Left counterpart somewhere else in the universe. They affect one another in subtle ways no matter the distance. Eventually they will meet—all the particles in the universe will find their counterparts eventually."

"How many of you are there?" Sonjaa asked.

"About three hundred billion of us are here in total. Some of us are over six billion years old. I'm one of the youngest, at just a couple centuries."

"Hundred billion... Where is here?"

"When Left and Right meet, they go to the next plane. That's where we are now. We are free to go anywhere we want, but we cannot affect anything in the previous plane. Only by separating our Left and Right particles again can we return and influence it."

"And... And what do you do here?"

"We explore the universe at the subatomic level."

Sonjaa blinked, again wondering how it looked to Lio.

"That is, more or less, where you are right now. You exist among the quarks and electrons. Your atoms are actually spread out across millions of light years right now, all connected through entanglement. Here, we need no food or water or external energy to keep us alive."

"How? What is keeping my particles together? How am I still conscious?"

"We're not sure."

"It takes energy to keep atoms together. The energy has to come from somewhere."

"It is one of the questions we still probe. You haven't learned how to comprehend this place as it truly is yet, but when you do, you will understand better. Mostly, however, we simply enjoy existing."

"But..."

Sonjaa looked up at the image of her childhood home-world. She hadn't really been there as a hatchling, but she still had a lifetime's worth of memories of that place and thus felt a twinge of nostalgia for it. The planet Ekest was a world of blue soil and green oceans. She was aware of every person on it, every atom vibrating.

"When I was a child," Sonjaa said, "it was mostly a rumor. Why don't you go down there and teach people about this place? Why aren't you guiding Left and Right together?"

"There are still many, many species who cannot handle it. Some of them are even contacted. When the paradigm shifts and everyone is capable of understanding this, they will be ready to join us. Otherwise, we would have a lot of panicked people here. People who cannot die. Cannot be isolated. Cannot be silenced. Again, you aren't aware of all the people around you right now. It can be overwhelming for someone who isn't an Archeon. Sometimes it's overwhelming for those who have been trained."

"So you're waiting for the universe to mature to where most everyone is a capable Archeon."

"It will happen on its own, when they're ready. Most of the Archeons in the contacted universe find their way here eventually. I can tell you still view your surroundings in familiar terms. How does it appear to you?"

"A flat sheet of glass extending into infinity. The sky is black. Things fill the sky when I walk."

"You are capable of understanding where you are without metaphors. I encourage you to try."

Sonjaa peered into the darkness. Suddenly her vision encompassed millions of light years from multiple directions. She recognized her atoms were spread out across this entire distance yet somehow she was seeing her surroundings all at the same time. She sensed gravity waves. She sensed electromagnetic waves—she saw the wave-particles speeding by. Panicked, she turned it out and maintained the projection. She became a theropod standing on a sheet of glass again.

"No. No. I... I like this better."

"You will navigate the universe much faster."

"Maybe later. This is fine for now. Much happier."

"You said you are not from this universe. I think it's time you told me what you meant."

Sonjaa sighed. "Have any of your Archeons been thinking about what what exists beyond the universe?"

"You mean outside?"

"Yes, an idea that the universe exists somewhere, going someplace, and that's what causes time."

"I have heard some concepts like that, but they are just theories. Are you suggesting you know the answer?"

"Part of one. The universe exists inside a place called the Lake. I understand it even less than this place, but we've been traveling in it for a long time. Friend's instincts send him into a panic. I've been teaching him how to channel those urges into finding imbalances in the universe, but he seems to have returned to destroying people again. He was doing so well. I was finally starting to think he had learned how to control it."

"Our calculations state there can't be anything beyond the universe. You must have some equations we do not."

"I'm sorry, but I'm not a typical Archeon. It was forced on me. I don't think in equations. I think in terms of language. Sounds. Music. Harmony. My mind is parsing the tones of the universe. Electrons make a sound, quarks make a sound. When they interact, they add up to a drone. It's different for every universe. Once everything merges I can create portals and antispheres. I can also hear when things disturb it."

"Antisphere?"

"Your turn."

"Does your home universe have Left particles and Right particles?"

"Nothing that sounds like this."

"It must have them. I can't comprehend an equation without them. The math states matter can have two electric charges with opposite spins."

"I'm sure it does, but whatever my universe has, it doesn't sound anything like this."

"How did you become an Archeon without knowing any of these things?"

"That's another long story."

"What do you mean he is your fox? What is a fox?"

Sonjaa's answer caught in her throat. Her killing claws stabbed the glass and she grieved.

"He was doing so well. He progressed so far. He hadn't killed anyone in ten landings. Maybe more. It's hard to remember. Now look at him. Without a raptor, he can't control himself. I need to be with him! I want to separate my Left and Right particles. Show me how."

"I'm sorry, but I can't. It may be years before you learn how to return to the Right and the Left."

Sonjaa snarled and screeched at the image of her homeworld.

"Friend, you are better than this! You were becoming stable! Everything I did for you, and you forget it the moment I'm not there! Let me help him! I can help him! I should be there for him!"

She collapsed and clawed the glass, slower and slower.

5

They had found Right Friend. He had eliminated the people on this world, leaving only himself. He snarled and paced and growled, as if still sensing people around him but unable to reach them.

Sonjaa watched, Lio at her side. Lio had told her there were over a hundred million people gathered around this planet in the Leftright plane, but she could only feel Lio. Sonjaa did hear a change in the tone of this universe as more people gathered, so she figured she was on the way to understanding where she was. She feared she would learn far too late.

Left Friend had hopped eight planets and eliminated all life on them. Sonjaa apologized profusely, but Lio told her nobody understood why she wanted to take the blame. All the people in the Leftright plane could do was watch. Sonjaa had warned them not to go there or they would not survive.

Both Friends snarled and paced in a panic, rolling in blood, screeching at the sky or the ground or at empty air. Sonjaa recognized the body language. He was trying to calm the anxiety physically, but it was not working.

"Why haven't they met yet?" Sonjaa asked.

"Even for Archeons," Lio answered, "it can be difficult to discern where the other half is. Sometimes it would require a portal calculation years long, as the distance is so far. Not everyone is capable of it. It can be a lifetime journey to reach a place they can find each other at all. They are only nine light years apart. I do not know what is taking them so long. Do you?"

Sonjaa observed them. Something seemed strange now. On other worlds, his awareness would have extended to thousands of planets by now in an expanding radius around him, but Friend's two halves had jumped to planets that were not within such a radius.

They were both pacing, holding their heads, snarling at nothing. She had seen him do this before.

"He knows how this universe works." she answered. "He is capable of destroying all life in the galaxy. His awareness might extend to the whole equation by now."

"But he is killing people."

Sonjaa willed the view to be closer. Both planets zoomed in to ground level, and now she stood with both Friends next to one another, superimposed on top of the glass surface. Both were huddled into themselves, covered in blood, in agony.

She had been focused on the deaths Friend was causing she hadn't noticed he wasn't killing anyone now.

"He knows what's wrong with the universe!" Sonjaa shouted. "He's holding back!"

Sonjaa stumbled backwards two steps, sending her eight light years away. At the same time, Left Friend snarled. Both Friends opened portals on top of her. They did not touch her. Both Friends seemed to be trying to speak, but their words devolved into garbled nonsense. She looked around and saw antispheres cascading around the planet alongside normal portals.

Then the portals changed.

She sensed quantum disturbances up and down the sheet of glass, finger-sized portals winking in and out everywhere.

She felt changes in the drone that comprised the universe. Uncomfortable changes. Now she felt hints of other people around here in this plane. Erratic movement. People were running away. Lio led Sonjaa away from the view of the planets, and when they stopped moving, they were in an empty section of spacetime. Sonjaa felt the lack of gravity.

"Sonjaa, did you feel any of that?" Lio asked.

"Yes. Friend can open portals here."

"They're smaller than an elemental particle! How is he doing this? It requires precise calculations—they take a lifetime to master!"

Sonjaa sat on the glass and stared at the vastness of spacetime.

"He always tries to help me catch up. He always tries to explain it. He can't speak this time. Was anyone hurt?"

"No. Portals just appeared everywhere. They didn't touch anyone."

"He's dropping pebbles in the pond. He's trying to show me how portals sound here. I need to go back."

"They've both hopped three worlds. Everyone is considering plans to keep them apart. They're going to kill him."

"No! Don't kill him!"

"Sonjaa, there is no other way. If he can open portals without having met his other half, we have no idea what he is capable of."

"Take me back to him!"

"They've already decided."

"He'll be even more dangerous if he's dead! He won't be able to resist killing everyone if he's in the Lake!"

Lio's presence moved away. "I'm sorry, they need me. It's going to take all of us to make this happen. We're can't leave anything to chance."

She felt Lio's presence fade.

"Lio, something is wrong with your reality! He's trying to fix it! It has something to do with—"

Sonjaa saw an antisphere open in front of her. It hovered for a moment and then winked out. Then a normal sphere appeared, Friend's snarling, rodent-canine face projected around it. The portal winked closed as Friend's language skills failed to surface through his anxiety.

Sonjaa heard more portals. They made waves in space-time. Those waves bounced off particles; Sonjaa now heard how everything interacted.

She remembered Friend never touched Deka, Kylac, or herself when he reverted like this, but this time had killed her Left half.

What if that had not been a mindless act of reversion? What if Friend had done it deliberately? He didn't know where her other half was, but he figured Left Sonjaa would find her from the Lake, just as she had done with Deka back in their home reality.

Friend's awareness extended far enough for his two halves to meet. He could have combined his Left and Right halves at any time. He could have opened spheres on top of both halves of himself and merged in the Lake, giving himself an easy way to calm his scent anxiety.

Sonjaa began running.

Galaxy clusters and stars and planets sped by. Friend was opening tiny portals everywhere in both the Leftright plane and in the plane where matter existed. Sonjaa took it all in from this vantage point. Subatomic particles that were somehow alive. Left and Right matter merging.

She had heard people talk about something like that before.

Matter and antimatter.

In her home universe, they destroyed one another, but what if, here, they combined into a new form of matter?

The universe sounded a bit more harmonious now, even as Friend opened more and more spheres and antispheres. They surrounded her, parted ways for her, never touching her, but coming very close.

"Hold on, Friend! I'm almost there!"

Matter and antimatter combined. Instead of converting into energy, they became new particles with different properties. The mass still existed, but where did it all go?

Sonjaa sped up. She watched every planet speed by. Every star. That breaking sound she kept hearing. That was the sound of matter and antimatter merging and popping into existence in this new plane, where the laws of physics were vastly different.

Breaking.

It was the only part that did not blend into the background drone. The sound of the universe fell apart around it—every time it happened, and it was happening everywhere, not always to people or groups of particles, but electrons and protons meeting all over the universe.

Sonjaa saw two of these particles colliding. The protons had traveled eight billion light years, and now, at last, they touched. Right and Left. Positive charge and negative charge. Sonjaa felt the universe become slightly heavier.

She slid to a stop and observed the new particle the collision had produced. It tipped the balance of the universe by exactly that much mass.

She thought about what happened when they met in her home universe, what she remembered when Friend tried to explain things like this in mathematical terms. The matter converted to energy, thus it maintained a balance.

Not so here. Sonjaa felt it now. Friend's portals were everywhere, flicking in and out of existence, the fox throwing rocks everywhere, hoping Sonjaa would hear the different sounds and form a mental map of her quantum surroundings.

Instead of converting to energy, mass converted into more mass. Now she understood.

Hundreds of billions of people in this plane. People who never died. Particles that did not decay. The energy had to come from somewhere, and that source must be the force the Lake exerted on this universe. Sonjaa knew enough about the equations to realize if this kept up, the universe will have so much mass it would collapse back in on itself.

Perhaps before anyone could leave it.

Reality fell into harmony with one bad voice in it. Sonjaa heard it clearly now. She found both of Friend's selves and blocked him. She sensed the entire population of people in this plane had gathered to try to kill her fox, but now they backed away when the portals ended. Sonjaa pushed their particles away. She opened a sphere on top of Left Friend and dropped him on top of his Right half.

The universe broke, and Friend popped into existence here, still snarling. Sonjaa saw him lying on the glass in front of her. He was a fox again, a touch of grey in his muzzle and tail cut off near the base. He stopped thrashing and snarling just long enough to speak.

"Took you long enough!"

Friend continued screeching and clawing the ground. His mind was trying to break free, but Sonjaa contained him. His voice died down. He caught his breath. Sonjaa willed him to be closer. She held out a hand. Friend took it and rose to his hind feet. He stood tense and stiff, arms spread, as Sonjaa embraced him.

"I don't care how long it takes! I am teaching you the math!"

She rubbed his back with the side of her snout. "I doubted you! I saw you killing people and I feared the worst! I'm sorry you were alone! I'm so sorry! I believed my own history and I wasn't there."

Friend leaned backwards as she pulled him close to her. "I resisted for eight days! Eight days of agony, and this time the imbalance was touching me all the time no matter where I went! Do you have any idea how that feels?"

Sonjaa pulled away and looked him over, sighing in relief. "I'm in pain every time you revert. But why were you killing people? I taught you better than that!"

Friend averted his eyes. "Not the people... Their particles. Think far enough ahead. All of those particles will eventually find their other halves. I ended their lives prematurely. That changes the course those atoms will take as the universe ages. Those planets I wiped out... I just extended the life of this universe by seventeen centuries."

"That's all?"

"If we do enough of them, the universe will last long enough for three people to leave it."

"Friend, we've been through this. That's scent anxiety."

Friend snarled. "It's a little different when the people themselves are the problem!"

Sonjaa became aware of Lio's presence next to her. She also became aware of the merged particles around her. The entire population of the Leftright plane had come to observe. Personal space did not exist here; everyone could exist on top of one another. Sonjaa chose to keep the projection of physical bodies on top of a glass surface. It made things easier. She wondered if Friend saw the same thing.

"Thank you for helping me catch up, but you are not ready to be alone. When did you remember?"

He was staring at the ground, panting through his nose. "Just a few moments before I killed your Left half. It was the only way I could think to help you remember yourself and understand how the universe works. My Right side thought of a few equations, and so did I. It triggered an antisphere. Everything rushed back to me. I figured out the equation. This one was easy. Matter and antimatter combining into new particles instead of just energy. These particles add mass to the universe. It's inherently unstable."

"So what can we do about it?" Sonjaa said, turning and walking about. A different galaxy came into view with each step but Friend remained where he was on the glass. "Somehow matter and antimatter create more massive particles when they combine, and they never decay. The universe is already too heavy. We have to find a way to release all this mass."

"I believe the merged particles are drawing extra energy from the Lake itself."

"How does that work?"

"The numbers imply matter and antimatter form energy singularities."

She turned to him. "Black holes? Here?"

Friend hadn't looked at her since they embraced. His muzzle curled into a bigger snarl. "Not made of gravity. Made of energy. Possibly kinetic. Energy from the Lake falls into the particles, and they keep growing. I thought about pulling all the mass from this plane and spreading it out across spacetime. That would ease the pressure so reality can spread out at a normal pace again. A few people could escape before it dissipates. The particles would not come back together before then. But... I stopped myself. I searched for another way, and I found it."

"Those are people, Friend."

"Think of them in big enough terms."

Sonjaa observed three galaxies colliding. "We don't have to remove any of the people from this plane. Entire galaxies found one another as well. We can isolate those particles and split them apart. We can take each half somewhere it can't meet its twin until the universe is old enough to let someone out. There's enough nonliving mass here to achieve the same thing. Deka and Kylac must also have believed their own histories, or we would have heard from them by now. I wonder what Deka became, and is he with his fox?"

"Sonjaa, this is a waste of time! I was working on a solution! Let me open ways above those planets. I can free up the particles and that will prevent them from adding more mass to the universe in the first place. Three people will leave it before it pulls itself back together."

"Friend, they are not just particles!"

Sonjaa felt the fox trying to break out of her control. Every time he sent out a sound to disturb spacetime, she sent a vibration of her own to cancel him out. He fought harder. He bared his teeth as he dropped to all fours and charged. Sonjaa braced herself on the glass. He collided with her. They tumbled, claws and teeth scraping flesh, but nothing was happening. When they separated, neither had a scratch on them.

Friend huffed as he rolled to his feet. "I resisted for eight days! I could have killed everyone, but I didn't! I remembered what you taught me and I found a better solution! I was hoping you wouldn't catch up until I was done so I could show you I can do it on my own now!"

She fanned her claws, ready for another attack, wondering how this looked to the people in the Leftright plane.

"Friend, if this is anything like back home, you'll always need a raptor to guide you. Rupi hadn't reverted in years, but she knew without me, she—"

The fox snarled and howled, collapsing to the glass. Sonjaa lowered her claws, tucking them in as she trotted up to him. She nuzzled his cheek. Friend swatted her away as he pounded and scratched the ground.

Sonjaa chirped and stared at him. He turned his back on her and sat on the glass, whimpering.

"What's wrong?"

He did not answer.

"Friend, you still need help diverting this into something that won't harm others."

He grumbled. "When will it be over?"

Sonjaa straightened up. "Over? What are you talking about?"

"You know what I mean!"

Sonjaa lowered her neck parallel to the glass. "Friend, I watch how you're progressing, and I am so proud of you. It brings me so much joy to have a fox again. It means everything to me. You may be the reason Rupi is gone, but you needed a lot of help and I'm so happy I can be the one to help you tame your old ways."

Friend did not answer. Sonjaa waited patiently. By now, Rupi would have bounded to her, overjoyed and grateful Sonjaa kept her away from the pit of her instincts.

The fox growled. "I've heard it all my life. I need a raptor. I can't live without one. I'll sink into the old ways. I never needed one before, and now you're always there. Always standing over me making sure I don't hurt myself. At least Rive let me hunt."

"What?"

"I am not reverting! Eight days I made a conscious decision! Why did I help you?"

Sonjaa shivered. It was like the moment she realized her hatchlings were gone. "Helping you means everything to me, Friend. You would have destroyed everyone, but you have learned so much."

Friend jumped to all four feet and faced her, fur raised. "Stop that! Stop talking to me like that!"

"Friend, you're my fox. I—"

"I'm not Rupi! Stop touching me stop making me lie down with you or lick your snout! This has been a nightmare and you think you'll always be here, always watching over me, always making sure I behave like a good fox! Go fuck everyone in sight, go fix this equation—it's all the same! You want it to last forever because you want Rupi back but she's dead! I can get my own drink of water! I can be in a crowd! Other universes in sight and I *still* need a raptor to help me reach them!"

Sonjaa swallowed the pain and rose to attack stance. "This isn't a nightmare for me."

His lips curled as he bared his teeth. "I never wanted Rive! How can you keep whining for a fox? When I was watching you on Earth I was jealous you were free. You had what I've wanted all my life and all you wanted was to be leashed to a fox again! You're worse than Rive because he didn't keep telling me I need to change my attitude! I didn't revert! I was in total control for eight days! I knew exactly what I was doing! I knew what I was doing back home, but the three of you keep telling me I'm dangerous and something is wrong me but nothing is wrong! You're trying to force me to care about these particles but that's all they are and I'm old enough to be your father and you're telling me all the time I should feel something for all these people but I feel *nothing!*"

He was trying to open thousands of portals on top of people all across the Leftright. Sonjaa was still stronger for now.

"I am so tired of pretending something is wrong with me—that's it's all animal instinct! Raptors have been telling foxes we're dangerous for generations because that's what you want us to believe! It makes you feel better about yourselves but all you do it hold us back and force us to pretend to care about other people when all we want is to get away —why the *fuck* is that so hard?! Why can't I just leave?! So many universes out there why can't I reach them without a raptor why can't I stay calm enough to get there on my own! Why isn't this over!"

Sonjaa opened portals on Friend's Left particles and sent them to a Left planet. At the same time, she sent his Right particles to a Right planet, thousands of light years apart. She took two steps and ended up facing the Left planet. She mentally traveled to the Right world. A view of it came into focus. She zoomed in and found them exactly where she had set them, both Relian canines, but with mirrored fur patterns. Neither was trying to open portals. She viewed them side by side.

"Better?" she asked.

Right Friend climbed to his feet as he answered. "Much... Much better."

Left Friend continued. "Bad enough being aware of the imbalance in the universe. Being made of the particles that cause the imbalance. That was unbearable."

Sonjaa's killing claws rose. She deliberated lowered them to the glass. "You meant every word, didn't you?"

Both Friends were standing now, panting and trying to lower their fur. They didn't hear her, but they were aware of her presence.

Left Friend answered. "We're sorry. We didn't mean to say it like that. We probably wouldn't be alive right now if not for you helping us."

"We wanted to tell you in kinder words," Right Friend continued. "It is still frustrating. The truth is... we have felt this way all our lives, but we never felt comfortable saying it out loud. Not even to Rive."

Left resumed. "This urgent desire to get away. We don't want to imagine doing this forever. Bound to a raptor. It scares us to think this won't end. That we won't ever become good enough to live on our own."

Sonjaa resisted making any grieving sounds. She gritted her teeth. "You wanted to leave Rive?"

The two Friends paused to trade thoughts. Then Left Friend answered. "The urge became stronger as the years went by."

"We would have abandoned him a long time ago, but... It didn't seem right. We didn't want to hurt him. He was still our raptor. Nobody understood us the way he did."

"We were stable. Rive taught us to have sex with everyone we scented, trained us to get hard every time someone came near. He made us obsessed with sex, but for what? To help us tame instincts we never felt. He turned us into something we were not. We always felt it. That we were supposed to be something else, and Rive was keeping us from becoming that."

"Yes," Sonjaa said, "from becoming a creature that lives to kill all scents in its territory. That's what we do."

"We are not reverting," said Left.

Right: "If we were, we'd have no control."

Sonjaa folded her hands, hiding her claws. "You want to break away for its own sake. You don't feel sorry about the people you've hurt. That's instinct, Friend. You know what you become when you're alone. You remember what you said all those times you reverted. Everything you can't explain."

Both Friends stared at the ground and sighed. Left spoke.

"Everyone tells us something is wrong with us, but that's not how it feels. The math is solid. It's painful and insulting to have to listen to you treat us like we're just a fox acting on instinct. We're not mindlessly appeasing animal nature."

Right: "No matter how hard we try, we still can't seem to break free. We should be able to, but it's always just beyond reach. It hurts to think that this may be it."

Left: "We may never be able to get away from this."

Right: "Back home, when we first saw the universe as a whole, we began to wonder why we let Rive hold us back. Leaving was possible at last, and we wouldn't be hurting him. We'd be giving him relief. Watching the new equations destroy planets had been a burden on him. We remember seeing his numbers. He would be happier without us. He didn't know it then, but he would realize it, too. It was better to part ways. Then while we were teaching Kylac about the Lake, the urge became stronger. That's all we wanted. Just to get away."

Left: "We made a choice. A conscious, reasoning choice. Once Kylac started blocking us from opening spheres, that's when we began to panic. Getting away from not just raptor scent but every scent. Leaving the universe seemed to be the only way to do it once we could see the universe as a whole."

Right: "And we couldn't. We were outside, but we still failed."

Left: "Other universes were out there, but we needed help. Now we escaped. At last we escaped, and we still have a raptor. It's the same no matter where we go. All the same. Always a raptor standing over us, never leaving us alone, telling us we should feel bad and we're dangerous and we need to be watched at all times."

Sonjaa craved to embrace her fox again. Rupi would have jumped her, pushed her to the ground and held on, licking Sonjaa's snout up and down, clinging to her until she fell asleep. Sonjaa would hold her fox as close as possible, embracing her with her arms and legs, and Rupi would huddle into her raptor, never wanting to let go of the one thing in the contacted universe that prevented her from becoming a mindless monster—always the sense that she could not show her gratitude enough and she had a bottomless reservoir of it which she could only express by keeping Sonjaa as close to her as possible.

"Friend, foxes have animal instincts. Some of the strongest in the contacted universe. They overpower your higher mind. That's what you're feeling."

Both Friends growled at the ground and looked everywhere but at her. Sonjaa continued.

"You met your instincts. You know they're part of you." She reached out to both of them. "Friend, I meant it. You are everything to me. When I lost Rupi, I had no purpose. Helping you has made me feel alive again. I would be happy to be your raptor forever if that's what it comes to."

Left Friend and Right Friend turned away from where they sensed Sonjaa was trying to touch them.

"This is not who we are!"

"We are not a normal fox!"

"We are what every Relian canine wants to be!"

"Stable! Happy! Never reverted!"

"This is not us!"

"This can't be us!"

"This can't last forever!"

"Rive turned us into a sex-obsessed animal!"

"It's not who we are!"

"He made us into this! Why can't we get away?!"

"Why can't we just leave!?"

"All we want to do is get way!"

"Entire universes out there!"

"We can't reach them!"

"Without anyone watching over us!"

"Pushing us to *fuck* everyone we meet!"

"There's nothing wrong with us!"

"We are in control!"

"We can't do this anymore!"

"We can't live with everyone telling us every day that something is wrong with us!"

"People making us feel guilty for everything we do when instinct isn't involved!"

"Even when we show we're in control, you still treat us like children!"

"You say we're acting on instinct no matter what we do!"

"So your hatchlings died."

"So Archeons died."

"We know."

"We don't feel anything."

"How is that wrong?"

"That's not instinct!"

"That is conscious reasoning!"

"And you keep telling us it's wrong!"

"That's why you don't think we're ready to be alone!"

"Even when we don't revert, you hold us down!"

"Rive did it, too!"

"Kylac wanted us dead!"

"Deka tried to kill us!"

"Everyone's telling us we are giving in to instinct!"

"We are conscious!"

"Reasoning!"

"Everything we have ever done has been for a greater purpose!"

"Not old ways!"

"We want to leave!"

"It shouldn't be difficult!"

"Just let us get away from everyone so we can be what we're supposed to be!"

The bottom fell out of Sonjaa's emotions. She reached out again. Both Friends jumped away. Sonjaa willed them to come closer, and they did, but they leaped away an equal distance. Sonjaa chased both of them over hills and meadows and through forests and over streams.

She realized she was not chasing Friend. She let the view pull out, and now she saw the planets as a whole again. The feelings she got from helping Rupi burned to a husk and sat in her gut. She felt alone. A raptor without a fox.

She thought back to all the times she brought Friend back or held him from destroying everything, and she realized she had been doing it for a long time. Ignoring what Friend was and seeing Rupi instead. He was nothing like her, and now Sonjaa couldn't pretend he might become so someday if she tried harder.

She stepped away from the planet and dropped to the ground. A moment later, she felt Lio's presence touching her. Sonjaa let the illusion of the glass plane and the planets fall away. Now she existed in the Leftright as it truly was.

It scared her, but she forced herself to look at it. Now she saw Lio as she truly was. Sonjaa reached out to her. Lio reached back. The embrace felt nothing close to what she wanted, but it was the kind she needed.

6

The foxes enjoyed the process. Every particle changed the equations in subtle ways. Moving a single electron resulted in an extra day this reality would survive, and the tangible feeling of a person about to leave it tingled on the tip of their noses. Friend wanted to move more and more. Kylac especially enjoyed the gradual changes that had large effects into the future.

The people in the Leftright plane had been watching for generations. From the Lake, the Relians barely felt the time go by. Separating the antimatter from matter returned both halves to the normal universe, and the Relians took each particle to opposite sides.

They still did not know why matter and antimatter combined into a form that had more mass than the sum of their parts, but now the universe would not become too heavy for another hundred billion years.

Mass leaving the Leftright and returning to the plane where antimatter and matter remained apart taught the people on both sides about the Lake. By observing how someone in the Lake affected their universe, they began to infer the equations that made it happen. The Relians concluded it would take generations to go from equation to true understanding, and for them it would not be a destructive process. It would be creative.

Friend was especially interested in why so many people were projected to leave this universe compared to others. Nineteen people was the highest number they had ever witnessed, and they wished they knew why. Deka guessed it had something to do with the Leftright forming a midway reality to the Lake, preparing generations of people for it.

Friend had never been able to resist breaking free this long, and Kylac felt relief being able to interact with the people of this world as he worked. Friend derived pleasure from gradually balancing this place, and he never once tried to break out of Sonjaa's control for the easy solution. They projected themselves into the universe often, and they had time to get to know people here.

In the Lake, Sonjaa sensed that Friend wanted to break free of her. He was searching for an opportunity to sneak away, and the longer he remained in this equation, the more likely he would find it. They could not stay forever.

Rupi would have recognized what Sonjaa had done for her, and that would have made Rupi delightfully clingy, and then she would take Sonjaa somewhere to do something exciting together.

She felt Friend beside her. She helped him become more than an animal. Knowing he didn't believe anything was wrong and she was trying to change him into something else tainted all memories of the past as well as the present. Even now, as he derived pleasure from watching a universe in better balance than the plan he had in mind would have yielded, he wanted to be as far away from her as possible.

Now the universe was as balanced as they could make it. Working with an audience had been such a wonderful change of pace for everyone, and knowing they would not be forgotten made the effort worth it.

The Relians had already said their farewells. Deka exerted force, and they allowed themselves to drift away. Sonjaa sent Friend positive vibrations. He had done very well, and she was still proud of him.

Friend gave her silence in return.

Sonjaa wondered if they would have to be together forever. She wasn't sure if she could do this for much longer. Taming Friend's old ways was work, not a relationship. Rupi had given her so much of herself, but thinking back on it, Friend hadn't given her anything in return. She had been pushing him into that since the beginning.

Sonjaa took one last look at Lio and all the other people in the Leftright, and then Deka pushed them to the side. They drifted away from this reality. Sonjaa promised to stop projecting Rupi onto Friend. Instead of thanking her, he sent her palpable relief.

Kronia

"Is it just me, or is the video wall busier than normal?"

Adam sat in a chair next to Sorven, beer in one hand, compensators detached from his body and resting on the floor behind him. Both his arms were different lengths and he was missing two fingers as well. The compensators were designed to wear out after ten years of use, and his were well past their expected lifespan. He only wore the visor over his eyes. His in utero exposure to the chemicals used to make the compensators caused his body to be in this state now.

"It's not your imagination," said the Krone. "Your subconscious has registered a change in the mood on Earth."

"What's the change?"

"There's a lot of anger brewing. It has been since long before broadcast television ended and the bandwidth repurposed to augment internet speed. The computers that create entertainment recognize people are watching shows with a lot of anger and rebellion in them, so they create more of the same. Since the systems are automated, they do not care that presenting this anger on screen helps people externalize it."

"It's been almost five hundred years since you founded the Church. You always say anger is brewing, and yet things keep going."

"Anger is always under the surface. People are inclined to work within the system they are given, to a point.

The anger comes from not being in control. It is human nature to submit to authority while at the same time trying to rise up and overthrow it, but only to a degree."

"What degree is that?"

"It varies from culture to culture and individual to individual. As long as a person can satisfy their needs, they will not fight the control. Individuals may, but as a whole, the system moves on. When the control becomes too detrimental to comfort, the anger of a society synchronizes and the people fight back all at the same time."

Adam laughed, took a drink. "Isn't five hundred years long enough?"

"Oh, but they did rebel. The collective anger synchronized in multiple places several times over the last few generations. But it only extended across a few countries. Sometimes riots forced the corporations to do something for the people to appease them. There were reforms. New policies, new protections. A few cities even burned to the ground, along with the companies that owned all the land, but new ones took their place. Things got better for a while, and people calmed down and went back to work, able to satisfy their needs again. Now here we are, as if those concessions never happened. Once that generation passed away, the next forgot about the oppression, and the companies began squeezing harder. The human lifespan is the largest detriment to progress. If human beings lived longer, these cycles would elongate to the point of being meaningless. Extrapolate that logic to an observer who has an initiate lifespan, and nothing that persists in human civilization would last. The corporations decide what's remembered and what isn't. If not for us retrieving information and keeping it alive, the oppressed would not remember better times. They would not be able to see the cycle and recognize it for what it is. The Church is the only thing stopping the owners of society from having total control of the population."

Adam had learned never to interrupt Sorven when he started talking like this. He always learned something. "So you're waiting for revolution to happen on a global scale. What makes you confident anger can spread across borders?"

"When things get bad enough, it will happen. It's only a matter of time before people make the connection between their suffering and the opulent lives of the wealthy. When they question the legitimacy of this divide, and the answer is plain and obvious and undeniable, that's when it will spread."

Adam took another drink as he watched the screens. The audio was mere noise to his ears, and the screens blurred into flashes of moving color. While they watched, another Krone wandered in.

"It's a good idea," she said as she passed, her voice clearer than the noise. "I know it's a good idea, but how can it be done without setting foot on Earth? I'm not sure. Well, think! We haven't got forever! We have a long time. Rushing never solves anything."

She walked into the next chamber. The skylight made her scales shimmer, and then she entered the shadow and walked out of sight.

Sorven spoke again. "You know what fascinates me?"

"Lots of things. What are you thinking this time?"

"Aliens were on Earth, and nothing changed. Science fiction writers portrayed first contact as the turning point in human history. The moment when everything changes, either for better or for worse. What does it say about humanity that absolutely nothing happened?"

The human laughed. "Something would have changed, but certain people were sitting pretty just the way things were. The corporate military defeated a fake Relian invasion over a century ago. Aliens still invade Earth from time to time. A real person has never seen one, but the news is full of sightings."

"And nobody has written science fiction since. Computers don't generate it anymore. People want to forget about alien life. Even if someone tried to write it, they find every implementation of every idea has already been copyrighted. The algorithms delete works in progress as infringement even before anyone finishes writing them. There is no outlet for creativity in any field. Music, art, writing, acting. All done by computer. It has left humanity a hollow shell."

"The anger would be directionless if not for the records the Church keeps. If only you'd come sooner. Maybe if we'd known this stuff as it happened, we could've stopped it early."

"What would you wish people five hundred years ago had known?"

Adam pondered that. He took a drink. "For the people of the late twentieth century to understand they were part of a great experiment. The idea that business had made government obsolete. That there were powerful people who believed governments were inefficient and rigid, and the people who controlled the giant corporations saw themselves as more qualified to make decisions."

Sorven smiled with both his mouth and his wings. "Many did realize it was happening. They noticed industry and commerce accomplish everything government and religion once had to do: keeping the people under control and busy while directing their labor into something for the benefit of the ruling families."

"More people needed to understand what it meant," Adam said.

"Some were aware of what they were doing, and they believed it was noble..."

While Sorven spoke, another Krone walked through the chamber, speaking French. Adam knew French, so he tuned out Sorven for a moment and listened to this Krone as he passed.

"I'm hungry. We just ate. It wasn't enough! We are not hungry. You're just used to eating three times a day. It's mental habit. It will take time to adjust. I do not understand how you can only eat every five days. How does your body survive on so little? The Krone have the most evolved bodies in the known universe. Our bodily systems are efficient. We waste very little. You are not hungry. Neither are you tired. Yeah, the sleep thing. It's so weird being awake for so long and then losing entire days sleeping. Your sense of time is adjusting."

They moved out of earshot. Adam listened to Sorven again. "...would find the worthy people among the masses. The good genes that should be nurtured. They really do believe the ability to rise out of the pit they created is a sign of being one of the true human beings. But the only way for a person to do that is to pull someone else down, place other human beings under that someone's control. The corporate owners are selecting their own exaggerated animal traits and magnifying them even more, so any new society they form will degenerate into the very thing they seek to escape. If humans ever left Earth in this state of mind, they would be a destructive force worse than a fox without a raptor. It will take time to undo the damage to the psyche as well as the body."

"Yeah. If enough people knew it, maybe we could have stopped it. Now here we are. There's no way to win. They're going to destroy the world. They're just waiting for a sign that the time is right."

Adam felt Sorven's mouth next to his ear. "You noticed those Krone, didn't you?"

"I did."

"Do you understand what's happening?"

Adam's mouth went dry. He took another drink. It didn't help. "I figured it out weeks ago."

"Say what is on your mind. It's already in your scent and body language."

Adam faced him, looked him in the eye. "I am dying of jealousy."

Sorven smiled. Many Krone bared their teeth to imitate a human smile. It helped the humans feel more welcome in the library.

"Every Church leader experiences it when they realize what the Krone are doing. Would you like to hear the whole story?"

Adam did not want to talk about it. "Tell me."

Sorven held eye contact. "Shortly after I brought all the Relians safely to Earth, I went back to Pryip and allowed them to examine me. Then, after my human half and my Krone half synchronized, I went back again. It gave them a complete understanding of what they did wrong the first time, and what it should feel like in the end. They were confident they could repeat the process. Safer this time.

"After I built this library, the Krone became curious about Earth, and they wanted to be part of it. They were also fascinated by what happened to me. They noticed I was enthusiastic, optimistic, social, and I even had a sex drive. They wanted what I had. I told them what I had to go through to get it, and they still wanted it, so they began to do something they had never done before. They socialized with individual humans, and they found people they actually got along with. Eventually, one Krone found a human he wanted to synchronize with. Others began doing the same. Almost all the Krone have a human inside them now, and the Pryip are happy to perform the procedure."

Adam sighed, looking down at his feet. "That's... That's wonderful."

Sorven's wings spread and folded back again. "I understand why you are not happy about it. I wouldn't expect anyone to be. We leave it up to the Church leaders whether to incorporate this into their sermons or not, but we also tell them to consider the consequences. There are fewer than two hundred Krone. We cannot rescue every human being. There is nothing anyone can do to deserve it. If you begin telling people it is possible for them to merge with Sorven's people, it will fill them with false hope. I would rescue them all if I could. The truth is we are doing it for selfish reasons. We are saving ourselves."

Adam chuckled and turned to the Krone again. "You need saving?"

Sorven laughed with his voice. He was the only Krone who did this. It sounded forced and strained—he actually was saying hah-hah-hah—but it helped.

"The Krone. The most evolved species in the contacted universe. What were we doing with our evolved bodies? Sulking in our caves, contemplating how hopeless everything is. That's why the Pryip join us with humans. They know how much we need it. Everyone in the contacted universe pitied us even as they stood in awe of us. I changed that. I showed the Krone another way to save a lone species. We can't force them to understand, but we can still help, and if we wait long enough, the Krone will be able to take over. The survivors of Earth will welcome us. They will realize what happens when humans are in charge and beg us to keep them from doing that again. Hopefully just us being on Earth will tame their old ways. If not, they will be ready to listen."

Adam zoned out facing the video wall. "I'm still jealous. No room in there for a third person?"

"I am happy with two minds in this body. I do not want to imagine what synchronizing a third would do to me."

Adam sighed.

Sorven continued. "Meditate on this emotion and think very carefully before you inflict it on other members of the Church."

"It's not really a choice then."

"When you know the right thing to do, there never is a choice. My concern is when a person intentionally makes the wrong decision for the sake of defying the control of someone else, even if the control is beneficial. That is why the human beings of Earth must remain on Earth. So long as they have this untamed urge to dominate others in order to prevent themselves from being under someone else's control, they cannot leave. We are here to preserve information and keep the human spirit alive, not fill people with false hope."

"They already have that." Adam took a long drink and then cleared his throat. "Corporations fabricate alien invasions everywhere, blaming extraterrestrials for everything from disease to cancer to crops failing to why we need compensators just to stay alive past the age of thirty. Sea levels have risen, more people are packed onto less land, weather patterns have changed, and we're supposed to believe Relians or some other made-up alien species are causing all of it, and the brave corporate-owned military has somehow been holding them back for centuries. Computers and machines do just about everything, and yet we still have to crawl over each other to make a living. Most of the jobs are in manufacturing compensators and chemicals to make technology and oil and processed food packets. Our jobs are to make the very things that keep us sick and miserable. Our work accomplishes nothing but keeping us busy so we don't have time to question why the owners of these corporations are building space stations. Everyone in the Church believes the end is near. They want the Krone to fly in and do something about it, since nobody else can."

"If we came now, we would still have to force our-selves on everyone. It would only be another oppressive regime."

Adam chuckled, finished the bottle. "So what would the Krone do with an entire planet to rule?"

"We would not be objects of fear. We would be your companion species."

"How? What does that mean?"

"You would help us as much as we help you. The Krone need a purpose. You need someone to break the cycle of oppression. I believe historians will remember the pre-Krone era as mere preparation for our arrival. All of human history up until that point will be summarized as yearning for a companion species, and humanity itself coming to realize what it is without one, so it would be ready to accept the Krone when we arrived. The Church has helped steer events to that end, as well. The information we disseminated into the population has sparked protests and rebellions and maintained knowledge of the past, but ultimately it has left the world unchanged except for the latent anger. That is the Church's true legacy. We have preserved a reason for people to be angry. Eventually, the anger will synchronize worldwide, and then humanity itself will understand exactly what is wrong with the world. It will be an epiphany on a global scale."

"I hope I live to see it."

"*I* may not live to witness it, but I am content with what I've accomplished. Watching other Krone synchronize with humans reminds me just how much has changed."

Adam laughed. "And Earth can look forward to being under the rule of benevolent dragon gods."

Sorven laughed with him. "Change is possible. Change is good. Pass me a beer."

Adam set the empty bottle down. He reached for another, popped the cap, and held it up to Sorven.

"Hah. For a moment I forgot I wasn't human. I love it when that happens. Chug it for me, Adam. I can't touch that shit."

The human upended the bottle and downed the whole thing as Sorven flapped his wings. He came up for air, set the bottle down, and reached for another. Sorven laughed with his voice, smiling with his mouth and his wings. Adam popped the cap and slouched in the chair. The noise from the wall sounded a little clearer now. He could pick out entire sentences from the computer-animated people on it.

Chaotic Landing

I

Sonjaa had just become conscious again. She heard screaming. She barely had time to comprehend her plated body as she bolted upright and faced Friend.

He was the same species as she was, similar to a Neben mammal, but bipedal, and his plating had swirls of red and black pigment over it. He stood on his hands and knees, tiny portals opening and closing around him. Sonjaa rolled to her hind legs and bounded to him.

"Friend?"

He snarled, gritting his jagged teeth as he turned to her while portals boiled. "I figured it out... before we... landed!"

"Help me catch up!"

"There are... so many..." The field of portals grew wider, and then higher.

Deka and Kylac, also plated bipeds, approached them.

Friend snarled and panted. Even more portals opened and closed around him. "Too many imbalances. Too many! This is— this is— this is—"

Deka and Kylac counted hundreds of different planets visible through the spheres. His awareness had spread light years in just the few breaths since they landed.

Sonjaa picked him up and stood him on his feet, holding him by the shoulders and forcing him to meet her eyes. "Help me catch up!"

Friend gritted his teeth and snarled at her. "Nothing is wrong with me! I can handle this!"

"No, you can't! You are not stable!"

Friend snarled louder. The portals around them fizzled and bubbled faster and larger. "I don't need a raptor to tell me how to calm myself! I know what to do!"

Portals began bubbling in front of Sonjaa, and she backed away to avoid them chopping her hands off. Spheres now surrounded the former fox, cutting him off from the other Relians. Sonjaa stood five paces away, holding his stare through the foam spacetime had become.

"Friend, let me through. We can fix this together."

The portals boiled faster. Every cubic claw's reach for five hundred paces in all directions held a tiny sphere spreading and collapsing, thousands of different planets visible in them. Friend grunted through clenched jaws.

"I haven't killed anyone. Their scents don't make me panic anymore. It's their place in the universe. They're not right. They're not— They're not— Not in the right place! Their end! Their end! It doesn't lead— Out!"

He hunched over, moaning. The portals seemed to moan with him.

"They're all imbalanced! Every planet I calculate—it's all part of it! It's huge! I can control myself until I know the entire equation!"

Antispheres mixed with the normal ways, opening and closing so fast they flashed. Deka and Kylac stood back to back. Sonjaa stood in front of Friend, the former fox just barely visible through the gaps he left between the portals.

"How far are you?" Sonjaa shouted.

"Almost half. The equation is falling into place!"

"Help me catch up before you lose control."

"I don't lose control! I am not like Kylac!"

"Friend, please."

The spheres boiled faster, the field extending outward to make room for more portals. Deka and Kylac stood in a small vacuole in the fist-sized portals appearing and winking closed just a claw's reach from their skin. They tried not to breathe. Sonjaa also stood in an empty space, facing Friend through a hole just wide enough for them to see one another. Friend spoke through gritted teeth.

"I'm anxious. Yes. I know, but it's a product of the conscious mind, not survival instinct. I'll prove it."

Sonjaa sensed the field of spheres encompassed the entire horizon. Her Archeon mind told her billions of worlds now appeared in the portals.

Friend did not speak.

Sonjaa held his stare.

Friend shivered.

Breaths passed. Friend hunched lower and shivered, as if the weight of all these portals around them compressed him.

"Everything..." he began.

Sonjaa waited a few breaths for him to finish. He did not. "Everything what?"

"Nobody will leave this universe. Nobody!"

"We can fix that."

"Nothing we do will fix it!"

"There's always a way."

"Not here! Not here! Not! Here!"

"Friend."

"I won't hurt anyone! I'm going to restore balance!"

"You're not ready for this."

"Stop telling me that! Stop treating me like that! This isn't instinct! I'm not a mindless animal and it's time you accepted it, Sonjaa! Everything feels right! I'm aware of multiple galaxies. Trillions of... Each... The same.... As the last.

All the same life. The same equations repeating over and over! How can there not be one person to leave it?!"

Friend howled. The portals vibrated and wiggled and expanded dangerously close to everyone's plated skin. Deka and Kylac squeezed closer together.

"The end— It's coming— The entire equation! I'm almost there!"

"Friend, you are only—"

"I'm at the end. The entire universe in an equation too large to write but comprehended in a single thought. I'm here!"

Sonjaa figured the entire planet must be bubbling with portals by now.

He snarled and screeched as he dropped to his hands and knees, the portals evacuating that space to make room for him.

Sonjaa dropped to her knees and held his stare at his eye level, the portals leaving to make room for her as well. "Find the closest imbalance and correct it. Start with something simple. Remove one atom, then stop and examine how that effects the equation."

"There will never be a contacted universe here! I can't — I can't— I can't think of a way to steer anyone to make one! Or discover the Lake!"

"Stop thinking of the whole universe. Make a small change, move on to another civilization, make another— take it one planet at a time."

Friend panted through his clenched jaw. "I hate the small changes."

"They work best. You've seen it many times."

He pounded the ground with both hands. "I can do this without someone watching me!"

"Friend, show me what's missing. When I catch up, I'll help you think."

"Easiest solution... Easiest... Easy... The only..."

Blood started pouring out from the portals. Deka and Kylac stood back to back as the spheres bled. A river of red flowed around Sonjaa. Friend now knelt in a puddle of it.

"...solution. Simplest solutions! Kylac likes the complicated ones, but they're a waste of time! I'm tired of wasting time."

The blood flowed faster. Pieces of organs also spilled out of the portals and fell into others below them, disappearing somewhere else. Blood found its way between the gaps in the spheres and hit the ground. It drizzled on Sonjaa, Deka, and Kylac.

"Friend..." Water fell from Sonjaa's eyes. A drop of blood hit her muzzle, mixed with the tear, and streamed off.

"This is my solution! It's all the same life form! The same equations on each planet! One solution! It will work! Planet... To... Planet..."

Organs and limbs and heads spilled out of portals, fell into other portals, chopped to pieces, and vanished somewhere else. They heard cries coming from the people on the other side of those ways. Breaths passed. Friend knelt and panted.

The universe bled.

Sonjaa sagged. Her plated body was drenched in blood, and the tears from her eyes had washed thin canals in the red. Deka and Kylac stood in place, also covered in blood, watching the universe in agony.

The portals thinned out and then dissipated. Friend and Sonjaa knelt in an ocean of blood a claw's reach deep that covered the ground from horizon to horizon. Deka and Kylac separated and relaxed. Tiny pieces of organs lay as far as they could see.

Sonjaa did not rise. "Friend... Did you?"

He opened his eyes. "The universe is balanced. It's peaceful."

"They're all dead."

"Look at me. Listen to me. I haven't reverted. I made a conscious choice. Now do you believe me?"

Sonjaa turned and surveyed the land and the awful stench of bodily fluids and severed flesh.

Friend rose to his hind legs. "All the intelligent creatures. They were the same species. The exact same species evolved independently on millions of worlds. They were holding this universe back. Without them, others can rise up. They will discover portals before the equation ends."

Sonjaa faced him. Blood dripped off her plating. She opened her mouth and screamed at him. She ran out of breath, glared, screamed again, leaped and smacked him on the snout. Friend fell to the ground and lay on his back in the blood.

"You don't understand now, but when you figure out the equation, you will. It was the easiest—"

Sonjaa snacked him again. She had no claws, and he was covered in armor plating, so she could not hurt him. Deka and Kylac looked on. Kylac leaned on his raptor. Deka leaned back. Sonjaa shouted in a mix of English and their new native language as she struck him again and again.

"You have learned nothing! Nothing! How many times did you say something was the only solution and how many times did I lead you to something else?! You didn't even try! This was scent anxiety! That's what just happened! The entire universe! Gone! Just to calm your *fucking* nerves!"

Sonjaa ran out of breath. While she caught it, she stood up straight, backing away from him and looking around.

"Well... Maybe this is a good thing. Yes, maybe it is! What's done is done, so let's be positive about this! Let's be *fucking* positive! You just ended life in this universe to save it, so that means there are no scents anywhere! Not big enough to make a difference at least. Now there's nothing to distract you from figuring out the Lake. So do it! Now you can make a portal anywhere you want, and it won't matter because there are no scents anymore! Maybe now that you finally did what you wanted to do from the beginning, you can figure out whatever the fuck this second subconscious is! Don't worry about us! When we figure this place out, we'll be waiting for you in the Lake, so you have the entire place to yourself. An entire universe to think. Nobody blocking you, nobody distracting you. Free to figure out the mysteries of the universe without all those scents making you nervous and distracting you because it's not your fault they make you anxious—it's their fault! For! Fucking! Existing!"

Sonjaa's voice cracked. She choked, gasped for breath.

Friend rolled to his feet, slowly straightening up, dripping in blood, facing the Relians. A sphere opened in front of him. Friend walked through. It shut.

Sonjaa collapsed to her hands and knees. Deka ran up beside her and held her. Sonjaa punched the blood and cursed in every language she could remember until she ran out of breath.

Kylac stood still, looking out over the ocean of blood. Millions of people filled his nostrils. Gone forever.

2

Eliminating the intelligent species from this universe would allow others to rise up, and this new group would discover portals. Deka, Sonjaa, and Kylac understood it now from the Lake, and they also saw the nearly infinite number of other ways to solve the problem without killing anyone.

They could have relocated a few hundred individuals who had been holding those sentient species back, and that would have allowed them to rise to consciousness and discover portal physics in a few hundred generations. By eliminating a few species of animal, or a few mountain ranges, they could have opened up chances for others to become companions to this intelligent species. All of this took more effort to calculate, but it was there. Sonjaa had shoved all of it in Friend's face, but it did not seem to influence him.

The only thing they blocked him from doing was making ways into the Lake. They watched him hop from planet to planet, essentially pacing around the universe. He had been doing this for years, surviving by eating whatever animals he wanted to kill. When he wanted meat, he opened a portal somewhere in the universe, brought a hunk of meat to himself, and he barely had to pause.

The Relians watched from the Lake, often spreading their particles to make time pass faster. They watched a species of animal achieve sentience. The moment coincided with neurons in the brain reaching a level of complexity, and then particles from the Lake began streaming into their minds.

The Relians felt Friend knocking on the barriers they set up from time to time. All three of them blocked him from leaving, just in case he couldn't be contained. He often spoke to them, but they never answered. Sonjaa wished they could kill him and be done with it, but the thought of wandering from universe to universe without the purpose of taming a fox's old ways scared her more than the Lake itself.

They had been tempted to leave him here and try to find a way home, but they feared Friend leaving this universe and finding another one. He remained stable so long as the universe felt balanced, and his idea of a balanced equation differed greatly from theirs.

They floated in the Lake, keeping one another together. On the third Relian year, Friend begged them to allow him to come to the Lake. To finish his calculations, he needed to be able to make portals into it. None of the Relians liked the idea, but they were confident they could intercept him before he tried to escape. They relaxed spacetime.

Friend opened an antisphere and stared at it. He thanked them and continued working out the equations. Now he frequently paced the universe, opening spheres around himself on a whim. He also made ways into the Lake, walked through them, emerged outside the universe, paced, and then made a way back inside and continued pacing from planet to planet. He did not seem fazed by the fact that he had not met another person in five Relian years. Sonjaa had hoped he would beg her to come back and tame him.

Friend intentionally opened unstable antispheres, destroying thousands of planets and allowing the unstable way to take him. He slipped inside, floated in the Lake for a while, and then made a way back, now with a new body.

He became anything he wanted, and his choice often showed his state of mind. When he felt normal, he became a Relian canine. When he felt overwhelmed, he became a Krone. He often took on the physical form of species they had been in other realities.

A few times he allowed several antispheres to intersect on top of him and tear his body apart. His conscious mind emerged in the Lake in pieces. The observing Relians began to recollect him, but to their surprise, Friend collected himself.

He told them they didn't need to contain him here. He had no intention of leaving, for this was the perfect place to think. He wished he had done it to their home universe from the beginning; it would have saved a lot of trouble. Sonjaa, Deka, and Kylac did not move from their positions outside the universe. Until that moment, they considered spreading Friend out across the Lake to be a last resort solution, but now they did not know if it would work anymore. Friend had become so aware of the Lake they worried he could recollect his pieces no matter how far they spread him.

The years continued to pass. Friend stopped speaking. He stopped wandering. He existed entirely within his own mind now. He made spheres to other planets, killed something, brought pieces of it into his mouth, and chewed.

No other sentient species emerged, but they would in time. The knowledge of them existing in the future didn't bother Friend now. The knowledge of the single sentient species that had emerged as a result of his purge did not bother him because it was so far in the future it didn't matter.

The Relians were unaware of his thoughts until he entered the Lake and swam around for a bit. His calculations were light years ahead of where they were, and yet he remained here. Deka did not want to disturb him. Kylac had projected himself down there, but Friend did not even know he existed, his mind so completely absorbed in the equation of the universe. The physical world meant nothing to him now. All that mattered was the Lake.

Sonjaa spent most of her time focusing on the new intelligent species that just emerged. She wanted nothing to do with him, but this universe was their prison as much as Friend's. If not for the time compressing techniques, these years would have been agony.

Years stretched into decades. The Relians did not block Friend at all. They remained here not to contain him, but in case he succeeded.

The only outward sign Friend made any progress at all was the state of his body. He let it go for longer and longer periods, sometimes reaching the point of death. Then he moved into the Lake, remade his body, returned to his thinking spot, and started the whole process over again.

They sensed his thoughts for those brief moments outside reality. His calculations were larger. He held more than one universe in his mind now, remembering the complete equations for several of the realities they had visited, but he did not reveal how he arrived at these conclusions, or for what purpose.

Deka understood the point: comparing universes as a whole to learn why those equations caused the Lake to create a reality.

He hoped Friend was close to an answer.

Sonjaa asked him why he hoped that.

Deka just wanted it to be over.

3

The raptor projected himself onto the planet, complete with his dark blue scales and red stripe. He stood before the decaying Relian canine. Friend had been sitting in this spot for six local years. He didn't eat or sleep. He just let his body wear out. It was simpler than dealing with physical needs. When his body became too decrepit, he sucked himself into an antisphere, remade it, and then sat back down in this one place, staring through space and time.

"Well?" Deka began.

Friend did not move. His mind was somewhere else. Deka sat down beside him.

"Is this really the next step?"

The old fox did not move.

"How many universes are in your mind right now? You think the more you hold, eventually you'll figure out how to take it from mere equations in the mind to becoming a reality, just like portals? The math manifesting in the physical world as a connection between two regions of spacetime. And eventually, you'll learn how to start from scratch. Taking raw numbers and stretching them into a full equation. Entire universes. But let me ask you something, since you never stay in the Lake long enough to talk. What is the purpose of creating universes? Why do they exist? Do you really hope the community of... of Superarcheons—*fuck*, I still hate that word—Do you think they will accept you when they figure out what you had to do to get there? What if they block you as well? Is that what you want?"

No answer. No movement.

"Do you want to go that far? When the other Superarcheons find out you think of life as an obstacle to understanding the Lake, what if they don't value that? What if you're an outcast? They will know you're dangerous. In spite of everything you've been through, you still consider a balanced universe one that does not trip your scent anxiety."

The wind blew Friend's ragged fur around. His most recent body had gone days without food. Insects had eaten parts of it to the bone.

"You only came this far because of Sonjaa. Now we can see the real you. This is what you are without a raptor. What you were the whole time you were with Rive. Maybe your raptor held you back more than I realized. Maybe he taught you how to care about other people, so you learned to resent him for it. I never would have guessed this is the person you were always meant to be. What will happen to you when you understand the Lake? How will the others react to you? Will your scent anxiety extend to every universe you can sense? The solution is simple: just wipe out everyone and start fresh. I don't think they will respect that."

An insect crawled out of Friend's skull and back in through the shoulder.

"Friend... It's been more than a century. I wish I could kill you now so we can work on finding a way home. It's what I wanted to do from the beginning, and you know what? I still would. I can understand a fox acting on instinct, but what I can't grasp is how you can feel nothing. How you can't care about what you've done. How you have justified it. No wonder Rive didn't want to face you. Maybe he knew this was you the whole time. You need help, Friend, but you choose to blame everyone else. To me, that makes you less than an animal, and if I could go back in time, I'd kill you on Vico and save us all from being stranded out—"

Friend's eyes opened. The insects crawled out and flew from his body.

A sphere opened, but not a black antisphere. It flashed a greyish color, and it had blue strings going through it. It didn't lead anywhere in this universe. It led somewhere else. Somewhere that wasn't the Lake.

The grey sphere quietly swallowed reality, and Deka also felt vibrations in the Lake. He retracted his projection and focused on the universe from the outside.

The sphere didn't exist inside reality. It existed in the Lake, leading outside it, cutting straight through the particles of consciousness, swallowing them, tearing chunks of the Lake away, and this reality with it.

Kylac and Sonjaa joined Deka and watched the new sphere. New equations and new vibrations spilled out of it, variables which underpinned the behavior of the Lake itself, and they perceived it had a causal structure supporting it as well. It appeared to be nothing to the Relian's senses, but they heard Friend snarling across the Lake as the new sphere grew and approached him.

It lost its spherical shape and collapsed into a blob with blue tendrils reaching out of it, whipping about and swallowing any piece of the Lake they touched. The expanding mass didn't touch the universe at all but the particles that supported it, and reality fell into the hole it made.

Friend's voice reached beyond reality. The wiggling mass stretched unevenly as it reached out.

It exploded.

A new universe emerged and flew outwards. Friend streamed out of this universe and chased the new reality. The other Relians held one another and swam after him. They caught up to the reality Friend had made and floated within the Lake that supported it.

Friend floated in the center of his new universe, visible through the particles of consciousness that congealed within it. He was still snarling.

Another grey sphere opened up, blue tentacles reaching out and trashing. It exploded just before it touched Friend, launching another universe into the Lake.

Inflation halted in this reality, and now the quarks began to come together into atoms and matter.

Friend howled, thrashing. Being present for the beginning of an equation meant he could calculate it to its ending. Life would emerge here, and this enraged him. Friend opened spheres over the particles that would react and eventually cause life to emerge eight billion years hence.

Friend floated in the Lake, calmer, now able to consider a new reality that existed behind the Lake, supporting it, causing it. He remained here for a while, the other Relians observing from a safe distance.

Another grey sphere opened in front of him, blue threads emerging from its interior and feeling around but not destroying any parts of the Lake yet. It relaxed into a blob, and now the threads became aggressive.

The mass exploded, sending another universe away.

The other Relians thought they should stop him, but they held back, observing.

Another grey mass opened, blue threads running through it, expanding at an unimaginable rate. It exploded again, sending another universe on its way.

An antisphere opened between them and inflated faster than they could perceive. It swallowed all four Relians, and they tumbled out inside a different reality, in their Relian bodies.

Deka stood on his feet next to Sonjaa and Kylac. Friend knelt in the distance, his mouth open and drooling, growls dying off as he ran out of breath. He seemed to be calm.

Deka slowly approached Friend. Sonjaa and Kylac looked around.

"That was an antisphere," Kylac said. "We emerged through a normal way into a different universe. I didn't make myself into a fox again. How did we get here?"

Sonjaa dashed for Friend as the fox rolled on the ground and hyperventilated. Deka had already caught up to him.

"What was that?" Deka asked.

Friend rolled to his back, looking at him with wide eyes. For the first time in a century, he existed behind them.

"The equations are alive! I can make them do what I want! Something is behind the Lake! I glimpsed it!"

Sonjaa held him by the muzzle. "Friend, you don't even understand the Lake, and you want to go beyond?!"

"Things in the Lake have numbers! They are calculable, too! They are... They are—!" His words dissolved into snarling growls.

A grey mass began spreading a few dozen paces away. Blue threads poked out of the mass and wiggled before them. Deka curled his neck and faced it. Sonjaa backed away.

"Stop it," she whispered, as if afraid raising her voice would make the new portal explode again. "Friend, stop it. You can close it."

"It's beautiful! It's starting to make sense!"

Lake particles fell into this unstable sphere. Reality fell away around them, leaving them floating in the Lake. It did not seem to tug on them. They remained in place as the Lake itself swirled around them.

An antisphere swelled and swallowed them, and they exited through a normal sphere into a new reality. It felt much different from the previous landing. They lay in a sprawling field of glasslike plants under a red sky. Transparent plant life filled the region, and glowing insects flew inside these hollow tubes.

Friend lay on his back, panting, mind a million light years away. Normal portals opened and closed around them. A few breaths later, those changed into antispheres. A few dozen more breaths later, those ceased, and a pinprick of grey appeared high in the atmosphere.

Sonjaa stood over him, grabbed him by his chest fur, and yanked him up to his feet. "What is this? What's happening?"

Friend grinned like a human. "You have numbers in the Lake. My mind is expanding to encompass it... the equations that make it work. Universes are as predictable as planets. You wasted so much time watching me. You should have been figuring it out, too, but then I always knew it would be me to join the people who live in the Lake."

Sonjaa shook him. "Make it stop!"

He snarled. "I wish I had left Rive years ago, when I found Reth. I wouldn't be here right now. If it takes fifty-six universes to get away from a raptor making me feel guilty for being a Relian canine, then that's what it takes."

The grey and blue mass pulled reality out from under all of them. Their bodies disappeared, leaving them as floating clumps of consciousness staring at a spreading hole in the particles of scattered minds.

Sonjaa already had Friend within her grip. The other two now surrounded the older fox and held him in place.

Friend pushed. He broke through, thinking they had numbers now. Everything did. As soon as he figured out the rest—

Another antisphere opened and swallowed them, and they emerged in another universe in their Relian bodies again. Now they stood on a planet that seemed to be made of atoms large enough to see with the naked eye. Their own bodies consisted of tiny beads that wiggled and jiggled in place.

Friend collapsed to his knees in front of them and held his head. The Relians looked around. Nothing seemed different, but Friend had reset. He hadn't figured out this equation yet, but in a few breaths he would.

They surrounded him and held him in place, waiting. Portals appeared everywhere, followed by a burst of antispheres. Now a new way appeared where this planet's star was. The star didn't fall into the new sphere. The Lake did, blue threads whipping in all directions in its place.

"Friend..." Kylac said. "How far will this go? How can this be worth it?"

The universe fell away. They braced themselves, and their bodies separated from their conscious minds. They enveloped the older fox, holding him while the giant mass of grey swallowed reality's foundation.

Sonjaa pleaded him to stop.

Friend said he won't stop now—things were just starting to make sense, and this is what mattered, getting away, leaving everyone—being alone in that universe was paradise and he wanted it again and something larger than a universe where he could be alone was within reach and this time he wouldn't let anything stop him.

Friend remained within them, but his awareness had grown. They sensed he had their numbers, which meant he could break free of them.

They tumbled through another regular portal onto a different planet. Their Archeon minds told them they were now in a universe where antimatter and normal matter existed side by side, touching all the time and yet did not annihilate one another. They stood in a shallow sea only ankle deep, particles of opposite charges washing around them.

Friend collapsed to his back and lay still while he panted. "The Lake is a universe! That's all it is! Its equation is huge, and it's starting to make sense!"

Sonjaa slashed Friend across the chest with her hand. The fox did not flinch.

"This is far enough!"

Friend laughed. "I knew it! I'm not reverting, but you still want to hold me down! It's what you do! No more! Never again!"

Sonjaa slashed him again.

Portals appeared. Sonjaa slashed him across the neck. Antispheres replaced the portals. She opened her mouth and twisted his head off. A grey blob replaced the antispheres, vacuumed up reality, and quickly left them floating in the Lake again.

Deka began moving forward. Sonjaa and Kylac caught up and swam with him. The three of them flanked Friend, but they could not make a single move he could not predict. The grey blob loomed, tentacles reaching farther and farther out.

Suddenly they spilled out of a normal way and onto another planet in a new universe. This region was dry, full of mesas and rust-covered rocks under a green star. It did not feel too different from home.

"What the hell is going on?!" Kylac shouted as he jumped to his feet.

Deka was already running up to the other fox. "I don't know, but he resets every time we do that! We have a few breaths to stop him before he has our numbers!"

Friend rose to his hind legs, but he could not move very fast as his mind was already a million light years away. Deka neared. Sonjaa and Kylac caught up to Deka and approached the tailless fox.

Friend stood in place, snarling and screeching. He opened portals over their bodies. Deka lost an arm. A toe. Part of his torso. Then Kylac fell into a heap of punctured flesh. Sonjaa collapsed in pieces into a puddle of her own blood. Deka now fell, headless and missing his hands and feet.

Friend dropped to the ground. He felt himself being pulled apart from the inside. He tried to resist, but his mind slipped through a hole in the universe, and he streamed out of his body. As he fell into the space between atoms, Friend felt particles holding him still. Deka, Kylac, and Sonjaa exerted force and tried to pull him in three directions.

He wanted to open antispheres over all of them, but they had been landing in disparate parts of the Lake, areas his conscious mind had yet to calculate as it worked out the equation for reality's foundation. Until his mind adjusted to that area, he was helpless in the grip of these three.

Deka screamed that he had had enough of Friend.

Friend screamed back that this is discovery and was no different from their determination that those planets he destroyed were worth it.

Sonjaa said Friend was beyond help.

Friend repeated that he did not need help. He never did. Everything he had done had a purpose, and everyone around him had done nothing but hold him back. That ended now.

His mind caught up to their position in the Lake, and antispheres began bubbling around them. Friend was just about to direct antispheres over the three Relians holding him when they fell onto a new planet in a new equation. Kylac had the feeling this universe wasn't too far away from the one they had just left.

Friend lay face down in a puddle of bubbling petroleum. He tried to raise himself, but he could not move. Friend struggled as he suffocated, his fur burning.

The other three stood on a ledge overlooking the tar pit. Volcanoes erupted around them. The planet rained acid, which stripped the scales off Deka and Sonjaa. Kylac's fur was melting. All three ignored the pain.

Friend opened thousands of portals around himself. Antispheres replaced them. Those closed, and then reality fell from underneath them. The grey mass had appeared in the center of this planet and ripped everything away.

The Relians surrounded Friend and carried him down to the mass. Friend struggled and thrashed. He thought that this was how he discovered the Lake, and he will discover what's beyond the Lake, and whatever lies beyond that if that's what it took to get away from people forcing him to be something he did not want to be. He thanked Sonjaa for helping him get to this point, but he didn't need her anymore. He was ready.

They swam toward the mass as it expanded, reaching out for them.

Friend was trying to find their numbers in the equations running through his mind, thrashing as they carried him. Their own particles began to separate.

Friend laughed. He was almost there.

Deka laughed. He sent waves to Sonjaa and Kylac. They agreed.

Friend began to open antispheres over their particles to scatter them to all corners of the Lake.

Just then they landed face-first on soft soil. Deka rose to his feet. Sonjaa and Kylac also stood. Friend lay in the moss, his weight compressing it.

He lifted his head. Spheres bubbled around him as his conscious mind reached through this equation. The onlooking Relians knew in a few moments Friend would find the Lake through the laws of this universe, and then he would find this region of the Lake and figure it out, too.

The old fox snarled, opening spheres over Deka's skull, then Kylac's, then Sonjaa's. Their lifeless bodies collapsed.

Friend climbed to his feet and dashed across a landscape with angular trees and rocks filled with helium. The second lightest element in the universe was friendly with other atoms here and bonded with almost everything, making so many substances float.

The tailless fox opened a portal in front of himself and dashed to a different planet.

He opened another portal and leaped to another, fifty light years away.

Friend jumped around the universe, sometimes only taking a single step on one world before landing on the next, an erratic path across the universe to outrun the three Relians trying to grab him.

Friend eagerly awaited another piece of the Lake's equation to fall into place.

Hundreds of planets went by in just a few breaths, some had breathable air, others did not. Some had weak gravity.

He felt pressure in his skull. Friend hopped six more worlds. The pressure increased. Pulling. His mind sinking out of reality. He kept running from planet to planet to planet to moon to gas giant to asteroid to star surface to—

He clutched his head and tried to open an antisphere around himself in the Lake, but his conscious mind ripped from his brain and drained. His body went to a planet of petroleum oceans. His mind did not.

Reality fell away, and now he floated in the Lake between Deka, Kylac, and Sonjaa's particles. They did not contain him. They exerted force and stretched him in three different directions.

Friend elongated. He resisted, but this time they were faster than he was.

Friend snapped.

A blue tentacle emerged from this planet's star, taking reality with it.

An antisphere opened and swallowed all of them. They tumbled out. Now the Relians sensed this region of the Lake was indeed far, far away from where they had just been.

They stood on top of a glacier of solid ice that felt boiling hot. Deka held Friend. A few paces away, Sonjaa also held Friend. Kylac also held a Relian canine that was missing a tail.

The fox Kylac held had no skin, and it moaned and thrashed. The old ways.

The fox Sonjaa held had no arms and lacked fur, and half its joints didn't seem to work. It looked around as spheres appeared around its head. The higher mind.

The fox Deka held had no muscle or bones underneath its sagging skin and fur, and it seemed to stare into nothing as a grey mass appeared.

The Archeons looked at one another. Without exchanging words, they reached the same conclusion: Deka's piece was the part that lay behind the second subconscious. The next layer of awareness. The Lakemind.

Deka ran in the opposite direction, carrying the limp fox in his jaw. Sonjaa's version began to open antispheres around itself erratically. Kylac struggled to hold onto

Friend's old ways as it snarled and reached out and snapped its jaws at everyone while sniffing the air.

Antispheres opened on top of everyone's heads, the Relians fell lifeless, and their minds drained into the Lake.

The skinless fox dashed and grabbed the higher mind's neck in its jaws. The Lakemind watched, wagging its tail. The old ways ripped pieces of flesh from the higher mind without a fight, and the particles of consciousness leaked into the Lake.

Sonjaa and Kylac caught the particles and collected them. Antispheres opened everywhere, but nothing touched the Relians. Deka swam up to them and enclosed Friend's higher mind.

In reality, Friend's Lakemind lay limp and helpless, waiting for the old ways to come for it next. It looked around. Blinked. It opened a grey mass. It laughed with its voice as the universe fell away, and now the three Relians moved toward the spreading hole in the particles of consciousness. They tossed Friend's higher mind into it. With no sense of self-preservation, it tumbled helplessly. A blue tendril slid from the grew mass and touched it. The higher mind dissolved.

Reality fell away underneath the two remaining parts of Friend, and now their particles floated in the Lake. The old ways swam for Friend's remaining part. The Relians felt the vibrations and moved to intercept, but they were too far away. The old ways merged with the Lakemind. The shockwave it sent through the Lake pushed the Relians backwards and almost scattered their particles.

They landed on an asteroid that had no atmosphere and weak gravity, floating six paces above the dusty ground as they choked.

The version of Friend that floated before them had no skin, and some of its muscles dangled from its bones, as if it had been picked apart by scavengers. It snarled and wagged its tail at them. They sensed it speaking to them, its voice traveling through the Lake particles and entering their minds directly, repeating that it was almost free, almost free, almost free, almost free.

Deka choked and gagged. Sonjaa tried to breathe harder. Kylac willed himself to die as quickly as possible. In moments, their conscious minds separated from the bodies that contained them, and they left reality.

Sonjaa was first to grip Friend's mind within his skull. She pulled. Friend did not resist, and she felt the vibrations coming from it.

It said that Friend had been wrong. His old ways hadn't been holding him back. His higher mind did. Instinct propelled him forward, but his higher mind had still been tied to reality as he knew it. Now it was gone, and he was free to understand without hindrance.

They pulled.

A grey sphere appeared. It did not collapse but stayed firm as the blue threads within swirled. It sucked up the Lake and stripped Friend of its body. It had caught up to this region of the Lake, and now it was about to open anti-spheres over the Relians to scatter their particles—

They dropped into another part of the Lake, manifesting underneath some kind of fluid. Their Archeon senses told them this was hydrogen under such great pressure it became liquid. The skinless thing that used to be Friend was missing some muscles as well, exposing some the bones in its arms, legs, chest , and skull. Blood leaked into the hydrogen fluid, sending red tentacles in all directions.

Deka opened his mouth. Kylac held his mouth open. Sonjaa held Friend's skinless muzzle closed and kept hers open. They counted the breaths until they died.

Just four breaths, and their conscious minds drained into the Lake. Friend still floated in the hydrogen, not too far behind them. They gripped it and ripped its consciousness from its container and yanked it in three directions. Friend split into two halves.

Deka's piece thrashed and struggled.

The piece Kylac and Sonjaa held sent waves of laughter in all directions.

A grey sphere appeared and quickly collapsed into a quivering blob. Kylac and Sonjaa swam toward the object that ate the Lake. The Lakemind lacked a desire to defend itself, so it did not struggle. They exerted force and threw it toward the grey mass as the tendrils emerged and wiggled in all directions.

This part of Friend laughed at them as it tumbled, sending loud waves through the Lake that said this is exactly where it wanted to go; it was free; it had shed its perception of reality and at long last it was ready to comprehend what had eluded it for so long—it remembered what they had done during their journeys between realities—the conversations that lasted decades, the arguing about whether Kylac and Friend could handle this imbalance or that one—whether they should land in this universe or that —if it had an imbalance or not—it was not afraid to comprehend the vast distance and the incredible timescale—it welcomed a perspective that would have driven Friend insane —it was now free of all limits—no more animal impulses filling it with anxiety and arousal—no more conscious mind limited to thinking about atoms and quarks—no more raptors trying to convince it to feel guilty about feeling nothing for the numbers that lived in reality—it was finally going somewhere nobody could follow—freedom to live its own life at last and reclaim the person that was stolen from itself so many years ago—

Two tendrils smacked together, dissolving half of Friend's particles. The rest tumbled onward. They connected with the grey portal and dissolved on contact. The threads retracted, and the mass collapsed.

Deka held the old ways as they thrashed. He sent them into the universe on a habitable planet that resembled Rel, with green grasses and trees growing everywhere. Deka followed the fox down and stood before what was left of him.

Friend's old ways had manifested as a skeleton with meat hanging off it. Its skull hung open, and the exposed brain leaked fluid. It lacked arms and legs, so all it could do was wiggle on its torso and snarl at Deka.

Sonjaa and Kylac descended into the universe. They beheld the animal separated from the part of the mind that comprehended the familiar reality and the part that understood the Lake. The antifox.

It turned to Sonjaa, snarling and wiggling in her direction. It caught Kylac's scent and snarled at him, trying to slash and claw him, blood leaking from everywhere.

Sonjaa walked up to it, grabbed its neck, and snapped it. The skeletal fox fell still.

She turned, stumbled a few paces, and sat. Deka approached her and nuzzled her snout. She bumped Deka's nose, shivering. Kylac walked up to Deka's other side and wrapped an arm around his neck. Then he reached out to Sonjaa. She reached back and rubbed his fingers with her claws.

Something rose from the ground in front of them. It grew to twice the height of a Relian, five legs unfolding from its underside. The head was shaped like a triangle, and all of its limbs had a triangular structure to them. Even its torso had three sides, and it resembled a spider if it had been carved out of marble using nothing but sharp angles.

Deka rose to full height. "Ein?"

"Well done, everyone!" said the creature standing before them. "Well done! I knew you would succeed! It was only a matter of distance! Sit! Sit, little aberrations in our perfect, harmonious math!"

Deka collapsed to a sitting position. So did Kylac. Ein lowered his abdomen, the legs tucking underneath.

"I wish you could understand how far you have traveled from home, but the distance would mean nothing to you. Friend was very close to figuring out every region of the Lake. We were running out of places to send you, but we knew you would kill him just in time. Your numbers predicted you would."

"Please..." Deka gasped as he panted.

"I understand you have come a long way. You deserve answers. In some of our more recent creations, a certain anomaly continuously appeared. We weren't sure what it was, or where it came from, but it affected our calculations every time. We left those equations alone, expecting some external force we didn't understand to balance everything again. All our calculations told us something would, but we couldn't tell what.

"Then you four showed up. The source of all those anomalies. We've been watching you since I told the others you were here. Sure enough, the four of you kept steering yourselves to these equations, and you corrected everything. It became your goal, which was fascinating to observe. I am sorry I couldn't be there for every instance, but my creation still needed me."

The Relians looked around as they listened, killing claws raised, fur bristled. Despite everything they had been through, it had felt too easy.

"You wanted him dead as much as we did?" Deka said.

"Everyone figures out the Lake in their own way, but he is the first to be destructive. The math implied he had a chance to turn away from this, but we had no way of knowing what he would do. The only way to kill him was to let him make a way to the place he didn't understand yet. We calculated you would send him there soon enough. In the meantime, his instincts restored balance to those realities. Thank you."

"Is he finally fucking dead?" Sonjaa said, the English word rolling off her tongue like warm water from an arctic mountain spring.

"You sent his higher mind and the part of him that understood the Lake to a place they were not ready to be. The Lakemind, as he called it, comprehends the Lake but not what lies beyond. His last task before becoming like me would have been to combine his new awareness of where the Lake exists with his higher mind, and then reconcile all the layers of calculations into one operation, but he lacked the discipline to overcome his animal ways. Only a mind fully aware of all the layers of mathematics survives in the Grey. He did not know how to preserve himself there, so his particles dissolved. They will never collect again."

Hearing someone else say it lifted the weight of the universe off the Relians. They breathed easier, and their hearts began to slow.

"So was he right?" Sonjaa said. "How many of you are there? Is there a society in the Lake? Or beyond?"

Ein laughed. "There are several million of us here. We do not call ourselves Superarcheons though. There is no word for what you would call us, but that will do. We ponder the math all of you have only glimpsed. The math that makes reality.

We create universes because it is the only place where the particles of consciousness move into something that is coherent and self-aware. Our goal is for all the particles in the Lake to have a permanent place.

"We do not live in the Lake, but in the realm you saw through the grey spheres. We only come here to create. We're searching for the right equations that will allow every person to rise from it before it expires, and for the particles of consciousness to shed their limits and join us in the Grey realm.

"As for what the Grey is, we still don't know. As you have guessed by now, the particles in the Lake are also shockwaves caused by particles in the Grey bouncing off it. It's full of mystery, just as your reality is still full of mystery to you. We are sure we can figure it out eventually. We are still exploring the unknown, even in the Lake. We don't know where it came from, but we think it is debris from some sort of cataclysm that occurred in the Grey region long ago. We believe all the particles of consciousness once existed in the Grey, but something scattered them. Everyone has a place in the Grey, a former life, and we want to collect these particles and restore life to its former levels of awareness. It has not been easy. The math which should allow all the particles to return to their former states eludes us."

"It doesn't look like a friendly place," Kylac said.

"It is a very different way to perceive reality. Friend was not prepared for it. It is my solemn duty to inform you that the three of you are incapable of understanding it. Friend was as well."

Kylac dropped to his side and curled up. "Good."

Deka rested a hand on his fox's shoulder.

"But I have better news," Ein continued. "Friend's thrashing nudged your reality onto a balanced course again. People will leave your universe and join us thanks to his attempts to understand it and your efforts to stop him. He was part of the anomaly from the beginning. That's why the one who created your universe moved on. The calculations said nothing else needed to be done because something would bring balance. Everyone who came into contact with Friend was part of it. Even those who died. Their minds flowed back into the Lake and will become part of a new creature in some other equation. Perhaps closer to where they belong.

"The four of you made quite a few waves here. It's not the first time something of this kind has happened. The math that manifests here is precise, yet the life that results still surprises us. We can calculate the movement of each particle to degrees of accuracy beyond your comprehension, yet life still does things that defy the numbers. Life means so much more beyond the math. It is worth saving, and we won't stop until we rescue all the particles of consciousness from this layer of reality and return them to where they belong. Perhaps we will reassemble everyone the way they were in the Grey, before they were scattered, and they will remember what happened. I look forward to meeting whoever leaves your universe. I'm sure they will be full of surprises."

The Relians caught their breath. Kylac spoke.

"So... Where is the one who created our universe?"

Ein laughed again. "I knew you would ask. You'll have to trust me on this, but everything will be much easier if you don't know that. I can tell you that it was no accident you and Deka ended up on Earth."

Deka and Kylac stared, minds blank.

Sonjaa clicked her claws. "So what now?"

"Now I send you home."

"Home?" Kylac shouted as he unrolled and sat up. "Like this?"

The life form rose to all five limbs, looking down on all of them. "None of you were ready to perceive reality this way. I will remove those parts from you. You will remember what you did, but not how." Ein turned to Kylac. "I can restore your mind to what it was before Friend forced you to comprehend the Lake. Would you like to be a Relian canine again?"

Kylac stood on his hind legs and gazed up at the creature. He swallowed. "I enjoy not needing sex all the time to keep my instincts calm. I don't think I could ever go back to that. I want my body but this is who I am now."

"As I expected."

The raptors now climbed to their feet.

"Sonjaa, would you like to remain an Archeon?"

She did not hesitate. "Yes. Friend forced me into this, but I fucking earned it. Will the universe scream at me now?"

"Without comprehending life as part of the equation, the universe will be so harmonious you won't hear it unless you choose to."

"That's what I want."

"I want to be an Archeon again," Deka said. "As I was before the disaster took it from me."

"We already took the liberty of finding the parts of your mind the disaster took away. It is an arduous process, even for us, but we felt you deserved it. Kylac, we will give yours back as well, and you, Sonjaa, will no longer have to exert effort to keep your mind contained inside your physical body. On behalf of everyone in attendance, thank you for restoring balance to our equations."

"Thank you for helping us kill that fox," Deka said.

"Think better of him. He is the reason your universe is balanced. We look forward to meeting whoever makes it out of your equation. We will know you again through that person, and we will never forget you. You still have long lives ahead of you. Enjoy the rest of your time in your physical bodies."

Before any of them could reply, an antisphere swallowed them.

Kronia

I

The sphere closed, and they stood on their feet under a black sky on a planet with weak gravity. Above them, a large gas giant took up most of the horizon, and around their feet grew miniature trees and shrubs. Labccr. A Relian-sized portal hovered a few paces away. It led into an internal structure they did not recognize.

This was where they had left the moon. The portal rested in the exact spot where Deka had walked headlong into an antisphere. In front of the portal, English words were written in the soil like a welcome mat.

Here There Be Dragons
This Way To Sorven
Wipe Your Paws

"Deka!" Kylac shouted. "It's gone. The equation that makes up this universe! It's gone!"

Deka examined the variables his mind took in. "Same for me."

"The universe is calm!" Sonjaa hopped up and down and clicking her claws. She pranced over to Deka and played his claws. "I can hear the universe! It's normal!"

She leaped around Deka, bumping him with her snout. Deka held her claws and danced with her, laughing.

"I feel... So good!" Kylac said, staring up at the gas giant filling the black sky. "It's not behind a subconscious. Deka, I can still calculate the universe. Just this universe. That's it. I'm an Archeon again."

Deka clicked claws with Sonjaa. "It feels good to share a laugh properly."

"Is it over?" continued the fox. "Is it really, finally, over?"

"Things feel normal," Deka said, turning to the portal. "Speaking of normal, how long has it been?"

"Let's find out." Sonjaa separated her claws from Deka's and approached the portal. She tucked her arms in as she walked through.

Deka turned to Kylac, who was rubbing himself.

"Kylac..."

"I'm trying something. Deka, how do I smell?"

He approached his fox, scented him up and down as Kylac rubbed. His penis wasn't coming out.

"Your scent is subdued."

"I feel normal, Deka, but... Are my instincts tamed? Are they gone?" He felt his head. One of his ears was still cropped. "It wasn't a dream."

Deka rubbed his claws. "This universe is in balance."

Kylac threw his arms around Deka's neck, wagging his tail. Deka wrapped his neck around Kylac's shoulders, rubbing his claws as loudly as he could.

"Home," said the raptor.

"Home," replied his fox.

Deka turned both of them around and walked them toward the portal. They emerged inside a stone structure. The center of the ceiling was made of a transparent crystal. The walls had shelves built into them. Several staircases led up to the three levels.

Dozens of screens hung from one of the walls, most showing human beings on them, but they seemed wrong somehow. The Relians stood on a ledge out of reach to everyone but a Krone. No ladder led to this crevice in the wall. Sonjaa jumped to the bottom level. Deka and Kylac followed, the fox landing on all fours. The room smelled of the many Krone and humans who had walked here.

Footsteps came around the door to an adjacent chamber identical to this one. A Krone with silver and yellow scales regarded them for a moment. Her wings stretched out and folded back again.

"Wait here. I'll get Sorven." She turned, muttering to herself. "Who are they? They are relics from an earlier time."

The two raptors turned in circles and surveyed the room. Kylac walked to one of the shelves behind them. Boxes and boxes of paper rested here, all marked by year and other descriptions. Boxes of cassette tapes, boxes of books, memory cards, hard drives, CDs, and so on around the whole room.

Deka watched the screens. All of them were in English, but the people looked off. They were nearly perfect in appearance and mannerisms, but subtle differences made it obvious these were not real people.

Sonjaa had joined Kylac at the shelves. Old scents of many humans covered them, something none of them thought they'd smell again.

Kylac pulled a small box halfway off the shelf and peered under the lid. Sonjaa looked with him. It was full of manila folders and papers.

Fast, heavy footsteps echoed from the next chamber. Kylac slid the box back as he turned to face the doorway. Sonjaa walked up to Deka and stood by his side, facing the sound. From this angle they saw through the arches to the next four chambers. A Krone cloaked in shadow ran around the corner of the last room and dashed forward on all fours, wings partially extended. He ran under the light.

His scale pattern looked much older than they remembered.

He ran into the shadow of the next chamber, then passed under its skylight. The light shined off his golden and green scales. He saw them, and his wings extended further.

"You motherfuckers have been gone for five hundred and forty-six years!"

"Sorven!" Deka shouted back.

The Krone crossed into the adjacent chamber and dropped to his stomach, sliding the rest of the way to them, muzzle coming to a halt just a pace away from them. The Relians converged on it and embraced it. Sorven's wings stretched out all the way, and he bared his teeth in an imitation of a human smile.

"Holy shit, you're real! Sonjaa! Deka! You— And you haven't aged a day!"

Kylac scented him as if he had found treasure. Deka and Sonjaa rubbed their necks over Sorven's head, speaking at the same time.

"You wouldn't believe where we've been—"

"Where are we?"

"What is this place?"

"What dialect of English is this?"

"Slow down, slow down," said the Krone. "I only have one mouth. I wish I were human again so I could hug you. Oh, it feels so good to smell all of you. I kept that portal open for five hundred years! Every time that side of the moon solidified, I went back and carved the message again. I thought you'd never find it."

They released him. Sorven raised his head and regarded each of them.

"Where is Friend?"

"The fucker is dead," Sonjaa said.

Sorven's wings flapped. "Friend is gone? It took you five hundred years to kill him?"

"It's a very long story," Deka said.

"I want to hear it. Every detail! I'm already three hundred years past my life expectancy, and once I hear this I think I can finally die! First let's find Rive! He's aged, too—he's losing memories and motor skills—the Multitude can't keep his body working forever."

"I already found him," said the yellow and silver Krone standing in the shadow in the next chamber.

Multiple winged lizards stood around the door, and several others looked on from the adjacent chambers, most in shadow. Everyone smelled strange, and it took the Relians a moment to realize why.

"Sorven," Sonjaa said. "Did every Krone—?"

"Yes, they did! Everyone's carrying a human in them now. God knows we weren't doing very well on our own! I'll tell you about it later—where's Rive? Rive!"

Metallic footsteps clanked across the stone floor between the Krone looking on. Moments later, the clanking stepped between two dragons, and a Relian reptile halted beneath the light.

"Rive?" Kylac said.

Deka huffed, clicked his claws. "You look like shit!"

Rive was completely metal except for his eyes. A few patches of him resembled raptor scales, but most of him was reflective grey. He opened his mouth and screeched. He dashed, slid to a stop among them, wrapping his neck around Deka's and touching Sonjaa's claws with one hand. Kylac ran up to him and held his neck. The metal raptor radiated heat.

When they separated, Rive looked them over. He scented them. Clearly his nose did not believe they were real, so he relied on his eyes.

"Five hundred and forty-six years," he said in English.

"You've aged horribly!" Deka said, swiping his claws down Rive's metallic arm. "What happened to you? And why are we speaking English?"

Sorven butted in. "You owe us a story first! Start with the moment you left Labccr! I saw Deka go through an anti-sphere and that's all I know! I don't care what comes out of your mouths—I will believe it!"

Dozens of wings extended and retracted.

2

They walked down the central avenue, spheres on either side of them, people walking to and fro. Tavax's portal hub had many Krone-sized spheres in it. Deka, Kylac, and Sonjaa remembered a time when no hub on any planet had a sphere that large. A few Krone walked about, hopping between worlds. All of them were capable of opening spheres on their own, but the Archeons of other planets took great pleasure in accommodating them.

A Zjr walked past them. Three metal legs, one leg made of skin and bone, metal wrapping around her wolf-like torso and jaw and partially capping her skull. The Relians turned and followed her with their eyes as she passed.

"The Multitude joined the contacted universe as metal explorers with the Zjr," Rive said.

Deka turned to Rive and scraped his claws down his metallic side. "Didn't we joke about that?"

Rive laughed with his voice like a human, which sounded strange. "It did not seem plausible at the time, but the Zjr suffered a decline in health a couple centuries later. The Selts saved them, but it required so much effort they had little time to do anything else. The Zjr could do nothing but stay alive as their tumors came back and disease wreaked them. The Multitude came just in time to help them."

"And what happened to you?" Sonjaa said.

"Survived a drone strike and a couple bio-weapons. You wouldn't believe the shit they have now."

"Tavax has become the preferred home for the Relians," Sorven finished.

A theropod with white scales walked past them, a fox in tow, and something else as well. The Relians stared at the apelike creature as she walked by. She walked upright on plantigrade feet, but she had thin coat of dark fur covering everything.

"Remind you of anything?" Sorven said as the group passed.

"*Planet of the Apes*," Kylac answered.

"Yes!" shouted the Krone, wings flapping, kicking up dust and annoying the others on the path. "The old movies, from when I was human, before computers remade them every twenty years! I couldn't believe it myself when I realized what was happening! Without all that pollution and pointless living for the sake of mere survival, the human body changed back into the form God probably intended."

Another Relian group passed. The new arrivals stared.

Rive: "They are only a few generations away from leaving the human species."

"What will we call them?" Kylac asked.

"Everyone already calls them Relian primates, so I'm sure it will be a variation on that. The Selts began caring for the humans centuries before the Zjr joined the Multitude. Since then, the felines of Selta travel the contacted universe caring for everyone. In a way, the Multitude freed them to become part of the contacted universe at last."

"Just as they did during the disasters oh so long ago," continued the Krone. "An improvement. Everyone seems happier now. Turn here. You must see this place now."

The Krone-sized sphere led to Neben. On the other side, everyone stood still and beheld the scene.

Spheres to the mountain range below lined the hub. Crystalline creatures swam about down there, and many walked on the surface, glowing blue with stored energy. Some appeared dimmer than others, indicating they needed to return to the water to recharge.

Metallic canines also walked everywhere, their jointless metal flexing and moving just as Rive's did. Birds with feathers that glowed green, and pangolins half as tall as a raptor milled about. Hundreds of offworlders mingled with everyone.

One crystal creature directed a few tiny bolts of electricity at a batlike Heeke from the planet Eiae. This individual must have gone through quite a bit of conditioning to be able to handle electromagnetic energy so strong. The Heeke raised a clay tablet and began writing S'rin symbols on it. The Eich read it, and then the two walked on together.

"The Eich learned how to lower their voices," Rive said. "Sometimes they can read the responses of others by direct touch. For everything else, S'rin's writing system has become a universal written language in the contacted universe thanks to Gruum's poem."

"I was about to ask about those symbols on the walls," Sonjaa said.

The Krone laughed. "Gruum himself carved it into the walls of my library. I was thrilled he said he would. His poem became so famous people started learning the language just so they could read it, and the S'rin written language became a standard."

"A language that isn't spoken but only meant to be internalized," Sonjaa said. "That by itself is poetry."

The Krone laughed harder. "It's a great pleasure telling people of Earth about that. They ask me to help them understand the poem. I tell them they must learn another language plus understand the mindset of two telepathic species. A handful of humans managed to do it. They started writing poetry and stories about comprehending the inexpressible."

Deka turned to Rive. "So if the Multitude is here, then you finished the portal."

"The Dekanites finished carving the caverns a long time ago," Rive answered. "I filled those caves with the Multitude's mountain range."

"I wish I could have been there for it," Deka said.

"A nonspherical portal that took centuries to calculate." Rive laughed with his voice. "Lots of people came to witness it. My mind feels empty without it."

"The mountain range is smaller than it was when Rive brought it here," Sorven said. "Many joined with the Zjr. Others chose to remain the mountain and commune with the Eich and anyone else who sought to learn their reality."

"Not many people can say they helped bring a non-compatible species into the contacted universe," said the metal raptor. "It took me centuries to teach them how to understand the basics of life in the physical universe. It took them even longer to teach me how they live. When my time ends, I believe I might be capable of joining them. It's my dying wish."

Kylac felt someone sniffing under his tail. He turned and looked down. A Zjr made of mostly metal stood behind him. He licked his nose, looked at Deka. The raptor had noticed him, and he clicked his claws.

"Kylac?"

The fox turned to the canine. "I'm flattered, but... No. I don't want it anymore."

The metal quadruped sniffed Kylac again. "Are you all right? You don't smell like a Relian canine."

"I'm not, and I feel fine like this."

The canine seemed more bewildered than disappointed. He sat down next to the fox and listened.

Sorven turned his head and snorted. "Damn, I was hoping to fuck you."

Kylac wagged his tail. "I think Deka finally tamed my instincts completely. I don't have desire anymore, and for the first time since Friend forced me to understand the Lake, I feel good about it."

Sorven's wings flapped. "Our humans gave us the curse of a sex drive. We fuck all the time now, and barely any eggs to show for it. I'm happy you finally found peace."

"Sorven," Sonjaa said. "What was that place? Have you been watching Earth for five hundred years?"

"Only on weekdays during business hours," Sorven said, lying on his stomach. "I work weekends if something big is happening. I've been watching and waiting for global revolution. It's coming. Centuries of corporate rule have brought us here; you were there for the very beginning of it. Everything we thought would happen in the distant future has happened, and anger has been brewing. Thanks to our Church, the revolution will be able to coordinate on a global scale. We are broadcasting real footage of the real riots, and the collective anger of mankind will finally boil over. Nuclear and biological weapons will be used on the protesters after the wealthy evacuate to private space stations. They will vote that it's time to get rid of what they call the surplus population and rebuild human civilization properly. When mankind brings itself to the point of death, the Krone will move in to fill the power vacuum, and humans will welcome us as their companion race."

Deka curled his neck. "This is our legacy on Earth?"

"Powerful people used fear of extraterrestrial invasion to further their goals," Rive answered. "It would have happened with or without us. If anything, our visit sped things up."

"Maybe in another five hundred years or so," Sorven continued, "the humans of Earth will be able to join the

contacted universe as well, assuming there's an uncontami-
nated piece of land left on the planet for civilization to start
over. If not, we have several worlds we can move them to. If
all else fails, we have a plan. The Dekanites have been making copies of every Church member's neural pattern since
the beginning. We have enough glass cubes to last the
Krone hundreds of generations, and give human beings a
second life to make up for the one they had to spend in mis-
ery here."

The new arrivals stared for a while. Deka sat and
looked at the ground. Kylac and Sonjaa followed.

"Enough about us." Rive sat down in the cool sand. "I
have to know. Did Friend get what he deserved?"

"He probably got off easy," Deka said. "But yes. We
ripped him apart and sent him beyond the Lake. He is
dead."

Rive sighed. "It fills me with enormous relief to know
he can't hurt anyone else."

Sonjaa sighed, killing claw idly poking the sand.
"From our point of view, it's only been a few hours since it
happened. No remorse. I wanted a fox again, but he didn't
want a raptor. Our relationship was one-sided. He all but
told me he only let me tame him because he thought it
would help him reach his goal."

Rive held his trembling hands apart. "It was me, wasn't
it? He wanted to get away from me."

Sonjaa growled, killing claw stabbing the ground. "He
liked you. He was happy, but he always felt an itch to run
away. He finally got what he wanted. Watching him for
that century alone in the reality he exterminated... I
thought it would be punishment and he would beg me to
tame him, but it was exactly what he wanted. He was
happy being alone. All he wanted was to live somewhere
without you, without me, without anyone around him. It
was the old ways. He felt them."

Rive held his claws together. "Scent anxiety. It's the only thing that made sense."

"He resented you treating him like a fox all those years. He hated you for turning him into a sex-obsessed canine. He didn't think he had an animal nature. Even after meeting it face to face, he couldn't accept it was part of him."

Rive looked down at the ground. "I'm old enough to admit I have been happier without a fox. So he was happier without me. The whole time he wanted to get away from me. We held each other back all those years. We stayed together because it was expected of us. Of course... All that time I wasted wondering what went wrong... I told the other Relians about us. How Friend wanted to break away from me, and maybe if I had not pushed him to be like all the other Relian canines, the disasters wouldn't have happened. I implored other raptors who had stable foxes not to feel so much pressure to divert their scent anxiety into sexual desire. That perhaps foxes are ready to divert their instincts into other things. Some raptors have begun doing so. It seems to have helped. It took me years to admit my part in the disasters that killed so many people. Years to consider maybe Relian society was too strict and wasn't equipped to handle foxes who had reached the point of not needing their raptors to tame their instincts anymore. I failed to recognize it."

"He wasn't tamed," Sonjaa said. "He had scent anxiety. He knew."

"If I had recognized his stability and not tamed him the way every other raptor tamed their foxes, maybe his instincts wouldn't have come out that way when he noticed the Lake. Maybe he wouldn't have been so determined to get away from me."

"He might never have found the Lake had you not tamed him the normal way," Sonjaa offered, "Don't blame yourself, Rive. Friend... He wasn't happy in Relian society, and he thought he didn't need to be treated like a Relian canine. Then he discovered he had instincts beyond his control. He never came to terms with that. He chose to take it out on everyone else instead of accepting he was a normal fox and he needed help."

Rive did not look up from his feet. "So many raptors have stable foxes, and the raptors are not pushing them to have sex with everyone. They seem to be stable. Honestly, truly stable. So much happier. Not pretending to be happy, the way Friend and I must have all those years. I wish I had thought to treat Friend differently. He was different, and I pushed him to be something he wasn't. I let him hunt, and I thought that was enough. Now I know... He really did resent me. I thought I was doing the right thing, but yes, now I know he hated me for raising him like a normal fox. And I hated him for keeping me away from other people. I could have been someone else, too, had I not been so afraid of leaving him alone. I became obsessed with conceptual concepts of physics for his sake. He met me there because that's what he felt he needed to do. He was doing it, too. Becoming someone else. It was there the whole time and I refused to acknowledge it. I tried to help him connect with other people, but he never enjoyed it, so I didn't push him. We connected with one another, and I thought that's all we needed but now I know he was always like that. The fox I saw on Reyno—the one who almost killed everyone to satisfy his scent anxiety because he didn't care about anyone else—that was the real Friend. The person he would have been if not for Relian society pushing us together. Now I know. I finally know what went wrong." He looked up and met her eyes. "Sonjaa, I'm sorry to tell you there are no foxes without a raptor right now. I hope you are content."

Sonjaa clicked her claws. "I spent centuries taming one fox. I wanted Rupi back. He couldn't give me that."

"My turn," said the Krone. "You didn't happen to meet the god of this universe, did you?"

"I don't think so," Sonjaa answered, "but things went according to plan. The disasters were part of the equation. Because of what Friend did, at least one person will leave our universe. He succeeded. We won't end up in oblivion. Nobody will be forgotten."

"And Ein told you what the meaning of life is!" Sorven laughed with his wings and his voice. "I knew there was a reason I'm still alive, and sure enough you came back to tell me!"

"I wouldn't go that far," Deka replied.

"Think about it! You left the universe, you met the gods, and one of them told you why the universe exists! And then this god told you to enjoy the rest of your time in your bodies!"

He laughed with his voice again, louder. Rive clicked his claws together, and he also laughed with his voice. Nobody could get a word in.

"Finally," Sorven continued. "The answer to the ultimate question, and it's just as disappointing as I knew it would be."

Sonjaa stared at the dirt as Sorven and Rive laughed like humans.

Kylac's eyes gazed at nothing.

Deka felt a chill run down his spine all the way to the tip of his tail. "Holy shit."

A Krone with solid green scales meandered between and over the Nebens and offworlders. Neben birds landed on her, making her glow so vividly she was difficult to look at directly. Deka, Kylac, and Sonjaa gazed at her. She stopped just inside their group.

"Sorven, Rive. It's happening."

The winged lizard rose. The metal theropod stood straight and began walking back to the hub. Deka, Kylac, and Sonjaa followed. The Zjr trotted to catch up to the fox and jogged at his side.

"I'm Ezir," he said. "If he's Deka, then you must be Kylac? I've heard so much about you! My father! He said he tied you once! His name was Ora."

Kylac's ear perked. "I remember him!"

3

Sorven lay under the skylight. Deka and Kylac sat on one side of him. Sonjaa and Rive sat on the other. The screens came from the net and over broadcast and satellite. The computer-animated anchors and analysts reported on "a few tiny uprisings in isolated places of the world." They blamed Relian invaders for agitating the populations. Some of the people on the screen discussed how overblown the situation was, and everyone should just return to work as usual.

Sorven laughed with his voice. "They say that every time a rebellion happens, but people have caught on. Remember the Mortons? People like that only got richer, and they did this to society deliberately, creating a crucible to find the worthy human beings. They believed having what it took to pull oneself out of the working world and amass large amounts of money was a sign of being a real human, and the rich think everyone who can get out already has. Some members of the Church have hijacked the signals, and they are transmitting the real footage of the riots so people can see they are not tiny, and they are not isolated. You may watch if you wish. It is so good to see all of you again, but I don't expect you to stick around. A lot has changed in the last five hundred years. You should get out there and explore it."

Rive continued. "The disasters allowed a few new species to join the contacted universe. I will take you to meet them later. You said the creators restored your minds to be Archeons again?"

"Yes," Deka said. "We haven't tested it yet."

"Well, go and try. You can bridge the cultures as if the disasters never happened. As if Friend never happened."

"Never forget him," Deka said. "For all the harm he did, he succeeded. Our universe won't be forgotten."

"I'm glad some good came out of all that. Makes me feel like less of a failure as a Relian."

A few channels began playing real footage of the riots. The real riots had something the computer-animated recreations did not: scope. Other screens showed people breaking into the homes of rich businessmen and setting fire to everything. More screens showed people setting fire to factories and banks.

People were yelling that these people made the world a living hell so they were going to pay. The computer-animated news, however, showed people in round-table discussion groups saying this whole thing was an overblown hoax and everything was just fine and business could continue as usual and the people needed to get back to work for the good of the economy—yes, the economy was the most important thing to consider because working was not merely an obligation but a virtue and people should be grateful for the employment.

Hacked video from satellites showed shuttles docking with space stations. The shuttles bore various corporate logos.

Sorven laughed with his wings this time. "They will push the button. The new nuclear weapons have biological agents in them as well. A few centuries ago, someone figured out C-Corn pollen survives a nuclear blast. They spliced those genes into viruses to make biological weapons that will decimate the survivors during the fallout. Some will live though. The Church has made sure of it. The people who own all the companies and the land plan to stay on those stations until the dust settles, and then they will move on to the Mars colony for a few centuries for Earth to recover and to give human civilization a fresh start with only the greediest, most selfish and sexually insecure people. The ones who managed to subjugate others in order to rise up and amass fortunes. They really do believe these are the real human beings. The only ones worth sparing. That's why they wanted the space program privatized in the first place. I will personally make sure they do not escape the consequences of what they are about to do."

All through the library came the sounds of riots in other languages across the globe. People were tired of endless work with no way out, and being told to be thankful for it. People would no longer stand for corporations having more rights than the people who work for them. People all over the world toppled the monuments to CEOs and company founders, whom history books remembered for their accomplishments, never their decision to employ slave labor and pollute entire countries, and certainly never the brutal governments they sponsored so they could continue to do so.

Deka rose. So did Kylac. Sonjaa stood with them. The dark blue raptor turned to Sorven.

"I've seen enough destruction to last a lifetime. I want to join the contacted universe again."

"I want to learn their languages," Sonjaa said. "The new species. They must have wonderful languages! And now I can make my own ways there. Permanent ways!"

Kylac wagged his tail. "I can't wait to meet them." He checked himself. "I'm not hard thinking about it. My instincts are calm. This is... I want to make portals and travel the contacted universe and catch up on all the things we missed! I want to meet the Selts again—and the Eich! And we can talk to the Multitude now!"

"I want to meet more Krone," Deka said, turning to face the exit into the desert.

"Don't be gone long!" Sorven called. "There's still so much more to tell you, and I know you haven't told me everything. I'll be here, or maybe on Earth."

"We won't be long," Sonjaa said.

"I have missed you so much. Thanks for coming back."

Deka turned to Rive. "Are you staying?"

"No, my wife is down there vaccinating people as we speak. She will need me."

Sonjaa stared. "Wife?"

Deka and Kylac froze in place.

Rive clicked his claws. "Her name is Elsa. Come back soon and you'll meet her."

Sorven laughed as he watched the riots. Several more internet streams now showed the real riots happening around the world. Entire cities on fire.

"Rive has had nineteen wives if you include CJ. Human women is all he's wanted! Elsa's way too young for him, but she is just like him, big thoughts all the time, and she thinks his metal body is sexy is hell."

Deka clicked his claws. Sonjaa clicked hers.

Kylac still stared at him. "You? Married?"

Rive laughed with his hands, met their eyes. "I married even before I taught the metal how to make my middle claw work again. I was a lousy Relian, but I found my people. It's what I really wanted to do. Without a fox, I was free to find them."

Kylac wagged his tail. "We'll be back soon. Maybe after the carnage is over. I'm in the mood for happy. Yes, happy. I haven't been happy in five hundred years. I think the universe owes me that."

"Couldn't have said it better," Sonjaa said.

Several screens showed wealthy businessmen leaving Earth on private shuttles for the space stations in orbit. The riots continued. More buildings of commerce and industry burned at the hands of the people they employed. More than half the screens displayed fire.

Kylac led the way across the library. They grouped up and walked to the door, now looking out over a desert on Kronia.

A Krone flew from the sky and landed fifty paces away. He trotted up to the library, nodding to them as he passed and smiling with his wings.

"Welcome home Sonjaa, Deka, Kylac."

Two more Krone walked out of the library side by side, past the three Relians. Their scents mixed. They had just coupled. They spread their wings and took off together, soaring into the sky and then fading into the clouds.

"So many Krone in one place," Sonjaa began.

"Laughing as a group," Deka continued.

"The Krone gaining a companion species," said the fox. "The Selts and the Zjr are not companions anymore. Sorven and Rive are alive—"

"Rive is married!" Sonjaa shouted, clicking her claws.

"The Krone revere us," Deka said. "This is the weirdest reality we've ever landed in."

Sonjaa was still laughing with her hands. "Sorven is right. We met the gods. We saw for ourselves there was a creator. We learned the meaning of life."

"And the purpose of the universe," Deka continued. "The purpose of life itself."

"We had the power to alter entire universes," Kylac finished, "and now..."

Sonjaa shivered, feeling the weight of what they had just been through.

Kylac felt the weight of it, too, which made him weak in the knees. He leaned on his raptor. "Can we possibly live normally again?"

"I am eager to begin." Deka turned to Kylac. "Do you want to make the portal to the hub, or should I?"

"Both!"

Deka began working on a way. The math seemed so complex. He remembered a time when the math for a portal to another part of the same planet had seemed so small and easy, but he could not remember why.

Kylac worked on a portal to the hub as well. He felt no mental scars from the disaster, or from the knowledge of the Lake. He felt no scent anxiety channeled into sexual desire, hence he felt no desire, and it felt so liberating.

Sonjaa pondered the pronunciation the Krone had used when they spoke. The English language as a whole had changed, and she clicked her claws in anticipation of hearing how all the languages of the contacted universe had evolved. That reminded her of something.

"Deka," she said. "The universe. It sounds like you."

The other raptor curled his neck. "Me?"

"When I found you on Xce, I promised to tell you how the universe sounds to me. It's your voice. I'm not sure why. Maybe..."

Deka nosed her neck, growling.

She bumped him with her hip. "It means I need to marry you. Deka, you meant what you've said all this time, haven't you? You don't mind if I stay? I'm not intruding on you and Kylac?"

He nuzzled her snout. "You never intruded on us."

"Relians come in threes now," Kylac said. "You'll help us fit in."

Sonjaa returned the affectionate growl. "Thanks. I don't think I'll ever take a fox again. A mate will have to do. After giving it some thought for five hundred years, I've decided I really have enjoyed being around you all this time, so it must be true. I like you for more than just the killsex. Let's make it official."

"I've enjoyed having you close all the time." Deka rubbed snouts with her. "For as long as you can tolerate me."

"What about me?" Kylac said. Deka turned to him. "My instincts are calm. Am I stable? Do I... Do I need a raptor anymore?"

He bumped muzzles with his fox. "Do you?"

"I can't imagine life without you. What am I if I don't need to be tamed anymore? I always wondered that. Taming foxes so they don't have these instincts. It's been the raptors' goal, but who are we if they actually achieved it?"

Deka rubbed Kylac's neck with his snout. "We can try it if you like. I trust you."

"I don't know, Deka. Could I? Could I be all right without a raptor? Who am I without you? I don't... I don't know."

Deka reached down and weaved his fingers between Kylac's, touching his claws. "I would enjoy visiting you and finding out what can do without someone helping you control your old ways."

Kylac's tail was between his legs, but wagging. "Who are the raptors? We can find other foxes who don't need sex to calm their instincts. Let's find out how it's changing the culture. Who are we if raptors and foxes don't need each other?"

Deka licked Kylac's snout. "I'm married now. I'll have someone to pull me to other worlds and go on adventures and help me tame *my* instincts. If you don't need me anymore, that would make me happier than—"

Sonjaa shrieked and backed away. "Deka! There's something else in that drone!"

An antisphere appeared five paces in front of her, swelling from a point to Relian-sized. The three of them glared at it.

"Shit," she whispered.

The three stared at it breathlessly, waiting for it to do something, but the antisphere merely hovered in place.

Another antisphere opened next to hers.

Kylac straightened up. "I hear it, too."

And another.

Deka uncurled his neck and rose from attack stance. "Yes."

The three exchanged glances.

"I thought Ein took this away from us," Kylac said.

Deka shifted from foot to foot as the antispheres stared at him. "I understand. Ein only took away the part that comprehended life as part of the equation. Ein wants us to remember the Lake."

Staring at the Lake wasn't terrifying. The antispheres were stable.

"It's part of the drone," Sonjaa said. She closed the way.

Deka closed his.

So did Kylac.

"Ein must have left us with this for a reason," Deka said. "We can do it properly now. We'll research it. We can teach others and prepare people for the Lake."

"Ein didn't say who would leave the universe," Kylac said. "If we ever get bored of this reality, could we leave it? When we're old, do we have to die? Can we just move somewhere else and start over?"

Deka bumped him with his shoulder. "One step at a time, Kylac. We don't want to doom the universe because we rushed in."

"I'm in no hurry," Sonjaa said. "Now let's go to Hithe. To celebrate our marriage, I want to feel those causeways again."

Deka growled, rubbing his claws in anticipation. "We'll start our union right."

Three spheres opened above the sand, both leading to the hub, now full of Krone-sized portals. A busy hub on Kronia looked even more alien than a universe in which space had liquefied.

Deka looked at Kylac. Kylac reached out and hugged his raptor's neck. Deka pulled Sonjaa up to his other side with his free arm. She rubbed his neck with hers, and then dashed through the portal she had made.

Kylac separated from his raptor, and ran through his own portal. He stood on the other side, looking around, taking in everyone's scents. The sphere closed.

Sonjaa and Kylac waited for Deka on the other side of his sphere. Deka clicked his claws as he walked through his portal. The contacted universe was open, and it was full of people he could not calculate. He wanted to meet them all.

First draft began on September 2013
Final draft ended on November 2016
Final edit made on November 2021

Would you like to know what's
wrong with your planet?

It's been a long journey. A childhood world made coherent thanks to an adult perspective. I have made that world my own. Thank you for sharing it with me.

—JLS

About the Author

James L. Steele has had the idea for the Archeon series in his head since the mid-1990s.

He has been published in various anthologies and magazines, including: *The Furry MEGAPACK®*, *Zooscape*, *Tall Tales with Short Cocks V.2*, *Fictionvale*, *The Reclamation Project*, *Claw the Way to Victory*, and *Shark Week*.

His sci-fi novel *Huvek* is published through Argyll Productions.

He lives in Ohio, where he pursues his hobby of becoming a wine connoisseur while laughing at his many existential crises.

Blog: DaydreamingInText.blogspot.com

Twitter: @JLSteeleAuthor